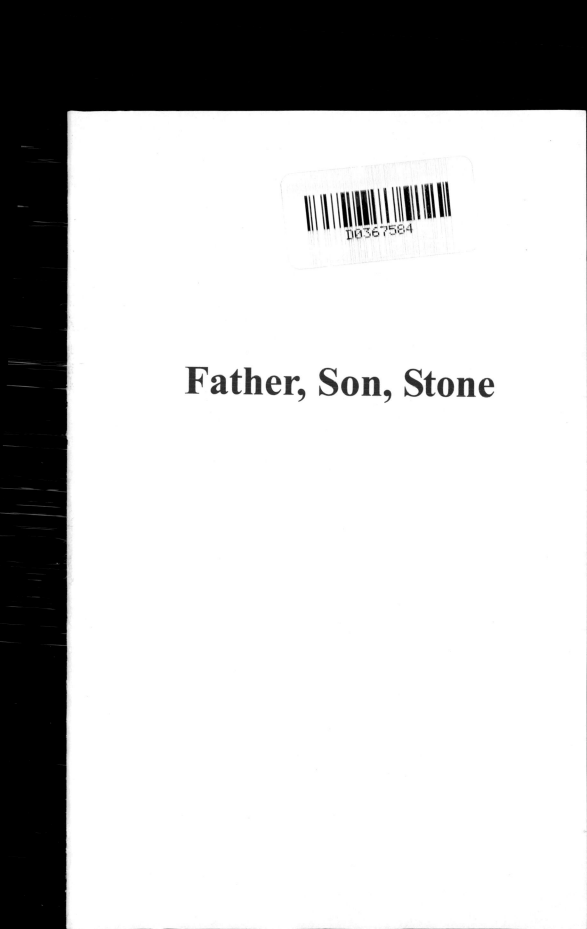

Father, Son, Stone

To Harriet and Herb —

Father, Son, Stone

Allan H. Goodman

Solomon Publications
Rockville, Maryland

Family is everything!

Allan H. Goodman
9/8/2014

Father, Son, Stone © 2014 by Allan H. Goodman

This is a work of fiction. While some characters and dialogue are historical, the story as a whole is created by the author. Any resemblance of the fictional characters to actual persons, living or dead, is entirely coincidental.

Cover art © Copyright 2014
Two Doves on the Kotel, Evalyn Cohn
Moon Over the Kotel, Matthew Saunders

Printed in the United States of America
Signature Book Printing, www.sbpbooks.com

First Printing, June 2014

Published and Distributed by:

Solomon Publications
P.O.B. 2124
Rockville, Maryland 20847-2124

www.solomonpublications.com

Library of Congress Control Number: 2014904245

ISBN-10   0-9670973-6-3

ISBN-13   978-0-9670973-6-7

To Susy

Abraham heard two words in the night wind.

"ab, ben, ab, ben, ab, ben."

"Father, son, father, son, father, son."

The voice became more urgent, until the two words merged into one, a terrifying command.

"aben, aben, aben, aben."

"Stone, stone, stone, stone."

Contents

Part One – War 1

Prologue 1

Chapter 1 3
Chapter 2 6
Chapter 3 11
Chapter 4 15

Part Two – Collapse 19

Chapter 5 21
Chapter 6 23
Chapter 7 28
Chapter 8 34
Chapter 9 37
Chapter 10 44
Chapter 11 51
Chapter 12 57
Chapter 13 60
Chapter 14 65
Chapter 15 71
Chapter 16 74
Chapter 17 77

Part Three – Section 614 89

Chapter 18 91
Chapter 19 96
Chapter 20 103
Chapter 21 112

Chapter 22 122
Chapter 23 127
Chapter 24 130
Chapter 25 139
Chapter 26 144

Part Four – Stone 147

Chapter 27 149
Chapter 28 156
Chapter 29 172
Chapter 30 176
Chapter 31 185
Chapter 32 189

Part Five – Testimony 197

Chapter 33 199
Chapter 34 210
Chapter 35 227
Chapter 36 234
Chapter 37 240
Chapter 38 249
Chapter 39 258
Chapter 40 275
Chapter 41 279
Chapter 42 287
Chapter 43 298
Chapter 44 306
Chapter 45 312
Chapter 46 323
Chapter 47 334
Chapter 48 345
Chapter 49 351
Chapter 50 366

Part Six – Realization 375

Chapter 51 377
Chapter 52 382
Chapter 53 388
Chapter 54 393
Chapter 55 405
Chapter 56 409
Chapter 57 413
Chapter 58 418
Chapter 59 424
Chapter 60 427
Chapter 61 431
Chapter 62 433

Epilogue 435

Afterword 437

Fact and Fiction in *Father, Son, Stone* 441

Historical and Fictional Characters 449

About Hebrew and Arabic 455

Bibliography 457

Acknowledgements 465

About the Author 467

Part One – War

Prologue

Jerusalem
November 2035

I am Nuri. I grew up in the holy city, al-Quds. When I was eighteen, my grandfather and I walked onto the Noble Sanctuary and into the courtyard between the Dome of the Rock and al-Aqsa Mosque.

We stood at the end of a long line, waiting to enter the Dome of the Rock. My grandfather, ninety years old, leaned on me and spoke in his halting, precise Arabic. Soon a security guard recognized my grandfather and escorted us inside ahead of the others.

"Stay as long as you like, please," the guard whispered to us.

The cool interior of the Dome of the Rock embraced us. My grandfather led me along the railing that surrounded the rock in the center of the dome, away from the tourists and other visitors.

"I need to tell you a story, Nuri."

I smiled. My grandfather was always telling me stories about his life.

"This one is a long one. I hope you have time today, and maybe some time tomorrow."

"I always have time for you, *jiddo*."

My grandfather hugged me and kissed the top of my head, as he had done countless times.

"You know that when you were a child, Jews used to pray next to the Noble Sanctuary."

"Of course," I said. "I studied it in school. They prayed in a plaza that used to be in front of al-Buraq's Wall. They called it the Western Wall. They stopped praying there when I was five years old. Everyone knows why."

My grandfather smiled.

"Everyone thinks they know why," he said. "But they don't know the whole story."

I looked at my grandfather, my eyes wide with wonder. He never ceased to amaze me.

"And you are going to tell me?"

He led me to a small bench against the wall. We sat and he began to speak.

Chapter 1

Monday, June 5, 1967

The morning sun was warming the runways at Tel Nof Airbase in Israel. The 55th Paratroop Brigade had been on alert since the previous evening after President Nasser's latest threats. Meir Bar-Aben knew war was imminent. His hand shook as he lathered his face to shave. He had performed training jumps, but he had never jumped in combat.

Amos Eitan, the brigade's junior intelligence officer, watched as Meir put down the shaving brush and picked up his razor. Meir's hands shook.

"Careful, Meir. Don't cut your own throat before the Egyptians get their chance."

Meir raised the razor, steadied his hand, and drew it across his face. As he did, he could hear the engines of the transport planes warming up on the runways not far from the paratrooper barracks.

Amos picked up his parachute backpack and other gear.

"Hurry up, Meir. We're heading out."

Meir dropped his razor in the sink and quickly wiped his face with a towel. Blood smeared from small cuts on his chin."

Amos laughed.

"The war hasn't even started, and you're bleeding already."

Amos was wrong. The war had started. A half hour earlier, Israeli jets had streaked west, emerging from the rays of the rising sun, destroying most of the Egyptian air force on its runways.

The paratroopers fell out onto the area adjoining the runway. The smell of fuel wafted in the air as the transport planes gunned their engines.

The men arrayed themselves with their gear in the morning sun and looked expectantly as the planes dropped their boarding ramps. The commander of the 55th Brigade raised his voice over the roar of the engines.

"Men of the 55th Brigade, you have been chosen for a special mission."

Meir and Amos craned their necks forward, trying to hear above the engine noise. Before the commander could continue, three large trucks rolled up next to them. The commander's next announcement sent the men reeling in disbelief.

"Leave your chutes on the ground where you stand. The trucks will take us to our combat assignment."

The paratroopers groaned. They could not believe this was happening to them.

Amos turned to Meir.

"Trucks. We're not going to get the red patch."

The red patch was the paratrooper emblem received by those who parachute jump during combat. During the Suez campaign in 1956, the 55th Brigade had jumped. Other paratroopers who had been airlifted into combat had not jumped and had not received the red patch.

The men of the 55th Brigade dumped their paratrooper gear on the ground and lined up next to the trucks. The commander of the 55th Brigade could see the disappointment on the paratroopers' faces.

"Men of the 55th, you have been chosen to liberate Jerusalem."

The men cheered as they raced to the trucks.

Jerusalem was a divided city. West Jerusalem was the capital of Israel, containing its seat of government, the Knesset. The Kingdom of Jordan had occupied East

Jerusalem, including the Old City, since Israel's War of Independence in 1948. Several veterans in the 55th Brigade had fought in that war. As the trucks moved northward to Jerusalem, everyone understood the importance of their mission.

Inspired by Egypt's false assertions of victory during the first day of the war, King Hussein of Jordan ordered the Jordanian Arab Legion to begin shelling West Jerusalem. The paratroopers of the 55th Brigade fought in the counterattack, encountering various pockets of the Arab Legion. By the end of the second day of the war, the paratroopers had captured East Jerusalem, except for the Old City. The 55th Brigade positioned itself outside the Old City. The defenders of East Jerusalem had retreated inside the Old City's walls.

Lieutenant General Mordechai Gur, field commander of the Israel Defense Forces—the IDF—stood on the terrace of the Intercontinental Hotel on the Mount of Olives, looking down at the Old City. The Roman Tenth Legion had camped at this location almost two thousand years ago while besieging Jerusalem. Gur had often read the historical accounts of the destruction of Jerusalem and the Temple. It was an utterly strange feeling for Gur now to be standing there. He was a Jewish general commanding a Jewish army, poised to retake what had been lost for two centuries.

His gaze focused on the Temple Mount where the Temple once stood. Known to Muslims as the Noble Sanctuary, the Dome of the Rock, with its gold dome, stood in the center, and al-Aqsa Mosque, with its silver dome, stood in the southwest corner. The presence of these Muslim holy sites did not dim Jewish longing for access to the Temple Mount, which remained as holy to the Jews as if the Temple still stood upon it.

The glow from the twin domes faded as the sun set.

Chapter 2

Wednesday, June 7, 1967

The third day of the war dawned clear and hot. The paratroopers of the 55th Brigade crouched just outside the Lions' Gate in the walls of the Old City. For the past half hour, Meir, Amos, and several others could not go forward because of Jordanian sniper fire. Amos was bracing himself against the wall to the right of the gate, transmitting their position and combat conditions to Commander Gur.

Meir breathed deeply in the increasing heat and gagged. "Donkey piss," he muttered. "This place reeks of donkey piss."

A sniper's bullet whizzed by his left ear, and he pulled his helmet down tighter over his forehead.

Commander Gur remained in his outpost on the Mount of Olives, gathering information from his intelligence officers near the fighting. As the sun rose over his shoulder and illuminated the city below, he received reports of intense sniper fire from the Arab Legion. His paratroopers outside the Old City could not remain there in constant danger from snipers. Finally, at nine o'clock, he received the orders from Minister of Defense Moshe Dayan that he had hoped to hear.

Amos, Meir, and the other paratroopers had maintained their positions in an alley outside the Lions' Gate since sunrise. Suddenly, the battalion's commanding officer received the order from Commander Gur over the radio.

"Proceed into the Old City. Secure the Temple Mount."

The commanding officer pointed his finger toward the Lions' Gate. Amos raised his rifle and fired directly over Meir's head, causing stone to ricochet into the narrow alley. This gave Meir cover, and he raced through the gate followed by about twenty of his fellow paratroopers.

Immediately after giving the order to take the Old City, Commander Gur and his driver began their descent from the Mount of Olives to the Lions' Gate in a half-track.

Meir entered the Old City and flattened himself against the wall of a building. Sniper fire was sporadic. The jets of the Israeli air force attacked and neutralized Jordanian artillery positions in the surrounding hills. Meir, Amos, and the other paratroopers advanced down the Via Dolorosa that paralleled the north side of the Temple Mount. Within minutes, Commander Gur arrived outside the Old City in his half-track. He directed his driver straight through the gate over a Jordanian motorcycle riddled with bullets. They proceeded down the Via Dolorosa and passed the paratroopers. The paratroopers gathered behind the half-track and followed.

A boy stepped into the narrow street from a doorway. Clad in a loose-fitting shirt and cotton pants, wearing sandals, he looked unconcerned at the advancing chaos and battle garb worn by the Israeli troops. He held up his hand, and the paratroopers stopped in amazement.

"*al-qubbat as-sukhrah? al-masjid al-aksa?*" the boy spoke in Arabic.

Amos understood. "He will lead us to the Dome of the Rock and al-Aqsa Mosque."

The boy pointed south through an alley. They could see the gold crown of the Dome of the Rock protruding from over a wall.

Commander Gur's half-track turned into the alley. The paratroopers ran ahead and burst into the courtyard on the Temple Mount between the two Muslim holy structures. The sniper fire had stopped. There was no resistance here.

Commander Gur radioed General Uzi Narkiss at Central Command.

"*har habayit bi yadenu!*" The Temple Mount is in our hands!

The paratroopers secured the Temple Mount. They found the door of the Dome of the Rock bolted with a heavy padlock. Two paratroopers approached and shot the padlock off. They entered and found themselves in silence. Heavy carpet muffled their steps as they searched for a way to the roof. They soon found a stairway that led them to a door at the dome's base. Opening the door and stepping onto a platform surrounding the dome, they could see the entire expanse of Jerusalem stretched before them. They raised an Israeli flag over the dome.

General Uzi Narkiss left Central Command in his jeep and headed toward the Old City. As he entered the Lions' Gate, he saw Rabbi Shlomo Goren, chief rabbi of the IDF, carrying a Torah scroll and blowing a shofar. He followed the rabbi in his jeep and they quickly found their way to the Temple Mount.

As they stood on the Temple Mount, Rabbi Goren turned to General Narkiss.

"Now is our opportunity to blow up the Dome of the Rock. Do this and you will go down in history."

General Narkiss was stunned. The consequences of destroying the Muslim holy site were unthinkable. General Narkiss did not reveal Rabbi Goren's remark until many years later.

Minister of Defense Moshe Dayan entered the Old City soon after and came to the Temple Mount. When he saw the Israeli flag flying over the Dome of the Rock, he realized this would be an inflammatory action if reported in the press. He ordered General Narkiss to direct his troops to remove the flag.

Meir watched several paratroopers rush to the edge of the Temple Mount. They found a spiral staircase descending into an alley. In several minutes, Meir heard shouts from below.

"*hakotel! hakotel!*" The Wall! The Wall!

Meir signaled to Amos. They rushed to the staircase and climbed down the narrow stairs. The stones of the Western Wall, *ha-kotel ha-maaravi,* usually referred to as the Kotel, loomed gray and white in a narrow alley bounded by houses. Rabbi Goren sounded his shofar as he squeezed into the alley. Some paratroopers reverently touched the Kotel. Others embraced it. Many wept.

Rabbi Goren began an ancient Hebrew prayer.

"Blessed are you, Lord, Our God, King of the Universe, who has kept us alive . . ."

The soldiers joined in, ". . . and sustained us, and enabled us to reach this day."

Several paratroopers hoisted Rabbi Goren onto their shoulders and twirled him as he blew a shofar again and again.

Meir felt numb, remembering that many of his fellow paratroopers had been wounded or killed in the fighting. He had no religious feeling for the capturing of the Temple Mount.

A paratrooper took a camera from his backpack. Amos pulled Meir next to him. Meir was oblivious as the paratrooper took their picture in front of the Kotel.

Chapter 3

Dusk settled over the Old City. The paratroopers closed alleys and streets leading into the Temple Mount. Moshe Dayan stood at the edge of the Temple Mount, looking down into the alley adjoining the Kotel, where Rabbi Goren was leading a group of paratroopers in evening prayer. He could hear the Muslim call to prayer, which would usually emanate from al-Aqsa Mosque, echoing from somewhere nearby. Moshe Dayan waited until Rabbi Goren concluded the evening prayers. Rabbi Goren finally closed his prayer book, kissed it, and ascended the staircase to meet Moshe Dayan.

"Rabbi," Moshe Dayan said softly, "we have some decisions to make, and we need to make them quickly."

Rabbi Goren nodded but said nothing.

"We can't sit here and celebrate, ignoring the millions of Arabs in this world who would gladly blow us off the face of the earth for doing what we did today."

Rabbi Goren cleared his throat and nodded again.

"We will be under pressure from our own people as well as the Arabs."

Rabbi Goren placed his hands on Moshe Dayan's shoulders, looked him directly in the eyes, and recited an ancient Hebrew prayer, "May the Temple of the Lord be rebuilt speedily in our day."

The Muslim call to prayer reverberated again through the evening air, as if in response to Rabbi Goren's prayer.

Later that evening, Moshe Dayan stood in the courtyard of the Dome of the Rock. A military reporter asked for a statement. Moshe Dayan said, "We have returned to the holiest of our sites and will never again be separated from it. To our Arab neighbors, Israel extends the hand of peace, and to the peoples of all faiths, we guarantee full freedom of worship and of religious rights. We have come not to conquer the holy places of others, nor to diminish by the slightest measure their religious rights, but to ensure the unity of the city and to live in it with others in harmony."

Meir and Amos stood guard at the bottom of the staircase leading from the Kotel to the Temple Mount. As Rabbi Goren and the paratroopers finished their evening prayers, the paratroopers dispersed. Several minutes after the rabbi returned to the Temple Mount above, a man emerged from the shadows of the Old City. He had his arms raised above his head. He came forward, raised his arms higher, and shouted in Arabic.

"*ana imam. ureedu tatakalumu lakum.*" I am a religious leader. I want to speak with you.

Amos motioned the man to come forward as the paratroopers held their guns steady. The man spoke again.

"*tatakalamu arabiyata?*" Do you speak Arabic?

Without hesitation, Amos responded in Arabic.

"*naam. jayidun jiddan.*" Yes, very well.

The man began speaking rapidly. Amos nodded and motioned to the paratroopers.

"He says he needs to speak to someone in authority. Check him, and then I can take him to the command tent."

Two paratroopers frisked the man. Amos escorted him up the stairway to the Temple Mount. He left the man with two guards and entered the command tent alone. Amos came out a few minutes later and took the man into the command tent.

Night had fallen. Meir looked up, observing the order of the night sky. He knew that the war was still raging on other fronts. Yet peace had come to Jerusalem. As Meir walked back up the staircase to the Temple Mount, he heard footsteps behind him. He turned to find two soldiers walking up the staircase with an Orthodox Jew wearing a long black coat and carrying a canvas bag.

The soldiers approached Meir. One spoke.

"This man says Rabbi Goren is waiting for him. Please escort him to the command tent."

Meir motioned the man to follow him.

When they reached the top of the staircase, Meir saw Amos standing outside the command tent as if he were waiting for someone.

Amos came to them quickly.

"Please follow me," Amos said to the Orthodox Jew as he led him into the command tent.

Meir stood guard outside the command tent with several paratroopers. About two hours later, Moshe Dayan, Rabbi Goren, and the Orthodox Jew left the command tent. They approached Meir and the other paratroopers.

"The Kotel is secure, I assume?" Dayan asked.

"Yes, sir," Meir answered. "There is a contingent below along the length of the Kotel."

Moshe Dayan, Rabbi Goren, and the Orthodox Jew descended the staircase. They came back up the staircase an hour later and returned to the command tent. Soon Amos came out with the Muslim man. Amos was speaking Arabic to him. He led him down the staircase and returned to the command tent alone. Several minutes later, Moshe Dayan and Rabbi Goren escorted the Orthodox Jew to the staircase, and several paratroopers led him away.

Amos joined Meir later that night as Meir was resting on a sleeping bag against the wall of the Dome of the Rock.

"You seemed heavily involved. What happened in there?" Meir asked.

Amos smiled and waved his hand.

"Nothing," he said, dismissing the question. "There's nothing I can tell you."

Amos remained in Jerusalem after the capture of the Old City to assist Moshe Dayan. Meir went north with the majority of the 55th Brigade to fight in the Golan during the last days of the war.

Chapter 4

Saturday, June 11, 1967

By the sixth day of the war, most of the fighting had ended. The entire nation was euphoric. Politicians and the public discussed many changes. Former prime minister David Ben-Gurion proposed tearing down the walls of the Old City built by the Ottoman Turks, so there was no division between the Old City and West Jerusalem. Others suggested building a replica of Rome's Arch of Titus—which depicted the aftermath of the Roman destruction of the Temple—somewhere in Jerusalem, with its Latin inscription of "Judea Captured" altered to read "Judea Liberated." Many wanted the song "Jerusalem of Gold," which had become popular shortly before the war, to replace *"Hatikva"* as the national anthem. None of these suggested changes happened.

The Knesset received many recommendations for naming the war, including The War of Life, The War of Survival, and The War of Peace. Ultimately, the Prime Minister's Office chose the Six-Day War, which is what the press had begun calling the war shortly after it ended. In hindsight, the name evoked the religious aura of the six days of creation and thus a renewal of the State of Israel.

On June 17, 1967, the first Shabbat after the war, the State of Israel now included the Old City of Jerusalem and the Temple Mount. In the previous week, the IDF bulldozed the Arab neighborhood in front of the Kotel, creating a large plaza for the multitudes eager to visit the historic landmark. The Kotel, no longer hidden from view by the narrow alleys created by encroaching buildings, stood stark and exposed.

Moshe Dayan and Amos Eitan, together with high-ranking military officers of the IDF, ascended the Temple Mount and walked toward al-Aqsa Mosque. The five members of the Waqf, the Supreme Muslim Council that had controlled what had previously been Jordanian-controlled Jerusalem, met the Israeli delegation at the entrance to the mosque. They ushered the Israelis inside, and everyone sat on a large prayer rug in the center of the mosque. Amos sat next to Moshe Dayan. The meeting proceeded with mutual respect. Moshe Dayan stated that the Temple Mount was an important part of the Jewish people's ancient past. Nevertheless, it would remain a Muslim place of worship under the control of the Waqf.

Thus, in a gesture of goodwill, the conqueror ceded back control to the conquered. The administrative control over the Temple Mount was to be the sole responsibility of the Waqf. While Israel now had access to the Kotel, the Waqf would continue to control the Temple Mount, just as it had done before the war.

That evening, Amos and Meir met at a small sidewalk cafe on King George Street overlooking the Old City. They hugged each other joyfully. Amos lit a cigarette and leaned back in his chair, admiring the view. They could hear the Muslim call to prayer from al-Aqsa Mosque.

Meir cradled his chin in his hands, staring at the Old City.

"It seems unreal, Amos. We're both twenty-two, and we've survived a war."

Amos exhaled slowly, reached under the table into his backpack, and withdrew a small package wrapped in brown paper.

"Remember the paratrooper taking pictures? He gave me this."

Meir opened the package. Inside was a framed photograph of himself and Amos at the Kotel.

"Thanks, Amos," Meir said. "What's next for you?"

"I'm not sure. I'm going back to my kibbutz for a while. What about you?"

Meir looked at Amos.

"I want to go to Hebrew University. I've always wanted to be an attorney."

Amos laughed. "You are always the one with the questions. You'll be a good attorney."

Meir was silent for a few moments, and then he leaned forward.

"I have to ask again, Amos. Who were the Muslim man and the Orthodox Jew? What did they say?"

Amos crooked his neck and puffed smoke rings skyward.

"I told you, I can't speak about what happened."

"But we risked our lives to capture the Temple Mount, Amos. We reclaimed our holiest place after almost two thousand years. We lost lives. Many were wounded. Then we gave it back. It doesn't make sense."

Amos nodded but remained silent. Meir looked him in the eye.

"Amos, what happened? Why did we give back the Temple Mount?"

Amos shook his head.

"Meir, please. No more questions."

Amos finished his beer, stood up, and dropped money on the table.

"The beer is on me. *l'hitraot*. I'll be seeing you!"

Meir stood up and shook hands with Amos. Amos turned and walked down King George Street. Meir sat down. His question reverberated in his mind as he saw Amos disappear into the crowd.

Why did we give it back?

Part Two – Collapse

Jerusalem
November 2035

My grandfather paused.

"Let's take a walk outside, Nuri. I need to stretch my legs."

As my grandfather stood and steadied himself, the security guard came over to us. He shook my grandfather's hand and spoke.

"Whenever you come back, come find me at the guard's station and you won't have to wait in line."

My grandfather said, *"shukran,"* and the guard smiled at me.

We walked out of the Dome of the Rock and into the morning sun. I led my grandfather to a bench shaded by a canopy. My grandfather sat and patted the bench next to him.

"Sit. We are going to be here awhile."

I sat close to my *jiddo.* I sensed he was anxious to continue with his story. He put his arm around my shoulder.

"I am not boring you, Nuri?"

"Never."

"Good. There is much more to tell. There is another person who fought in the war who is important to the story. Do you remember Ezer Zadok?"

"He was prime minister when I was born, *jiddo.*"

My grandfather nodded.

"We are going to move ahead to 2014, several years before you were born, when he was prime minister."

We sat, and my grandfather continued his story.

Chapter 5

Hassan ibn Sadik pressed his forehead against the prayer rug covering the floor of al-Aqsa Mosque. He rose to his knees and continued to pray. He was oblivious to those around him. By the time the morning prayers ended, Hassan and the other worshippers had assumed all the positions taught to Muhammad by the angel Gabriel.

As the mosque emptied, those close to Hassan could smell the perfumed rose water he had bathed in that morning. They whispered, "*shaheed, shaheed,*" as they averted their eyes so as not to draw attention to him. Several touched him on the shoulder and murmured, "*allah hu akbar.*"

A soft breeze brushed his face as he came out of the mosque. He felt that the virgins in paradise were already kissing his cheek.

Hassan hurried back to the small apartment in the Old City and changed his clothes. His two companions strapped the explosives to his chest and helped him button the clean white shirt. He pulled on dark pants and looked at himself in the mirror. The rest of his clothes were in a small canvas bag. Without saying a word, all three descended the narrow stairs to a small courtyard.

Hassan climbed into the back of a battered van with no side windows. As he put on the rest of his clothes, the two men in the front seat fought for the rearview mirror and began to laugh. Hassan sat in the back of the van dressed as an Orthodox Jew.

"Shut up, you sons of donkeys," Hassan said under his breath.

They left the Old City and drove to Ben Yehuda Street. Hassan opened the rear door and jumped out. He walked down the street, merging with those waiting at a bus stop.

As the bus approached, he huddled together with the others waiting on the curb. No one glanced at him as he boarded the bus and sat directly behind the driver.

The driver closed the passenger door and pulled away from the curb. Hassan opened the book he was carrying and pretended to read. The bus crept through afternoon traffic, stopping several times. Hassan waited until the bus was full and several passengers were standing in the aisles. He slowly put his hand inside his dark coat and fumbled for the detonator. Looking out the window, he saw a couple holding hands. Behind them, a woman pushed a baby carriage.

He looked at the sky and remembered his handlers' words: "He who dies in battle enters paradise."

He activated the detonator. Before he could catch sight of the beautiful *djinn* who would escort him into the life to come, he entered a black, painless void.

Chapter 6

Prime Minister Ezer Zadok sat in his office at the Knesset, trying not to light another cigarette. He had already smoked three since he had been informed of the of the bus bombing an hour before. He was waiting for the casualty report.

To divert himself, he had started to read a report from Hiram Aitza, the Director of the Israel Museum. Zadok had recently ordered the report from a team of museum archaeologists because of construction activities by the Waqf under the Temple Mount.

Beginning in the 1990s, the Waqf had excavated an area under al-Aqsa Mosque, creating a large prayer hall called the Marwani Mosque. The excavators had dumped seventy trucks of material into the Kidron Valley to the east of the Temple Mount. Many Israelis believed that the Waqf was systematically destroying evidence of the Temple that might remain under the Temple Mount.

The courts had considered the excavations twice. In 2000, a court had rejected a petition to halt construction. Ehud Olmert, the mayor of Jerusalem, then issued an order to halt the project. The Waqf had ignored the order and continued with the construction.

In 2007, a private organization on behalf of a group of Israeli citizens had filed a petition in the Supreme Court of Israel. The petition claimed that the Waqf was illegally attempting to eradicate all evidence of Israel's ancient connection to the Temple Mount. The organization argued that the Waqf's excavations were a religious, cultural, and archaeological crime. In 2010, shortly after Zadok's election as prime minister, the

Supreme Court had dismissed the petition, holding that the private citizens did not have standing to block the excavations.

Zadok had then ordered the museum archaeologists' investigation to discover the extent of the destruction below the Temple Mount. He found the report very disturbing.

The report concluded:

This demolition of the strata of the Temple Mount was the most extensive since the construction of the Dome of the Rock in the seventh century C.E. The demolition proceeded without archaeological regulation or oversight. Many artifacts dating to the First and Second Temples and the Crusades were covered up, destroyed, or removed. Since the excavations, a large bulge in the Kotel has developed. Because our archaeologists do not have access to the caverns under the Temple Mount, they could not determine the actual cause of the bulge.

Zadok slammed his hand down on the desk. How could the bulge in the Kotel *not* be caused by the Waqf's excavation? He threw the report against the wall, scattering the pages on the floor.

He picked up the phone and called Hiram Aitza on his direct line. The phone rang once.

"Ezer, don't tell me you are canceling the poker game tonight."

"No, I need your money, Hiram. I'm calling about this report on the Kotel."

"What about it? You've known about the excavations for years. The protests, the press exposure, and the court cases could not stop it. They drilled, crushed, and dumped the material in a pile. Our archeologists have rescued the material and are sifting it for artifacts that might have survived."

Ezer slammed his hand on his desk again.

"I'm not talking about the excavated material. I'm talking about the bulge in the Kotel. This is the first time I've heard of that. How can we allow that to happen?"

Hiram laughed.

"Ezer, Ezer, those stones have been standing for two thousand years. Even the Romans couldn't knock them down when they demolished everything else. Relax. I'll see you tonight. You'll win as usual and go home with some extra shekels."

"I'll see you tonight, Hiram."

Zadok hung up and stared out his window. He felt a strong connection to the Temple Mount. As a member of the 66th Battalion of the 55th Paratroop Brigade, he had been severely wounded during the early morning of July 6, 1967, during the battle of Ammunition Hill outside the Old City. He had lost consciousness and had been evacuated with other wounded. When Zadok had regained consciousness in the hospital on the last day of the war, he learned that thirty-six soldiers in his battalion had died in battle.

His wounds and the loss of his friends had sent him into a deep depression. Hiram Aitza was in the bed next to him, recovering from wounds he had received in combat in the Golan Heights. When Zadok heard that Moshe Dayan had returned the Temple Mount to the Waqf, Hiram had to restrain Zadok from rising from his hospital bed and destroying furniture. During the next few weeks, Hiram's upbeat personality had pulled Zadok out of his depression. They had remained close friends ever since. Hiram had attended Hebrew University and become an eminent archaeologist.

Zadok was twenty-two years old when the Six-Day War ended. He had decided to remain in permanent service in the IDF after the war, and he had fought in the Yom Kippur War in 1973. By 1980, he had reached the rank of major. In 1982, he lost a leg below the knee when he was wounded during the IDF's "Operation Peace for Galilee" invasion of Southern Lebanon.

Zadok never had any desire to enter politics, but the press and the public followed his rehabilitation closely. He had given interviews from his hospital bed in the early days after his injury. The press filmed and broadcasted his first halting steps on his prosthesis and his determined facial expressions. He revealed his innermost feelings to the microphones and cameras, resolving that his days as a warrior were over. He had expected to return to the kibbutz in the Negev, collect his military pension, and watch his grandchildren grow up. What he did not expect was the public adulation that followed him everywhere.

His frankness and honesty were political assets that could be cultivated. He ran for a seat in the Knesset and won the election in 2000 when he was fifty-five. He served as a bridge among the various political parties, until he became the obvious choice for prime minister in 2010.

Today, as he waited for the casualty report, Zadok leaned back in his chair and breathed slowly. He lit his fourth cigarette and puffed smoke rings. He was about to gather the scattered papers on the floor when his secretary called him from the outer office. Zadok picked up the phone.

"They have just issued the preliminary casualty report from the bus bombing, sir. Ten dead, fifteen severely wounded."

Zadok breathed heavily into the phone. He reached down and massaged his knee.

"Have the press secretary meet with me to prepare a statement, please."

"Something else, sir," his secretary said. "One of the seriously injured is Ori Bar-Aben."

"Bar-Aben? Is he related to . . .?"

"Yes, sir. He is the son of Meir Bar-Aben, the newest justice of the Supreme Court."

Chapter 7

Almost three years passed since the day Hassan ibn Sadik had killed himself and others on the bus on Ben Yehuda Street.

The morning sun shone brightly on the building that housed *beit hamishpat haelyon medinat yisrael*, the Supreme Court of the State of Israel. Built of luminescent pink Jerusalem stone, the Supreme Court's building rose as a natural outcropping of the hill on which it stood.

Justice Meir Bar-Aben stood at the window in his chambers and looked down into the central courtyard of the building, known as the Courtyard of the Arches. A little more than three years ago, shortly after Meir's appointment to the court, a few weeks before Ori had died, Meir's wife, Channah, had given him a framed scroll. The scroll contained the verse from the book of Psalms that had inspired the architects when they designed the courtyard.

The verse read, "Truth will spring up from the earth and justice will be reflected from the heavens." The construction of the courtyard visually expressed the verse by its stone floor and a small channel of water that ran through the center. The stone represented the solidity of law, and the sky—reflected in the water— represented justice.

Meir turned from the window, scanned the Hebrew script of the scroll, and shook his head. He had never seen truth spring up from the earth, nor justice reflected from the heavens. He had spent a good portion of his life with the responsibility to discover truth. Before his appointment to the Supreme Court, he had been a district court judge and an attorney in private practice.

In court, as in archaeological excavations, truth had to be extracted from layers of compressed historical rubble. Truth was like sunlight, reflecting from the sea or the desert. Depending on what it struck, and who was watching, sunlight could be brilliant, subtle, distinct, or vague. A judge sifted through testimony, documents, innuendo, ambiguity, faded memory, and bias. Even then, it was difficult to determine what was true. Meir doubted that truth would ever spring up in front of him, as the psalm suggested.

He returned to his desk and sat down. He was trying to gain enough mental momentum to finish drafting a decision he had started several days ago. His secretary, Ruth, had reminded him several times last week that his deadline for producing a first draft had passed.

He stared at the computer screen. His phone rang. He knew it was Ruth calling from the outer office.

"President Heifitz is here to see you."

Meir hung up and walked toward the door. Eli Heifitz, the chief justice, did not visit his colleagues for social reasons. He was standing at the door when Meir opened it.

"Justice Bar-Aben, good morning."

"Mr. President. Please come in and have a seat." The staff and justices always called the chief justice by his official title, President of the Court.

Eli Heifitz sat in one of the two chairs facing Meir's desk. Meir sat behind his desk and waited. The chief justice was not one to waste time.

"I'm concerned about the Kleinman decision."

"Mr. President, I'm working on that decision now."

Eli Heifitz looked around, not seeing evidence of work in progress, except for a document displayed on Meir's computer screen. Meir's colleagues were all aware of his compulsive neatness.

"I'm actually more concerned about you."

"Because?"

"Your docket is not current."

Meir nodded.

"Mr. President, the Kleinman decision is the only decision that is late. I have read the record, and I'm writing the decision. You know my methodology."

Meir could write the most complicated decision relying upon his memory of the written record and the oral arguments. He wrote one draft and then circulated it to the other justices.

The chief justice shifted in his chair.

"You are working on the Kleinman decision?"

"I'm probably a week away from finishing it."

"And how is Channah?"

The chief justice always shifted to personal subjects when he finished his business agenda. Meir knew the conversation was over.

"Channah is fine."

"Good. Glad to hear it," Eli Heifitz said, as he rose from his chair and headed to the door.

Meir followed, closed the door of his office, and returned to his desk. He felt a twinge in his right arm. He reached with his left hand to massage it. This pain came at moments when he felt particularly stressed.

Meir's pain always evoked memories of his father, who had escaped Poland in 1939 to Romania. That same year, with a group of Romanian and Polish Jews, Meir's father had boarded a ship that sailed from the Romanian port of Constanta. After sailing at night for twenty-two days, the ship had anchored off the Tel

Aviv beach and the illegal immigrants had swum ashore in the moonlight. By the time Meir had been born in 1945, his father had abandoned the *tallit*, *tefillin*, prayer, the Commandments, and his Polish name, and had taken the name Chaim Bar-Aben, which meant "life, son of stone."

When Meir had asked his father why he had chosen to be called Chaim Bar-Aben, Chaim had replied, "The night I swam ashore on the Tel Aviv beach, I buried my past. I felt reborn, even though the State of Israel was still just a dream. I am not a son of Abraham. I am not a son of Europe. I am not a son of Poland. I am strong because I survived. I live, and I am a son of stone."

While Chaim had suppressed the memory of his life in Europe, his musical ability had been his legacy to his son. Chaim had been a professional violinist in Poland, and he began to teach Meir the violin when Meir was six. Even though he had had no desire to play professionally, Meir studied the violin diligently with his father. One night, when he was seventeen, Meir had played one of Heinrich Ignaz Franz von Biber's *Mystery Sonatas* several times.

He had woken the next morning unable to lift his right arm. Meir had injured himself, and his doctor told him he could not play the violin for six months until it healed. Meir had tried to play after the six-month hiatus, but the pain returned. During his military service, law practice, and the demands of family life, Meir would occasionally think that he should play his violin, but he never did. When the pain erupted during stressful moments, Meir would remember the many hours he had spent studying the violin with his father.

As Meir sat at his desk, he massaged his aching arm, willing himself to relax. The pain was too familiar to be anything other than his normal pain. He stretched both arms in front of him and then placed his hands behind his head. This usually dulled the pain, as it did this time.

He closed his eyes and breathed slowly, his mind drifting to the legal principles and the facts of the Kleinman case. He stared at the draft decision he had started. His hands felt heavy on the keyboard, his fingers numb.

Meir looked at the framed photograph of Ori, tanned and healthy, on the beach at Eilat. Meir rose from his chair and locked the door. Ruth heard the lock click softly and knew not to disturb him until he opened the door again. Meir crossed the office and slowly collapsed into a large leather chair near the window. He closed his eyes and gave himself up to the pressure in his chest and the tears that followed. After several minutes, he forced himself back to his desk and continued to work.

Meir did not make much progress on the Kleinman decision that morning. When he emerged from his chambers a few minutes after noon, Ruth was gone. Friday was a half day at the court, as most employees left by early afternoon to prepare for Shabbat. Meir stayed until four, then turned off his computer and put the Kleinman file in his cabinet, returning his office to its pristine state of neatness.

The afternoon sun beat down as Meir came out of the underground parking garage. He opened the sunroof of his Mercedes and breathed the dry air that usually cleared his head. *Don't focus, don't concentrate, stay loose.*

Despite his attempt to relax, Meir could feel the sensation of a flashback building. As he gripped the wheel, his arms suddenly became heavy, and he pushed forward to maintain his grip. He sucked in his breath and held it, then exhaled. He slowed for a red light, coming to a stop behind a bus packed with commuters. He closed his eyes, knowing that self-imposed darkness would not prevent the vision of what was about to burst inside his head.

Even with his eyes closed, he could see the bus explode in a massive fireball followed by dense black smoke. As the flash subsided, he saw that the top of the bus had peeled back and the sides had puffed outward. Body parts were strewn on the street, and mangled bodies were tossed inside the bus. Some were hanging out of the blown-out windows. He could feel the force of the blast hit his car and throw him against the seat. The smell of smoke and burning flesh filled his nose and throat.

He could not stop himself from screaming, "Ori, Ori!"

When he opened his eyes, the flashback was over. He saw crowds of shoppers, several couples holding hands, and a group of tourists staring at maps and street signs. The light changed to green, and the bus slowly accelerated, its exhaust wafting through his sunroof. He bent forward and placed his forehead on the steering wheel. The honking horns behind him urged him forward. When Meir raised his head, the bus had already turned the corner and was out of sight.

Chapter 8

As Meir was driving home, Zara lay on her bed in her parents' house in the Jerusalem neighborhood of Silwan, where she lived with her husband, Hamid. Hamid sat working at a desk in the corner of their room. He looked up and noticed the clothing that Zara had draped across a chair in front of the bed.

"You have lost your mind, Zara," Hamid said.

Zara ignored Hamid. She had several hours to relax before she dressed to go out that night. She reached into the drawer of her night table and removed a tattered newspaper article.

"Don't read that again, Zara. You've read that a thousand times in the last three years."

"Read it to me, Hamid. Please."

Hamid sighed. He got up from the desk and sat on the bed next to her. He took the article and began to read.

"Son of Supreme Court Justice Killed in Suicide Bombing. . . ." As Hamid read the article, Zara turned on her side and listened to him. By the time he was finished, she was asleep.

Zara woke two hours later. Hamid was asleep next to her. She rose from the bed and dressed quickly. She sat at a small vanity and removed a wig from a box. She put the wig on, looked at herself in the mirror, and smiled. She was twenty-three, with dark eyes and olive skin. The wig covered her long black hair, and, together with the clothes, dramatically changed her appearance. She turned and found Hamid awake and staring at her. She stood and turned in a circle.

"How do I look?" she asked.

Hamid sat up and placed his head in his hands.

"Jewish," he said. "Very Jewish."
"I'm ready," Zara said.

Zara glided through the door of the Rambam Synagogue in the Jewish Quarter of the Old City of Jerusalem. "*shabbat shalom*" bubbled from the group of women bunched at the door, kissing and pinching the faces of young children. Men in large black hats and white shirts whispered to each other. Some talked about business and sports in low tones, while others quieted their minds to contemplate the arrival of the mystical Shabbat Queen.

Just moments before, her heart had skipped as the security guard wanded her from head to toe. She had been careful not to wear any jewelry, not even her wedding ring. She had clutched her chest involuntarily, and the tall guard had put his hand on her shoulder with a look of concern.

"*aht beseder?*" Are you okay?

"*ken, ani beseder.* Yes, I am okay. The Hebrew glided from her tongue as if it were her native language.

She had calmed immediately when the soft lights of the synagogue bathed her at the entrance. She looked around at the seats, the raised platform in the center of the room, and the Holy Ark that held the Torah scrolls. The room looked crowded even without people in it. Zara was used to the larger expanse of the mosque, rugs on the floor, people finding their prayer places on the floor, pillars holding a high ceiling. She found an aisle seat in an empty row near the back. Someone began a slow chant, and everyone began to take their seats.

Zara closed her eyes and prayed silently, her lips not moving.

"*bismallah arrahman arraheem.*" In the name of God, the Compassionate, the Merciful.

She clutched her arms tightly around her.

I must do what I must do, Zara thought. She looked around. Everyone was praying, welcoming the Shabbat Queen. No one was paying any attention to the young woman who had easily breached their security.

Hamid paced outside the Dung Gate of the Old City. When he had failed to persuade Zara not to go to the synagogue, Hamid could not stay at home and wait. He had walked several paces behind her to the wall surrounding the Old City. He had watched Zara disappear into the Jewish Quarter dressed as a Jewish woman.

What had possessed his wife to do this? Nothing he had said could dissuade her. He had pleaded with her, but Zara shook her head and insisted that God would protect her.

An hour later, the sun had set and the stars and moon cast a faint glow. At first, Hamid did not recognize Zara as she walked through the Dung Gate in the dim light. She looked radiant, happy, like the Jews looked on Shabbat. He could not believe this was his wife. She looked at Hamid and walked past him toward Silwan. He followed behind and prayed that God would free his wife from her obsessive plan.

Chapter 9

Samir ibn Abdullah awoke before dawn the following Monday morning. His wife, Jamilah, slept soundly next to him. He slipped out of bed and reached for his robe on the chair near the door. He was jolted into full wakefulness as his bare feet curled at the feel of the cold stone floor. Samir padded down the hall to the kitchen and turned on a small electric heater under the kitchen table. The chill of the Muslim Quarter of the Old City had seeped into the stone walls and floors.

He sat down and inched his bare feet toward the heater. He hated wearing slippers. They kept him from waking up. How many pairs had Jamilah given him? They were all in their boxes in his closet. Samir waited until his feet were warm and then went to the sink. He opened the cabinet above and grasped his large tea mug. He put two pinches of tea leaves into the bottom of the mug and filled it from the instant hot water dispenser. What a luxury! No more waiting for hot water to boil. No more screeching teapots to wake Jamilah.

Samir, eighty years old, still looked forward to his Monday duties at al-Aqsa Mosque. He reached for the honey and mixed two large spoons of it with the hot water and tea. The tea was just an excuse to drink the honey. The honey coated his throat and allowed his voice to explode from his lungs. He sipped the tea and honey while he stood at the kitchen window. In the distance, dawn tinted the gold and silver domes.

Samir dressed quickly and left Jamilah in bed. He stepped out into the narrow streets. Monday was his day to deliver the *adhan*, the call to prayer. The Muslim Jumuah, Jewish Shabbat, and Christian Sunday were over. Shops were still shuttered, and the streets were dark. He entered the Noble Sanctuary and walked south around the Dome of the Rock. Even though he had walked this path for more than fifty years, he stopped and looked at the mosaics that adorned the outside of the dome.

Yazir, the blind beggar, was sitting cross-legged in his usual spot in the courtyard. He recognized Samir's footsteps.

"*sabah al-chaeer, ya samir.*" Good morning, Samir.

"*sabah al-nur, ya yazir.*" May your morning be full of light, Yazir.

Samir's greeting was the traditional response, but Samir always felt odd responding so to Yazir. As usual, Yazir cackled a toothless laugh, accepting the irony of Samir's words.

Samir walked quickly toward al-Aqsa Mosque. His eyes caressed the silver dome in the dim gloom. He sprinted up the winding stairs before the sun rose. Standing on the small platform at the top of the minaret of al-Aqsa Mosque, he caught his breath and inhaled deeply. He let the cool air soothe his vocal chords. This was his time to be alone.

The gold dome of the Dome of the Rock floated to the north as dawn approached. To the west, he could see down into the plaza in front of al-Buraq's Wall, where the Jews were gathering for their morning prayers. Below him to the south, the ruins of the Umayyad Palace dropped away. He looked at his watch. It was five minutes before sunrise. He closed his eyes and clutched his ears with his hands, facing the Holy City of Mecca. Inhaling deeply, he began the *adhan.*

"allah hu akbar."

"God is greater."

Samir continued with the call to prayer.

"asshadu anna muhammadan rasul allah."

"I bear witness that Muhammad is the messenger of God."

He particularly liked the phrase added to the morning call.

"assalatu haran min a nawm."

"Prayer is better than sleep."

As Samir issued the call to prayer, Rabbi Ashur Avidan arrived at the Kotel. He greeted his regular *minyan,* his prayer group. Another half hour passed until everyone arrived. Rabbi Avidan led the group in their morning prayers. When the prayers concluded, he approached the Kotel and pressed his head and hands against one of the large stones. He closed his eyes and tried to calm himself by offering a personal prayer. He could not dispel the tension he had felt after the phone calls the night before. Seventy-one rabbis were advocating action to rebuild the Temple on the Temple Mount. Why was he not willing to join them? Why was he ignoring those who deemed themselves the most learned men of his generation?

Rabbi Avidan could not give them an answer they would accept. His ancestor had fled from this very spot almost two thousand years ago before the Romans had reduced Jerusalem to rubble. He was concerned that the Waqf had conducted excavations under the Temple Mount and created the mammoth Marwani Mosque under al-Aqsa Mosque. Nevertheless, he believed that rebuilding the Temple was a physical and political impossibility.

After Rabbi Avidan finished his prayer, he walked across the plaza in front of the Kotel and up the stairs to the Jewish Quarter of the Old City of Jerusalem.

Zara could not sleep. She woke before dawn in her bedroom in her parents' house. Hamid was still sleeping. He was exhausted from celebrating the news that Zara had shared with him the night before. She had told him that she was pregnant. She did not want to tell her parents or anyone else until she had been to the doctor.

When Zara heard the call to prayer from al-Aqsa Mosque, she rose from her bed and dressed quickly. She left the house and walked the narrow streets upward toward the gold and silver domes in the distance.

As she approached the Dung Gate, she again was determined to have courage to do what her heart urged her to do, even at the expense of causing pain to her parents and her husband. She was almost ready, until yesterday when she discovered she was pregnant.

Now, as Zara approached the Noble Sanctuary, her course became clear again. She would execute her plan soon. Even the new life within her would not keep her from her goal. Emboldened by her visit to the synagogue last Friday night, she entered the area above the Kotel and walked toward the checkpoint. The security guard had just finished screening a large group of American teenagers. He wanded Zara, checked her bag, and waved her through.

Zara descended to the plaza below and walked into the women's area in front of the Kotel. She ignored an offer of a prayer book and approached the wall. Placing her hands against the stones, she leaned toward the wall and rested her face against it. People of all religions were welcome to visit the Kotel. Many Jewish women from the Muslim countries did not look different from her. She did not need to dress as an Orthodox Jewish woman to avoid suspicion here.

The soft murmurs of prayer rose and fell around her. Zara pressed her body against the stones, feeling her heart beating slowly and steadily. She stood there for more than an hour. No one paid attention to her, as many spent hours standing near the Kotel. Finally, as she turned to leave, she saw a large contingent of paratroopers entering the plaza. She left quickly, passing through the Dung Gate to return to Silwan.

Samir climbed the minaret again at 9:00 a.m. He knew that the plaza in front of al-Buraq's Wall was very festive on Mondays. The Jews read from their scroll of the law. They conducted bar mitzvahs in the plaza in the men's sections in front of the wall, and bat mitzvahs near Robinson's Arch. Samir looked down into the plaza and could see many praying against the wall. A rank of soldiers began to form in the middle of the plaza, and the crowd surrounded them. It looked as though a military ceremony was going to take place.

Suddenly, Samir felt disoriented and reached for the railing to steady himself.

What is wrong? he wondered. Then he felt it again.

The minaret had lurched. He looked down and saw that the Jews' bobbing and swaying prayer motions had stopped. The crowd stood frozen. Samir gripped the rail tighter as the minaret seemed to drop from under him. This time he felt his stomach jump and his eyes blurred.

Then he heard it. It started as a low-pitched moan, and he thought that the Jews had begun to pray again. Then he saw the crowd begin to back away from the wall.

Rabbi Avidan was sitting in a café in the Jewish Quarter, waiting for a friend to join him, when the ground lurched beneath him. His dishes rattled on the table, and his water glass spilled. A woman walking by fell forward onto the sidewalk. He heard a large cracking sound, and the ground shook again.

Twenty minutes had passed since Zara had exited through the Dung Gate. She walked slowly, enjoying the cool morning air. As she walked through Silwan, she approached the Visitor's Center on concrete stilts above the excavations of the City of David. A long line of tourists waited on a ramp leading up to the Visitors' Center, while others on the opposite side of the building walked down another ramp into the excavations below. When she was a child, her parents would often take her to a playground there. She still shuddered in horror when she remembered the day five years ago when Israeli bulldozers demolished the playground and the Silwan Community Center next to it to clear the area for the Visitor's Center to be built over the excavations.

Just as she passed the Visitor's Center, the ground shook, and the wind carried a moaning sound. One of the stilts buckled, and the ramp leading up to the building tilted. Several tourists leaning against the railing fell several feet to the ground. Zara walked into the middle of the road and waited for the ground to stop shaking.

Meir was in his office early. He was determined to complete his overdue decision. Ruth was already sitting at her desk in the outer office.

"Good morning, Justice Bar-Aben," she said, without looking up from her computer.

"What are you looking at so early in the morning?"

"The Kotel Cam. The live Internet feed from the Kotel."

"What's going on at the Kotel this morning?"

"My nephew is being inducted into his paratrooper brigade."

Meir bent over her shoulder and looked at the screen. The plaza in front of the Kotel overflowed with worshippers and tourists. A contingent of paratroopers stood in the plaza.

"*mazal tov*, Ruth."

Meir walked into his office and closed the door. He turned on his computer and logged onto the network. He saw two new cases on his docket. Ruth had left copies of the petitions on his desk. He read the first one and realized that he was delaying his work on the Kleinman decision. He put both petitions in his desk drawer and began to work on the decision.

Ruth walked in without knocking.

Meir looked up from his desk, annoyed that she had interrupted him. She was breathing deeply.

"What's wrong?"

She gestured out the door toward her desk.

"Come look. Hurry!"

Meir followed Ruth into the outer office. The live feed from the Kotel Cam on Ruth's computer showed a blurry, dust-filled image of the plaza in front of the Kotel. Ruth moved the mouse and clicked. The image filled the entire screen. Clouds of dust obscured the Kotel. People were screaming.

"What happened?" Meir exclaimed.

Ruth pointed to the image at the midpoint of the screen."

"The Kotel has collapsed!" she gasped.

Chapter 10

Hiram Aitza remembered sitting on the cool marble floor of his parents' apartment when he was young and stacking his plastic blocks into a pile. He would stare at the pile from all sides, then stand up and look down. He would memorize the different colors, and then he would topple the blocks. He was only about three years old, yet he would pick up each block and stack all of them in their original order.

His parents would watch him manipulate the blocks, changing the shape of the stack every time, and marvel at his ability to rebuild what he had created and then scattered.

"An engineer," his father said proudly.

"An architect," his mother would say.

Hiram had not fulfilled his parents' dreams. After a distinguished career as an archaeologist and professor of archeology at Hebrew University, he had been the director of the Israel Museum in Jerusalem for the past ten years. This morning he sat in his office watching the news of the Kotel's collapse. The security cameras had captured the collapse from various angles, and more than one tourist had already sold footage to the media. Hiram watched the ashlars collapse again and again, focusing on the irregular piles formed by the huge blocks.

His phone rang. He answered without taking his eyes off the screen.

"Aitza here."

The screen changed to a hospital scene of injured arriving in ambulances. Hiram changed the channel.

"Mr. Aitza, this is the Office of the Prime Minister. Please hold for Prime Minister Zadok."

As Hiram waited with the phone to his ear, he grabbed his camera from his desk and began to unplug his laptop.

The prime minister came on the line.

"Hiram, I'm sure you've seen the news."

"Yes, I'm watching it now."

"I'm sending a car for you."

Hiram descended in the elevator to the ground floor of the Israel Museum's main building, which was a five-minute drive from the Knesset. When he reached the entrance to the building, he wasn't surprised to see Amran, the prime minister's personal security guard, waiting in a small Ford. Hiram opened the rear door, dropped his laptop on the seat, and then got into the front seat next to Amran.

Amran, usually a man of few words, spoke first.

"No poker tonight, Professor Aitza."

Amran knew Hiram was an old friend and poker buddy of the prime minister. Hiram nodded.

"Probably no poker for a while."

Amran put the car into gear and drove off.

"The prime minister says to take you up there, let you walk around, take pictures. Take your time."

Amran lit a cigarette and rolled down the window.

"I'll get you through security. Don't talk to anyone. Stay close to me. Don't answer any questions. Don't take notes. But first, we're going to your apartment."

"My apartment? I don't need anything there."

Amran turned to him. "You need to put on an IDF uniform. I have one for you. I hope it fits."

"Why do I need to wear an IDF uniform?"

"The press knows who you are. The prime minister wants you to wear a uniform, helmet, and sunglasses, and not to look like an archaeologist."

As they approached the Old City, Hiram was strangling in the IDF uniform, which was much too small for him. Amran parked the car, and they entered the Old City on foot. The army had set up a security checkpoint inside the Dung Gate. Amran flashed his ID and was waved in with Hiram.

A cloud of stone dust drifted over them as they walked from the Dung Gate in eerie silence. Approaching the plaza in front of the Kotel, Hiram grasped the enormity of the collapse. The television images could not capture the size of the ashlars that lay jumbled in the plaza. The ambulances were gone. Anyone lost under the stones would not need medical attention.

Hiram was fascinated by the large hillside that now lay exposed, sloping upward. Muslim officials stood at the top of the hill, on the same level as the Dome of the Rock.

Amran nodded toward the top of the hill.

"Those are members of the Waqf."

IDF soldiers ringed the fallen ashlars. A crowd had formed behind the soldiers. They gazed in awe at the destruction that even the Romans had failed to accomplish almost two thousand years before.

Hiram crossed the barrier of soldiers and slowly circled the fallen stones. He was oblivious to the crowd on the plaza and the watchful gaze of the Waqf officials above. He took pictures, looked for foundation points for his equipment, and calculated loads and slopes. He walked around the pile of ashlars closest to the Temple Mount to look at the bare slope from where they had fallen. He examined the ashlars carefully, taking detailed pictures of the exposed sides of the ashlars that had been turned toward the hillside for centuries.

After three hours, he approached Amran.

"I'm ready to go home."

Amran drove Hiram to his apartment. Hiram thanked him and trudged up two flights of stairs, his tight army uniform plastered with dust and sweat. Entering his apartment, he stripped and hurled the uniform into a plastic garbage bag. Hiram headed into the bathroom and turned on the shower. As he waited for the water to get hot, he reached for his cell phone and dialed. The line rang once.

"Zadok here."

"It's Hiram."

"What can you tell me?"

"I need an IDF uniform that fits."

"And what else?

"We need to meet. Can I come to your office?"

There was a long pause.

"I will be at your apartment in an hour."

Hiram hung up and took a shower. Fifteen minutes later, he was dressed and uploading the pictures from his camera to his laptop. He was lost in thought until he heard the knock.

When he opened the door, Prime Minister Ezer Zadok walked in with Amran behind him. Zadok was somber and to the point. He had just reviewed the casualty report. Fifty-two people were not accounted for, presumed crushed under the fallen ashlars.

"What can you tell me?"

Hiram balked and looked at Amran. Zadok turned.

"Amran, please wait for me in the car."

Hiram and Prime Minister Zadok sat at the kitchen table staring at thumbnail views of Hiram's photos on his laptop screen. Hiram clicked and expanded several photos and arranged them on the screen.

"These stones were next to each other before they fell."

He moved his cursor across the screen, pointing at various places on the photos. Zadok shook his head.

"What is that on the stones?"

"I'm not sure," Hiram said.

He zoomed in on the photograph.

"Interesting, but I can't tell you what this is. I need to go back and do more analysis."

Zadok shrugged. "That's fine, but I'm not really interested in archaeology. Right now, you need to figure out how we can put this back together."

The prime minister left Hiram's apartment an hour later. Amran was waiting in the car, ready to take him home. The prime minister got in the back seat.

"Take me back to the Knesset, Amran. Then you go home. I'm going to be there all night."

The next morning, Amran arrived with a new uniform that fit Hiram perfectly. Amran drove Hiram to the Kotel before dawn. During the night, the IDF had constructed a barrier in the far corner of the plaza for those who came to the Kotel to pray. A long flatbed truck lumbered into the area with timber and canvas sheets. Thirty construction workers from the IDF Engineering Corps arrived. By noon, the fallen ashlars were hidden with a cube of timber and canvas and surrounded by soldiers. Hiram ducked under the canvas and went to work, determined to complete his examination. He urinated into a bottle and ate pita and energy bars. When darkness fell, he continued his examination by flashlight.

At 4:00 a.m. the next morning, he packed up his camera and computer and ducked under the canvas. Amran was waiting for him. As they left the Kotel, Amran turned to Hiram.

"We're being followed by a TV truck. Hang on."

Amran floored the car, drove through an alley, and exited the Dung Gate. The streets were almost empty, but Amran had evaded the truck following them.

"Where to, Amran?" Hiram asked.

"The PM has a private suite at the King David Hotel for visiting dignitaries. We're going there."

Amran drove into the hotel's underground parking garage and escorted Hiram to a service elevator. They took the elevator to the top floor, to a door without a room number. Amran punched a code on a keypad next to the door, and they entered. Hiram found Prime Minister Zadok seated on the sofa in the living room of the suite.

Hiram was too exhausted to say anything. He dropped his laptop case onto the desk next to the window and sat in an armchair facing Zadok. Amran excused himself and left the suite.

Hiram turned on the laptop. As it was booting up, Zadok waved his arms impatiently.

"Just tell me, Hiram. Can we put it back together?"

Hiram nodded. "I have mapped the stones and compared them to previous photos. I know exactly how to reposition them. It will take about three months or more—working around the clock with the proper engineering. I can supervise it."

Hiram opened a design program on his screen that showed numbered grids. Another window opened with photos of the individual fallen ashlars with corresponding numbers.

"See, we can put the ashlars back from where they fell."

"What about the backs of the stones?"

"I'll have to analyze what is there. Whatever it is, once the reconstruction is finished, no one will ever see it."

"And no one but you has seen this since the collapse?"

"You know I have been the only one allowed under the canvas. Whatever the markings on the stones are, they will be hidden from view again."

Zadok exhaled slowly. "Good. I don't want any archaeological curiosity. We just need this put back together as quickly as possible. Let's have a drink."

He went over to the bar and opened the cabinet.

Hiram stood. "Mr. Prime Minister, it's five o' clock in the morning. I'll pass."

Zadok poured himself a drink and raised his glass.

"To the reconstruction and the reconstructor. Go home and get some sleep."

Hiram headed to the door.

"By the way," Zadok said, "can we say for sure what caused the collapse?"

"There was no earthquake activity before the collapse. The damage in the surrounding area seems to be the result of the shock wave from the ashlars falling. You read our report before the collapse. The bulge didn't occur until after the Marwani excavations. I would say that the instability created by the excavations led to the collapse. Too bad it happened while you are prime minister."

"Thank you, Hiram," Zadok said. He wasn't feeling sorry for himself.

Chapter 11

Wednesday, March 22, 2017

Prime Minister Zadok and Amran left the King David Hotel at 7:00 a.m. The prime minister relaxed in the back seat.

Amran looked at the prime minister in the rearview mirror.

"You look tired, sir. Do you want me to take you home and bring you back to the Knesset later?"

"No, Amran. I have a meeting at nine this morning that I have to prepare for. We need to go to the Knesset now."

Two weeks ago, when Zadok had scheduled the meeting with Rabbi Tarfon, the head of the new Sanhedrin, he had thought of it as a political obligation. Now, with the collapse of the Kotel, everything had changed.

Zadok opened a file that contained background information for the meeting. He found a photograph of Orthodox rabbis in black hats and robes seated at several large semicircular tables. The caption on the bottom read: "Sanhedrin, Tiberias." The file also contained two newspaper articles. The first was dated thirteen years before, in 2004.

SANHEDRIN REESTABLISHED AFTER 1600 YEARS

The Sanhedrin, the religious-legal assembly of seventy-one sages that convened during the Holy Temple period and for several centuries thereafter, was the highest Jewish judicial tribunal in the Land of

Israel. This great assembly sat in session in the Temple in Jerusalem. After the destruction of the Temple in 70 A.D., the Sanhedrin met in Yabneh and Tiberias. Recently, the Sanhedrin reestablished itself for the first time in 1,600 years, at the site of its last meeting in Tiberias.

The members of the revived Sanhedrin stress that the Torah mandates the existence of the Sanhedrin. The ordination of Rabbi Ezekiel Tarfon, a rabbi agreed upon by many prominent rabbis in Israel, initiated the reestablishment of the Sanhedrin. Rabbi Tarfon, considered to have received authentic ordination as handed down from Moses, was then able to ordain seventy others, making up the seventy-one members necessary for the Sanhedrin.

Years before, when Zadok had first heard that a group of rabbis had revived the ancient Sanhedrin, he had dismissed it as another fringe religious occurrence. He did not believe the past could be revisited in this way. The members of the new Sanhedrin could reenact history if they wished, but Zadok doubted that any attempt to gain ultimate religious authority over world Jewry would be successful.

Zadok read the second article, which detailed the efforts of the new Sanhedrin since its reestablishment. This article was more recent, dated 2012.

SANHEDRIN CALLS FOR REBUILDING THE TEMPLE

The Sanhedrin was a 71-man assembly of rabbis that convened adjacent to the Holy Temple before its destruction in 70 A.D. and outside Jerusalem until about 400 C.E. Since its reestablishment in this century, the Sanhedrin has met monthly in Jerusalem.

The new Sanhedrin is calling upon all groups involved in Temple Mount research to prepare detailed plans for the reconstruction of the Temple. Several organizations headquartered in the Jewish Quarter of the Old City of Jerusalem have focused their efforts in recent years on reconstructing ritual objects and priestly garments used during Temple worship.

The call for an active movement to actually rebuild the Temple has followed the election earlier this week of a leading Talmud scholar as head of the Sanhedrin, which now is attempting to establish itself as Judaism's highest legal-religious tribunal.

Despite the election of a head of the Sanhedrin, which adds important rabbinic legitimacy to the body, many major religious authorities have resisted joining this group or offering support.

The Sanhedrin has announced that it will enlist an observant group of design professionals to draft plans for rebuilding the Temple—an effort that is certain to provoke religious controversy and aggravate the already volatile political climate that surrounds the Temple Mount. It is calling on the Jewish people to contribute funds to acquire materials for rebuilding the Temple—including the gathering and preparation of prefabricated construction elements to be stored and ready for rapid assembly.

Zadok knew that groups advocating the rebuilding of the Temple had existed for years. One, the Temple Mount Faithful, had clashed with Israeli authorities when it had marched to the Temple Mount and attempted to lay the foundation stone of the Third Temple. Another, the Temple Institute, had recreated the ritual objects of the Temple, including the Menorah and the priests' robes, anticipating the day when the Temple would stand again on the Temple Mount. The

Temple Institute's website had a virtual tour of the rebuilt Temple. Now, the new Sanhedrin was advocating prefabricating the actual structure of the Temple for quick rebuilding.

Zadok arrived at the Knesset as he finished reading the two newspaper articles. He went immediately to his office. As he did every morning, he read the daily intelligence briefings from the Shin Bet and Mossad. He showered in his private bathroom and changed his clothes. His secretary called and told him that Rabbi Tarfon had arrived.

Rabbi Tarfon was waiting with two other rabbis in the prime minister's conference room. The meeting lasted an hour. The rabbis talked passionately. Zadok was surprised to see that they had blueprints for rebuilding the Temple and a model of the Temple from the Temple Institute.

"And what about the Muslim holy places on the Temple Mount?" Zadok asked.

"We should have removed them in 1967," Rabbi Tarfon said. "Moshe Dayan missed his opportunity. Who knows? Maybe they will collapse next."

Zadok was surprised by the rabbis' determination. Even so, their desire seemed unrealistic.

"Does the entire Sanhedrin wish the Temple to be rebuilt?" he asked.

"The rabbis of the new Sanhedrin are unanimous. But a very influential rabbi refuses to join and support the rebuilding of the Temple."

"Who is he?"

"Rabbi Ashur Avidan."

"Why is he so influential?"

Rabbi Tarfon hesitated noticeably.

"He has a rather distinguished ancestry, and there is a rumor about him."

"What is the rumor?"

"That he convinced Moshe Dayan to return the Temple Mount to the Waqf after the Six-Day War."

"Who started the rumor?"

Rabbi Tarfon looked uncomfortable.

"I don't know. I heard it when I was studying for the rabbinate. Many believe that Rabbi Goren, the chief rabbi of the IDF during the Six-Day War, was the one who first said it. I don't know how he knew."

"Did Rabbi Goren know Rabbi Avidan?"

Rabbi Tarfon shrugged.

"Again, I don't know. Rabbi Avidan is still alive. He is more than one hundred years old."

Zadok shook hands with the three rabbis.

"Thank you for coming. This has been very informative."

"May the Temple be speedily rebuilt in our lifetime," Rabbi Tarfon replied.

Prime Minister Zadok walked out of the Knesset and sat on a bench in the sun. He had had enough of offices and conference rooms. As a military man, he had made most of his major decisions in the field. Fresh air and sunlight enhanced his thinking.

He had always been angered by the return of the Temple Mount after its capture in 1967. This was Zadok's opportunity to complete the historical landscape and take back what the Romans, Early Christians, Muslims, Crusaders, Fatimids, Ottoman Turks, and Jordanians had withheld for two thousand years.

He did not want to rebuild the Temple. He had no interest in reviving the Temple ritual, animal sacrifice, and Levites playing lutes and flutes. It was a matter of national pride. He knew that crisis created opportunity.

Roosevelt had Pearl Harbor. Bush had 9/11. Zadok had the collapse of the Kotel.

He returned to his office and stretched out on the sofa. He told his secretary not to disturb him for the next hour. When he woke up from a quick nap, Zadok called his secretary into his office.

"Please locate Rabbi Ashur Avidan. I need to meet with him immediately."

Chapter 12

Since Ori's death, Meir had struggled with free-floating anxiety and malaise. The collapse of the Kotel had a jolting effect on him, and he began to feel unusually productive and focused. At noon, the day after the collapse, he had asked Ruth to bring him a falafel wrap and frozen yogurt from the cafeteria when she came back from lunch.

She raised her eyebrows.

"Working through lunch?"

"You know I don't stop when I get going."

Ruth nodded. This hadn't happened in a long time.

"Hot sauce or tahini sauce on the falafel?"

"Both."

"Chocolate or caramel sauce on the yogurt?"

"Both."

Meir consumed his lunch as he worked. The hot sauce, tahini, chocolate, and caramel fueled his brain to a fever pitch. The fog of depression lifted, and a familiar warmth swept through his head as his fingers flew over the keyboard. Facts began to combine with legal principles in a cogent, concise draft.

Thursday, March 23, 2017

Three days after the collapse of the Kotel, the Israeli government issued an official report blaming the Waqf's excavations under the Temple Mount for destabilizing the Kotel and causing the collapse. The Waqf denied the accusation, stating that Israeli archaeologists exploring ancient tunnels under the

Temple Mount had weakened the foundation and caused the collapse.

The Arab press escalated tension by speculating that Israel was planning a covert mission to damage the Grand Mosque in Mecca. The fringe press reported that the Mossad's use of a HAARP weapon aimed at the Dome of the Rock misfired and caused the Kotel to collapse instead. Another tabloid reported a massive UFO perched over the Temple Mount immediately before the collapse. A noted evangelical Christian broadcaster predicted that the collapse of the Kotel was the precursor of the end time and the return of Christ.

Hiram Aitza began the supervision of the effort to reconstruct the Kotel. Worshippers and tourists were allowed on the plaza but kept away from the area of reconstruction. Prime Minister Zadok made a heavily publicized visit, during which he assured the nation that the Kotel would be "rebuilt quickly and protected from any future damage."

Meir had continued to work on the Kleinman decision. His mood allowed him to review draft opinions from other justices as well. By Thursday afternoon, he completed the draft. He printed it out and moved to his leather armchair to proofread. He had almost finished proofreading when a knock at the door made him jump. He rose as Ruth entered.

"Sorry to interrupt, but Amos Eitan is on the line. He insisted that I put the call through."

"*Amos Eitan?*" Meir felt the pain under his armpit grab him.

"He spoke as if you know him."

"I do. I just haven't heard from him in a long time."

"Do you want to pick up? He is on the public line."

"Tell him to call me back in fifteen minutes."

"He was rather insistent and —"

"Just tell him to call me back. Ring it through when he calls, please."

Ruth nodded and closed the door behind her. Meir watched as the light on his line stopped flashing, indicating that Ruth was speaking to Eitan. Then the light went out. Meir had not spoken to Amos Eitan in almost fifty years, but he knew that Amos would not wait fifteen minutes to call him back. Five minutes was more probable.

Meir walked over to a bookcase filled with framed pictures. He reached for a stone frame that contained a faded photograph of himself and Amos in battle gear at the Kotel. Memories of the Six-Day War flooded through him as he waited for the phone to ring.

Chapter 13

The ringing phone interrupted Meir's memories. He put the picture on the desk and let the phone ring three times. He picked up the receiver, knowing he would not have a chance to say hello.

"Meir? It's Amos. *ma nishma?*" How are you?

His voice was upbeat, friendly, with no hint of their almost fifty-year hiatus.

"Amos, good to hear from you. How are you?" Meir's voice was flat. Amos paused.

"Meir, I'm sorry about Ori. I heard, but I didn't call. I should have."

Yes, you should have, Amos.

"What can I do for you, Amos?"

Amos was upbeat again.

"All in good time, Meir. Or should I say, Justice Bar-Aben?"

Meir laughed as he sat down behind his desk.

"Meir will do, unless this is somehow related to official business."

"Actually, I am calling to tell you that we will meet again soon. We'll have a chance to catch up."

"And why will we be meeting soon?"

Amos laughed.

"I can't tell you now. *l'hitraot.*" See you soon.

Amos hung up.

Meir leaned back in his chair. His mood crashed and his sugar-induced euphoria snapped. Amos mentioning Ori was enough to induce an anxiety attack. Meir's heart began to race. He tried to breathe slowly. He decided to finish proofreading the Kleinman decision tomorrow. He put the decision in his drawer and spent the next few minutes cleaning up his desk.

He passed Ruth on his way out.

"Done with the decision?" she asked.

"For now. I'll finish proofing it tomorrow."

Ruth raised her eyebrows and shook her head.

"The president will be pleased, finally."

Meir shrugged.

"I think I'll go home early."

Meir called Channah on her cell phone. She answered on the first ring.

"Channah, I'm leaving early today. I'll probably be home when you get there."

"Is everything okay?"

He heard the concern in her voice. She was overly protective of his emotions, as he was of hers.

Meir paused.

"Everything is fine."

"Well, you don't sound fine. Drive carefully."

Meir drove home without seeing a bus and having an anxiety attack. He entered the underground garage and eased into his parking space. The space on the other side of the column was empty. Channah wasn't home from work yet. Meir walked to the elevator and pushed the button for the tenth floor. He was glad when the elevator rushed upward without stopping until it reached his floor. He entered his apartment, and, out of habit, he walked into the kitchen. Despite his lunch, he was hungry. He hesitated. If he ate now, before Channah came home, she would be angry if he sat with her and didn't eat dinner. He opened the refrigerator. Two large containers of vanilla yogurt sat on the top shelf. One was half full, left over from his breakfast that morning. He grabbed a banana from a bowl on the counter and sat down at the small table in the kitchen. This would take the edge off his hunger until dinner.

He popped the lid off the yogurt container and peeled the banana. Esther, their Persian cat, recognized the sound of the yogurt lid and flopped from the windowsill onto the floor at the entrance to the kitchen. She came toward Meir, purring, her tail held high.

"Good evening, Your Majesty."

Esther did a dance around his feet, rubbing her head against his calves. Meir looked down into her wise gray eyes. He broke up the banana with his fingers and dropped the pieces into the half-full yogurt container. Channah would have his head on a plate if she saw him do this.

Esther meowed loudly.

"Okay. I'll give you some if you don't tell."

He scooped a spoonful of yogurt onto a paper napkin and placed it on the floor. Esther licked it rapidly, devouring it in seconds. Then she scrunched the napkin into a ball and batted it under the table with her paws. She looked up at him and winked.

Meir reached down and patted her on the head. Esther loved vanilla yogurt, and it was against Channah's rule. Cat food was for cats, people food for people. The first time Meir had broken the rule, he was in the kitchen early one morning. He had not slept well the night before, pondering a particularly difficult case. As he ate his yogurt from the container, he noticed Esther sitting in the sphinx position in the corner—hind legs tucked under and front paws extended in front, head erect, and with her eyes half shut, meditating.

Meir spoke softly to her.

Chapter 14

Meir sat on the sofa and motioned Channah to sit beside him. He put his arm around her shoulder and buried his face against her neck under her shoulder-length brown hair.

"How are you?" Channah asked again.

"My mind is racing around in circles."

"Your mind is always racing. You never relax. The only time you do is when you're asleep."

Esther jumped onto the couch and curled herself in a tight ball next to Meir. This was her favorite spot. To show her satisfaction, she slowly whisked Meir's knee with her tail.

Channah switched on the TV and clicked the remote control, avoiding news channels.

"We're not going to watch news. The Kotel collapsed. They are putting it back together. There is nothing more to know. Let's find something else."

She clicked on an American animated show she liked—*South Park*.

Even though Channah's English was almost fluent, she had trouble understanding the high-pitched mechanical voices, so she relied on the Hebrew subtitles. Last week's episode had certainly distracted her. Americans had a very strange sense of humor.

Meir ignored the TV and tried to relax. His day had started in a sugar-induced frenzy that had him momentarily productive and relaxed. The phone call from Amos had jolted him back into his usual agitated state. He closed his eyes and willed himself to breathe deeply.

After about ten minutes, Meir was calm. He opened his eyes and glanced over at Channah. Her face was flushed, and her mouth was wide open in an expression of disbelief as she stared at the TV screen. Meir looked at the one-dimensional *South Park* characters. He had not paid attention to the story line, but a cylindrical brown character with arms was speaking, standing on top of a toilet. He turned again to Channah, who covered her eyes with her hands and shook her head.

Meir looked again at the screen.

"Is that what I think it is?"

Channah nodded, without uncovering her eyes.

"Why in the world are you watching such nonsense, Channah?"

Channah let her hand drop from in front of her eyes and laughed.

"To understand the United States. This show has been very popular there for years."

Meir stood up.

"Americans have too much time on their hands."

Channah clicked the remote and turned off the TV.

"You seem distracted. Did something happen today?"

"Well, someone called me. Someone I haven't heard from in a long time."

Channah motioned Meir to sit down, and she hugged him.

"That's not unusual. Why did it upset you?"

"I guess I expected to hear from him when Ori died. I knew him in the army."

"Have I ever met him?"

"No. You've seen his picture on my desk in my office. Amos Eitan. I haven't heard from him since the war."

"Of course. Your picture at the Kotel. Why did he call you?"

"I'm not sure. He just said I would see him again soon."

"So when was the last time you saw him?"

"Right after the war. It seems strange that he would call me after the Kotel collapsed."

"You never saw him again?"

"No. Remember, I missed the Yom Kippur War, and our paths never crossed during reserve duty.

"Maybe the collapse made him think of the war, and he wanted to reconnect. What has he been doing since the war?"

"I don't know. I know he grew up on a kibbutz, and he was going back. We lost touch."

"Well, I remember from the picture that he was very handsome. You still have the picture in your office, don't you?"

"Yes. Every time I look at it, I'm reminded about something that happened during the war that I have never understood, and I always thought he knew the answer."

"And you never mentioned it to me?"

"No."

"But this is something you have thought about often?"

Meir was silent. Channah elbowed him lightly in the ribs.

"But you're dying to talk to me about it now, I'm sure."

"I'll tell you while we eat."

Channah prepared a light dinner and opened a bottle of wine.

Meir raised his wine glass and drank.

"You already know that I was in the paratroop brigade that took the Temple Mount. It's what happened after that I don't understand."

Channah looked at him over her wine glass.

"Should I put you under oath?" she intoned in a solemn voice.

Meir laughed.

"You never have since we've been married. It's probably too late now."

"You're probably right. You may proceed."

As they ate, Meir told Channah in detail how his paratroop brigade captured the Temple Mount.

"And Amos Eitan? Where is he from and how long had you known him?"

"He grew up in Kibbutz Regavim in the Galilee. He emigrated with his parents from Morocco in the early fifties. His parents spoke Arabic and French, so he was fluent in both. He was an intelligence officer, because he had a facility for languages. We were the same age. We had both completed our mandatory service in early 1967. We met when we were assigned to the 55th Paratroop Brigade as reservists. We became friends during jump training. We always watched out for each other."

Channah poured another glass of wine for Meir. He told her about the Muslim man who entered the perimeter that night.

"How old was he? Young, old?" Channah asked.

"I'd say he was thirty, more or less," Meir said.

"He wanted to speak to someone in authority. Moshe Dayan and Rabbi Goren were there. Amos went into the command tent, and I don't know what happened in there."

Meir sipped his wine. He had hardly touched his food.

"Then another person appeared, an Orthodox Jew. He was older. I'd say he was in his late forties or early fifties. They escorted him into the command tent, too. Later he, Moshe Dayan, and Rabbi Goren went down the staircase to the Kotel and came back. Then they all left.

Channah pointed at Meir's plate.

"You need to eat something, before it gets cold."

"It's chopped salad, hummus, and pita. It should be cold."

"I'm glad you noticed. Eat."

Meir pushed the chopped salad and hummus into the pita.

"Do you know who those men were?" Channah asked.

"No. They were in the command tent for a long time. I was on guard duty on the opposite side of the Temple Mount when they left. Amos was in there. He has to know who they were and why they were there."

"When was the last time you saw Amos?"

Meir raised his glass.

"When I asked him a question that he refused to answer."

Channah was enjoying her role as examining attorney.

"Please continue."

"We met at a café the Shabbat after the war. I asked him if he knew why we gave the Temple Mount back to the Waqf."

"Did he know why?"

"I don't know. He wouldn't answer the question. It just seemed strange to me that we captured the Temple Mount after two thousand years, these two people appeared, and then Moshe Dayan just gave it back. Like we hadn't fought for it and lost lives in the process."

Channah reached across the table and stroked Meir's wrist.

"So he never answered your question?"

"No. I don't know if he knew the answer. The meeting in the command tent may have had nothing to do with it. He acted cryptically, as if he knew. But that was always his attitude. He was an intelligence officer."

"But you think the answer to your question may involve the two people who showed up that night on the Temple Mount?"

"I don't know. Possibly."

"So why did Amos call you today?"

"I don't know. Not yet."

Channah smiled. "People don't call after so long just to chat. I'll bet you'll see him soon, for some reason."

A loud meow from under the table, which Channah and Meir both recognized as Esther's "yes," shattered their silence.

Meir found his head involuntarily nodding in agreement.

Channah patted Meir's hand. "She knows you as well as I do."

Meir reached down and scratched Esther's ear.

Maybe better, he thought.

Chapter 15

Talking to Channah gave Meir an unexpected catharsis. He was able to put the phone call from Amos out of his mind. Since he and Channah had moved into their condominium three years ago, they had stayed home most evenings. At about ten o'clock, Meir made his usual visit to Ori's room. Ori never lived there, but his furniture and premarital possessions presented a neater version of his usually scattered room at their previous house. Ori's first computers were stacked under his desk, containing electronic thoughts that would never be retrieved by their author again.

Channah had put photos of life's milestones on the dresser. There was a soccer championship, Ori's bar mitzvah, a family hike in the Negev before he entered the army. In all of these, it was the same pose, with Ori in the middle between Channah and Meir. Ori's and Sarah's wedding pictures were in the den, but in this room, there were only pictures of Meir, Channah, and Ori.

Meir sat on the bed and rubbed the back of his neck.

Channah stood at the door and looked in at him. Her face had that end-of-the-day expression when all pretenses were gone.

"I'm going to call my sister. Why don't you go to bed?"

It was more of a command than a question. She knew when Meir was ready to shut down.

Meir went down the hall to the bedroom, took his clothes off, and got under the sheets. His nightly ritual was to watch the television news channel muted so he wouldn't hear the newscaster's spin. He thought he could understand the day's events as much as he needed to from pictures, captions, and videos without the commentary.

This evening, there was certainly no need for sound. The camera panned the plaza in front of the Kotel, showing the piles of ashlars separated by a newly constructed barricade. A large crowd pressed against the barricade. Some swayed in prayer, as close as they could get to the Kotel, while others raised cell phones or cameras over the barricade to snap photos.

The screen faded to a video clip of a large room filled with Orthodox Jews. On the wall of the room, a large photograph of the Temple Mount had a graphic of a soaring white building superimposed in the center, a representation of the Temple. Videos of riots in Muslim countries came next. Many Muslims believed Israel intentionally caused the destruction of the Kotel to encroach on the Waqf's control of the Temple Mount.

As Channah was speaking with her sister, Tamar, she heard a beep and looked at the call-waiting display on her phone.

"Tamar, Sarah's calling. I need to talk to her."

Channah hadn't talked to Sarah for several weeks. She clicked the phone and answered.

"Sarah, you're calling late."

"Channah, I need to talk to you." Sarah was crying.

"What is the matter, Sarah? Tell me."

"I can't tell you over the phone. I've done something, and I can't keep it from you anymore. Can we meet for coffee about three tomorrow afternoon after school?"

"Yes, but you are scaring me. Can't you at least tell me what this is about?"

"I can't. And please, don't tell Meir I called. At least, not before you hear what I have to tell you."

Meir dozed off. He woke up as Channah turned off the television. She came to his side of the bed to turn off the light on his night table. He grabbed her hand.

"I don't want to turn off my light," he said.

She bent down and kissed him on the nose.

"I know, I know. I don't either. But we have to."

She turned off his light, then got into bed next to him and turned off her light. Darkness filled the room.

Meir turned his face away from her. His tears came silently. He breathed deeply and willed himself into oblivion, hoping for dreamless sleep.

That same night, Zara lay in bed as the waves of nausea rocked her. Hamid brought her a glass of cool mint tea, and he stroked her forehead as she sipped it.

"Stop this, Zara. This is madness. You are risking everything."

Zara looked into his eyes. She put her hand on her heart, took a deep breath, and calmed herself.

"I am at peace, Hamid."

Hamid lay next to her and turned out the light. He looked out the open window at the moonlit sky. Zara turned to him.

"Sleep, Hamid. Don't worry about me."

"You need to go to the doctor. I will make an appointment for tomorrow. And then we will tell your parents the good news."

"Tomorrow is jumuah, Hamid."

"I know, Zara. But your doctor will see you early in the morning. No arguments, please."

Zara reached for Hamid's hand and squeezed it tightly. Within minutes, Hamid was asleep. Zara lay and thought about the *shaheed*, until her resolve returned and her nausea disappeared.

Chapter 16

The next morning, Zara and Hamid walked down a narrow alley in Silwan and entered a doctor's office. Three pregnant women were sitting alone in a small waiting room. They nodded and smiled at Zara. Hamid sat down next to Zara, glad that he was able to come with her.

A doctor came into the waiting room and motioned Zara to follow him into an examining room. The doctor closed the door and hugged Zara tightly.

"You look wonderful, Zara."

Zara laughed.

"I am pregnant, Kal Da'ud." Da'ud, Zara's uncle, was her mother's younger brother. "My parents don't know. I will tell them after my appointment today."

"That is wonderful, Zara! Dr. Jamal will call for you soon. I just wanted to see you first. Your parents worry so much about you."

"I know. Nothing I say or do stops them from worrying. You can tell them to stop, can't you?"

"Of course. I can also tell the sun to stand still in the sky."

Zara returned to the waiting room and sat next to Hamid.

"Your uncle is well, Zara?" Hamid asked.

"He is."

"I hope he told you that you need to stay close to home."

"No, he just said that my parents worry about me."

"They should."

Dr. Jamal entered the waiting room and smiled at Zara. She rose and went to him. Several minutes later, Zara's uncle came out and asked Hamid to follow him. They walked down a corridor into Da'ud's office. Da'ud sat on a small sofa, and Hamid sat next to him.

"How is she, Hamid? I am worried about her."

Hamid shuddered.

"I am afraid for her. Sometimes it is as if she is someone else, and then she is Zara again. Maybe having the baby will bring her out of it."

Da'ud leaned forward.

"I will ask Dr. Jamal what he thinks after he examines her. Tea?"

Da'ud reached for a pitcher of iced tea and poured two glasses.

Hamid sipped his tea in silence. Da'ud made a phone call. Several minutes later, Dr. Jamal knocked on the door and entered.

"Ah, Hamid, I thought you would be in here. Can you come with me? I have some news for you."

Hamid urged Zara to go home and tell her parents the news, but she was so excited that she wanted to first pray *salat aljumuah* in al-Aqsa Mosque and thank God for their good fortune.

When they came out of the mosque after praying, they followed a group of tourists inside the Dome of the Rock. As they approached the rock, Zara turned to Hamid and whispered to him, "You know that the Jews believe that Ishaaq, not Ishmael, was to be sacrificed on this rock by Father Ibrahim."

"I know, Zara. Your fascination with Judaism is becoming overwhelming."

"But, Hamid, you are much more like Ishaaq than Ishmael."

Hamid looked at her, not understanding.

"Why, Zara?"

"You don't know what happened to Ishaaq after Ibrahim was stopped from sacrificing him on this rock?"

"What, Zara?"

Zara grasped his arm and squeezed tightly.

"He became the father of twins!"

Hamid hugged her and said, "*alhamdu lillah.*" Praise God.

Chapter 17

Meir continued to work efficiently during the following week. He finished the Kleinman decision and began to work on other cases. Ruth brought him lunch in his chambers every day. Some afternoons, he went out for ice cream. He came home early for dinner, and he and Channah relaxed in the evening. Channah refused to allow Meir to watch the news. She was afraid that anything might destroy his mood. He forgot about Amos Eitan's phone call.

Sunday, April 2, 2017

Meir slid quietly from the bed and left Channah sleeping. He went into the kitchen. Esther wrapped herself around his bare foot as he ate berries and yogurt. She knew that the creamy treat would not be hers this morning, because Meir and Channah were home together. She marked Meir's foot with her nose. He shook her off without reaching down to pet her.

Feeling rejected, Esther slunk down the hall to the bedroom and jumped on the bed. She walked on Channah's head until Channah woke up. Channah got out of bed and put on her bathrobe without scolding Esther. Esther curled in the vacant warm spot.

Channah found Meir sitting in the kitchen with the empty yogurt container in front of him. He was surprised to see her.

"Why are you up so early, Channah?"

"Esther was apparently feeling ignored, so she did her head dance. Anyway, I want to tell you something before you leave."

"What?"

"I'm surprising you today. I'm having lunch with you."

Meir laughed.

"We have never had lunch since I was appointed. Where are we having lunch?"

"In your chambers. I'll bring it."

"Well, why did you tell me? It's not a surprise anymore."

"Coming to have lunch was enough of a surprise. I didn't want to show up without warning. You'd probably have a major anxiety attack."

"You're probably right. How about noon? And how about being on time?" Channah was always late.

"I'll be there promptly at noon, with lunch."

"And what will you bring?"

"*That* will be a surprise."

"Great. Bring enough for Ruth."

When Meir left, Channah was sitting at the desk in the study, opening mail from the day before. He kissed her on her forehead.

"I'll be ready at noon. Remember, don't be late."

Channah was late, but Meir didn't notice. He wasn't keeping track of time, and he was feeling unproductive. He had spent the morning reading a brief in a particularly uninteresting case. After reading the brief for the third time, he put it aside and hoped the attorney would be clearer during oral argument.

Meir leaned back in his chair and took off his reading glasses. He consciously blinked, trying to start some moisture in his eyes. He was hungry and didn't care what Channah brought for lunch. He called Ruth on the intercom.

"Is Channah here yet?"

"Not yet, but the guard downstairs just called. Mr. Eitan wishes to see you. Can you see him?"

"He's here?"

"At the front entrance."

"Tell Yossi to escort him here."

He hoped Channah was bringing enough food.

Meir waited in Ruth's outer office for Amos. Yossi Chernitzki, the security guard, arrived quickly with Amos. Amos came toward Meir and grabbed him in a tight hug. Meir hugged him back.

Amos had barely aged since Meir had seen him last. He was slim with a full head of curly hair. Except for traces of gray at his temples, Amos looked as if he had been frozen fifty years ago and thawed yesterday. Meir mused on his own receding hairline and the wrinkles around his eyes from too much reading.

Ruth stood up to excuse herself for lunch. Amos broke his grip and turned to her.

"This must be Ruth. A pleasure to meet you."

Ruth looked into his piercing blue eyes and found herself blushing.

"My pleasure, Mr. Eitan."

She turned to Meir.

"I'll be back in an hour, Justice Bar-Aben."

Good. Amos can eat your lunch.

She left, closing the door behind her.

"Meir, let's go out to lunch. We can —"

Meir cut him short.

"My wife is bringing lunch. Join us."

Amos laughed.

"That sounded more like a command than an invitation."

"Channah's on her way, and, believe me, she'll insist. Besides, she knows who you are, and she wouldn't want to miss this opportunity to meet you."

Amos was suddenly somber.

"She knows I had called you?"

"You're an old friend I hadn't heard from since the war. I have nothing to hide from her, do I?"

Amos gave him a faint smile.

"Not yet."

Channah's knock interrupted them. Meir opened the door, and she stood there with a large bag from the Best Falafel and French Fries in the Whole World, a food stand outside of the building. She put the box down on Ruth's desk and turned toward them.

"Meir, I brought enough for Ruth . . ."

She stopped in midsentence as she saw Amos.

"Channah, this is Amos Eitan."

She knew he would eventually show up. She extended her hand to Amos.

"Amos, you must have lunch with us. I insist."

Channah spread out the food on the table in Meir's conference room.

"I knew you'd like this, Meir. You've said it's the only place you eat when you leave the building," Channah said.

Channah had asked for three different flavored tahini sauces, which they poured over their falafel and the chips.

Channah turned to Amos.

"So, Amos, you haven't seen Meir since the Six-Day War. What have you been doing with yourself?"

"Working hard."

Channah laughed.

"Doing what?"

Meir gave Channah his back-off look, which she ignored.

Amos smiled a charming smile, reached into his pocket, and handed her a business card.

"'Amos Eitan, Publisher. Arkridasio Publications.' So you're a book publisher. What books have you published?"

"All the books are listed on the company's website."

"How did you get into publishing?"

"I like books."

"Well, my divorced sister likes books, and she's ten years younger than I am. Are you married?"

"No."

"What else can I tell her about you?"

Meir interrupted.

"Okay, Channah. As they say on television, you are badgering the witness."

Amos laughed. "Thanks, Meir. I've survived worse."

"You don't know her, Amos. She is just getting started."

They ate and talked. Amos told Channah about the capture of the Temple Mount without mentioning the two visitors and the meeting in the command tent. As they mopped up the last of the tahini sauce with the chips, Channah took four large portions of baklava from another bag. Meir started a pot of coffee in Ruth's office. Amos leaned back and put his hands behind his head.

"Hey, Meir, do you still have that photograph of us at the Kotel?"

"I do. It's in my office."

"My picture? Here?"

Channah stood up.

"Go get the picture, Meir. I'll get the coffee."

Meir went into his office and returned with the picture. He handed it to Amos, who stared at it intently.

"I lost my copy many years ago. I hoped you had it."

Channah came back with a tray of coffee cups.

"Interesting picture. You look almost the same today, Amos. Meir looks like he has jumped ahead a generation."

Amos nodded his head but didn't look up. He turned the picture over and looked at the frame.

"Nice frame, Meir. Jerusalem stone?"

Meir looked at Channah.

"Yes. Appropriate, isn't it?"

Amos handed the picture and frame back to Meir.

"Meir, I can't believe we haven't seen each other since."

Channah interrupted.

"I am going to leave you two alone to reminisce some more."

Amos smiled at Channah.

"A pleasure to meet you."

She shook his hand and kissed Meir on the cheek.

"I'm going shopping with my sister. You're on your own for dinner."

Meir kissed her again.

"See you later. Why are you so dressed up to go shopping?"

She smiled.

"I was at the Supreme Court for lunch. Remember?"

Channah walked out of the building toward the main street. She dialed her sister on her cell phone. Tamar answered on the first ring.

"Tamar, I'm leaving now. Come pick me up and take me to meet Sarah, please."

Her sister was silent for a few moments, then responded.

"Channah, are you okay?"

"I'm fine. I just don't want to drive. Just remember, Tamar. You and I went shopping today."

Meir led Amos into his office. Amos scanned the room. "Very neat. Everything in place. Impressive. I've never met a Supreme Court justice."

Meir sat in a chair opposite a small couch and motioned Amos to sit on the couch.

"I've never met someone who pretends to be a book publisher. Why don't you tell me about yourself."

Amos chuckled.

"Okay. You're going to find out soon enough. I'll fill you in about me since I saw you last."

"The last I remember, you were going back to your kibbutz."

"Well, I didn't stay there long."

Amos leaned back on the couch and crossed his legs.

"I went back to my kibbutz, not knowing what to do next. I didn't see myself as a student, so the university wasn't in my future. I could never sit still in class during high school on the kibbutz, and there was no reason why I thought it would be any different. I didn't feel more mature after the army."

Meir nodded. "But you were fluent in Arabic, French, and English. Whatever happened with that? I always thought that was a marketable commodity."

Amos laughed. "I didn't know then what a marketable commodity was. I just knew I could pick up girls in all of these languages. But you're right. I turned it into one."

"How?"

"It happened rather quickly. Several weeks after I returned to the kibbutz, I was working in the banana fields."

"You, in the banana fields?"

"It was always my favorite work on the kibbutz. It was tough work, too. When the trees sprout bunches, you had to prop up the tree stalks with large trimmed branches so the banana bunches wouldn't drag the tree down. Also, it was dangerous. Poisonous snakes like banana fields. I would slice them in half with my machete."

"So what happened?"

"One day, I came back from the fields to the kibbutz dining hall for lunch and a man was waiting for me. He was dressed as a kibbutznik—in a work shirt, shorts, sandals, and a cloth hat. I thought he was from another kibbutz. He came up to me and said, 'Amos Eitan, I need to talk to you about your service to the nation. Can I join you for lunch?'"

"Your military service?" Meir asked.

"I wasn't sure. I had finished my compulsory service, like you, and I wasn't scheduled for reserve duty again until the next summer. Anyway, we had lunch, and he recruited me into Shin Bet to help administrate the new territories. My kibbutz days were over."

Amos described to Meir how he had soon begun intensive training in the *sherut habitachon haklali*, the General Security Service, known by its abbreviation, the Shin Bet. Immediately after the Six-Day War, Israel found itself administrating a greatly expanded Arabic-speaking population in the West Bank and Gaza. Amos became an agent in the Arab Affairs Department. His early fluency in Moroccan Arabic from his parents and his knowledge of colloquial Palestinian Arabic served him well. After twenty years in Shin Bet, Amos's facility in Arabic made him more valuable to Israel's national intelligence service, *hamossad lemodiin uletafkidim meyuchadim*, the Institute for Intelligence and Special Operations, known as the Mossad, or "The Institute."

"I always wondered if you made use of your language facility, Amos."

"Well, it's certainly more interesting than publishing books. I know a tremendous amount about publishing, since it's my cover. Would you like to know how to format a manuscript to be published as an ebook?"

Meir laughed.

"Not really. You told Channah you aren't married. Have you ever been?"

"Never. Too busy." Amos grinned and leaned forward, with his elbows on his knees. "By the way, Meir, where were you during the Yom Kippur War? I thought I would see you when we reported for duty."

Meir shrugged.

"I was in the hospital. I had an emergency appendectomy the night before. I thought I would see you during reserve duty, but I never did. Did your employment relieve you of that obligation?"

"No, but I served my reserve duty as an intelligence officer, so our paths never crossed. When did you get married, Meir?"

"In 1976. I met Channah when I was a young lawyer, and she had just finished her IDF service. She was just twenty-one, ten years younger than I. Ori was born three years later."

Amos leaned forward and his face became serious.

"Look, Meir, I should have said something when Channah was here. I'm sorry about your son. Several times during the past three years I meant to call you. I have no excuse."

Meir shrugged and nodded. He was through absolving late condolences.

"I know he was killed by a suicide bomber on a bus."

Meir exhaled slowly. "Ori and I had a routine. He would call me when he left work and wait at the bus stop. If I could leave in the next few minutes, I would pick him up before the bus came, but if the bus came, he would get on it. He called one afternoon, but I was delayed here. He got on the bus, and I was a minute behind. I saw it explode."

Amos put his head in his hands and shook his head.

"Was Ori married?"

"Yes. He was thirty-five, and he had been married for three years. He and Sarah were trying to have children. After Ori died, Sarah told us she had miscarried several months before."

Amos looked at Meir, stunned by what Meir had told him.

"I'm so sorry for your loss. Is there somewhere we can go so I can smoke a cigarette, Meir?"

"Let's take a walk. I can get ice cream, and you can smoke and tell me why you're visiting me."

Tamar drove while Channah sat in silence next to her.

"Talk to me, Channah."

Channah shook her head.

"Sarah called me last night when I was talking to you. She wanted to meet me today. But she told me not to tell Meir. I don't know why."

Tamar was silent. She sensed that Channah did not feel like talking. She drove to the Mamilla Mall next to the Jaffa Gate of the Old City.

"Thanks, Tamar," Channah said. "Sarah should be here soon. I'm meeting her at Roladin for coffee. I'll call you later to pick me up."

Tamar leaned over and hugged her sister.

"Just call me when you're ready."

The ice cream calmed Meir, but he was still wondering why Amos had come to see him. He and Amos sat on a bench in the afternoon sun. Finally, Amos turned to Meir.

"So, you saw the bus explode. I can't imagine seeing that."

Meir flinched. He thought they had finished talking about Ori's death.

"He died in the hospital later."

Amos sighed. Meir changed the subject.

"Amos, why did you come to see me?"

Amos lit his cigarette and looked across the street toward the Knesset.

"Well, soon, your boss and the prime minister will visit you. And after that, you and I are going to be in a very messy situation not of our own making. Just like 1967, except then we were trying to end a war."

Amos tossed his cigarette on the ground and stamped it out.

"And now?" Meir asked.

"Now, we might start one."

Part Three – Section 614

Jerusalem
November 2035

The *muadhin* called the faithful to noon prayer at al-Aqsa Mosque. My grandfather paused in his story and hugged me to him again.

"Go, Nuri. I will wait here for you."

I went first to the vendor across the courtyard and bought my grandfather his favorite orange soda. I hurried to him with the soda as I heard the call to prayer again.

"Go," he said again. "I will nap here on the bench and be ready to continue the story after *salat*."

I entered al-Aqsa Mosque and found my place in the prayer hall. I prayed for the continued health of my grandparents, my parents, and my sister.

I returned and found my grandfather dozing on the bench in the shade. I waited for several minutes until he woke. He smiled at me, refreshed, and drank some of his soda.

"Nuri, what I am going to tell you next concerns a Section 614 proceeding. Do you know what that is?"

"Yes, *jiddo*. When I was young, an unidentified high government official leaked to a newspaper reporter that the Supreme Court of Israel had the authority to conduct secret hearings. We read the reporter's investigatory series of articles in school, but there wasn't much detail in the articles."

"Well, Nuri," my grandfather said," this story involves a Section 614 proceeding that the public does not know about."

I shook my head in wonder.

"And you are going to tell me, *jiddo?*"

"Yes."

He put his arm around my shoulder and continued in a low voice.

Chapter 18

Meir watched as Amos walked toward the Knesset for another appointment. Despite Amos's cryptic warning, Meir spent the rest of the afternoon feeling productive. He began researching and drafting another decision. Ruth left at four. By five, Meir began winding down, reviewing what he had written and drafting a research assignment for one of his law clerks. Just when he was relaxed and ready to leave, he heard someone enter the outer office of his chambers and knock on his door.

"Meir, *shalom*. It's Eli Heifitz."

Meir opened the door.

"Mr. President, what brings you here so late in the day?"

He motioned the chief justice toward the sofa. The chief justice walked into the office but did not sit down. He had a large red file in his hand.

"I have something for you. It's the background information for a Section 614 case."

In his three years on the Supreme Court, Meir had never presided over a Section 614 proceeding. He knew other justices who had, but they could never discuss it.

Meir looked at Eli Heifitz, and his heart began to beat faster.

Three years before, soon after Meir began serving on the Supreme Court, Eli Heifitz had visited Meir in his chambers and told Meir about the existence and purpose of Section 614 of the Basic Laws of Israel. Section 614 does not appear in printed editions of the *sefer hachukkim*, the Book of Laws. Only the Supreme

Court justices, the prime minister, and select members of the Knesset, Israel Defense Forces, and the Israeli Intelligence Services know its text.

Enforcement of Section 614 is within the authority of the Supreme Court sitting as *beit mishpat gavoah letzedek*, the High Court of Justice, as a court of first instance deciding the legality of state action. Section 614 authorizes one justice of the Supreme Court to sit in special session to decide the legality of a proposed action that the Office of the Prime Minister believes to be vital to the security of the State of Israel. If the sitting justice finds the proposed action to be legal, the state may proceed without authorization by the Knesset.

Extraordinary events that cause the Office of the Prime Minister to propose unprecedented state action are the reason for Section 614 proceedings. The proceedings take place under strict security, in a courtroom in the basement level of the Supreme Court building. All sessions are closed, not recorded, and never reported. The presiding justice issues the decision verbally to the prime minister. The president of the Supreme Court sits in the hearing as an alternate in the event that the presiding justice is not able, for whatever reason, to render a decision.

The prime minister presents a statement supporting the recommended action and remains throughout the hearing. No attorneys participate. The presiding justice hears evidence directly from witnesses. The chief justice randomly selects the presiding justice.

After describing the purpose of Section 614, Meir and Eli Heifitz had gone to the justices' dining room for lunch. As they began to eat, Eli Heifitz leaned back and looked at Meir.

"There is something else you need to know, Meir. A justice is allowed to preside over a Section 614 hearing only after that justice submits a written statement to the prime minister in which the justice explains why this law is designated as Section 614."

Meir toyed with his food as he listened to all of this.

"Mr. President, is this a quiz?" Meir smiled to hide his nervousness.

Eli Heifitz reached for his water glass and took a long swallow, then wiped his beard with his napkin.

"There is an ascertainable reason. Don't be concerned about it for the first few months. Spend your time learning your job and getting comfortable with it. But remember this: Section 614 hearings are only called when an issue vital to the security of Israel is at stake, and you will want the opportunity to participate."

"So I will need to determine why it is called Section 614?"

The chief justice stood up.

"Yes. I would prefer that you do so sooner rather than later."

Eli Heifitz left, and Meir reached for his dessert, a chilled strawberry yogurt with thick whipped cream. He knew he was going to have to control himself. The food in the justices' private dining room was abundant and enticing. As he licked the whipped cream from his spoon, he felt like a student who had received a homework assignment.

Several evenings after his conversation with Eli Heifitz, Meir and Channah met Ori and Sarah for dinner. As Channah chatted with Sarah, Ori told Meir about the new software he was developing. Meir was always fascinated with his son's profession as a software engineer.

"Computer programming language is like a foreign language, *abba*. It has its own grammar and vocabulary. It uses a logical mathematical scheme."

Meir remembered his conversation with Eli Heifitz.

"A mathematical scheme? Let me ask you something, Ori."

Ori leaned forward. He always liked it when his father asked him questions. Before Meir's appointment to the Supreme Court, whenever he had said, "Let me ask you something," Ori knew the question was important. Now that Meir was on the Supreme Court, Ori knew the question must be very important.

"Is this one of those questions that you can't tell me why you want to know the answer?" Ori asked.

"Yes."

"Ask me."

"I can't really give you the context of this . . ."

"Just ask, *abba.*"

Channah and Sarah stopped talking and turned to listen.

"Let me ask all of you. Does the number 614 have any significance to you?"

Ori shook his head.

"Not really. It's just a number without a sequence leading up to it. It is difficult to extrapolate the significance of a random number. Maybe if you could just tell me —"

Sarah patted Ori on the wrist.

"I know I'm just a nursery school teacher, but let me try. Is this a legal question, Meir?"

"You might say that."

"Well, we were singing the 'numbers song' in nursery school today. One God, two tablets, three patriarchs, four matriarchs, twelve tribes of Israel, forty years wandering in the desert, and we finish with the big number—six hundred and thirteen commandments in the Torah."

Meir's eyebrows arched. Sarah continued.

"Number 614 would be the next commandment, if there were one."

Meir reached for the check.

"Good point, Sarah."

"Was that what you were looking for, Meir?"

Channah and Ori answered in unison.

"He can't answer that."

As he was not an observant Jew, Meir had needed to refresh his understanding of the commandments. The next day, he had researched the commandments and written Eli Heifitz a memo:

The Torah contains 613 commandments. The rabbis say the 248 positive commandments are for each bone and organ of the male human body, and the 365 negative commandments are for each day of the solar year.

I believe that Section 614 of the justice code is so named to signify the 614th commandment—preserve the security of the State of Israel.

Eli Heifitz had sent the memo that afternoon in a secure courier pouch to Prime Minister Zadok's office at the Knesset. The next day, Meir was eating dessert in the justices' dining room when Eli Heifitz tapped him on the shoulder.

"Grab an extra dessert and celebrate. You have your Section 614 clearance."

Ori died a month later. Meir had not thought about Section 614 again until Eli Heifitz knocked on his door three years later.

Chapter 19

Eli Heifitz handed Meir the red folder. He didn't wait for Meir to ask questions.

"Some preliminary instructions. First, I am appointing you as the presiding justice in this proceeding. Second, I already know what this is about. Once you review the petition, if there is any reason why you do not think you are capable of presiding, let me know immediately. You know that I will be sitting through the hearing as an observer and an alternate. The decision will be yours alone."

Meir looked down at the folder.

"What do I —?"

The chief justice interrupted.

"You can't remove the petition or any other documents you receive about this case from this building, and you can't work in your chambers. Let me show you where you will work on this."

They left Meir's chambers and walked to the hall elevator. They took the elevator to the basement level. At the end of the basement corridor was a metal door. Eli Heifitz tapped on a keypad next to the door, and the door opened. They entered a small room where a young man in black pants and a casual open-collar shirt sat reading a book. The man snapped to attention. Meir had never met him before.

"Meir, this is Amran. He is from the Prime Minister's Office. He will be in charge of security for this case. From now on, he will always be here at this entrance. Amran, Justice Bar-Aben."

Meir nodded and smiled. *Why was it that security officers never gave their last names?*

Amran nodded but didn't smile.

On the wall opposite the door they had entered was another door with a sensor shaped like a hand. Eli Heifitz motioned Meir to that door.

"Put your right hand here."

The sensor read all five fingerprints, and they could hear the door unlock. Meir grabbed the door handle and pulled the door open. They entered another hallway with a locked door at the end. Again, the chief justice pointed to the hand sensor on that door for Meir. The door opened, and they entered a nicely furnished but windowless office. Meir was feeling mildly claustrophobic. Eli Heifitz motioned to the chair behind the desk.

"Sit down and we can talk about how you are going to handle this."

Meir sat behind the desk. Eli Heifitz reclined into a comfortable leather chair facing the desk. Meir looked at the bare concrete walls. Eli's voice echoed slightly even though he talked in a low voice.

"As you have just seen, the hand sensors on the entrance door and this office are set to your fingerprints. For now, until the hearing begins, you are the only one allowed into this corridor, unless you accompany someone into the corridor. Any documents you review or notes you write are to remain in this room. A safe under your desk is also keyed to your fingerprints. There is paper in the safe. If you need to take notes, use it. You can't bring anything else down."

Meir shifted in his chair.

"What else will be submitted to me before the hearing begins?"

"You will receive a summary of several witness interviews after the interviews are conducted. The hearing will be verbal, presented by the prime minister and witnesses. When you are finished reviewing the petition and witness interviews, you should put them in the safe in this room."

"I want to stay here and read the petition. Is there a phone down here to call Channah?"

"Yes. It's inside the safe, and it has a secure line."

The chief justice left. Meir opened the safe and pulled out a red phone. He placed it on the desk next to the red folder. He dialed home, but there was no answer.

He looked at his watch. It was a quarter past five. The red folder was sealed with tape. Meir opened the desk drawer and found a pair of scissors. He cut the tape and opened the folder. The petition for the 614 proceeding was the only document in the folder. He began to read.

Before the Supreme Court of the State of Israel, sitting as the High Court of Justice
Pursuant to Section 614 of the Basic Laws of Israel.

Violations of Law

The Office of the Prime Minister of the State of Israel alleges as follows:

The actions of the Waqf, by excavating under the Temple Mount to construct the Marwani Mosque below al-Aqsa Mosque, and removing and disposing of a significant amount of excavated material from under the Temple Mount during these excavations, has resulted in the destruction of historical archaeological material sacred to the history of the Jewish people and the recent collapse of the Western Wall of the Temple Mount.

These actions of the Waqf have violated the following provision of the Basic Law of Israel known as the Law of the Holy Places:

Jerusalem, Capital of Israel: The Holy Places shall be protected from desecration and any other violation and from anything likely to violate the freedom of access of the members of the different religions to the places sacred to them or their feelings toward those places.

<u>Relief Requested</u>

Therefore, the Office of the Prime Minister seeks a determination, based upon the foregoing alleged actions of the Waqf, that the Law of the Holy Places has been violated.

In addition, to prevent further desecration of the Temple Mount, and to protect the archeological and historical value of the Temple Mount, the Office of the Prime Minister further requests that this Honorable Court approve the proposed action by the Government of the State of Israel to take back unto itself from the Waqf the administration of the Temple Mount to allow people of any faith free access to visit and to pray there.

Respectfully submitted,

Ezer Zadok, Prime Minister of the State of Israel

Meir finished reading. He leaned back in his chair, closed his eyes, and breathed deeply and slowly. The petition asked the court to make a decision that could have frightening consequences. Even so, Meir felt calm. Before Ori died, the enormity of this case would have sent him into a state of excitement, if not anxiety. Today, he had no emotional attachment to the collapsed Kotel, or the upwelling of religious violence that threatened the region. He put the petition back in the red folder and locked the folder in the safe. A few minutes later, Meir left the office and walked the short corridor. He went through the door and found Amran waiting for him.

Amran rose.

"Justice Bar-Aben, I'll follow you home tonight. Starting tomorrow, I will be your driver. I will pick you up in the morning and bring you home."

Meir nodded and didn't object.

"Don't follow me too closely, Amran. I tend to make sudden stops."

Amran followed Meir out of the Supreme Court's parking garage. He kept his SUV behind Meir's Mercedes, not allowing any other car to separate them. Meir fixed his eyes on the car in front of him. The drive home was always the hardest part of the day. He turned on the radio and then switched it off. He saw a bus two cars ahead of him and gripped the wheel hard. He breathed in and out, steadying himself.

The bus discharged passengers and turned the corner, out of sight.

He forced himself to press the accelerator and turn the corner. The bus was already a block away. Meir looked in his mirror to make sure Amran was behind him.

When Meir arrived at his building, Amran pulled up next to him and rolled down his passenger window.

"Tomorrow morning, I'll be waiting for you in the parking garage next to your car, Justice Bar-Aben. We already arranged for me to have a pass to get into your building. What time would you like to leave?"

"Seven."

"Don't come out of the building. Wait until seven and meet me in the parking garage."

Meir nodded and drove into the garage. He pulled into his parking space and leaned his head against the steering wheel. He waited for almost ten minutes before his breathing steadied. The sound of another car entering the parking garage roused him, and Meir quickly got out of his car and walked to the elevator.

He was glad Channah wasn't home. He wasn't hungry, but she would have forced him to eat. Esther glided out of the kitchen and stared at him. She sensed his lack of hunger and resigned herself to eat cat food. Meir headed toward the bedroom.

Before Amran drove away, he scanned the café across the street from Meir's building. Five people sat outside. He took a picture of them with his camera and emailed the picture to a central database. Zara was sitting alone at one of the tables.

Amran called another Shin Bet agent.

"Agent Aleph, anything to report?"

"The wife's sister dropped off the wife at the Mamilla Mall. The wife met her daughter-in-law at a coffee shop. The sister came back later after the daughter-in-law left. The wife and her sister are wandering around the mall now."

Amran hung up and dialed another number.

"Agent Bet, anything to report?"

"The daughter-in-law met the wife at the Mamilla Mall then went home. I followed the daughter-in-law home, and she hasn't left the house again."

Amran hung up and drove home.

Meir was in bed, watching a DVD of Itzhak Perlman performing the Mendelssohn Violin Concerto. Meir, having learned the concerto when he was a child, occasionally closed his eyes and visualized fingering the notes on the neck of the violin. Esther stretched out across his stomach, facing the television.

The phone rang at eight o'clock.

"Meir, I'm out to dinner with Tamar. I'll be home around nine."

"I'll be up. I'm in bed with the Queen."

He heard the door open a little after nine o'clock. Channah came into the bedroom and looked at him. Her mood from lunch had vanished.

"Bad day shopping with Tamar?"

She shrugged as she began to undress. Channah slipped on her nightgown and climbed into bed.

"Tamar doesn't have much expendable cash these days. We walked around Mamilla Mall but didn't buy anything."

"Where did you eat?"

"At Luciana. You know, Tamar likes Italian food. Anyway, that Amos is quite a good-looking guy."

"Always has been."

"I can't believe he's a book publisher."

Meir was silent. She turned on her side and shooed Esther off Meir's chest. She reached for his hand and brought it to her lips, kissing it lightly.

"Actually, I don't believe he is a book publisher."

"What do you think he is?"

"Someone with a reason to come see you."

Meir laughed.

"How about this. I won't tell you anything more about my day, and you don't have to tell me about yours."

Channah lowered her head onto Meir's chest, closed her eyes, and hugged him gently.

"That's fine with me," she whispered.

Chapter 20

Monday, April 3, 2017

Amran was waiting in his SUV in the parking garage next to Meir's car. He was reading the newspaper when Meir climbed into the back seat.

"Good morning, Amran."

Amran nodded, folded the newspaper, and drove out of the garage. Apparently, he wasn't a morning conversationalist.

Meir called Ruth into his chambers. He decided that the less he said, the better.

"President Heifitz has given me a special assignment. For the next few weeks, I'll be working in the building but not in chambers. If you need me, leave a message on my voice mail. I'll check it during the day."

Ruth had worked at the Supreme Court for twenty-five years for two other justices before Meir. Both justices had worked out of chambers several times during their tenure. One was exhausted for a month after his return and had not written a decision for several months afterward. Another had taken a long vacation without pay.

"I understand, Justice Bar-Aben. *mazal tov.*"

Ruth had offered and Meir understood the congratulatory expression with its literal meaning—"good luck."

Meir took the elevator to the basement and found Amran at his post, immersed again in the newspaper.

Eli Heifitz was waiting for him with another red folder and a portable video player.

"More information for you to review. There is a video disc attached to one of the documents."

Meir took the folder and video player. Eli Heifitz left.

Meir placed his hand on the sensor to enter the secure corridor, and again to enter his office. He put the video player on the desk and sat down. He opened the red folder and removed several documents.

The first document was titled "Causation Analysis of the Collapse of the Western Wall." It was a detailed report prepared by a team of archaeologists and structural engineers. Meir turned the pages, looking at mathematical calculations, photographs, and computer-generated diagrams. He skimmed the technical narrative, knowing that he would return to it later. Finally, Meir turned to the last section of the report and read the conclusion.

The construction activities and excavation conducted by the Waqf under the Temple Mount destabilized the structure of the Western Wall and directly and proximately caused the collapse. The accompanying video disc contains a computer-generated simulation of the progress of construction activity and excavation, the resulting destabilization over time, and a simulated collapse.

Meir put the video disc into the video player and watched. A narrator conducted a brief orientation of the Temple Mount from above and from four sides, with grids superimposed on aerial and vertical layouts. Based on analysis after the collapse occurred, scenes shifted to time-lapsed excavations under the Temple Mount, with arrows showing the change in geological pressures as the excavation proceeded. Finally, an animated collapse occurred, which the narrator described as inevitable, based upon the Waqf's actions.

The next document in the file was titled "Interview of Rabbi Ashur Avidan." Meir was surprised that Prime Minister Zadok had conducted the interview. A photograph was attached to the interview summary. Meir noted that the man in the photograph appeared very old with his long white beard, but alert with piercing eyes.

The interview summary stated that Rabbi Avidan was *one hundred and one years old*. He could trace his ancestry back to the time of the Second Temple. He had been born in Vilna, Lithuania, and studied Torah and Talmud at one of the great yeshivas there. During World War II, when the Nazis had occupied the city, he had escaped into the forest and joined Russian partisans. Rabbi Avidan had immigrated to Israel in 1949 when he was thirty-three years old. He was the only member of his family who had survived the Holocaust.

That same morning, Rabbi Avidan awoke shortly before sunrise. An hour before, his wife, Leah, had returned to bed from nursing Jacob, their one-year-old son. The rabbi closed his eyes and said his first prayer of the day, thanking God for returning his soul to his body after another night of restful sleep.

He slowly removed the blanket and eased himself out of bed, stretching the blanket over his wife. He looked at Jacob, lying in the crib next to their bed. He had always known life was a miracle, but his young wife and newborn son attested to this. He had outlived three wives, ten of his twenty-one children, and several of his grandchildren. Counting grandchildren, great-grandchildren, and great-great-grandchildren, he had over a thousand descendants. Why God kept him alive, and still procreating, was a mystery.

Rabbi Avidan walked softly into an adjoining bedroom and dressed quickly. His small apartment in the Jewish Quarter of the Old City of Jerusalem was not far from the Kotel. When he left his apartment, he was joined by others heading to the Kotel for morning prayers. The worshippers reached the stairs that led down to the plaza in front of the Kotel. Rabbi Avidan could see that the first rays of dawn had already illuminated the top of the Dome of the Rock.

Rabbi Avidan joined his usual group in the area where worshippers and tourists were still allowed. He looked at the canvas tent covering the ashlars. He wrapped his prayer shawl around himself and began the morning prayers. Doves that used to roost in the cracks between the stones, cooing along with the prayers, had migrated to the courtyard of the Dome of the Rock. Rabbi Avidan closed his eyes and swayed his body in unison with his fellow worshippers, praying for guidance. As he prayed, his concentration was shattered by gasps and cries from tourists and others who were descending into the plaza, seeing the collapsed Kotel covered under canvas. Some wept, others cursed, drawing sharp looks from those praying.

Rabbi Avidan had been startled to receive a call from the Prime Minister's Office soon after the collapse of the Kotel. His meeting with the prime minister at the Knesset had been cordial. The prime minister had told him that Rabbi Tarfon of the new Sanhedrin had mentioned that many believed he, Rabbi Avidan, had convinced Moshe Dayan to return the Temple Mount to the Waqf after the Six-Day War. *Was this true?*

Rabbi Avidan had spent hours with the prime minister. At the end of the day, the prime minister requested that Rabbi Avidan testify at a secret hearing before a justice of the Supreme Court. When the prime minister had explained the purpose of the hearing, Rabbi Avidan had shuddered with awe and dread.

This morning, Rabbi Avidan prayed the traditional prayer of thanksgiving.

"Blessed are you, O Lord our God, who has kept me alive to reach this day."

Then Rabbi Avidan said another prayer, this time more fervently, for the justice of the Supreme Court who would conduct the hearing.

It was almost noon when Meir finished reading Rabbi Avidan's interview. He took off his reading glasses, rubbed his eyes, and exhaled slowly. After fifty years, Meir now knew that. Rabbi Avidan was the Orthodox Jew who had appeared on the Temple Mount the night it was captured. Meir left his office and found Amran reading a newspaper.

"I'm going to the dining room to eat lunch. Can I bring you anything, Amran?"

"No. Thank you, sir. I am going over to the Knesset to meet with the prime minister briefly. I will return soon."

When Meir came back to the basement office an hour later, Amran was sitting at his post reading a novel. Meir entered his office and sat down at the desk. He began to read the next document in the folder entitled "Interview of Samir ibn Abdullah." Again, a photograph was attached. Mr. ibn Abdullah was eighty years old. Since 1965, he had been a *muadhin* of al-Aqsa Mosque, calling the faithful to prayer on Mondays. Meir began to read.

That morning, as Rabbi Avidan was praying at the Kotel, Samir looked up at the minaret of al-Aqsa Mosque. Every Monday, as dawn broke, he would stand overlooking al-Quds, putting the tips of his forefingers in his ears to amplify his voice, and begin the call to prayer.

From his earliest youth, Samir had always wanted to be a *muadhin*. By the time he was six years old, he had memorized many *suras* of the Quran. One afternoon, Samir had returned from his morning study at the madrasa. He and his mother Sabah were in the open courtyard of their home. She was kneading the dough for the daily pita. Samir was reciting the new *suras* he had learned that day, and he paused to look at his mother.

"I need to tell you something, *mama*."

Sabah continued to knead the dough. She could do almost anything while she kneaded. She could gossip with friends, boil a pot of tea, nurse Samir's younger brother. There was hardly any reason to stop the kneading.

"I decided today that I will be a *muadhin*."

Sabah stopped kneading and nodded knowingly. "I am not surprised, Samir. You can't remember what happened on the day of your birth, but from that day, I knew that you would be a *muadhin*."

Samir laughed the easy laugh of a child who thought his mother was just humoring his wish.

"How do you know that? Did I tell you even though I could not speak?"

Sabah did not laugh. Her expression became very serious, and she rose from her knees in front of the kneading stone and stood above him. She reached down and placed her hands over his ears.

"You were born at dusk, after I had been trying to birth you since that morning. When you were handed, crying, to your father, he sang into your ear the *adhan*. Do you know what happened then?"

Samir laughed again.

"No, *mama*, I really can't remember."

Sabah did not smile.

"When your father began with 'God is greater,' you stopped crying. When he said 'I bear witness that Muhammad is the messenger of God,' you cupped your hands over your ears, as the *muadhin* does. When he said, 'Prayer is better than sleep,' you smiled and then stayed awake for a whole day and did not cry."

"And why did that mean I would be a *muadhin*?"

"Because you stayed awake to make sure that the faithful would be called to prayer. From that day, we knew the desire of your heart that even you did not know."

Today, as Samir climbed the stairs to call the faithful to morning prayer, his legs ached. For the past several months, he had suddenly begun to feel his age, as if his life force were ebbing slowly away. Perhaps the collapse of al-Buraq's Wall was an omen for him. He hardly noticed the large tent draped over the stones in the plaza below.

Samir faced east and began to chant. He could see groups of men and individuals crossing the courtyard to enter al-Aqsa Mosque. As he completed the call to prayer, he watched the last of the worshippers hurry toward the mosque.

Samir had hoped to live into his old age in his usual rhythm, working in his shop, climbing the minaret, soaring above the crowds, and projecting his now-failing voice over the ancient stones. Last week, the Monday after the collapse of al-Buraq's Wall, he had climbed down after morning prayers and found himself face-to-face with someone he had not seen since the day the Israelis captured the Noble Sanctuary in 1967.

The man's curly hair had a touch of gray, but he still seemed young. They went to a coffee shop in the Muslim Quarter, where they sat and drank thick bitter coffee. The *yahudi* spoke Arabic as if he were a cousin.

Samir looked at the *yahudi* and whispered, "The rabbi, the other one who came that night, is he still alive? He must be over a hundred years old."

"He is. And he remembers you."

Samir felt relief flow through him.

"Good. I think he is the only one alive who believed me," he said.

Then the *yahudi* told him something he could not believe.

"The prime minister wants to interview me? So I can testify at the Supreme Court?"

"Yes," the *yahudi* replied. "And I will be your interpreter."

Meir read the entire interview slowly even though he had only intended to review it briefly. Like Rabbi Avidan in his interview, Samir had offered long narrative answers. Now, Meir knew the identity of the Muslim man who had appeared on the Temple Mount. When Meir finally looked at his watch, it was six thirty.

Amran must be furious. Channah was sure to be furious.

Meir found Amran at his station, reading a book.

"Sorry, Amran."

Amran actually smiled.

"My job is to conform to your schedule, Justice Bar-Aben. There's nothing to be sorry about."

During the drive home, Amran was silent as he had been that morning. Meir sat in the back seat with his eyes closed and thought about the interviews. Before he knew it, Amran arrived at his building. Meir realized he hadn't looked out the window for the entire ride.

Before Amran drove into the parking garage, he looked over at the café and saw the same woman he had seen the evening before. This time she was with a man. When Amran came out of the garage several minutes later, he stopped at the curb and took a picture of the woman and the man.

Channah found it difficult to hold her tongue as she watched Meir rummage in the refrigerator.

"I didn't hear from you, so I just ate a salad. Otherwise, I would have cooked dinner."

Meir took a container of yogurt and some orange juice from the refrigerator and sat down at the kitchen table.

"I'm sorry. I lost track of time. But you haven't been home recently, anyway."

Channah was quiet. Meir looked up at her. She had turned her back on him.

"Recently, I never know where you are or when you plan to be home."

Channah turned toward him.

"Look, Meir. You can't work like this, whatever it is you've been doing lately. We've been living on the edge for more than three years now. You're going to be wiped out before this thing, whatever it is, is over."

Meir ate the yogurt slowly. Esther circled his leg in one direction, rubbing her face against his leg, then switched direction.

"Want some, Channah? There's plenty."

"You eat. I'm going to call my sister."

Chapter 21

Meir and Channah ate breakfast together the next morning. Meir broke the silence.

"Channah, I'm sorry. I'm working on a case that is going to take more time than usual. I'll be working late."

"Can you tell me anything about it?"

"Not now. I'm not sure if I ever can."

"That big, huh?"

"As big as it gets."

"Are you sorry you are working on it?"

"No."

"Then don't worry about it. Just get it done. I won't ask any questions. By the way, I am seeing Sarah this afternoon. She called me and wanted me to go shopping with her."

"Give her my best," Meir said.

After he arrived in the underground office, Meir read the interviews of Rabbi Avidan and Samir ibn Abdullah again. He finished just before noon. As he exited the secure corridor to retrieve his lunch from Amran, he found Eli Heifitz waiting for him at Amran's station.

"You have a lunch guest in your chambers."

Meir winced.

"Do I really have time for guests? Who is it?"

"'Guest' is a relative term. It's Prime Minister Zadok. I'm having lunch sent up. You go and I'll join you soon, just to say hello. You've met him before, I believe."

"Briefly, at Ori's funeral. I've never had a conversation with him."

"Well, I'm sure you will today."

Meir took the elevator to his chambers. Ruth did not flash him her usual smile. Instead, she stood up and motioned toward the conference room.

"We have a guest."

"I know."

"He's waiting in there."

Meir found Prime Minister Zadok seated at the table in the conference room, leafing through a volume of court opinions that he had randomly selected from the shelf. He rose from his seat as Meir entered the room.

"Justice Bar-Aben. A pleasure to see you again."

"Likewise, Mr. Prime Minister."

They shook hands.

Zadok was at least six feet five inches tall. He was very thin and fit from constant exercise he imposed upon himself. The scent of Zadok's cologne was overwhelming. Zadok was also a smoker, and he reeked of cigarettes.

"This is an unexpected break for me, Mr. Prime Minister. I assume you know that I have been working out of sight, so to speak."

Zadok nodded and smiled.

"I wanted to give you my thoughts before the hearing begins," Zadok said.

As they sat down at the table, Ruth appeared with a tray of salads and fresh pita from the justices' dining room. She placed it on the conference table and filled water glasses from a pitcher. She closed the door behind her as she left.

Meir and Zadok filled their plates and began to eat. Meir felt the need to speak first.

"Mr. Prime Minister, the basis of your petition to the court is the allegation that the Waqf's activities caused the collapse of the Kotel and violated the law of the holy places. You have submitted evidence of the cause of the collapse. Do you intend to have those who prepared the report testify, or am I supposed to accept the report's conclusion without testimony?"

Prime Minister Zadok shrugged.

"Do you not accept the conclusion of the report, Justice Bar-Aben?"

"It's not a question of whether I accept the conclusion or not. The usual procedure is for an expert to explain an expert report to the court, and for the opposing party to have an opportunity to present an expert to challenge the report. In this case, there is no opposing party. So, are you willing to submit the report to me without any further guidance?"

"We are submitting the written report without supporting testimony," Zadok said. "We don't want those who prepared the report to have knowledge of this proceeding."

"So, why have a hearing, if you believe the report proves the cause of the collapse and the violation of the law? From reading the interview summaries, I don't understand how the testimony of the two witnesses can support your case."

"I believe the witnesses' testimony will support my office's petition for revocation of the Waqf's authority over the Temple Mount, even if you find that the Waqf's action did not cause the collapse of the Kotel."

Meir was puzzled. "That is not apparent to me from reading the interview summaries," he said.

"It will become apparent at the hearing," Zadok said.

"I will wait to hear the testimony. Also, I'm curious, Mr. Prime Minister. How did you know Rabbi Avidan and Mr. ibn Abdullah came to the Temple Mount that night during the Six-Day War?"

Zadok told Meir about his meeting with Rabbi Tarfon and the other members of the new Sanhedrin.

"After Rabbi Tarfon showed me actual plans to rebuild the Temple on the Temple Mount, he told me a rumor that has persisted since the Six-Day War. Many believe that Rabbi Avidan convinced Moshe Dayan to return the Temple Mount to the Waqf. I interviewed Rabbi Avidan, and he told me about a meeting he had with Moshe Dayan and Rabbi Goren the night the Temple Mount was captured in the Six-Day War. He told me that Mr. ibn Abdullah and an IDF intelligence officer, Amos Eitan, were also there. I then interviewed Mr. ibn Abdullah, with Amos Eitan translating during the interview."

"I will be very interested in their testimony," Meir said. "Let me raise another issue, Mr. Prime Minister. Since Amos Eitan was present that night, shouldn't he be a witness?

"He will be."

"I don't have an interview summary for him."

"Mr. Eitan is a Mossad officer," Zadok said. "The agency will only allow him to testify at the hearing. He won't be interviewed. We thought it prudent to have him serve as translator when I interviewed Mr. ibn Abdullah."

Meir and Zadok stopped talking and ate for several minutes, until Meir spoke again.

"You know that this court refused to halt the excavations under the Temple Mount when they began years ago."

"I remember," Zadok said. "But that was a petition brought by private citizens. This is the state seeking to find legal violations and reclaim the Temple Mount."

"Certainly a much more explosive situation than just halting excavations," Meir said. "So, please explain to me. Is your petition to take back the Temple Mount meant to further the agenda of the new Sanhedrin? Will you have dynamite and bulldozers ready to level the Dome of the Rock and al-Aqsa Mosque if the petition is granted?"

"No. I am not interested in rebuilding the Temple," Zadok said. "But I have never understood why Moshe Dayan returned the Temple Mount to the Waqf. He did not decide to capture the Old City until several days into the war when a ceasefire was considered. He used paratroopers so no holy sites would be damaged. He made a statement the evening the Temple Mount was captured that we would never again be separated from our holiest site. Then he returned the Temple Mount after our troops were killed and wounded. The Temple Mount is our heritage. We should control it. The damage inflicted by the Waqf 's excavations cannot be tolerated."

Meir listened patiently.

"When do you think we can proceed with the hearing?" Meir asked.

"I need to make several arrangements before we can begin," Zadok answered. "I will let you know soon."

Meir leaned back in his chair.

"I have to disclose several matters, Mr. Prime Minister, to make sure you do not object to my serving as the presiding justice in this case."

"Please do."

"First," Meir said, "I am not religious. My father escaped Europe before the Holocaust. He was not religious. When I was eight years old, he took me to the tomb of Shimon bar Yochai, the author of the *Zohar*—a major text of the kabbalah."

Zadok nodded.

"Yes, I have been there. It is in Meron, in Upper Galilee."

"Then you have seen what happens there," Meir said. "As we approached the tomb, women were weeping and wailing, mourning the death of Shimon bar Yochai. I was eight years old, and very scared. I asked my father why the women were crying. He told me they were crying because a great man had died. 'When did he die?' I asked. My father told me that the great man had died more than eighteen hundred years ago."

"What was your reaction to that?" Zadok asked.

"I asked my father why they were still crying. Wouldn't he have been dead by now anyway? My father said they were crying because they had nothing better to do. That was my first and last lesson in religion."

"This case is not about religion," Zadok said. "I told you, I am not interested in rebuilding the Temple."

"Second," Meir said, "I was in the 55th Brigade that took the Old City and the Temple Mount during the Six-Day War."

"I know," Zadok said. "You probably know I was in the 66th Battalion and was wounded in the Battle of Ammunition Hill. I don't see a problem. We both fought to liberate Jerusalem."

"Third and fourth," Meir said, "I knew Amos Eitan, and I saw Rabbi Avidan and Samir ibn Abdullah on the Temple Mount that night."

"I am aware of that. Mr. Eitan has told me that he served with you, and that you were there and probably saw both of the witnesses. You can corroborate that they were there. I still do not see a problem. Is that all?"

"Yes."

Zadok spooned chopped vegetables into a pita and took a large bite.

"Let me be blunt. I initiated the proceeding. The excavations under the Temple Mount have been a continuing problem. Now, with the collapse of the Kotel, I thought it was necessary that Israel protect the Temple Mount. I believe that the only way we can do this with any degree of certainty is to take it back from the Waqf. I agree that if you grant the petition, it will be an explosive decision."

Meir didn't respond. He looked at the prime minister. Zadok continued.

"I have been in the military and politics. I am used to fighting and talking. You're used to reasoning and deciding and taking a long-range view of consequences."

Meir leaned forward.

"I have learned that I must hear all the evidence before I can even begin to decide a case."

"I realize that. But I came to tell you something today. There are those who would prefer that your decision be based on historical right," Zadok said.

Meir was beginning to feel uncomfortable. The prime minister's attempt at subtlety seemed blatant and improper.

"Mr. Prime Minister, my job is to determine if the petition has a valid basis and decide accordingly. If this were a matter of preference, we would have an election, not a decision under Section 614."

Zadok reddened and breathed in sharply. He wasn't smiling now.

"I want to pose something to you, Justice Bar-Aben. The *shaheed* who murdered your son prayed in al-Aqsa Mosque the same afternoon your son died. Since al-Aqsa Mosque stands on the Temple Mount, do you think you are able to rationally and objectively deal with this case? Wouldn't it be better for you if you recused yourself and allowed another justice to preside?"

Meir felt his heart pounding and willed it to slow. He had never connected Ori's death to the Temple Mount. A politician connecting dots where there was no connection would not bully him.

"Mr. Prime Minister, whoever the murderer was, I never associated him with al-Aqsa Mosque or the Temple Mount. So, to answer your question, I will not recuse myself."

Zadok nodded slowly.

Meir had calmed himself.

"Another question, Mr. Prime Minister."

"Please."

"Since this is my first Section 614 hearing, I know that your office files the petition, but who actually will present the case for your office?"

"In this case, I do."

"We should finish eating lunch, Mr. Prime Minister. President Heifitz is going to join us soon."

Meir and Zadok had the catharsis of speaking their minds. Zadok was a slow eater, as he maintained a monologue of small talk. Israeli politics, based on numerous parties of competing interests, is at its best complicated and intriguing and at its worst a cacophony of mind-numbing trivia and backstabbing. Zadok's one-sided conversation vacillated between the two extremes.

As they finished eating, Eli Heifitz came in to say hello. Zadok left with him. Meir took a walk outside and let the noon sun warm him thoroughly. The fresh air cleansed the scent of Zadok's cologne and cigarettes from his nostrils.

Meir did not have any additional information to read for his Section 614 proceeding. He worked on other cases in his office. Amran drove him home at the end of the day.

Amran had resumed his silence during the drive home. Meir sat in the back seat with his eyes closed. He remembered that Channah would probably not be home so soon. She had told him that she was going shopping with Sarah. As much as Channah had been out lately, Meir couldn't argue with Channah spending time with Sarah.

Meir looked out the window and saw a bus. He closed his eyes again and breathed deeply.

Channah and Sarah had not spoken since they left the shopping mall. As Channah drove the car up to the entrance of Sarah's condominium, she spoke.

"I don't think I can meet him yet, Sarah."

"He wants to meet you. I want you to meet him. I think this is real."

Channah was chagrined.

"I just cannot believe this, Sarah. I want to meet him, but not now."

"Not yet. Soon."

Sarah leaned over and kissed Channah.

"Just remember, Channah. I loved Ori. I will always be a daughter-in-law to you and Meir. But this can be a part of your lives, Channah."

Channah hugged Sarah.

"It seems we don't have a choice. But I could never tell Meir now. He is very busy on a difficult case."

"Think about it. This can make you happy if you let it."

"I will have to think about it, Sarah. This is so sudden. I am just overwhelmed and confused right now. I have the appointment at the hospital tomorrow. And Meir is so busy."

Sarah hugged Channah.

"I'm sure the appointment will calm you. At least you will know for sure. Is Tamar going to drive us?"

"Yes. We'll see you tomorrow."

Sarah got out of the car and waved good-bye. Channah drove away.

Zara stood at the bus stop across from Sarah's building. Her heart pounded as she saw Sarah enter the lobby. The other two women at the bus stop ignored her, tapping text messages on their phones. Dressed again as an Orthodox Jewish woman, she hummed a Hebrew tune as Channah drove away.

Amran was returning to the Knesset to drive Zadok home when his cell phone rang. It was Agent Aleph.

"Amran, we have a situation. The wife and the daughter-in-law were together this afternoon. Agent Bet and I have been following them. When the wife drove the daughter-in-law home, we spotted the woman we had seen at the café across from your man's apartment. Today, she is dressed as a *haredi*. She is outside the daughter-in-law's building."

"Don't approach," Amran said. "Just follow her, and don't let her get close to the wife or the daughter-in-law."

Chapter 22

Prime Minister Zadok returned to the Knesset after meeting with Meir. He had scheduled a second meeting with Rabbi Avidan that afternoon at the rabbi's request. At the conclusion of their previous meeting, Rabbi Avidan had seemed tired, and had asked that they continue their discussion on another day. Zadok had sensed that the rabbi had more to say, and he wanted to conclude the interview before the hearing began.

Rabbi Avidan arrived shortly after Zadok returned. Zadok's secretary brought him to a conference room adjoining Zadok's office. They greeted each other and sat down.

Rabbi Avidan began.

"I showed Moshe Dayan something that night that had been in my family for generations. I believe it made an impression on him. If we can find it, it will support my testimony at the hearing."

"You don't have it now?" Zadok asked.

"No. But I believe I know where it is."

Zadok was puzzled.

"What is it, and how can we find it?"

Rabbi Avidan smiled. "It's a stone, and I think it is in the Israel Museum. At the end of my testimony at the hearing, I will tell you why it is important."

Zadok returned to his office and left Rabbi Avidan in the conference room. He called Hiram Aitza. Hiram answered on the first ring.

"Poker this week, I hope?"

"No, but I need your help. I can't tell you why."

Hiram was intrigued.

"What can you tell me?"

"There may be something in the museum that is relevant to a matter I am dealing with."

"What is it?"

"An artifact."

"That certainly narrows it down, Ezer. We have a few of those at the museum."

"I know the exhibit number."

"That's helpful. What is it?"

"It's in the Second Temple Period Exhibit Hall. Exhibit number 114."

"I can't just lend it to you," Hiram said. "There are rules and procedures for removing exhibits from the museum."

"First things first, Hiram. I want to come to the museum now with someone to examine the artifact."

Hiram searched the museum catalog on his computer.

"I see that it's a stone, easily portable. I will need an hour to remove the stone from the exhibit. Come directly to my office."

"We'll be there in an hour."

Hiram was standing outside the museum entrance when Zadok's car arrived. He led Zadok and the rabbi to the entrance hall past a long line of tourists and into a side corridor leading to a private elevator. When the elevator door closed, Zadok introduced Rabbi Avidan.

"Rabbi Avidan, this is Hiram Aitza, director of the museum."

"A pleasure, Mr. Aitza," the rabbi said.

"I have the artifact ready in the conference room, Rabbi."

They entered a windowless conference room. A rectangular stone lay on a rubber pad in the middle of a table. It was approximately twelve by six inches and an inch thick.

"This is what you requested to see," Hiram said to Zadok. Hiram waited for an explanation, but none was forthcoming. He turned to the rabbi who was standing over the stone.

"Rabbi, do you have a particular interest in the Second Temple period? We have many other artifacts from that era."

Rabbi Avidan looked at Hiram and smiled.

"May I touch the stone, Mr. Aitza?"

"Of course, but first, would you put on the gloves, please?" Hiram pointed to a package of latex gloves on the table.

"If you don't mind, this won't take long. But I prefer not to wear gloves."

Hiram looked at Zadok.

"Please, Mr. Aitza," Zadok said. "This stone has survived thousands of years before latex gloves."

Hiram nodded.

"You don't have to wear gloves, Rabbi."

Rabbi Avidan rubbed the top of the stone with two fingers. He turned it over and rubbed the other side. He stared at the stone for several seconds and sighed.

"This is not what I am looking for."

"We have many other similar stones from this period that might interest you, Rabbi," Hiram said. "If you could tell me exactly what you are seeking, I could search the catalog."

"This is the only one I wanted to see, Mr. Aitza. I understand it is from the collection of Moshe Dayan."

"Yes," Hiram said. "The museum purchased most of his extensive collection of antiquities after his death. He was an avid collector."

"Most of the collection?" Zadok asked. He turned and looked at the rabbi.

"Where are the artifacts that the museum didn't purchase?" Rabbi Avidan asked Hiram.

"Auctioned in the United States years ago. A prominent Jewish philanthropist bought the entire lot. I'm not sure if it is still intact."

"Is there any way you can find out what happened to the rest of the collection, Mr. Aitza?" Rabbi Avidan asked.

"I could try, I suppose. Can you give me any more information about the artifact you are looking for, Rabbi?"

"It is a stone from the Second Temple period similar to this one, from Moshe Dayan's collection," Rabbi Avidan said, pointing to the stone on the table. "That is all I can tell you."

Before Hiram could speak, Zadok spoke.

"Mr. Aitza will do everything he can to help locate Moshe Dayan's collection that was sold in the United States. You'll let us know as soon as possible, Mr. Aitza?"

Hiram nodded.

"It may take some time, but we will begin immediately."

"Please do, Mr. Aitza," Zadok said. "We don't have much time."

Hiram and Zadok escorted Rabbi Avidan to the museum entrance. Zadok's car was waiting.

"My driver will take you back to the Old City, Rabbi."

Rabbi Avidan shook hands with Hiram and Zadok and got into the car. Hiram and Zadok walked back into the museum to Hiram's office.

Hiram sat behind his desk as Zadok lowered himself onto the couch.

"So you want me to look in the U.S. for the rest of Moshe Dayan's collection, Ezer?"

"You heard me tell the rabbi you would."

"And you can't tell me why?"

"I couldn't if I wanted to, Hiram. I don't know why it is so important to him."

Hiram shrugged. He knew when to stop asking.

"Anything else I can do for you today, Ezer?"

"Actually, there is. Let me ask you a hypothetical question, Hiram," Zadok said.

"I suppose you can't tell me why you are asking. But please ask."

"If you needed an expert to establish the Jewish claim to the Temple Mount, before al-Aqsa Mosque and the Dome of the Rock were built, who might that be?"

Hiram thought for a moment and then shook his head slowly.

"That's actually an easy question, Ezer. One of my former students is now a professor of history at Hebrew University, and she is certainly an expert on this subject. I've read her publications and attended her lectures."

"Who is she?"

"Professor Fatima al-Fawzi."

"She is Muslim?"

"Yes. Her concentration of study is the century of the first Muslim conquest of Jerusalem. She is quite a scholar."

"How can she establish the Jewish claim to Jerusalem?"

"Well, my understanding is that the Muslims built al-Aqsa Mosque and the Dome of the Rock on the Temple Mount because they believed that was where Solomon's Temple stood. She will explain it, I'm sure."

Zadok returned to his office in the Knesset. He called Amos Eitan.

"Eitan here."

"This is Prime Minister Zadok. I have someone else I need you to contact and interview so she can testify at the Section 614 proceeding. I'll explain tomorrow."

Chapter 23

Channah wasn't home. Esther stretched out on her window seat facing the afternoon sun. She opened one eye as Meir entered the family room. Apparently not hungry, she shut her eye and resumed cat sleep. Meir's head ached. He walked down the hall into Ori's room. The pillows were propped against the headboard. He kicked off his shoes and reclined on the bed. The pain knifed through his skull, radiating from between his eyes. He tried to slow his breathing.

As the throbbing subsided, he opened his eyes and looked at the photographs on the dresser. Meir jolted upright as he saw one that Channah must have recently framed. It was just of Ori, wearing his favorite tee shirt—black with white zeroes and ones randomly filling a circle on his chest. Meir remembered it was something about computer programming. It was the shirt Ori was wearing the day the bus exploded.

Meir felt his pulse begin to race. He closed his eyes again, and the flashback began.

Meir saw himself running down a hall, frantically looking behind curtains. A doctor was following him, urging him to return to the waiting room. Meir threw back the last curtain. Ori was sitting in a large chair with a blanket around his shoulders, his head leaning forward. A nurse was checking his vital signs. He looked fine, and he was wearing his tee shirt. Meir was ecstatic, overjoyed to see him. The nurse turned to Meir. Before she could speak, Ori looked up and saw Meir.

"*abba*, how did you know I was here?"

Ori spoke loudly.

"I was right behind the bus. I saw it explode."

Ori didn't seem to hear.

"Is Sarah coming? Did you call *imma*?"

There was urgency in his voice. Meir reached for his cell phone to call Sarah and Channah.

"I'll call them."

Ori squinted at Meir's lips. He was clutching his laptop computer to his chest, the way he used to hold his stuffed bear when he was a child.

"I'm tired, *abba*. Really tired."

Ori's words were slurred. His head slumped forward on his chest. His arms opened and his computer fell to the floor with a loud crack.

Some die immediately from a bomb blast. Others farther away from the concussion may not look injured, but they receive an immediate death sentence. Their ears ring or their eardrums are punctured and they cannot hear at all. Internal bleeding from pulverized organs quickly saps their strength as their blood pressure drops and oxygen is not delivered to vital organs. They become increasingly lethargic and ultimately comatose.

When Channah and Sarah arrived together, they found Meir with his head buried in his hands, sitting next to Ori's bed in the trauma center. The doctors had put Ori on a respirator, as he was not able to breathe on his own. The nurse hovered over him. A hospital gown had replaced his tee shirt, so Channah didn't know Ori had been wearing the tee shirt in the photograph.

Several hours later, Ori's brain began to swell and his breathing became labored. The doctor told Meir, Channah, and Sarah that Ori's brain functions were diminishing rapidly. Sarah asked to speak to the doctor alone. When she returned, she told Meir and Channah that she had discussed Ori's living will that allowed her, as Ori's next of kin, to authorize the removal of the respirator if Ori's brain stopped functioning. Ori survived for three days as his condition declined. In the middle of the third night, Sarah called Channah and Meir and told them she had authorized the removal of life support.

Before a funeral begins, when the grieving family is alone, they recite a prayer which states, "*adonai dayan haemet,*" that "God is the True Judge." At Meir's parents' funerals, he had recited the prayer with no thought as to its meaning.

When Ori died, Meir had been a judge and was a recently appointed Supreme Court justice. Meir knew that the duty of a judge is simply to listen and understand when everyone else involved may not be listening or attempting to understand. That is why King Solomon prayed for an understanding heart.

Meir did not remember much about Ori's funeral. He had been lost in his thoughts and pain.

Today, as his flashback ended, Meir finally believed that he understood the meaning of the "True Judge" prayer. Being the True Judge must mean that God understands why Ori had died even though Meir would never understand why.

Chapter 24

As the sun rose the next morning, Fatima al-Fawzi sat at her desk in her apartment, typing furiously on her computer. She had been up since four, working in her usual frenzy. Three cigarette butts floated in her coffee cup next to her keyboard. As the light became brighter in the window next to her desk, she stopped typing and lit her fourth cigarette of the morning.

Her apartment, not far from the Mount Scopus campus of Hebrew University, overlooked the Old City. As Fatima deeply inhaled the cigarette smoke, she leaned her elbow on the desk and braced her chin in her hand. She could see al-Aqsa Mosque and the Dome of the Rock slowly beginning to glow. Watching the gold and pink wash across the roofs of the Old City, she tried to relax. She exhaled and dropped the half-smoked cigarette into the coffee cup.

Fatima had no classes to teach today. She was preparing for tomorrow's class by revising her lecture notes from the previous year. She had felt fine while she worked before sunrise, but her calm had fled with the daylight. She saved the file and switched off her computer.

She wasn't hungry, and her mouth tasted lousy from the coffee and cigarettes. She opened the window next to her desk to let in the morning air. She went into the bathroom, brushed her teeth, and dropped her bathrobe to the floor. She looked at herself in the full-length mirror on the back of the door.

She was forty-one and did not flinch when she looked at herself in the mirror. She could pass for her early thirties. She would often catch her male students zoning out in class, looking at her. Fatima knew they weren't lost in the details of Islamic history.

Fatima turned on the shower and waited until the hot water began to flow. She put her two towels on the sink and stepped into the shower stall. As the warmth caressed her shoulders, she began to relax. Her tension faded, but she was still anxious about her appointment this morning.

Yesterday afternoon, the voice on her office phone had sounded official. Speaking in Hebrew, the man had identified himself as "being with the government," and that he needed to speak with her in person.

Fatima had said that she would look at her calendar and call him back, and that was when his voice had changed.

"Professor al-Fawzi, there is no need to look at your calendar. I will see you tomorrow at ten in your office."

Fatima was not used to dealing with officialdom other than the academic administration.

"Very well, I can see you at ten. Let me tell you where I —"

"I know where your office is. Building 10 on the Hebrew University Campus, Room 7211. I will see you at ten tomorrow. Before jumuah begins. *ila likaa.*"

He had referred to the Muslim day of rest and used the Arabic good-bye greeting, which meant "until we meet." Fatima had hung up the phone feeling very uneasy.

Amos was in his office early, reviewing Fatima al-Fawzi's background file. A photograph, enlarged from her Hebrew University ID card, showed an attractive woman with dark hair, olive skin, and a pensive smile.

Another series of photographs had captured her on the campus of Hebrew University: talking to students, sitting on a bench reading a book, walking alone across campus.

Amos read the biographical data. Fatima had been born in 1976. She was an only child who lived with her mother, father, and maternal grandmother in the Muslim Quarter of the Old City of Jerusalem, where she grew up. She received top grades in high school and graduated from Hebrew University fluent in Arabic, Hebrew, French, and English. She had walked the precarious line of an Arab Muslim student in the predominately Jewish academic environment. Fatima was not politically involved. Shin Bet operatives at the university monitored her closely and found that her focus was strictly academic.

When she graduated at twenty-four, she was a teaching assistant to the chair of the Department of Islamic History. After receiving her doctorate three years later, her own professors, including Hiram Aitza, now the director of the Israel Museum, strongly endorsed her, and she was appointed as an assistant professor. She settled into the routine of university life. When she was thirty-five, she became a full professor, the only Muslim to achieve this position at the university.

Her grandmother had died soon after Fatima began her teaching career, and her parents were now deceased. She had never married and was currently living alone.

As a student and professor of Islamic history, her file noted that "she had a passionate, inexhaustible interest in the history of Jerusalem during the period of the Arab conquest." Her research, supplemented by archaeological excursions, resulted in numerous articles detailing life in that period.

The file included her articles, tabbed with a cover sheet listing the titles. Amos read the titles and turned to one of the more recent—"Construction of al-Aqsa Mosque and the Dome of the Rock: Origins of Muslim Religious Practices in Jerusalem."

Amos scanned the article, published in Hebrew and Arabic. It was a meticulous combination of archaeological research and historical analysis, with numerous footnotes. By the time Amos finished reading the article, he could visualize the construction of the Muslim holy sites.

The file contained a genealogy, tracing Fatima's family back through the centuries. He read it slowly, fascinated by the details of her ancestry. When he finished reading the genealogy and the explanation of it, he exhaled slowly, closed the file, and put it in his briefcase.

Fatima arrived at the entrance to the Hebrew University campus on Mount Scopus after a ten-minute walk from her apartment. The walk had calmed her nerves, and she wasn't even annoyed when the young guard who knew her asked to check her faculty ID card.

"*boker tov*, Professor al-Fawzi."

Fatima smiled as she opened her backpack for the guard.

"A man was here a few minutes ago asking directions to your office. The one you put on the list yesterday."

Fatima tensed. Mr. Eitan was early. She had hoped to straighten up her office and make coffee. She zipped her backpack shut and slung it over her shoulder. No need to rush to her office now. Let him wait. Her hair was still wet from her shower, and she was sweating from the short walk in the morning sun. She would cool off in the cafeteria in the basement of the faculty office building.

She entered the campus and slowly walked toward the office building. Students drifted by wearing shorts and sandals, carrying backpacks. Some waved to her. Male students blatantly stared at her. She smiled back at them.

At the faculty office building, another guard whom she had known for more than three years checked her ID again and also rifled through her backpack.

"Your ten o'clock appointment is here, Professor. He wanted to go to the cafeteria, but I told him he needed to be a faculty member to escort him. I sent him up to the receptionist on your floor."

Fatima headed down a stairwell to the cafeteria. She needed a cup of coffee. In the cafeteria she encountered the head of the history department, Samuel HaNasi. Her heart sank as she knew that she was at least five minutes from getting her coffee.

"Sidereal Sam," as he was called, was very careful to position himself so that you could not see the large bald spot on the back of his head. If you moved, Sam would move, preventing you from glimpsing the bald spot, just as the moon moved, keeping the same face to the earth. Sam's colleagues soon learned it was better just to stay rooted to the spot where you met him.

Fatima endured several minutes of Sam's ramblings, unable to extricate herself from his recitation of faculty politics and administrative trivia. Fatima was taller than Sam was, and she could see that his bald spot was closely approaching the breakthrough point in the middle of his forehead. By the time she filled two cups of coffee and found tops to fit, it was five minutes to ten. There were no cardboard trays, so she had to carry a cup in each hand. Her heart was pounding as she squeezed into an elevator with five other people. She asked the person next to her to press the button for her floor. At least her hair had dried.

When the elevator opened, Fatima walked down the hall to the reception area. The man sitting in one of the three chairs against the wall was chatting comfortably with Anit, the student receptionist. Anit seemed enthralled. Amos was suntanned and muscular, with a full head of dark hair with streaks of gray. When he saw Fatima, he immediately stood up.

"Professor al-Fawzi. Good morning." He spoke in Hebrew, and it was not a question. He knew who she was.

"Mr. Eitan?"

"Yes. Pleased to meet you."

Fatima extended a cup of coffee to him.

Amos took the coffee without taking his eyes off Fatima's face.

"I'm right down the hall."

She turned and Amos followed. Her name was on her door in Hebrew, Arabic, and English. Fatima slung her backpack off her shoulder and dropped it on the floor. She bent down, unzipped the front compartment, and fished for her keys, holding her coffee cup over her head. She could feel Amos staring at her. She noticed he was carrying a slim briefcase. He looked more like an academic than whatever he was.

Fatima opened her office door, and Amos followed her in. She turned and closed the door behind them.

"Please have a seat, Mr. Eitan."

Amos sat in a comfortable leather chair in front of her desk. Fatima sat behind the desk.

"Milk or sugar?" Fatima opened a small refrigerator on the floor behind the desk and placed a small container of milk on her desk.

"Neither, thank you." Amos had switched to Arabic.

Fatima did not look at him, but poured milk into her coffee and stirred it slowly. Amos looked around the office. It was typical academia, with a large bookcase filled with books and photographs of archaeological sites, a computer on the desk, a lone plant on the window sill.

Fatima raised her eyes and looked at Amos. Rarely was she on the defensive in her own office, which she believed she was at this moment. His unaccented Arabic had caught her off guard, adding to her confusion. She decided she would not say anything until he spoke.

Amos reached into his pocket and placed his ID card on her desk. Fatima picked it up and scanned it. His name and the IDF logo were on the card, as well as his picture. There was no rank or title. She placed the ID card back on her desk, and he picked it up and put it back in his pocket.

Amos continued in Arabic.

"Professor al-Fawzi, I am here today as an agent of the Supreme Court of Israel. This involves a matter of national security, and you should discuss this matter with no one else."

Amos sipped his coffee, and Fatima felt confused. She was a scholar, not a political activist, and she had maintained a low profile at the university. She was sure that the Mossad or Shin Bet or whatever organization this man actually worked for had investigated her. Fatima put her elbows on her desk and leaned forward. She spoke in Hebrew.

"Mr. Eitan, whatever this is, I am just a history professor. I'm not sure what assistance I can offer."

Amos placed his coffee cup on her desk and leaned back in his chair. He switched back to Hebrew.

"Professor, you concentrate your studies in a certain period of history, I believe."

"Yes, I have a particular interest in the period of the Arab conquest of Jerusalem, during the seventh and eighth centuries of the common era, the first two centuries of the Islamic calendar."

Amos was silent. Fatima began to feel uncomfortable, and she began talking just to calm herself.

"I use the term 'common era' rather than A.D. Non-Christian scholars date findings and events as B.C.E., 'before the common era,' and C.E., 'common era.'"

She stopped again and waited. Amos Eitan obviously knew the focus of her scholarship, so what was this about?

Amos leaned forward.

"Professor, you are directed to appear before a special proceeding of the Supreme Court of Israel to offer testimony. You are not under investigation or a suspect in this proceeding."

"Testimony? About history? If I have written anything helpful to your proceeding, why not just read it to whomever needs to know. This is very confusing. What is the proceeding about?"

Amos shook his head.

"Right now, I am not able to tell you that."

"Well, what more *can* you tell me, Mr. Eitan?"

Her tone of voice and flashing dark eyes told Amos that he had better offer some more information.

"I can tell you that the court needs the benefit of your knowledge."

"Do I need to hire a lawyer?"

"You are not on trial, Professor. You don't need to hire a lawyer. In fact, you should not even speak to one. The proceeding is classified."

"When will this proceeding take place? Where will it be? Just tell me something . . ."

Amos sensed her agitation, and he tried to calm her. "Fatima . . . may I call you Fatima?"

Fatima looked at him.

"Yes."

"You can call me Amos."

Amos put his palms flat on her desk.

"I know this is surprising and confusing for you, Fatima, but you should not be afraid or concerned."

She leaned back and spoke slowly.

"Mr. Eitan, I am going to testify at a top-secret hearing *somewhere* I don't know where, *sometime* I'm not sure when, about *something* I'm not sure what, and you are telling me I shouldn't be concerned."

Amos smiled and nodded. He opened his briefcase and took out a notebook.

"You shouldn't be concerned, Fatima. We are going to discuss the subject matter of your testimony, and then I will ask you how you acquired the knowledge that supports your testimony All you have to do is tell the truth."

Fatima felt her stomach lurch. *Did they know the truth?*

Chapter 25

During the previous days, while Meir had been absorbed reading the interview files in his underground office, he had not let his mind wander ahead to the actual proceeding. As he was riding to work the morning that Amos was interviewing Fatima al-Fawzi, he realized that he had never seen the courtroom for the Section 614 hearing.

"Amran, I'm curious about the courtroom. Have you seen it?"

Amran looked at him in the rearview mirror.

"I was in there yesterday."

No further explanation. Typical Amran.

"What does it look like in there?"

They came to a stop at a traffic light, and Amran scanned all four corners of the intersection. A few commuters were standing at the bus stop on one corner, and soldiers in uniform were everywhere, as usual.

"You will find it to your liking."

"What does that mean?"

"President Heifitz can show it to you."

Eli Heifitz joined Amran and Meir in the basement of the Supreme Court. Another door in the secure corridor was keyed to Meir's fingerprints. He placed his fingers on the sensors. The door swung inward and they walked in. The lights blinked on as they entered.

Meir could not believe what he was seeing. He had expected to find a small underground chamber expediently furnished. Instead, he found himself staring at a courtroom familiar to him.

The five courtrooms on the upper level of the Supreme Court building were patterned after synagogues around the world during various periods in history. The underground courtroom where he now stood was two stories high. Instead of windows, lighting behind panels of opaque glass simulated sunlight.

The courtroom was furnished in the same motif as the one Meir preferred to use upstairs. Of the five courtrooms, Meir felt most comfortable in one designed as a synagogue in Toledo, Spain, before the Inquisition and expulsion. He found that the architecture struck a chord in his soul. Meir scanned the room, noting the duplication of details from the room above. All was familiar, from the flowing geometric designs to the construction of the platform where the justice would sit. As he viewed the courtroom, he knew that he would ask for his high-backed orthopedic chair that he used in his chambers and during hearings to be brought down. He had picked the dark blue fabric of the chair to match the blue in the Israeli flag, which was to the left of the justice's chair, on the side where the justice's heart beat.

Meir always felt a calm sweeping through him when he entered a courtroom. The courtroom was an arrangement in time and space to allow information to be transmitted to him. Whatever emotions might course through the other participants, he would sit at the center of the controversy, knowing that his goal was to focus only in the moment, to listen intently, and ultimately to reach a decision.

Eli Heifitz stood behind Meir and tried to gauge his reaction. He approached the raised platform where the justice would sit. He turned and faced Meir.

"Passover begins next week and concludes the following week. The prime minister has informed me that the hearing will begin in two and a half weeks, on

Yom HaShoah, Holocaust Remembrance Day. Will you be ready by then?"

Meir walked forward and ascended the platform. He sat in the justice's chair and swiveled from right to left, sweeping the courtroom with his eyes. A gavel rested on the desk in front of him. Meir picked up the gavel and pounded it firmly onto the wooden base. The sound reverberated from the walls.

"I'll be ready. I'll just need a few good nights of sleep before the hearing."

The chief justice laughed and pointed to the Hebrew inscription from Psalm 121 on the wall above Meir's head.

"henaay lo yanun v'loyishan shomer yisrael."

"Here the Guardian of Israel neither rests nor sleeps."

Tamar picked up Channah shortly after Meir left that morning.

"I wish you would tell me what you think is wrong, Channah," Tamar said.

"Nothing is wrong, Tamar. Sarah and I just need you to take us to the hospital."

"Why wouldn't you be able to drive home?"

"Let's just say I've been a little shaky lately, and Sarah doesn't have a car."

Sarah was waiting in the lobby of her building when they arrived. No one spoke during the fifteen-minute drive to Hadassah Hospital. Tamar pulled up to the entrance, and Channah and Sarah got out.

"Please wait in the car, Tamar. I don't think we will be here long," Channah said.

"I'm going to park and stand outside, smoke a cigarette, and check out the doctors," Tamar laughed.

Channah was in no mood for her sister's upbeat nonsense. Tamar was ten years younger than Channah, and she acted like a perpetual teenager.

"Doctors don't like women who smoke," Channah said. "Just sit on the bench over there and don't smoke."

Channah and Sarah walked into the lobby and went to the information desk.

"We're here to see Dr. Nathaniel Halevy."

The woman at the desk jotted their name on a list. Channah thanked her, and they headed toward the elevator. They squeezed in with three Bedouin women who were very excited. Apparently, someone had just had a baby. The Bedouin women got out on the second floor, and Channah and Sarah were left alone on the elevator.

When the elevator opened on the third floor, they walked out. Channah stopped suddenly. She felt weak and confused. Sarah grabbed Channah's arm and steadied her. They walked down the corridor to the doctor's office.

A half hour later, Channah and Sarah came out of the hospital. They found Tamar sitting on the bench, laughing and smoking cigarettes with a nice-looking doctor. Tamar watched them approach. Channah looked drained. Sarah was silent. Tamar stood up, dropped her cigarette on the sidewalk, and scrunched it with her foot.

"Channah, are you okay?" Tamar asked.

"Let's go, Tamar," Channah answered.

"What happened? Sarah, did something happen?"

Sarah stared and said, "Tamar, let's go."

"Okay, sorry. This is Dr. Mughrabi. We just met."

The doctor nodded, but he didn't speak.

"A pleasure to meet you, Doctor, but we need to leave," Channah said.

Tamar turned to the doctor.

"It was fun. Sorry we have to go."

As they walked away, Tamar whispered, "He *likes* to smoke. *And* he's a proctologist."

Channah's head was spinning. Tamar's self-centered nature seemed to reveal itself at the most inappropriate moments.

"That's *wonderful*, Tamar. *And* you need to drive us somewhere; anywhere but home. I told Meir I wouldn't be home for dinner. We have a long day ahead of us."

As Tamar drove out of the hospital parking lot, agents Aleph and Bet followed in their cars.

Meir spent the rest of the morning and early afternoon in his basement office preparing for the hearing. He walked out at two o'clock to get some fresh air and buy falafel and chips, with Amran following discreetly at a distance. When Meir returned to his basement office, Eli Heifitz delivered another sealed file. It contained Amos's written summary of his interview that morning with Fatima al-Fawzi. Meir spent two hours reading the summary and taking notes. At the end of the interview summary, Amos Eitan had noted that the interview had terminated when Professor al-Fawzi had refused to answer further questions.

Meir finished reading the interview summary and locked it in his safe. The day had passed quickly, and he was ready to go home.

Chapter 26

As they left the Supreme Court's parking garage, Meir settled in the back seat and closed his eyes. Before he had a chance to relax, he was jolted by Amran's voice.

"Sir, how long have you lived in your building?"

"A little over three years. Why?"

"Do you know your neighbors?"

"No. The building has four apartments on each floor and four elevators. I usually come and go through the parking garage and rarely see people in the elevator. We don't have any friends in the building."

"So you wouldn't necessarily recognize someone as living in your building?"

"No. I don't even know who lives directly above or below me."

When they arrived at Meir's building, Amran came to a stop in the driveway in front of the lobby.

"Justice Bar-Aben, please turn your head slowly to the right, as if you are talking to me. Do you see the man and woman across the street, next to the fruit stand on the corner?

"Yes, but I don't know them. Should I?"

Amran shook his head.

"Should I be concerned, Amran?"

"No. We've been watching your building since you started the case. Just making sure everything is okay."

Amran drove into the parking garage and let Meir out. When he drove out of the garage, Zara and Hamid were no longer standing next to the fruit stand.

Amran called Zadok on his cell phone.

"They were here again today, sir. Agents Aleph and Bet have seen them both following the wife and the daughter-in-law. The justice says he doesn't know them."

There was a pause on the line.

"They are being investigated," Zadok replied. "Don't let them get too close."

Amran hung up and headed home for the evening.

Channah had left a note that she was meeting Tamar for dinner. There was a plate of roast lamb and vegetables in the refrigerator. Meir heated it in the microwave, mixed the contents of the plate together, and wrapped all of it in two small loaves of pita, into which he poured a thick tahini sauce. Esther sat on her haunches and gave him a you-know-you-shouldn't-be-eating-that wink. He cut up a small chunk of lamb and threw the bits on the floor, hoping that breaking the cat-feeding rules might conjure Channah's presence. No such luck. Meir picked up a magazine and thumbed through it. By nine thirty Channah still hadn't come home.

Meir went to Ori's room and turned on the lights. He stifled an urge to lie down on the bed, then walked into his bedroom, slipped out of his clothes, and got into bed. He clicked on the TV.

The screen filled with a large crane hoisting a stone of the Kotel into the air. The camera panned downward to a group looking up at the stone.

Meir turned off the volume. His review of the interviews had removed him from current events, while the country was fixated on the reconstruction of the Kotel. He felt disconnected from the collapse. He lay on his back, breathing deeply, and felt Esther jump onto the bed, knead the covers on his stomach with her paws, and curl on his stomach. Meir reached out and stroked

Esther's back. She swished her tail across his stomach, and he drifted off to sleep.

Channah came home after midnight. She came into the bedroom and found Meir asleep. Her eyes were soft, the anger from yesterday gone. She undressed quietly and got into bed. Meir didn't wake up.

Part Four – Stone

Jerusalem
November 2035

My grandfather paused.

"We need to eat, Nuri."

I had been so absorbed with the story that I had ignored my hunger pangs.

"Let's walk to the Cardo and have lunch, *jiddo*."

My grandfather had a favorite restaurant in the Cardo, a shopping area in the Jewish Quarter excavated from the Cardo Maximus, the Roman main street of Jerusalem after the destruction of the Temple.

"I can tell you a little more, Nuri, while we walk."

As we descended the stairs from the Noble Sanctuary, my grandfather continued his story.

Chapter 27

Thursday, April 20, 2017

Two weeks passed. Hiram Aitza supervised the reconstruction of the Kotel and visited his office occasionally to attend to routine administration of the museum. When he had estimated the time to reconstruct the Kotel, Hiram had failed to include a work stoppage for four days during Passover. Yesterday, when work had resumed after Passover, the crane's engine had seized, and they had lost another day.

Today, a new crane arrived at the work site in the morning, but it was not ready to use until noon. When work finally began, Hiram yelled orders to the crane operator, running in front of the crane and waving his arms.

As Hiram continued to shout, one of the worshippers approached the barrier that divided the work area from the rest of the plaza and called to him.

"Sir, please be quiet. This is a holy place."

Chastened, Hiram nodded to the man, then turned back toward the crane and motioned the operator to come down and speak to him. Hiram gave the operator precise instructions for lifting the next three stones in place, and then he went back to a drafting table that held a plan of the completed Kotel. As he leaned on the table to mark the progress of the work on the plan, his cell phone rang. He could see from the caller ID that it was his assistant, Rita. He answered without a greeting.

"Rita, what is it? I am very busy today."

Rita was used to Hiram's harried attitude.

"I thought you'd like to know that I think I found what you are looking for."

Hiram was puzzled.

"What are you talking about, Rita?"

"You asked me to look for something, remember?"

Hiram was looking at the plan on the table in front of him, shaking his head.

"Just tell me. Whatever it is, I'm not remembering."

"Two weeks ago, you asked me to look for a stone from Moshe Dayan's collection. Well, I think I found several fitting the description you gave me."

Hiram hung up and called Zadok.

Several hours later, Hiram returned to the Israel Museum and found Zadok and Rabbi Avidan waiting in his office. Zadok was pacing back and forth, while the rabbi sat patiently.

"What have you found, Mr. Aitza?" Zadok asked without greeting him.

"Well, why don't you have a seat, and I can tell you. And good morning, Rabbi Avidan," Hiram said.

"Sorry to take you away from the reconstruction, Mr. Aitza," Rabbi Avidan said.

Hiram sat at his desk and began typing on his computer keyboard.

"The Jewish philanthropist who purchased a portion of Moshe Dayan's antiquities collection died in 2005. His estate sold the collection at auction in 2007 to private collectors. My assistant has only been able to track thirty of those artifacts. A private collector donated them several years ago to the Freer Gallery of Art in Washington, D.C. The museum's catalog is digitized and viewable online."

Hiram pointed to his computer screen.

"Rabbi, you might want to see these three stones that I believe fit your description."

Rabbi Avidan stood and walked behind Hiram. He stared at the screen.

"This one," Rabbi Avidan said, pointing at the screen. "By the dimensions under the photograph, it's the only one that might be the one I am looking for. The others are too large. Can you arrange to have it brought here?"

Hiram looked at Zadok.

"Absolutely," Zadok said. "Mr. Aitza can arrange it."

Zadok walked Rabbi Avidan to the museum entrance where Amran was waiting to take the rabbi back to the Old City.

"The hearing begins next week," Zadok said. "We will bring the stone here as quickly as we can. I'm going to discuss it with Mr. Aitza."

Rabbi Avidan shook hands with Zadok and got into the car. After Amran drove away, Zadok walked back into the museum to Hiram's office.

Hiram sat behind his desk as Zadok lowered himself onto the couch.

"So you want me to call the museum in the U.S. and arrange a loan of that stone, Ezer?"

"Yes."

"And you can't tell me why?"

"I told you before, I don't know why it is so important to him. Even if I did, I couldn't tell you."

"So how should we proceed?"

"Tell the museum in the U.S. that you will arrange a courier to bring the stone here. When it arrives here, you can confirm receipt. We will pick it up when we need it and return it to you after we are finished with it. You can send it back to the U.S. the way you usually send exhibits between museums."

"If it is so important, what makes you think we will return it, Ezer?"

Zadok shrugged. "Let's not get ahead of ourselves, Hiram."

"Well, what do I tell the director of the Freer Gallery? Why do we want this stone?"

"I don't know what you will tell him. You are the director of the Israel Museum. Tell him something a museum director will believe. To be safe, tell him you need to have it for a few months."

"I assume the rabbi is just going to examine the stone. Nothing invasive or destructive, I hope."

Zadok nodded.

"Just arrange for the loan of the stone. We need it early next week."

"Next week? Ezer, I don't know if that's possible," Hiram said.

"Anything's possible, Hiram. Let's see what you can arrange."

Hiram looked at his watch. It was already four in the afternoon.

"It's morning in the United States. Wait here, Ezer," Hiram said.

Hiram walked down the hall to Rita's office.

"Rita, do you know the name of the director of the Freer Gallery of Art in Washington, D.C.?"

"He is Robert Haskell. He was actually here last summer when you were on vacation. He had his family with him. I arranged a private tour. He was very appreciative."

"Good. Can you get him on the phone for me? I'll be in my office."

Hiram returned to his office and waited with Zadok.

"Rita is getting the director of the Freer Gallery on the line, Ezer. It seems he was here last summer, and Rita arranged a private tour. He owes us."

Hiram's phone rang.

"Mr. Haskell is on the line. I'll add him on."

Hiram heard the line click, and Rita spoke.

"Mr. Haskell, Mr. Aitza is on the line."

Hiram spoke in English.

"Mr. Haskell, good morning. This is Hiram Aitza, the director of the Israel Museum. I need a favor."

"Of course, Mr. Aitza."

Hiram explained that the Israel Museum was preparing a special exhibit of Second Temple era artifacts and wanted to feature examples from Moshe Dayan's collection. While the Israel Museum had a large portion of Moshe Dayan's collection, it did not have many artifacts from the Second Temple period. Hiram had noticed that the Freer Gallery had several artifacts from Moshe Dayan's collection, and the Israel Museum wanted to include the one stone in its exhibit.

"We would need it very soon, by early next week. We would send our courier and take full responsibility once we pick it up. Would a two-month loan be possible, Mr. Haskell?" Hiram asked.

He listened as Haskell responded.

"One moment please, Mr. Haskell," Hiram said. He pushed the mute button on the phone so Haskell could not hear him.

"Ezer, he's agreeable. As a favor to me, he can expedite all the arrangements and have it ready for pick up early Sunday morning. The gallery has an exhibit opening Monday, and he is working over the weekend with the final preparations. He will be there on Sunday by 7:00 a.m."

"That's fine, Hiram."

Hiram unmuted the line.

"Everything is fine, Mr. Haskell. We will arrange a courier and send you his information."

Hiram continued to listen and then laughed.

"Of course, Mr. Haskell. We can discuss that later."

Hiram hung up.

"What was so funny?" Zadok asked.

"He said maybe we could arrange a loan of one of the Dead Sea scrolls as an exchange."

"He was kidding, I hope," Zadok said.

"I don't know him well enough to know if that was a joke or not. I need to know the details of the delivery, Ezer. This is my responsibility and the museum's reputation if anything should happen to the stone. I'm not feeling comfortable with this."

"Stop worrying, Hiram. We'll have a courier pick it up, fly to Ben Gurion Airport, and deliver it here. I'll tell you the details once I make arrangements."

Zadok left Hiram's office and waited at the entrance of the museum for Amran to return. He called Amos Eitan on his cell phone.

"Eitan here."

"Mr. Eitan, this is Prime Minister Zadok. I need you to arrange a courier from the United States for something relating to next week. Come to my office, and I will explain."

Fairfax, Virginia

Later that day, Aaron Kragen sat in his home office reviewing new accounts for security systems. After only two years, his company, Home Fortress America, had over two thousand customers in the Washington, D.C., area. Aaron had recently put the legal wheels in motion to franchise. He had just turned thirty-five, and he hoped to retire in ten years if the franchise did well.

Aaron sat at his desk, eating lunch and multiplying his new accounts by the installation costs and yearly maintenance fees. He was reveling in his financial success when the phone rang. He answered the phone without taking his eyes off the computer screen.

"Hello, this is Kragen."

"Mr. Kragen, this is Account 199. We have a service issue. It will require a local pickup and a visit to our home office."

Aaron sucked in his breath.

"When is the pickup?"

"Sunday morning. Please meet our representative Sunday at 7:00 a.m. for instructions. Your flight to the home office will be at 3:30 p.m."

Aaron hung up the phone. He had to cancel his Sunday plans. This account demanded his immediate attention.

Chapter 28

Washington, D.C.
Sunday morning, April 23, 2017

Aaron drove into Washington, D.C., and parked his car on a side street near Dupont Circle shortly before 7:00 a.m. He walked to the park at Dupont Circle and spotted the old man wearing a red baseball cap, a torn Washington Redskins tee shirt, and tattered jeans sitting on a bench next to the water fountain. Aaron sat down next to him.

"My instructions?" Aaron asked.

The man responded in Hebrew, almost in a whisper. When the man finished speaking, he stood and walked away. An envelope was on the bench where the man had been sitting. Aaron picked up the envelope, knowing it contained airline tickets. He returned to his car and headed south on Connecticut Avenue.

Thirty minutes later, Aaron parked on the National Mall near the Smithsonian Castle. He walked quickly to the entrance of the Freer Gallery of Art and called a number on his cell phone. The door opened, and a uniformed officer ushered him to the information desk.

"I'm here to see Mr. Haskell. He is expecting me. I am Aaron Kragen, a courier."

"Your identification, please."

Aaron showed him his Home Fortress America identification card.

The officer struck an official pose, looked over the rim of his glasses at Aaron, and picked up a phone and dialed.

"Mr. Kragen is here." He listened, raised his eyebrows, and then hung up.

The officer motioned to Aaron.

"Follow me, please."

They walked down a corridor in silence to an elevator. The elevator opened and a man was waiting.

"Mr. Kragen?"

Aaron nodded.

"I'm Robert Haskell."

They took the elevator to the second floor and walked down the corridor to Mr. Haskell's office.

"You're here early on a Sunday," Aaron said.

"We're preparing an exhibit that opens tomorrow. We've been working around the clock for a week," Haskell replied.

Haskell went to his desk and handed Aaron a rectangular pouch about eighteen inches long, eight inches wide, and four inches thick made from very heavy black material. There was a zipper on one end and a shipping document attached in a plastic pouch.

"Be careful with this, please. They told you what it was, I assume."

"Yes, I was told it is a stone artifact. I will be careful, Mr. Haskell, I can assure you."

"One more thing, Mr. Kragen. Export and customs information is on the shipping document."

Aaron nodded. He knew the procedures. El Al security would meet him when he arrived at JFK Airport, and he would clear customs in Ben Gurion Airport in Tel Aviv.

Aaron signed a shipping manifest indicating the time and date of receipt, then he shook Mr. Haskell's hand.

"Thank you, Mr. Haskell. I will make sure this is delivered safely."

Aaron put the package in his backpack, returned to his car, and drove to the airport.

It was Sunday afternoon in Israel. Hiram Aitza sat in his office staring at the request manifest he had sent to the Freer Gallery. Zadok had described the delivery arrangements in detail. The courier would arrive at Ben Gurion Airport early Monday morning and bring the stone directly to Hiram at the Israel Museum by one o'clock. Zadok would be unavailable that morning, but Hiram was to call Amran and confirm receipt of the stone when the courier arrived at the museum. If there were any delay, the courier would call Amran.

Even with Zadok's assurances, Hiram was apprehensive about the entire situation. If something happened to the stone, his career would be over. He, therefore, had made his own arrangements to monitor the delivery.

Hiram checked his email until he received a message from Robert Haskell confirming that the courier had received the stone and left for the airport.

Hiram picked up the phone and dialed.

Joshua Galilee was asleep in his apartment in Brooklyn, New York, jet-lagged from a recent trip. His cell phone rang, and he answered it before he realized he was awake.

"Joshua Galilee."

"Joshua, it's me. The courier has picked up the stone. You'll see him go into the El Al security office before he checks in. His name is Aaron Kragen."

"Okay. Thanks."

Joshua set his alarm for 10:00 a.m., rolled over, and fell back asleep. When the alarm rang an hour later, he ate breakfast, dressed, and then packed his carry-on bag.

Aaron pulled into a long-term parking lot at Reagan National Airport at 8:30 a.m. and quickly found a parking space. He locked his car and opened the trunk to get the small roller bag that he had packed. He walked to the shuttle bus stop and waited. The bus arrived within five minutes and took him to the terminal.

When he arrived at the terminal, Aaron went directly to the security station. He placed his backpack and roller bag on the scanner. The bored TSA guard waved him through. Whatever the package showed on the scanner, it was not enough to alert the TSA. Fast walking brought him to the gate just as boarding began.

As Aaron boarded the plane, he noticed a group wearing red tee shirts occupying a section of the plane. Aaron found his seat on the aisle toward the back of the plane, behind the red tee shirts. Across the aisle, a woman unwrapped a steaming steak and cheese sub that she had purchased before she boarded. The smell of grease and onions exploded around her.

Aaron stored his roller bag overhead, stuffed his backpack under the seat in front of him, and tried to relax. No one had occupied the two seats next to him, and the plane was almost ready to take off. He was feeling lucky.

Aaron noticed that the red tee shirts were starting to get agitated. They were straining their heads over the seats in front of them, looking toward the door of the airplane. Aaron was catching snatches of their anxiety.

"Where is Reverend Crosby?"

"I hope he makes it!"

"We can't go without him."

Suddenly, two more red tee shirts appeared at the doorway. One was an elderly man with a full head of white hair, and the other was a much younger woman. Their traveling companions erupted in applause.

"Here he is!"

"We knew you'd make it."

Someone stood up near the front of the group.

"Here's your seat, Reverend."

The man immediately sat down. The woman looked at her ticket and started down the aisle toward Aaron. She was brunette, slim, late thirties, nice eyes, but with a cautious look on her face. Aaron could now see that the lettering on her tee shirt read "Zion Baptist Temple." She stopped at Aaron's row and looked at her ticket again. She spoke with a heavy Southern accent and a slight smile, pointing with her free hand and clutching the backpack over her shoulder with the other.

"Excuse me, that's my window seat."

Aaron stood up and let her squeeze past. She dropped her backpack under the seat in front of her just as the flight attendant closed the doors. Aaron looked across the aisle to see the woman with the steak and cheese sub pop the top off a can of diet soda, then turned to the woman next to him.

"You're in a tour group. Going to New York?"

She shook her head.

"No, I'm with my church group. We're flying up there on our way to the Holy Land."

"The Holy Land? Israel?"

She nodded.

"Yes. Israel. How about you?"

"Well, as a matter of fact, so am I. What flight are you on?"

"A three-thirty flight on the Israeli airline."

"El Al?" Aaron asked.

"Yes. That's the name."

"Well, I'm on that flight, myself. I'm Aaron Kragen, by the way."

She started to speak, but the flight attendant announced the beginning of the safety lecture presented on the video screens in the cabin. The plane began backing away from the gate. When the video screen went dark, Aaron turned to the woman in the window seat.

Her head tilted away from him, her hair covering her eyes, and she was breathing deeply. Her unbuckled seat belt lay across her lap.

"You need to buckle up," Aaron said.

She whispered a soft "thank you," but did not open her eyes. She buckled her seat belt.

"By the way, I'm Amy. Amy Collins."

Aaron looked again, but her eyes were still closed.

At 9:30 a.m., the plane accelerated down the runway and took off.

Joshua Galilee left his Brooklyn apartment and hailed a cab to JFK Airport. He arrived in plenty of time before his flight to Israel was to depart. He went immediately to the El Al Terminal to check in. Wearing a long black coat and fur-trimmed hat with his beard and wire-rimmed glasses, he was indistinguishable from other Orthodox Jews flying to Israel from JFK.

"Welcome back, Mr. Galilee. You have your aisle seat," the ticket agent said, as she handed him his boarding pass. "You're very early, as usual."

Joshua smiled.

"I'm going to sit here and relax."

He knew that most of the passengers on the flight would arrive in several hours. He sat in the terminal and waited.

The flight to New York was uneventful. Amy dozed until the plane began its descent into JFK Airport. When the flight attendant started cleaning up the cabin, Amy woke up and looked around.

"Are we landing already?"

Aaron smiled.

"Yes. You slept all the way."

"Oh, I'm sorry I was such a sleepy head. I was so excited that I hardly slept last night."

"Have you ever been to JFK Airport, Amy?"

"No. I hear it's huge."

"Do you have any checked luggage?" Aaron asked.

"Yes. We have to reclaim it before we go to the international terminal."

"Well, Amy, I'll see you at check-in for the flight to Israel."

They landed at 10:45 a.m., and Aaron headed to the international terminal.

A half hour later, as Joshua Galilee sat reading *Haaretz* on his iPad, Aaron entered the El Al terminal. Aaron went to the check-in counter and asked to speak to a security agent. An El Al security agent approached him and took him aside, speaking Hebrew in a low voice.

"Your account manager has already cleared you for boarding. We need to see the delivery. Please follow me," she said. Joshua watched as the security agent led Aaron into the security office next to the check-in counter. When she closed the door, Aaron asked in Hebrew, "The code word, please?"

The security agent repeated the word the person in Washington, D.C. had given Aaron when he gave him the delivery instructions.

Aaron took the package from the museum out of his backpack.

"I am authorized to open the package," the security agent said.

Aaron nodded

The security agent opened the zipper at the top of the package, withdrew an object wrapped in heavy plastic, and placed it on a table. She removed the plastic, revealing a piece of stone.

"Beautiful. Jerusalem stone," she said.

The security agent wrapped the stone in the plastic and put it back in the package. She put an El Al security sticker on the package and handed it back to Aaron.

"Have a good trip."

Aaron put the package in his backpack.

"I have a favor to ask," Aaron said. "I would like to sit next to one of the passengers on my flight. She's with the church group."

Joshua Galilee saw Aaron exit the security office and sit down in the waiting area of the terminal. He waited and watched.

Forty-five minutes later, Joshua saw a group wearing red tee shirts and baseball caps streaming through the waiting area. He was surprised to see Aaron stand up and wave to a woman in the group, then walk over and join her and the rest of the group in the check-in line.

The check-in procedure at El Al was very thorough. The El Al personnel asked each passenger a barrage of questions and searched all hand luggage. As the line moved forward, Amy seemed tired.

"Long trip from home today?" Aaron asked.

"Our bus left our church in Virginia about four this morning," Amy said. "I almost didn't go. When we planned the trip a year ago, I didn't know I was going to go alone. My divorce became final last week."

When the ticket agent waved Amy up to the counter for questioning, Aaron waited for the next agent.

Amy was cleared quickly, as she was traveling with the group.

Aaron was next. As he came forward, Amy stopped him.

"I'm in 33A. Maybe you could get a seat near me." She walked to a bench and sat down to wait for Aaron.

Aaron spoke rapidly with the ticket agent in Hebrew.

"I would like to sit next to the woman who just checked in."

"I know," she whispered. She had received instructions in her earpiece from the security agent who had inspected the stone. She had already shifted the person assigned next to Amy to another seat.

"Enjoy your trip, sir," she said, as she handed Aaron his boarding pass for seat 33B.

By the time the passengers boarded, Joshua Galilee had seen no other passenger escorted into the security office. He was now sure that Aaron was the person he was supposed to watch.

The plane had 2-5-2 seating in economy class. Amy was surprised that Aaron was sitting next to her.

"I thought Earl was sitting here," she said, pointing to a member of her group sitting two seats in front of her.

Aaron shrugged.

"Would you rather sit with Earl?"

Amy rolled her eyes and shook her head.

Amy took the window seat with Aaron next to her. Aaron put his backpack under his seat. Most of the Zion Baptist Temple group sat in the middle section in the rows across the aisle. Reverend Crosby was in the aisle seat across from Aaron. An older, graying couple in red tee shirts came down the aisle and took the seats in front of Reverend Cosby. The husband saw Amy and came over to her.

"I thought Earl was sitting with you."

"I guess not, Joe."

"Do you want me to talk to the flight attendant? There must have been a mix-up in the seating."

"Don't bother, Joe," Amy said. "I'm perfectly fine."

Joe returned to his seat.

"That's Joe and Emma Mason," Amy whispered to Aaron. "Real busybodies."

Reverend Crosby stood up and led his group in prayer for a safe journey. Amy had already turned her head to look out the window. Aaron saw some heads in the group turning in Amy's direction and whispering.

The passengers included many black-hat American Orthodox Jews, Israeli families returning from the United States with young children, and several synagogue groups. Even so, the plane was not full, and empty seats were scattered throughout the economy section. Joshua Galilee was one of the last passengers to enter the plane. He sat four rows behind Aaron and Amy in an aisle seat in the middle section.

Immediately before takeoff, a flight attendant made an announcement in Hebrew, followed by groans from those who understood it, and then repeated the announcement in English, causing more groans.

"Ladies and Gentlemen, in observance of Yom HaShoah, Holocaust Remembrance Day, there will be no movies, music, or other entertainment during the flight."

Amy looked questioningly at Aaron. Aaron explained to her that the flight would be during Holocaust Remembrance Day, observed tomorrow when they arrived in Israel. Since the Jewish day begins at sundown and continues until sundown the next evening, there would be no movies, music, or other entertainment during the flight.

"Gosh, we didn't know that when we booked this flight. Did you?"

Aaron shook his head.

"I really didn't have a choice."

El Al Flight LY028 to Tel Aviv took off at 3:30 p.m. and headed over the Atlantic. Captain Yaffi Ron performed a series of imperceptible zigzag maneuvers for the first forty minutes of flight. He was always wary of a terrorist attack by missiles from the shoreline of Long Island. Finally, the plane was out of range of any missiles, and Captain Ron allowed his co-pilot to take over the controls. Captain Ron always slept for the first part of the flight, allowing his co-pilot to fly the plane and monitor the autopilot.

Amy fell asleep immediately, as she had on the flight to New York. Aaron noticed Joe and Emma Mason watching him from across the aisle. He stared back and cracked a big smile. They nodded, thin-lipped, and turned away.

Aaron closed his eyes. He was soon lulled to sleep by the droning of the engines, and he began to dream. He found himself standing at a window in the living room of a large Victorian house. He saw expanses of green meadow and trees stretching to the horizon. He suddenly realized that he was trapped in the house. The house was filled with all the merchandise from the Airline SkyMall Catalog. Everywhere he looked he saw a different charging station for his cell phone. He wandered into the bedroom. On the dresser was a collection of watches with dials that told everything from the phases of the moon to altitude. On the floor, he saw a cat food and water dispenser and an automatic litter box that scooped cat litter into a sealed bag.

The basement was loaded with all types of exercise equipment to turn his body into a superhero in three months, or he would get his money back. The backyard was animal and insect free from a solar-powered mole repeller, a glass wasp trap on a pole, and a bobblehead fake owl. The home office had a desk with a clock that told time, temperature, wind speed, humidity, and whether it would rain tomorrow. The shower had ten different showerheads that could hit any conceivable body part with accuracy. Aaron continued to drift through the house until he heard the doorbell ring. When he opened the door, a large package from SkyMall was on the porch. Aaron waved his hand, and the box opened, revealing a large garden statue of Voldemort from the Harry Potter series. Aaron stared at Voldermort and then willed himself to wake up.

When Aaron awoke, the sun had set. He got up, picked up his backpack, and walked down the aisle toward the back of the plane to stretch his legs. Joshua Galilee saw Aaron walk past him. He rose and followed Aaron. A group of Orthodox Jews had gathered in the back of the plane to say evening prayers. They had put on their prayer shawls and were leafing through prayer books.

Aaron stood respectfully near the group. He had not prayed since his father died ten years ago. Every morning, for a year, after his father died, he had gone to synagogue for morning prayers, reciting the special prayer for mourners.

Joshua Galilee stood in the aisle near Aaron. As the group turned toward the front of the plane and began to pray, Aaron turned and noticed Joshua standing in front of him.

The leader of the prayer group spoke in a low voice.

"For Yom HaShoah, we all say *kaddish*."

All were requested to say the mourners' prayer, since today all mourned the dead. Aaron recited the prayer silently. In the darkened cabin, he felt part of this anonymous congregation.

"Magnified and sanctified is His glorious name," the group began.

Aaron murmured the ancient Aramaic prayer by heart, ending with "May He who gives peace in Heaven, may He grant peace upon us and upon all

Israel." Several of the passengers in the darkened rows whispered, "Amen."

As the prayers concluded, Aaron realized that the man standing in front of him had not prayed with the group, nor had he worn a prayer shawl. Joshua Galilee walked down the aisle, and Aaron followed him as he returned to his seat. Joshua continued down the aisle and sat in an unoccupied seat several rows in front of Aaron and Amy.

Aaron noticed that Joshua had not been sitting in front of him before. Amy slept on. Aaron tried to sleep again but could not.

About an hour later, he watched as Joshua Galilee stood and walked toward the rear of the plane. Aaron waited for several minutes, then stood and walked down the aisle to the restroom. He saw Joshua Galilee sitting with his eyes closed in an aisle seat near the rear of the plane.

Several hours later, the cabin lights turned on as the smell of breakfast wafted from the galley. Many of the passengers began to stir even though it was still dark outside the plane.

Aaron saw Amy begin to wake up next to him.

"Good morning, Amy. Breakfast!"

Amy looked at him and shook her head.

"I feel like I've been sleeping forever."

"You've been sleeping most of the time since I met you, Amy."

Breakfast trays were unceremoniously plopped in front of them. Amy eyed the glistening, plastic-looking omelet and miniature bagel. Her throat and eyes were dry from the pressurized cabin, and she had the beginning of a headache. She reached for a small cup of orange juice and tore the top off. Gulping it down, she turned to Aaron.

"I'm not such good company. I'll be better now."

"There's no need to apologize. Relax," Aaron said.

"Have you been to Israel before?"

Aaron nodded while he spread cream cheese on his bagel.

"My mother's parents are Israeli. I learned Hebrew from my mother as a child. I spent summers as a teenager visiting my grandparents in Israel and working on their kibbutz. You know what a kibbutz is?"

"Like a communist farm, I think."

"Well, more like a socialist farm."

"Are your grandparents there now?"

"My grandfather died five years ago."

"I'm sorry. Are you going to visit your grandmother?"

"First, I have some business to do, but after that I'll visit my grandmother."

"That's nice, Aaron. It's so different for my group and me. It's a religious experience."

"You'll enjoy it, Amy. For me, it's like going to California on an expense account."

He bit into his bagel and chewed slowly.

Aaron's service to Account 199 had started four years before when he was working for a small government-contracting firm that had submitted a proposal for a security system for the Israeli embassy. Because he had obtained a security clearance for work on U.S. Government contracts, he was on the team that made the initial site visit. Two security personnel from the embassy were chatting with each other in Hebrew near Aaron and his team.

Aaron interrupted in Hebrew, "Excuse me. I speak Hebrew."

Taken aback, the Israelis were thankful for Aaron's disclosure. Aaron's company received the contract, and Aaron headed the system installation team. When the installation was almost complete, Aviela, one of the embassy's security personnel, asked him out to lunch to show her appreciation for a job well done. Four hours later, after lunch at the Palm and an afternoon spent in a luxury room at the Mayflower Hotel, she thanked him again for a job well done.

"I knew when we hired your firm that this contract would have a successful conclusion."

Aaron laughed.

"So now I have fulfilled all the contract requirements?"

"With—how do you say in English—all the colors flying?"

Aviela got out of bed and headed for the shower. Aaron followed.

"Just like on the kibbutz, huh? Community showers."

As they were getting dressed, Aviela became serious.

"You are in the security business, and you speak Hebrew. We have some other contract work you could do for us."

"What? You already need upgrades to the security system?"

"No. From time to time, we need items delivered to Israel."

"What kind of items would you need delivered? And why would you need me to deliver them?"

"Letters. Documents. Valuables. Nothing that can't ordinarily pass through security at airports. Nothing that can get you in trouble. But sometimes it is better to have individuals not connected to the embassy or the Israeli Government transport whatever it is. It is quicker and less complicated."

"For money?"

"For love and money. We would pay all your expenses. I'm sure you would enjoy an occasional free trip to Israel."

The delivery procedure had been easy. Twice since that afternoon, Aaron had picked up a package in the United States with instructions, dropped off the package in Israel, and then visited his grandmother at Kibbutz Alonim. He would report to Aviela at the embassy, and they would go out for a long lunch and an afternoon at the Mayflower Hotel.

Chapter 29

As the passengers ate breakfast, Israeli children walked up and down the aisles, laughing and giggling. The Orthodox men moved about the cabin, murmuring greetings and speaking in guttural Yiddish and Hebrew undertones. The Zion Baptist Temple group gawked at them, as if they were ghosts from the Middle Ages. Joshua Galilee moved again to another unoccupied seat in front of Aaron and Amy. Aaron noticed Joshua walk past and sit across from an Orthodox couple with two young children. As the sun rose, the Orthodox Jews gathered in the back of the plane for morning prayers. Joshua Galilee pulled his hat over his eyes and pretended to sleep.

Eight and a half hours into the flight, the co-pilot gently shook Captain Ron awake. The captain opened his eyes and stretched his arms out in front of him. The co-pilot said, "We're making good time and are going to land in Tel Aviv a half hour early in about ninety minutes."

The co-pilot spoke to Shoshana Misrachi, one of the flight attendants, on the intercom at the flight attendants' station.

"Make the announcement, please."

Shoshana stood at the front of the economy cabin and picked up the microphone to broadcast over the PA system. She spoke first in Hebrew, then in English.

"Ladies and Gentlemen, thirty minutes from now, we will begin our final approach to Tel Aviv. We should be landing in ninety minutes. Please ring for a flight attendant if you have any last-minute requests."

As Shoshana walked toward the rear of the plane, she noticed that the Orthodox woman sitting directly across the aisle from Joshua Galilee appeared to be upset.

Shoshana stopped, leaned over, and whispered to their mother.

"What is wrong?"

"The man sitting across the aisle upset my children."

Shoshana turned and looked. The man was sleeping. She looked at the two boys.

"Did you talk to the man sitting there?"

Both boys shook their heads no. The younger one looked at Shoshana, his face very pale.

"He wasn't nice."

Shoshana looked into his brown eyes and cupped her hand under his chin.

"How was he not nice?"

"He didn't say the morning prayers. He slept through them."

The mother frowned at Shoshana and shook her head.

Aaron looked at Amy, who was browsing through a magazine.

"Hey, Amy, do you have your itinerary for the tour?"

Amy nodded and pulled her purse from under the seat. She rummaged through it and found a sheet of paper.

"Here it is. Our group had a meeting at the church to talk about it."

Aaron skimmed the sheets.

"Your group is going to spend a couple of days in and around Jerusalem and then go north into the Galilee."

"Yes. Reverend Crosby says, first, we need to see how the Jew has returned to his homeland and rebuilt it, just like the Prophets said."

Aaron looked at her.

"The Jew? Amy, there's more than one of us."

"I'm sorry, Aaron. It's just an expression."

When Aaron flipped through TV channels on Sunday morning, he often saw Christian religious leaders expounding their views on current events and Bible prophecies. When they referred to "the Jew," it was as if they were referring to a Godzilla-like creature plodding through the Christian world, spreading unbelief in its wake.

He looked at Amy's itinerary again.

"It says here that you are going to see the Knesset and the Supreme Court."

"Yes. The Knesset is like Congress, right? We have some lawyers in our group who really want to see the Supreme Court. I'm more interested in the ancient stuff."

Aaron laughed.

"There's plenty of ancient stuff in Israel, that's for sure."

Aaron read the rest of the itinerary.

"Amy, I see you're staying at the Hotel of the Seven Arches."

"Yes. It's on the Mount of Olives."

"Yes," Aaron said. "It has a great view of the city."

"Where are you staying in Jerusalem tonight, Aaron? I know you said you were going to visit your grandmother."

"I'm not sure. I have an appointment in the early afternoon, and then I am on my own. My grandmother isn't expecting me. I was going to surprise her."

Aaron stood up. He saw Joshua Galilee sitting towards the front of the plane.

"Amy, I'm going to take a walk and stretch my legs."

Aaron walked towards the front of the plane and stopped at the front of the economy cabin. He stood for several minutes, then turned and walked back towards his seat. As he passed Joshua Galilee, who appeared to be sleeping, Aaron noted Joshua's row and seat number.

He returned to his seat and relaxed. Soon, the engines decelerated and the plane began its descent over the Mediterranean Sea toward the coast of Israel.

Chapter 30

Earlier that morning, as El Al Flight LY028 flew through the night, Leah Avidan opened her eyes. Rabbi Avidan lay next to her on his stomach, with his arm draped over her midsection. Leah did not want to turn her head to look at the digital clock on the night table. Even the slightest move might wake her husband. Leah thought that he looked so peaceful when he slept. She folded her arms across her chest and stared into the darkness.

Leah remembered the day in school when she had read about the death of Moses. One of the last verses of the Torah intones: "He was one hundred and twenty when he died, but his eyes were not dim, nor had his moistures fled." What were his moistures?

Leah was twelve when she read this, and she and her best friend Chen had pondered the meaning of this sentence. Chen had consulted her older sister that night. The next day, as they sat next to each other at the long table in study hall, Chen had whispered into Leah's ear. Leah still hadn't been sure what Chen was talking about.

Now she knew. On their wedding night, in their darkened bedroom, where she could not see but only feel her husband's body, she thought that perhaps a younger man had slipped into the room and taken his place.

For the first few months of her marriage, Leah had fantasized that she was married to a vigorous man in his mid-twenties trapped in the body of an old man. She soon realized that she was just married to a vigorous man who was not trapped at all. Married to one of the oldest men in Israel, she had learned to love her husband, his burning intelligence and exuberance for life, but she often wished that his "moistures" would flee, at least for a short while.

Leah dozed off into a dreamless sleep. She did not know that her husband had been awake for several hours. Rabbi Avidan looked at the clock and saw it was 5:00 a.m. He listened to Leah's breathing. He could tell that she was asleep. He eased his naked body out of bed, put on his bathrobe, and walked down the hall to the bathroom.

Several minutes later, Leah awoke feeling restless and alert. She rolled on her side toward and reached for her husband. She touched the empty blanket. She whispered "Ashur, Ashur," as she rose from the bed. Rabbi Avidan had stepped into the shower and turned on the hot water. He let the hot water drench him. With the water running, he did not hear Leah come into the bathroom. The door to the shower stall opened. He turned and saw her in the faint light.
     "Leah, what . . .?"
     Leah stepped into the shower stall and embraced her husband. As they stood under the falling water, Rabbi Avidan felt as if they were Adam and Eve under a waterfall in the Garden of Eden. All of his anxiety about the day ahead quickly dispersed in the sensations that followed.

A half hour later, Leah went back to the bedroom to check on their son, Jacob. Rabbi Avidan put on his bathrobe and padded quietly into the kitchen. He cooked himself his usual breakfast of hot oatmeal and a banana. He took his breakfast into his study and turned on his computer. His morning routine was to eat his breakfast while he reviewed his business receipts from the previous day.

One of the secrets of the Jewish Quarter was that Rabbi Avidan was wealthy. In fact, he was very wealthy. After the Six-Day War, he had quietly begun purchasing real estate in the Jewish Quarter and other neighborhoods. All of his property was debt free; most was income producing. He had one employee, a property manager who reported directly to him and never discussed the identity of his employer with anyone.

He reviewed his morning report, thinking about how his early investments had slowly turned into substantial wealth. Several minutes later he finished his breakfast, shut off his computer, and went to his bedroom to get dressed.

Rabbi Avidan dressed quickly as Leah sat in the rocking chair, nursing Jacob. Leah watched as her husband put on his white shirt and dark coat. He brushed the coat vigorously with a lint brush.

"Today, I need to look utterly respectable, Leah."

Leah laughed.

"Ashur, you always look utterly respectable. Besides, you are the highest authority in the room."

"Well, today, I may not be."

Leah rose and straightened his collar.

"You may know the mysteries of the kabbalah, but you still need a woman's touch."

"I'll be home for dinner," Rabbi Avidan said.

Leah nodded. If there was one constant in the universe, it was that Ashur Avidan was never late for dinner.

He kissed Leah on the cheek and was gone.

Meir slept soundly through the night. He woke before sunrise feeling rested and alert. He rolled slowly out of bed so he would not disturb Channah. Esther lay sprawled in the hallway. He stepped over her and went out onto his terrace. The horizon glowed a soft pink. The air was clear. He stood and inhaled deeply, calming himself for the days ahead.

When he turned around to go inside, he found Channah in the doorway with tears in her eyes.

"I couldn't sleep."

She came to him, and he held her. He could feel her muffled sobs.

"What's wrong?"

She buried her face in his chest.

"You are so preoccupied with whatever it is you are doing. Will you be home for dinner tonight?"

"I hope so."

Channah hugged him tightly.

Rabbi Avidan left his house and walked through the Jewish Quarter of the Old City to the steps that descended to the plaza in front of the collapsed Kotel. He had been told to meet Amos Eitan. Even though the rabbi had not seen Amos since 1967, he recognized Amos immediately when he saw him standing in the plaza.

"Good morning, Mr. Eitan. It has been many years."

"Many, many years, Rabbi Avidan. You look well."

"And you do also, Mr. Eitan. I will be ready to leave after morning prayers."

Rabbi Avidan noticed his usual *minyan* standing next to the cordoned prayer area away from the collapsed ashlars. He joined them and removed his *tallit* from a velvet bag he carried under his arm. He wrapped himself in the *tallit,* then rolled up his sleeve and wrapped one of the *tefillin* around his left arm and the other around his forehead.

Amos watched as the rabbi joined the group of men waiting in the plaza. He continued to scan the worshippers, moving closer so he could keep the rabbi in his line of sight. He watched as the rabbi's group began the morning prayers, their chanting drifting through the breeze.

"Hear, O Israel, Adonai is our God, Adonai is One."

The Muslim call to prayer drifted from the minaret of al-Aqsa Mosque.

"There is no God but God. God is Greater."

Amos closed his eyes for a moment, letting the Hebrew and Arabic chants soothe him. The warm rays of the morning sun pierced the plaza. He thought about the hearing that was going to begin later that morning. He began to recite the morning prayers, something he had not done since he was a child.

Rabbi Avidan finished his prayers and shook hands with his *minyan*. He had been meeting with some of them for many years.

Yitzchak, his friend and neighbor, shook the rabbi's hand and looked into his eyes.

"You seem very preoccupied today, Ashur. Is everything okay?"

The rabbi looked at his friend.

"You know me well, Yitzchak. Right now, everything is fine. Tomorrow, who knows?"

"And it is tomorrow that you are thinking about."

Yitzchak said it as a statement, not a question.

"As I said, Yitzchak, you know me well."

As the rabbi turned to go, a crowd of about fifty people began descending the stairs into the plaza. They carried a large banner that read: "Rebuild the Temple."

Yitzchak nodded toward them.

"Ashur, you should leave now before they recognize you."

Amos watched as the rabbi suddenly turned and walked quickly toward him. He was anxious to get the rabbi into his car and to the Supreme Court. Amos met him in the middle of the plaza.

"Are you ready to go, Rabbi?"

Rabbi Avidan turned to look back toward the plaza, then grasped Amos's arm.

"I'm ready."

Amos drove slowly out of the valley surrounding the Old City. Ashur noticed an Arabic newspaper on the seat between him and Amos.

"I know you speak Arabic, Mr. Eitan. How did you learn it?" Amos stopped at a traffic light.

"From my parents. I grew up speaking Arabic, French, and Hebrew. Sometimes I have to remind myself which language I am speaking."

The rabbi stopped talking, lost in his thoughts. Soon they turned into the large driveway leading to the Supreme Court building. Amos drove past the main entrance to the large metal door of the parking garage. He flashed his ID to a video camera. A voice sounded through the small box under the camera.

"Enter, please."

The metal door swung slowly backward, and Amos guided his car down the ramp. When they reached the bottom level, he parked it next to the elevator door. There were no other cars on that level. Rabbi Avidan opened the passenger door and got out of the car. He looked around at the empty garage.

"Private parking? Not bad."

Amos pointed to the elevator door.

"We've got a private elevator, too."

Amos punched the keypad next to the elevator door. The door opened, and they entered.

"Have you ever been in this building, Rabbi?"

"Once, soon after it opened. It is quite impressive."

Amos pushed a button on the wall, and the rabbi felt his stomach drop as the elevator descended.

"We are going down?"

Amos nodded.

"I haven't seen this part of the building."

"Not many people have."

The elevator continued to drop.

"Why are we going so far below the earth?"

"Security."

"I would like to speak with Justice Bar-Aben before I testify."

"I think that can be arranged."

The elevator came to a halt, and the doors opened.

Meir had entered his basement office several minutes before. He took off his suit jacket and reached for his black robe draped across his desk. While most judges in Israel wore their robe open, Meir preferred to zip the front almost closed, leaving the top of his tie exposed. He opened the door of the closet, where a full-length mirror hung on the inside. He looked at his reflection and breathed slowly.

He remembered the first time he had put on a judge's robe. He had looked in the mirror and found his head and legs sticking out from the flowing fabric. He wondered if he would feel comfortable wearing it. By the end of the first day on the bench, he had understood the purpose of the robe. It told the world that he had authority and was entitled to respect. When he spoke, the attorneys and parties listened. The Torah commanded the Children of Israel to appoint judges in all the tribes, and the judges were to fulfill the *mitzvah*, "Justice, justice, you shall pursue."

As he left his chambers and walked to the courtroom at the beginning of each day, the feel of the black cloth swishing around his body had a calming effect on him. "Justice, justice, you shall pursue," echoed in his mind. As he entered the courtroom, he would always add his own prayer. "Please, God, let me get it right."

Amran was waiting for Amos and the rabbi as they exited the elevator.

"Mr. Eitan, everyone else is here. Justice Bar-Aben is in his office, and the prime minister and the president of the court are already in the courtroom. We have deactivated the sensors to the courtroom corridor so we can allow witnesses into the courtroom without the assistance of Justice Bar-Aben."

"Fine, Amran. Rabbi Avidan wishes to speak to Justice Bar-Aben."

Amran called Meir. "Mr. Eitan and Rabbi Avidan are here. The rabbi would like to speak with you before the hearing starts."

Ordinarily, parties or witnesses would not be allowed to speak privately with the presiding justice, but this was not an ordinary proceeding.

Amran backed out of the doorway as Meir opened the entrance to the office corridor and motioned the rabbi to enter. They went into Meir's office.

Meir ushered Rabbi Avidan into his office and extended his hand.

"Rabbi Avidan, Meir Bar-Aben. A pleasure to meet you."

Rabbi Avidan shook Meir's hand firmly and looked up into his eyes.

"Justice Bar-Aben, you have a difficult task in front of you."

Meir marveled at the rabbi's tight grip and the sparkle in his eye.

"Thank you, Rabbi. You wanted to tell me something before the hearing begins?"

The rabbi stepped back and looked piercingly at Meir.

"When Moses became weary of settling the disputes of the Children of Israel wandering in the wilderness, his father-in-law Jethro suggested that he gather the elders of the tribes to help him judge the people. God then commanded Moses to gather seventy elders for this task."

Meir listened respectfully.

The rabbi continued. "Do you remember what happened to Moses after he appointed the seventy elders to help him?"

Meir shook his head.

"Unfortunately, no. Please tell me."

Rabbi Avidan's face became stern.

"It didn't get any easier for Moses. The Torah says that after Moses appointed the elders to help him, Moses only decided the hard cases."

Meir laughed.

The rabbi grasped Meir's hand again and squeezed it firmly. His manner remained somber.

"Justice Bar-Aben, it's not every day that I meet someone who has the responsibility of Moses."

Meir felt comforted by the rabbi's presence.

"I wish I had the wisdom of your years, Rabbi."

"I'm sure you have sufficient wisdom. What is equally necessary for those who are chosen to enforce the law is strength."

The rabbi grasped Meir's hand again and uttered the worshippers' declaration in the synagogue at the conclusion of the reading of each of the five books of the Torah.

"*hazak, hazak, v'nithazek.*" Be strong, be strong, and let us be strengthened.

It was time for the hearing to begin.

Chapter 31

Meir opened the door to the office and gestured to Rabbi Avidan.

"Please follow me."

As they entered the hallway, they saw Amos standing at the door to the courtroom with Prime Minister Zadok and the president of the court, Eli Heifitz. The prime minister extended his hand as his scent of tobacco and cologne wafted over Meir.

"Justice Bar-Aben. A pleasure to see you again. We are finally ready to begin."

Zadok turned to the rabbi.

"Rabbi Avidan, a pleasure to see you again."

Rabbi Avidan shook Zadok's hand.

Eli Heifitz looked at his watch. It was 9:30 a.m.

"Justice Bar-Aben, it is time."

The beginning of the hearing was very informal. Meir, the rabbi, the prime minister, the president of the court, and Amos entered the courtroom and stood for a moment. The rabbi scanned the several rows of empty seats, and his eyes gravitated to the justice's platform and witness chair. The prime minister walked forward, seated himself in the first row behind the podium, and crossed his legs.

Meir turned to the rabbi.

"Please go down and sit next to the prime minister."

The rabbi nodded and walked down the aisle.

Meir nodded to Amos.

"Are you ready for this?" Meir asked.

"I never thought it would come to this. From the Temple Mount to the basement of the Supreme Court," Amos responded.

Amos walked forward and sat with the rest of the group. Meir took his place on the justice's platform. He leaned forward and spoke into the microphone.

"This hearing is called to order. I am Justice Meir Bar-Aben, presiding justice in this matter. The prime minister will examine all witnesses at this hearing. I will ask clarifying questions. Mr. Amos Eitan will serve as translator as needed."

"The proceedings of this hearing will not be recorded or transcribed. Those present are not to disclose what occurs. The following individuals are now present in the hearing room—Prime Minister Ezer Zadok, President of the Supreme Court Eli Heifitz, Rabbi Ashur Avidan, and Mr. Amos Eitan. The court notes that the state has requested Mr. Eitan's presence as a witness in this matter."

"This case has been initiated by a petition from the Office of the Prime Minister of the State of Israel pursuant to Section 614 of the judicial code. The court recognizes Prime Minister Ezer Zadok for the purpose of presenting the petition to the court."

Prime Minister Zadok rose and walked to the podium facing the justice's platform. He placed several sheets of paper on the podium, adjusted the microphone, and began to read.

"May it please the court—we are here to present evidence regarding a matter of national security. It involves the destruction of a place that has been holy to the Jewish people since the beginning of our existence.

"I am referring to the Temple Mount. In 1967, the Israel Defense Forces reclaimed the Temple Mount for the first time since it fell to the Romans almost two thousand years ago. Very soon thereafter, Israel returned the administration of the Temple Mount to the Muslim authority, the Waqf.

"The Office of the Prime Minister initiated the petition in this case because of the Waqf's extensive excavations under the Temple Mount to enlarge the lower level of al-Aqsa Mosque, creating the Marwani Mosque. The government of Israel has never been allowed to conduct archaeological excavations in this area. The excavations undertaken by the Waqf appear not to be archaeological excavations—but construction excavations. The Waqf transported the excavated materials by dump trucks to a landfill. Many archaeologist and others are outraged by the destruction of the Temple Mount. There has been an ongoing project to retrieve any artifacts of archaeological significance from the landfill, but many artifacts may have been destroyed.

"We have submitted evidence to the court, a report by noted archeologists and engineers, which concludes that the Waqf's excavations resulted in the collapse of the Kotel.

"The newly reconstituted Sanhedrin has called for rebuilding the Temple on the Temple Mount. While the Office of the Prime Minister is not advocating the rebuilding of the Temple, we believe that the collapse of the Kotel requires action by the state to prevent further destruction of our history and a place holy to the Jewish people."

The prime minister rested his hands on the podium and paused. He looked up at Meir.

"The Code of Law of the State of Israel requires that, with regard to Jerusalem, 'The Holy Places shall be protected from desecration and any other violation and from anything likely to violate the freedom of access of the members of the different religions to the places sacred to them or their feelings toward those places.'

"We believe that the actions of the Waqf have violated this legal provision, and we will prove the violation in this proceeding.

"Therefore, the Office of the Prime Minister requests this honorable court to hear the evidence, to determine that the law has been violated, to revoke the authority of the Waqf to administrate the Temple Mount, and to direct the government of the State of Israel to assume the administration of the Temple Mount."

Chapter 32

At 8:30 a.m., Tel Aviv time, an hour before the hearing had started at the Supreme Court, Reverend Crosby shouted, *"Halleluyah,"* as the plane landed. The plane taxied on the runway for ten minutes before arriving at the terminal. Aaron deplaned with Amy and the Zion Baptist Temple Group.

After they entered the arrival hall at Ben Gurion Airport, they made their way to passport control. Joshua Galilee had followed and stood near the group, keeping his eye on Aaron.

When they arrived at passport control, Aaron looked at his watch. It was only 9:00 a.m. He had plenty of time to make his delivery.

"I need to go to another line, Amy," Aaron said. "I'll see you over at baggage claim." Aaron walked to the line in passport control on the far right. As with his past two deliveries, he was required to pass through this line when he arrived.

Agent Tzion was in the Mossad office in Ben Gurion Airport near passport control, watching a closed-circuit transmission from a camera monitoring the passport control line through which Aaron was required to pass. Facial-recognition software on Agent Tzion's computer identified Aaron Kragen. As the border control agent swiped Aaron's passport, other software on Agent Tzion's computer confirmed Aaron's passport information. Agent Tzion continued to watch the closed-circuit transmission as Aaron opened his backpack and placed a black package on the counter.

Agent Tzion called Amran, who was waiting in the underground hallway as Rabbi Avidan was meeting with Meir.

"Please tell Mr. Eitan and the prime minister that the courier has arrived. The plane landed early, and the courier is passing through passport control. He should be on his way soon."

Agent Tzion looked back at his computer screen as the border control agent issued Aaron a standard border control pass, which had his entry date and an image of his photo from his passport on it. Agent Tzion was surprised to see Aaron still talking to the border control agent. He watched the border control agent make a phone call and then wave Aaron through. Then the border control agent made another phone call. Agent Tzion's phone rang.

"Agent Tzion, we have a situation here. I need your assistance. Meet me at line 2."

Agent Tzion watched as the agent closed his station and proceeded to stand in front of line 2, where cleared passengers entered the terminal.

Agent Tzion turned to Agent Halevi, who was sitting at the next desk.

"Do me a favor," Agent Tzion said, pointing to Aaron on the screen. "Keep your eyes on this person heading toward baggage claim. His name is Aaron Kragen, and he's one of our couriers. Follow him on video and make sure he gets in a taxi and gets away from the airport quickly."

Agent Tzion left the Mossad office and entered the passport control area.

Joshua Galilee had followed Aaron and was standing in line 2 in passport control. As Joshua's line moved forward, he kept Aaron in sight. When Aaron exited passport control, Joshua was next in his line. He was finished with his assignment. Once he cleared passport control, he would call Hiram Aitza and let him know that the courier had arrived and was ahead of schedule.

Joshua handed his passport to the border control agent in line 2 and smiled. He had come through Ben Gurion Airport many times before, and he recognized the agent. The agent scanned Joshua's passport, issued him a border control pass, and spoke.

"Mr. Galilee, I am going to ask you to pass through and speak to another agent who is waiting over there." He motioned towards the border control agent to whom Aaron had spoken.

Joshua was puzzled. He passed through the line and approached the other border control agent.

"Mr. Galilee," the other border control agent said, "we need to talk to you."

At that moment, Agent Tzion arrived. The border control agent turned to Agent Tzion.

"Agent Tzion, we have a security breach. You need to wait here with Mr. Galilee until El Al security arrives."

Aaron wheeled his roller bag to baggage claim. Reverend Crosby and the Zion Baptist Temple group had quickly cleared passport control and most had already claimed their luggage. Amy came toward Aaron.

"I enjoyed traveling with you, Amy," Aaron said. "I'll walk with you and the group outside and grab a taxi."

"That would be nice, Aaron," Amy said. She hesitated, then continued.

"Aaron, if you need a ride to Jerusalem, you can ride with us. I asked Reverend Crosby, and he said it would be okay."

Aaron looked at his watch. It was 9:30 a.m. He could take the bus to the hotel on the Mount of Olives and grab a taxi from there.

"Are you sure it's okay, Amy?" Aaron asked.

"Sure. Ask Reverend Crosby yourself if you want."

Aaron walked faster and approached Reverend Crosby.

"Sir, Amy said I could catch a ride to Jerusalem on your bus."

"Sure, son. There are twenty of us and twenty-four seats on the bus," Reverend Crosby said. "Climb aboard."

Reverend Crosby reached into his own backpack and extracted a baseball cap with ZBT on it, identical to those worn by the group.

"Now you're one of us!" he shouted, as many in the group clapped.

Joe and Emma Mason looked on, frowning.

Standing inside the door was a man in shorts and sandals holding a large sign that read "SHALOM, ZION BAPTIST TEMPLE." Reverend Crosby approached him.

"Shalom, Avi, shalom."

The man grinned.

Reverend Crosby turned to his group.

"This is Avi, our bus driver. Let's give him a loud 'shalom.'"

"Shalom, shalom!" the group yelled.

They waited another ten minutes until everyone collected their luggage. Reverend Crosby led the group in a short prayer service, giving thanks for a safe arrival in the Holy Land. He turned to Avi.

"We're ready, Avi. Show the way!"

"Follow me, please," Avi said, waving his arm toward the terminal door.

Fifteen minutes later, Agent Tzion returned to the Mossad office. Agent Halevi was drinking coffee and reading a magazine.

"Did you follow Aaron Kragen through the terminal?" Agent Tzion asked.

"I did. You should see this," Agent Halevi said, pointing at his computer monitor. "I recorded the video transmission for you."

Agent Tzion watched as Aaron walked inside the terminal with a group wearing red tee shirts and baseball caps. Aaron was wearing a baseball cap and walking next to a woman who was significantly younger than the rest of the group. They appeared to be traveling together.

As they exited the terminal, the transmission from another camera showed the group approaching a small bus. The driver quickly loaded the luggage, the group boarded, and the bus departed.

Agent Tzion was puzzled. He turned to Agent Halevi.

"He left with a tour group?"

"It sure looks that way. Are you sure that was the person you were tracking?" Agent Halevi asked.

"I'm sure. He had the package, and he is very smart. He inadvertently identified one of the undercover El Al security agents on the flight."

"What happened?"

"When he came through passport control, he told the border control agent that the person standing in the next line had acted suspiciously during the flight. Border control is required to act on the information. The border control agent notified El Al and called me to detain the El Al security agent and speak to El Al security, since our courier was the source of the information. I waited until El Al security came, and they took their agent away to debrief him. Their agent was very unhappy about being identified."

Agent Halevi shook his head.

"I'm sure El Al will take care of it. What do you need to do now?"

"Well, El Al needs to debrief our courier as to how he identified their undercover security agent. Since he is our courier, I need to bring him back for debriefing."

"Why didn't you just take our courier to make the delivery and bring him back?" Agent Halevi asked.

"He told border control that he had a deadline for his delivery, so border control just waved him through. By the time I arrived in passport control, and El Al told me they needed to debrief him, the courier was gone."

"What are you going to do?"

"The bus dispatcher knows where every bus is going. I am going to catch up with him at their destination. He's not that far ahead of me."

The Zion Baptist Temple tour bus had pulled away from the international arrival terminal at Ben Gurion Airport at about 9:45 a.m. Reverend Crosby stood at the front of the bus with the microphone for the PA system in his hand, looking at the sea of red tee shirts and baseball caps. As the bus swayed back and forth, he steadied himself and pressed the button on the microphone.

"I want to say again: praise the Lord for our safe landing. Let me say it in Hebrew. *halleluyah.*"

The group raised their hands above their heads.

"*halleluyah. halleluyah!*"

"We're in safe hands with Avi, our driver, who will be with us for our entire tour. Let's give him a round of applause."

The group clapped and whistled. Avi raised his hand in salute without taking his eyes off the road. He cruised through the airport gate and eased the bus onto the highway. The Zion Baptist Temple group turned their necks from one side of the bus to the other, trying to catch their first glimpses of the Holy Land. Hoping to see camels and idyllic herds of sheep on rolling hills, they saw tall buildings and construction cranes on the sides of the busy highway. Cars whipped past the bus with no regard for the speed limit. Reverend Crosby pointed out the window.

"This is the main road to Jerusalem. We're about an hour or a little more from our hotel. Sit back, relax, and enjoy the view, or you can sleep. Avi is going to turn on the radio, and we can listen to some music."

Avi turned on the radio over the PA system, and the group was surprised to hear Frank Sinatra crooning "My Way."

Aaron sat at the back of the bus next to Amy. Joe and Emma Mason looked disapprovingly at Aaron and Amy from across the aisle.

Aaron pulled his baseball cap down over his eyes and quickly fell asleep. Several minutes later, Aaron was jolted awake by an announcement on the radio in Hebrew, followed by the sound of a loud siren. Avi hit the brakes and pulled over. Everyone in the bus looked out the window and saw traffic halt on the highway.

"What's happening, Aaron?" Amy asked.

Before Aaron could answer, Avi picked up the microphone and announced over the PA system, "For Holocaust Remembrance Day, a siren blows at ten in the morning, and the whole country observes two minutes of silence for the victims of the Holocaust. We will wait here and be on our way in two minutes."

Everyone sat silently on the bus.

Joshua Galilee sat in the El Al security office at the airport, waiting to speak to his superiors. He called Hiram Aitza on his cell phone.

"It's Joshua. I've landed in Tel Aviv. We landed early."

"Good. Is the courier on his way?"

"Yes. He should be there on time."

"Any problems, Joshua?" Hiram asked.

Joshua paused.

"The delivery should be fine," he said, as the siren sounded in the airport.

Part Five – Testimony

Jerusalem
November 2035

My grandfather and I arrived at the restaurant in the Cardo. My grandfather was tired.

"What time is it, Nuri?" he asked.

"It's late, *jiddo*. You must be starving."

My grandfather, always the stoic, just smiled.

"Let's eat, Nuri. We can save the rest of the story for another day. Do you have classes tomorrow?"

"No," I said. "Can we meet for coffee early tomorrow morning?" I was eager to hear the rest of his story.

My grandfather laughed.

"Of course. There is much more to tell. Meet me at the coffee shop next to al-Buraq's Wall."

I met my grandfather the next day at Antony's Coffee Shop. I knew he would be there when I arrived. He was an early riser. When I was little, I would spend the night with him and my grandmother. I would wake up, and he would already be making breakfast.

I found my grandfather drinking his second cup of coffee, hunched over a newspaper. He had a huge piece of baklava cut in half on a plate in front of him. I sat down as he looked up and smiled at me.

"Nuri, eat." He pushed the plate toward me.

"I will, *jiddo*. Let me get some coffee."

I went to the counter to order. I stood in line and waited. Two tourists were in front of me. They were staring at the wall behind the counter. The illuminated menu hung on a huge ashlar framed by drywall. The coffee shop, like the other shops in the row, was built against the wall Jews used to call the Kotel. The street outside and the rest of the crowded shops were built on the plaza where Jews used to pray. A small portion of the wall was still exposed.

I got my coffee and sat down with my grandfather. He had already finished his baklava. He put his newspaper aside.

"Eat, Nuri. I will continue our story. While the courier with the stone was on the tour bus, the Section 614 hearing continued."

"I don't know much about the legal world, *jiddo*. You know I am studying engineering. Will I understand what you are telling me?"

"There is no 'legal world.' There is only the world that we all live in. People talk, listen, and hopefully try to understand. Whatever you do in this life, Nuri, never stop listening and trying to understand."

The coffee shop was cool and comfortable. We could sit all morning and stay for lunch. My grandfather continued his story.

Chapter 33

Meir leaned forward as Prime Minister Zadok concluded his opening statement. From the day he had read the petition, he knew that he was to decide whether the State of Israel would take back the Temple Mount from the Waqf. Hearing Zadok articulate it drove home the magnitude of the decision he had to make.

"Thank you, Mr. Prime Minister. I have some questions for you with regard to the petition. Mr. Prime Minister, you have submitted a report that allegedly proves that the Waqf's excavations under the Temple Mount caused the collapse of the Kotel. However, the witnesses you are going to present have no connection to the Waqf's activities. Can you explain the purpose of the witnesses' testimony?"

Zadok responded.

"Of course. I have reviewed the classified military summaries of what occurred when the IDF took the Temple Mount during the Six-Day War. There is very little information. Minister of Defense Moshe Dayan filed a brief report stating that those present made a detailed analysis of the situation. We know that on the night after the IDF captured the Temple Mount, Minister of Defense Moshe Dayan met with the chief rabbi of the IDF, Rabbi Shlomo Goren. Both are deceased. Upon further investigation, we found that Moshe Dayan and Rabbi Goren met with Rabbi Avidan and a Muslim cleric who will testify in this hearing. We also discovered that Amos Eitan, at that time an IDF intelligence officer, was present during that meeting.

We have, therefore, requested his presence here to offer testimony.

"It is the understanding of the Office of the Prime Minister that you, Justice Bar-Aben, were also in the brigade that took the Temple Mount. We have no reason to believe that you have any knowledge of the discussions that occurred that evening."

"That is correct, Mr. Prime Minister," Meir said. "Please continue."

Zadok spoke in a firm voice.

"In addition to violating the law that prohibits the desecration of the holy places, we suspect that the excavations performed by the Waqf violate an agreement between Moshe Dayan and the Waqf after the Temple Mount was captured by the IDF during the Six-Day War. If that is the case, the violation of that agreement would be additional legal justification for retaking the Temple Mount."

"You did not mention the violation of any agreement in the petition," Meir said. "Do you have any evidence that such an agreement exists, Mr. Prime Minister?"

"We believe Mr. Amos Eitan knows what Moshe Dayan negotiated with the Waqf. That is why we requested that he testify in this hearing."

"And there are three other witnesses—Rabbi Avidan, Mr. ibn Abdullah, and Professor al-Fawzi. What is the relevance of their testimony, Mr. Prime Minister?"

"Their testimony will support a third basis for the relief sought in the petition. That basis is the Jewish people's historic right to the Temple Mount."

"You did not mention that basis in the petition either, Mr. Prime Minister," Meir said.

"May it please the court—I move the court to amend the petition to include the violation of the alleged agreement and the historic right to the Temple Mount."

Meir smiled.

"Well, there is no opposing party here to respond or object to your motion. The motion is granted. Before we continue, let me clarify this, Mr. Prime Minister. Your office is presenting three causes of action justifying revocation of the Waqf's authority over the Temple Mount—violation of the law of the holy place, violation of an alleged agreement between the Waqf and Moshe Dayan, and the Jewish people's historic right to the Temple Mount."

"Yes, I have submitted a report on the collapse that supports the violation of the law of the holy place. It is possible that Mr. Eitan's testimony will support the violation of an agreement between Moshe Dayan and the Waqf. The testimony of Rabbi Avidan, Mr. ibn Abdullah, and Professor al-Fawzi will support the Jewish people's historic right to the Temple Mount."

"Thank you, Mr. Prime Minister," Meir said. "Please present your first witness."

Zadok spoke.

"The State of Israel calls Amos Eitan to testify in these proceedings."

Meir motioned to Amos.

"Mr. Eitan, would you please come up and sit in the witness chair."

Amos stood beside the witness chair, and Meir administered the oath.

"Please be seated, Mr. Eitan," Meir said.

Meir turned to Zadok, who had remained standing.

"Mr. Prime Minister, you may examine the witness."

Zadok began.

"Mr. Eitan, we will dispense with the usual introductory questions. We can stipulate that you are an employee of the state."

"That is correct, Mr. Prime Minister," Amos answered.

Zadok continued.

"Mr. Eitan, where were you in June 1967?"

"I was an intelligence officer in the IDF, in the battalion that took the Temple Mount. Justice Bar-Aben and I served together."

Zadok continued.

"What was your involvement, if any, in discussions the night the Temple Mount was captured and later discussions between Moshe Dayan and Muslim authorities with regard to the Temple Mount?"

Amos answered, "I am fluent in Arabic. As an intelligence officer in the IDF, I served as translator during the discussions with a Muslim cleric who appeared on the Temple Mount that night. Moshe Dayan was fluent in Arabic, and he conversed with the Muslim cleric in Arabic. I translated the Arabic conversation into Hebrew for Rabbi Goren, and Rabbi Goren's Hebrew into Arabic for the Muslim cleric. During subsequent discussions with the Waqf, Moshe Dayan spoke Hebrew. I translated his Hebrew into Arabic for the Waqf members, and the Waqf members' Arabic into Hebrew for the Israeli delegation."

"Were you instructed not to reveal the content of those discussions?"

"I was. By Moshe Dayan himself."

"If this court directs you to reveal this information, would you do so today?"

Amos shifted in his seat. He looked at Zadok, then at Meir.

"I believe any information I know concerning the night at the Temple Mount can be told more accurately by Rabbi Ashur Avidan and Samir ibn Abdullah. They spoke with Moshe Dayan and Rabbi Goren. As for discussions with the Waqf, I can speak to that if directed."

Meir and Zadok both looked at the rabbi. He was sitting calmly, waiting.

Meir spoke to Zadok.

"Mr. Prime Minister, I would prefer to have the order of testimony in chronological order. Let's focus on the meeting on the Temple Mount before we discuss the later negotiations with the Waqf."

Meir turned to Amos.

"Mr. Eitan, you are excused for the moment. Please remain in the courtroom."

Prime Minister Zadok remained standing at the podium facing Meir.

"The State of Israel calls Rabbi Ashur Avidan to testify as a witness in this proceeding."

The rabbi walked forward. Meir looked down at the short and ancient figure as he approached the witness stand. A sense of unreality overwhelmed him.

Rabbi Avidan sat in the witness stand and placed his hands on his lap. Meir administered the oath.

"Mr. Prime Minister, you may examine Rabbi Avidan."

Zadok turned to the rabbi.

"Rabbi, would you state your full name please."

"Ashur Avidan."

"Where do you live?"

"Rehov Hayai Olam, in the Jewish Quarter of the Old City of Jerusalem."

"And your age?"

Rabbi Avidan smiled and looked at Meir.

"One hundred and one."

"And are you employed?"

"I am a rabbi. I do not lead a congregation. I offer rabbinic advice to those who seek it. I am also self-employed in some worldly ventures, mostly real estate. But before I begin my testimony, Mr. Prime Minister, may I offer some advice to you and Justice Bar-Aben?"

Zadok was taken aback. He looked at Meir, who smiled at the rabbi.

"Rabbi Avidan, the court would welcome any advice you have to give," Meir answered.

The rabbi spoke.

"I have been a student of the Talmud my entire life. As you know, the Talmud, the compendium of oral commentary on the Torah, contains the discussions of rabbis over a period of five hundred years, from about one hundred years before the destruction of the Temple to four hundred years after the destruction. The Talmud was reduced to writing by the rabbis who lived in Babylonia and became the foundation for Jewish life in whatever country the Jews lived."

Rabbi Avidan paused. He turned first to Prime Minister Zadok and then to Meir, as if to confirm his authority to offer the advice he was about to give.

"I want to emphasize to the court that the study of the Talmud is a method of analysis that takes nothing for granted. I believe that is a good principle to apply in the law, as in life."

Meir smiled and spoke.

"Thank you, Rabbi. I note that it is almost ten o'clock. We won't be able to hear the siren for Yom HaShoah in this courtroom. Let us stand now for two minutes in silence, and then we will proceed."

Everyone in the courtroom stood. After two minutes, Meir sat down.

"Mr. Prime Minister, you may proceed," Meir said.

The prime minister continued his examination of the rabbi.

"Rabbi, I think it would be helpful to the court if you give a brief history of the Temple Mount."

Rabbi Avidan leaned forward, resting his elbows on the ledge in front of the witness stand. He turned slightly sideways so he could address Meir. He cleared his throat softly and wrinkled his brow. The rabbi framed his thoughts carefully, outlining his answer in his mind before beginning to speak, the method he used when he taught Torah and Talmud. He looked at the prime minister, and in typical Talmudic fashion, taking nothing for granted, critiqued the question.

"A good question. A very good question. The place where the Temple ultimately stood was important at the very creation of the world. We know this because the Torah tells us that Adam was created at this very spot. Generations after Adam, when men became wicked and the Flood was sent to destroy them, Noah returned to this place and offered a sacrifice to God.

"The next event on the Temple Mount has to do with the patriarch of the Jewish people, Abraham. He was the first to believe in One God. Abraham came from Ur of the Chaldees. He had two sons, Ishmael and Isaac. Ishmael was the firstborn, from a slave named Hagar, and he was the ancestor of the Arab people.

"Abraham's wife, Sarah, was barren, but when Abraham was ninety-nine and Sarah eighty-seven, the Torah tells us that God told Abraham that Sarah would conceive and bear a son. And she did conceive, and she did bear a son, Isaac—which means 'laughter,' because Sarah laughed when she found out she would have a son."

"And Isaac was the ancestor of the Jewish people?" Zadok asked.

"Yes, Isaac was the first person to fulfill God's covenant, the *brit,* with Abraham to be circumcised on the eighth day after birth. When Abraham entered into this covenant, he circumcised himself at age ninety-nine, and then Ishmael—who was already thirty-seven—but Isaac was the first to fulfill the letter of the covenant. And Abraham circumcised his eight-day-old son with a steady hand when he was a hundred years old."

Pride swept Rabbi Avidan's face. Not long ago, the newspapers in Israel had pictures of the rabbi officiating at his own son's circumcision when the rabbi was the same age as Abraham.

"Rabbi, when was the next important event at the place where the Temple was later built?" Zadok asked.

"Thirty-seven years later."

"What happened then?"

The rabbi paused. A look of pain crossed his face.

"Sarah's laughter turned to tears. According to the Torah, God commanded Abraham to sacrifice his son Isaac. God led him to the place of sacrifice. At the last moment, while Abraham raised his knife, a messenger from God appeared and stopped him, as his sacrifice had been fulfilled by his obedience to God."

The rabbi sighed.

"Jews today believe that the place where Abraham brought Isaac to be sacrificed was the place where the Temple was later built. Indeed, many believe that the large rock under the Dome of the Rock is the rock where Abraham tied Isaac. Isaac lived and fathered Jacob, also known as Israel. And Jacob had sons whose descendants became the Twelve Tribes of Israel, or the Children of Israel."

The rabbi paused, waiting for the next question. Zadok continued.

"When was the Temple first built?"

"Many centuries later, the twelve tribes descended from Jacob, Isaac's son, migrated to Egypt and were enslaved there. Moses led them out of captivity into the wilderness of Sinai, and he received the Torah on

Mount Sinai. After wandering in the wilderness for forty years, they entered the land of Canaan, conquered the Canaanites, and settled the land. Eventually, they established monarchies in the north and south. The focal point of religious worship was the portable Tabernacle containing the Holy Ark. The second king of the southern kingdom was David, who wished to build a permanent home for this Ark, a Temple to God in Jerusalem. God did not allow David to build a Temple, because David was a man or war. That task fell to David's son, Solomon, a man of peace. He built the Temple in the year 830 before the Common Era or in the year 830 B.C.E."

Zadok leaned forward.

"We are covering a tremendous amount of history in a few sentences, but I am leading to a question I want to ask you. First, tell me, the Temple was destroyed by the Babylonians, was it not?"

"Yes, in 420 B.C.E., the Babylonians captured Jerusalem, destroyed the Temple, and took the Jews into captivity for seventy years, until Cyrus the Persian conquered the Babylonians and allowed the Jews to return home. They rebuilt the Temple, which was later enhanced by King Herod in the first century before the Common Era. The Great Sanhedrin, the body of sages that ruled the country, convened in the Temple. At that time, the land was known as Judea, a province of the Roman Empire. After a civil war between Jewish factions and a subsequent revolt against the Romans, the Romans destroyed the Temple in 70 C.E."

The rabbi paused again and waited for the next question.

"Thank you, Rabbi. This brings me to my question. You are aware that recently a group of rabbis has reconstituted the Sanhedrin, appointing themselves as members and electing a head rabbi."

Rabbi Avidan nodded solemnly.

"I am aware of this."

"And you are aware that the new Sanhedrin is in favor of rebuilding the Temple on the Temple Mount."

"I am."

"I have read that you have resisted the new Sanhedrin's request that you join it, Rabbi."

"I have."

"And why have you resisted the new Sanhedrin's request that you join it, Rabbi?"

"I am in favor of some things that the new Sanhedrin advocates, but not everything. I am a man of peace, and I believe that rebuilding the Temple will not bring peace. And, by nature, I do not join groups. I keep my business to myself."

Zadok thought for a moment, and then he changed the subject of the examination.

"Rabbi, on the evening in June 1967, after the Temple Mount was captured by the IDF, did you go to the Temple Mount?"

"Yes."

"And why were you there?"

"I had been summoned from my home by Rabbi Shlomo Goren."

"Why had you been summoned by Rabbi Goren?"

"I was his friend."

"You were a friend. But what caused him to summon you?"

"I had told him that if I lived to see the day that Israel reclaimed the Temple Mount, I wanted to be one of the first to return there."

"Rabbi, I'm sure many wished to be among the first to return there. Why did Rabbi Goren honor your request?"

Rabbi Avidan paused. He looked at Meir and then turned to Prime Minister Zadok, who was looking intently at him.

"Rabbi Goren knew that I am a direct descendant of Rabbi Jochanan ben Zakkai, who was a member of the Great Sanhedrin and survived the Roman destruction of Jerusalem in the first century of the Common Era. I had told Rabbi Goren that I had an extreme interest in being one of the first to set foot on the Temple Mount if Israel ever reclaimed it."

Zadok continued his questioning.

"So you spoke that night with Moshe Dayan and Rabbi Goren?"

"I did."

"Was Amos Eitan there that night?"

"Yes."

"So Mr. Eitan heard what you are about to tell the court?"

"Some he heard. Some he did not."

Zadok hunched forward on the podium.

"Rabbi, please tell the court what you told Rabbi Goren and Moshe Dayan that night."

Rabbi Avidan turned to Meir.

"Justice Bar-Aben, what I told Rabbi Goren and Moshe Dayan that night was an abbreviated version of what I wish to tell the court in this proceeding. I believe it would help the court if I explained in greater detail."

"Rabbi Avidan, the court welcomes whatever you wish to say," Meir said.

"Thank you, Justice Bar-Aben. Let me tell the court what has been handed down through my family from generation to generation, beginning with my ancestor Rabbi Jochanan ben Zakkai."

Rabbi Avidan began to speak, sweeping those in the courtroom into the past.

Chapter 34

Jewish Calendar, 3858
Christian Calendar, 69-70 A.D

Rabbi Jochanan ben Zakkai rose before the members of the Great Sanhedrin in the Chamber of Hewn Stone. Hunger gnawed at his belly, and he steadied himself with a long wooden staff. The seventy elders sat in four large semicircles in front of him, scarcely breathing. Their robes hung loosely from their frail bodies. Rabbi Jochanan felt as if he were addressing spirits rather than men of flesh.

"What started as senseless hatred between brothers has sparked civil war in Judea. The Zealots' revolt against our occupiers has now brought the full wrath of the Roman legions to our gates. The Zealots have destroyed the peace of our nation."

The elders nodded helplessly. A group of Jewish revolutionaries had defied authority, threatening the entire nation. Yet the elders clung to their hope that the Temple of God would survive, and the nation would be saved.

Rabbi Jochanan continued.

"I am one hundred years old. I have lived to see the death of my parents, the death of my son, and the death of my wife. The Zealots who have revolted against Rome now think they are secure in the Romans' Antonia Fortress they have captured even though the Roman legions have surrounded Jerusalem. We are starving. Many of us have not been able to resist the taste of the flesh of unclean animals that the Roman catapults have hurled into our midst. Those who do not perish soon will see the destruction of the Temple."

Some of the elders shifted uneasily in their seats. Who could resist the taste of swine when slow starvation was the only alternative?

Rabbi Gamliel rose from his seat and pointed a bony finger at Rabbi Jochanan.

"You speak as if the Temple has already been destroyed, as if the unbroken chain from Moses to the members of this body has been broken. Do you believe that Rome will accomplish what the Egyptians, Syrians, Babylonians, and Greeks could not? *adonai* will save us from destruction. The Temple of God will stand."

Rabbi Jochanan had heard this before. Violence and hatred had plunged Judea into a death struggle with Rome, and the elders could not see that the end was near. Desperate men always believed that the Temple would save them. Rabbi Jochanan had long since dismissed this edifice of stone as a protector. Had not the sons of Aaron turned the Temple to their own devices for wealth collection? Many rabbis believed that the *shechinah* no longer dwelled within the Holy of Holies.

Rabbi Jochanan stared at Rabbi Gamliel, waving his hand in front of him.

"General Vespasian sees our Temple as the ultimate prize. The Romans will soon capture the Temple wealth. Our sacrifices will finance the armies of Rome."

Dizzy and faint from hunger, Rabbi Jochanan gestured to his students, Rabbi Yehoshua and Rabbi Eliezer. They rose and escorted him home through the empty streets of Jerusalem.

The rabbi and his two students entered the rabbi's home. The rabbi sank wearily onto a small couch.

"I cannot wait, powerless, for death to overtake me. My pleas to *adonai* for peace have gone unanswered. If we are to survive, to study Torah and live in this land, I have no choice but to make a plea to the one who holds the fate of our nation in his hands."

"But the Zealots have forbidden anyone to communicate with the Romans or leave the city," Rabbi Yehoshua said. "How will you do this, Rabbi?"

"There is only one reason why the Zealots will open the gates of the city, and I will give them that reason," Rabbi Jochanan answered. "Prepare. We will leave tomorrow evening."

The next day, news spread through Jerusalem that Rabbi Jochanan ben Zakkai had died in his sleep. Many of the starving population envied him. By late afternoon, the Zealot guard was almost too weak to open the gates of the city for the rabbi's two students and the cart carrying his coffin.

Flavius Vespasian, commander of the Roman Army in Judea, stood on the Mount of Olives overlooking the city of Jerusalem. Five years before, Emperor Nero had sent him to quell the local uprising in Judea. Vespasian had spent the first two years crushing the revolt in the northern towns of the Galilee. For the past three years, the siege of Jerusalem had been a respite from the fierce fighting in the north. While Vespasian fought the Judeans, Nero committed suicide, and five more emperors had ruled Rome.

Vespasian thought that these Judeans were a strange people. They did not live in forests like barbarians, nor were they by nature a warring people. They were farmers, merchants, artisans, and city dwellers. Many of them spoke Greek, having lived for centuries under Greek rulers after Alexander. They were highly educated and lived in a system of law. Even so, they had rejected the *Pax Romanus*, the peace and order that the Roman system had brought to the rest of the world.

Every evening, since he had laid siege to the city, Vespasian left the camp of the Tenth Legion on the summit of the Mount of Olives and looked down upon the Judean Temple. The Temple rose white and gold from a huge platform, soaring into the sky, catching the rising and setting sun. The Romans had methodically denuded the hillsides of trees for miles around, stripping the walled city of any hiding place or cover for anyone entering or leaving the city. As the food supplies gave out, the population began to die. During the night, those who had not starved to death the day before threw the bodies of those who had from the city walls into the valleys below.

This evening, an hour before sunset, Vespasian watched two men lead a donkey pulling a cart carrying a coffin up the Mount of Olives. No doubt, the coffin contained the body of a starved inhabitant, someone important enough for burial. Vespasian walked back to his tent where his meal was waiting for him. He left a centurion standing at the edge of the mount, keeping an eye on the procession below.

Inside the coffin, Rabbi Jochanan ben Zakkai was lying on his back, praying. The vibrations of the carriage wheels on the rocky trail rocked him from side to side. He could feel himself tilting backward as the trail sloped upward. He hoped that the donkey pulling the carriage was strong enough to reach the summit.

Rabbi Yehoshua and Rabbi Eliezer, thin and gaunt from gnawing hunger, walked beside the donkey cart. As they climbed higher, the wind cleansed their nostrils of the stench of death below and tortured their starving stomachs with the smell of roasting meat from the Roman camp above. They passed the first section of graves and continued, wondering how long it would be before the Roman guards sounded the alarm.

The bored centurion leaned on his lance, watching and waiting for the cart to stop and deposit its load. The donkey strained, whining and grunting, as it passed the last section of the cemetery before the summit. The rabbis urged the donkey forward, toward the entrance of the Roman camp at the top of the mount. Finally, the centurion reacted, walking slowly down the mount to meet the rabbis. He did not bother to point his lance at the starving skeletons, but stood in the middle of the narrow trail, forcing the cart to a halt.

Rabbi Eliezer bowed in greeting, speaking Latin.

"We must see Vespasian."

The centurion shrugged. He had been instructed to allow any communication from the city from whatever source. Any intelligence was better than no intelligence, but he was not in a hurry.

"You can't take that coffin into the camp."

The rabbis nodded and guided the donkey and the cart off the trail. The donkey stood exhausted, bending its head to eat a few blades of grass. Feeling confident that they could not be seen from the city below, the rabbis raised the lid of the coffin. Rabbi Jochanan ben Zakkai slowly sat up from the confines of the coffin. The two younger men helped him out, and he stood shakily before the centurion, speaking in Latin.

"We must see Vespasian."

The authority in the old man's voice startled the centurion. The centurion pointed toward the entrance of the camp and motioned the three men to follow him.

Vespasian sat in front of his command tent, carving strips of roasted flesh from a large pig spitted above an open fire. The centurion approached with the three men behind him.

"General, these men have asked to speak with you. This one"—he pointed to the older man—"was in the coffin you saw coming up the mount."

Vespasian chewed on the pig flesh and squinted past the flames at the men. He focused on the man from the coffin. Despite the old man's appearance, Vespasian recognized him immediately as a member of the Sanhedrin. He had met this man several years ago, in the delegation that had asked the Romans to allow burial in the cemetery on the Mount of Olives. Vespasian spoke in a welcoming tone.

"Rabbi Jochanan ben Zakkai. We have raised you from the dead? You and your friends should sit and eat with me."

The rabbi's face blanched as he looked at the spitted carcass roasting in front of him.

Vespasian knew well that pig flesh was forbidden to these Judeans. He could understand why a people could worship a God with no earthly form, but how could they reject succulent, tasty pig flesh? He wiped the grease from his chin and took another bite from the chunk of meat on the tip of his knife.

Rabbi Jochanan stood at attention, his eyes sunken in his thin face, with his two companions on either side. He made no move to sit down.

Vespasian put down his knife and rose. He towered above the three rabbis. None of them spoke. He was becoming impatient.

"Why the funeral procession, Rabbi?"

Rabbi Jochanan looked into Vespasian's eyes and spoke.

"Many believe that we are in a struggle to the death, and there should be no discourse with the enemy. Only the dead and those who bury them are allowed outside the city walls."

Vespasian turned to the centurion.

"Bring our dead friend and his burial party fresh water and bread."

The centurion left them and walked into the center of the camp to the food wagons. Vespasian knew that the Judeans would not eat his meat, but they would not refuse water and flour.

Rabbi Jochanan continued.

"I am tired of the starvation and death. The defenders of the city will not surrender. I have come to ask a favor of the Emperor Vespasian."

Vespasian was startled.

"You must be ravenous from hunger, Rabbi. Emperor Vitellius reigns in Rome. I am not the emperor."

The rabbi shook his head and pointed at Vespasian.

"I know that in the final battle, our Temple will be destroyed. Our prophets tell us that our Holy Temple will only fall by the hands of a king. So you will soon be the king who will seal its fate."

As Vespasian was speaking with Rabbi Jochanan, a messenger arrived at the camp. The young soldier dismounted from his horse, and the guards at the perimeter of the camp escorted him to Vespasian's tent. The centurion had returned with water and bread. The three rabbis sat with Vespasian, trying to eat slowly while their hunger burned. Vespasian rose to meet the messenger, while the rabbis continued to eat.

The messenger saluted Vespasian and unrolled a scroll. This was unusual, as most messengers delivered verbal messages containing news of recent battles fought by Roman legions in the vicinity. Vespasian motioned him toward the fire so he could read by the light.

The messenger read from the scroll.

"Hail Emperor Vespasian. Emperor Vitellius is dead. Long live Emperor Vespasian and the empire."

Vespasian's jaw dropped.

The remainder of the message contained details of events in Rome, including the murder of Emperor Vitellius by Roman legions loyal to Vespasian and the declaration of loyalty by the legions to Vespasian as emperor.

Vespasian turned to Rabbi Jochanan.

"You seem to have a grasp on what the future will bring. What is the favor that you would ask from me? I cannot save Jerusalem from its doom."

Rabbi Jochanan rose, his hunger sated momentarily by the Roman bread.

"I have one favor that is certainly within the power of the emperor to grant."

Rabbi Yehoshua and Rabbi Eliezer rose to stand next to their elder. Rabbi Jochanan spread his arms in front of Vespasian.

"I ask that you spare me and all of my students who survive the destruction of Jerusalem to establish an academy of study in the city of Yabneh. We will not fight against the power of Rome."

Vespasian almost laughed.

"An academy? To study? What will you study when we destroy your Temple and the city that you hold so dear?"

Rabbi Jochanan responded swiftly in a strong voice.

"We will study how to live according to our own laws, regardless of who rules the world."

Vespasian shrugged. These starving people lived in a world of dreams.

"You may have your academy. Rome will rule forever."

The sun was setting as the three rabbis walked back to the summit of the Mount of Olives. Rabbi Yehoshua carried a bucket of water and a bag of grain to feed the donkey. Rabbi Eliezer dumped the empty coffin on the ground. They unhitched the donkey from the cart, and, strengthened by the Roman bread, gazed below at Jerusalem for the last time. As the sun sank below the horizon, its last rays struck the golden roof of the Temple.

Rabbi Jochanan stood with Rabbi Eliezer to his right and Rabbi Yehoshua to his left, waiting. Rabbi Eliezer, sensing his teacher's calm, could not understand why they tarried.

"We should go, Rabbi."

Rabbi Jochanan pointed to the sky. They stood for half an hour, until the full moon rose. Rabbi Jochanan raised his hands in front of him, with his right hand blocking the Fortress Antonia—where the Zealots had barricaded themselves—from sight. He framed the Temple between his hands, and cried, *"If I forget you, O Jerusalem, let my right hand wither."*

Vespasian had ordered his soldiers to let Rabbi Jochanan and his two companions pass through the camp and travel along the road that led south. The donkey loped slowly through the camp. Rabbi Jochanan bent forward with his arms around the donkey's neck. The two younger rabbis walked by its side.

Vespasian went immediately to his tent and ordered his personal guards to saddle his horse. His son, Titus, second in command, was waiting in the tent; Titus embraced him warmly.

"Hail Emperor Vespasian!"

Vespasian basked in the praise of his son and his personal guards. He put his arm around his son and gave him specific instructions about the siege of Jerusalem.

"I have granted a request from a member of the Sanhedrin, Rabbi Jochanan ben Zakkai. He has escaped with his life to Yabneh, to start an academy for study.

He knows that we will soon prevail. When the time comes, and the city's inhabitants are too weak to defend it, destroy the city but leave the Temple standing. Send me the contents of the Temple, disperse the population throughout the empire, and send the strongest of the captured fighters to Rome as slaves. The rabbi can study with any who escape to Yabneh."

Titus laughed. He had seen the old man on the starving donkey pass through the camp with his two companions. They had been smart to flee from the power of Rome. To found a school was as good an excuse as any for saving their skins.

Titus helped Vespasian strap on his leather armor and mount his horse. Father and son saluted each other.

"The city is yours to conquer, but save the Temple for Jupiter, my son."

"May Jupiter and Mercury guide your path swiftly to Rome, my father."

Vespasian urged his horse through the camp and onto the road leading south. Within minutes, he saw the donkey loping ahead, with Rabbi Jochanan riding and the two students walking by his side. Without slowing his horse, Vespasian hurtled past them. The rabbis did not look up, nor did Vespasian acknowledge them.

Titus was ecstatic. His father was emperor, and the conquest of Jerusalem was inevitable. The Tenth Legion remained camped on the Mount of Olives to the east of the city, and three more legions arrived soon after Vespasian's departure. The Fifth, Twelfth, and Fifteenth Legions camped to the west, raising the fear of the Judeans to utter despair.

Rabbi Jochanan and his two companions were the last to escape the city before the destruction. With four Roman legions camping outside the walls, escape was impossible. For the next nine months, Titus regularly sent messengers within earshot of the walls to proclaim an opportunity for the inhabitants to surrender, but he received no response. After each messenger returned, Titus was not surprised and secretly delighted. He wanted nothing less than to rid the city of rebels, to return to Rome in triumph, and to live out his days as a member of the ruling family. If the treasure and slaves he brought back from Jerusalem were great enough, he might even become emperor himself when his father died.

The siege was a waiting game, but ultimately the city would have to be taken. As the time to assault grew closer, fear circulated through the camps of the four legions. Unlike the Romans, these Judeans only worshipped one god, and word passed from soldier to soldier that the Judeans' god was all-powerful. This god had whispered laws to a man who had stood on a mountain in the midst of thunder and lightning. The man had returned unharmed after carving the laws on two tablets. The Roman soldiers feared that this god would defeat any enemy that came against his holy city.

The Temple stood gleaming in the sunlight, its walls white and its roof covered with gold. The Roman soldiers never saw a bird on the roof of the Temple. Whatever mysterious power could keep birds from alighting on the Temple would surely protect it from the Roman arrows.

When Titus heard of his soldiers' fears, he called the generals from the four legions to his tent. He swept his hand across the horizon, pointing to the Temple and the walled city in the distance.

"Tell your legions they have nothing to fear. I have consulted our camp historian. He tells me that the kingdom of Babylonia destroyed Jerusalem five centuries ago, burning the Temple to the ground and sending the Judeans into exile. Even though the Judeans were allowed to return and rebuild their city and their Temple, nothing will stop us from destroying it again."

One of the generals spoke in a hesitant voice.

"But the birds, the birds . . ."

Titus looked at him, anger welling in his eyes.

"What about the birds?"

The general looked down, afraid to look Titus in the eyes.

"The men say that the birds never —"

Titus stopped him with a wave of his hand.

"The birds never land on the Temple? Is that what bothers our men?"

The general nodded.

Titus laughed.

"The Judeans have placed one million golden pins on the roof to protect the Temple from birds. We are not birds. We are the might of Rome."

Titus signaled his legions to begin the assault on Jerusalem. The Judeans watched in horror as the soldiers built great earth ramps to support assault towers and battering rams.

The Roman legionnaires worked in shifts. Those who were not constructing the ramps drilled constantly in formation in the valleys surrounding the city, chanting a mysterious word repeatedly, in time to their marching feet.

"Hep, hep, hep, hep, hep."

Once the earth ramps were in place, the fighting began. In the heat of the Roman month of Iulius, and the Jewish month of Tammuz, the Romans breached the walls and poured into the city, fighting hand to hand in every street and alley. Their primary goal was to retake Fortress Antonia, which loomed to the north of the Temple. After the Romans annihilated the Zealots holding the fortress, they used the fortress as a staging ground for attacks on the city and the Temple. They slaughtered the inhabitants who resisted. They captured the remaining inhabitants and delivered them outside the city walls to be sold as slaves.

In the Roman month of Augustus and Jewish month of Av, in the final days of battle, the remaining defenders retreated into the compound that surrounded the Temple. Titus himself stood before the gates of the Temple, speaking into a hollow bull's horn.

"I am Titus Flavianus, commander of the armies of Rome, son of the Emperor Vespasian. Your nameless, faceless god cannot save you. Surrender your Temple and you will live. Continue to fight and you will die."

Titus truly hoped for surrender. He did not wish to slaughter these brave fighters who would make excellent slaves. His father had commanded him to save the Temple, as Vespasian wanted Titus to dedicate the snowy, golden-topped building as a temple to Jupiter.

The gates to the Temple remained closed. Titus turned to his soldiers, raised his sword, and shouted, "*Hep.*"

The legionnaires immediately began their drilling chant, which wafted over the burning city and over the Temple gates.

"*Hep, hep, hep, hep . . .*"

The defenders locked inside the Temple puzzled at the meaning of the chant, which they had heard for weeks as the legions had drilled outside their walls. They did not know that it symbolized a promise that would be fulfilled that very day.

It was the ninth day of the Jewish month of Av. On this same day of the Jewish calendar five hundred years before, King Nebuchadnezzar of Babylonia had destroyed Jerusalem and the Temple built by Solomon.

Now, Titus gave the signal to the Tenth Legion to set
fire to the gates of the Temple. Within an hour, the
gates had burned through, and the Tenth Legion
stormed into the courtyard of the Temple, slaying its
defenders. Then, unexpectedly, a steady wind whipped
the fires out of control, and the flames consumed the
Temple.

Rabbi Jochanan ben Zakkai sat in the heat of the
evening in front of his cottage, hoping the breeze
from the Middle Sea would soon reach Yabneh and
cool the night. His eyes were weary from studying
his Torah scroll. Tonight, before the sun set, he had
read the portion of the Book of the Levites that
described the sacrifices. As he reached to extinguish
his candle, Rabbi Eliezer entered the cottage with a
young man.

"Rabbi, Reuven has escaped from Jerusalem."

Reuven's face was covered with dirt and tears. He
hung his head and looked at the floor. The words of
defeat choked in his throat.

"Rome has conquered. The entire city is destroyed.
The night sky in Jerusalem is as bright as day."

Rabbi Jochanan cradled the Torah scroll to his chest
and whispered, "The Temple?"

"Consumed by fire."

Reuven reached into his shoulder bag and removed
a stone. He dropped it on the table in front of the
rabbi. Rabbi Jochanan looked up, his face wet with
tears.

"The Roman Legions pried the stones of the Temple
apart to its very foundation, searching for the remnants
of the Temple treasury that melted in the fire," Reuven
said. "They drove the Zealots from the Fortress Antonia
and leveled it. The rest of the city is devastated.

Thousands are dead. The strongest who survived will be sent as slaves to Rome."

The rabbi reached for the stone on the table. He picked it up, clutched it to his chest, and wept.

Ten days later, Emperor Vespasian was enjoying dinner in his palace in Rome with his mistress Caenis when his steward ushered a messenger into the dining room. The steward was apologetic.

"Titus sent him. The messenger demanded to deliver his message immediately."

The messenger seemed uncomfortable. Vespasian urged him to speak.

"I have come from Judea, ordered by General Titus to deliver to you a single word."

Vespasian raised his eyebrow in anticipation.

The messenger raised his hand in salute and shouted loudly, "*Hep!*"

Vespasian clapped his hands and laughed. Caenis looked at him in amusement.

"And what is the meaning of this message from your son?"

Vespasian laughed again.

"I used to play a game with him as a child when he was learning to read. I would give him the first letters of a phrase, and he would have to guess the words they stood for. Now, he is doing it to me."

Caenis frowned.

"You are playing a game?"

"No. The night before I left Judea, he made me a promise. He is telling me he has kept that promise."

"And do I have to guess what the promise was, or will you tell me?"

"No, you don't have to guess."

Vespasian raised his wine glass.

"*Heirosylma est perdita.*" Jerusalem is fallen.

Monday, April 24, 2017

Rabbi Avidan paused in his testimony and reached for a glass of water. Meir leaned back in his chair and took a deep breath. The interview summary he had read had contained the bare structure of the testimony. It had described the rabbi's expertise, his ancestry, and his familial memory transmitted over the centuries. Nothing had prepared Meir for the sheer force of the rabbi's personality and ability to transmit information. Meir had been mesmerized, as if he had been a witness to the final days of Jerusalem and the Temple. As the rabbi stopped speaking, Meir returned to the present. The courtroom came back into focus.

Prime Minister Zadok continued.

"Rabbi, on the night you met with Rabbi Goren and Moshe Dayan on the Temple Mount, you told them what you just told us?"

Rabbi Avidan nodded.

"Yes. I have told the court the same story in much more detail."

"Mr. Eitan was there. I am sure he remembers."

Zadok turned again to the rabbi.

"And was this all you told them?"

"No. I also told them about my other ancestors. While Rabbi Jochanan ben Zakkai was a witness to the destruction of Jerusalem and the dispersion of the Jews, my other ancestors were fortunate to return after the Muslim conquest of Jerusalem almost six hundred years later."

"So there is more to this story?"

"Much more. But there was another person at the Temple Mount that night who should tell his story first. I don't know if I am at liberty to reveal to you who he is."

Zadok looked at Meir.

"Justice Bar-Aben, you've read the summaries of the witness interviews. That person is the witness who will testify this afternoon."

Amos stood at his seat.

"Yes. I am going to pick him up and bring him here."

Meir reached for his gavel.

"It's eleven thirty. Let's adjourn until one," Meir said.

He banged the gavel and rose from his chair.

Chapter 35

As the Zion Baptist Temple tour bus reached the outskirts of Jerusalem, Avi shifted the bus into low gear to begin the hilly ascent into the city. The members of the tour group had long since given up hope of seeing pastoral biblical scenes. The bus climbed higher, and they marveled at the modern apartment buildings that ringed the surrounding hillsides.

Reverend Crosby made an announcement over the PA system.

"If you are sleeping, wake up! We are arriving in Jerusalem."

Aaron woke up. He knew they would be at the hotel soon. As the bus turned onto Jaffa Road, Amy pressed her face to the window and stared into another place and time. She saw Meah Shaerim, the neighborhood of One Hundred Gates and the ultra-Orthodox. She had first seen the bearded, black-coated Orthodox men on the flight. Now, despite the heat of the Middle Eastern summer, the men wore the long black coats and fur-trimmed hats, as if they were still living in the winter snows of Eastern Europe. Young boys wearing small black caps, black pants, and long-sleeved shirts ran through the streets. Women in ankle-length dresses and scarves covering their heads drifted along.

Amy could see a large sign in English and other languages stretched over one of the narrow streets.

"Daughters of Israel. The Torah commands you to dress modestly."

The signs on the shops were written in what she assumed was Hebrew. Soon the bus turned south, and the population changed. People in casual clothes strolled down King George Street. Many were dressed in shorts and tee shirts. Some of the boys and young men wore small black caps, but most were clean shaven.

In a few minutes, the bus turned east and dipped into a valley. Reverend Crosby grabbed the microphone again.

"We're passing through the new part of Jerusalem. If you look to your right in a minute, you will see the Old City, where Jesus walked."

Soon the walls of the Old City came into view. Amy recognized the gold Dome of the Rock—prominently floating above the walls—from the slide show that she had seen in church when she had signed up for the trip. The bus cruised past the walls of the Old City and began ascending the Mount of Olives.

The Hotel of the Seven Arches commands a sweeping view of the Old City from the Mount of Olives, where the Roman Tenth Legion had camped before the destruction of Jerusalem. It was here that Vespasian and the Roman centurion stood the evening Rabbi Jochanan ben Zakkai and his two students escaped from the city.

Yair, a professional tour guide, stood at a podium at the main entrance. At 11:15 a.m., he heard the deep growl of a large vehicle in low gear, and soon he saw the Zion Baptist Temple's bus crest the hill. His friend Avi had radioed ahead. Avi's back was killing him. He had offered Yair a third of the tips he had collected when he loaded the luggage if Yair would help him unload.

Aaron had dozed off in the last few minutes. He sat with his head on Amy's shoulder and his eyes closed. As the bus approached the hotel, Avi pulled off the road

onto a point overlooking the Old City. Reverend
Crosby stood up without the microphone.

"We're right across the street from our hotel. Let's
get out and enjoy the view."

Aaron opened his eyes and raised his head.

"Wake up, sleepy head." Amy's lilting voice had
developed a soft croon.

Aaron reached to the floor and picked up his
backpack. He turned and grabbed his roller bag that he
had placed on the empty seat behind them.

As they got off the bus, Reverend Crosby waved
everyone into a circle around him. He pointed down the
valley toward the Old City.

"Folks, we are almost standing where Jesus stood
the night before he was crucified. Look down there.
That is the Garden of Gethsemane, where he prayed and
sweated blood."

The group leaned forward and looked down below.

"You can see the domes of the two Arab mosques,
the gold and the silver ones. The blue one with the gold
dome stands right where the Jewish Temple stood,
where Jesus threw out those evil money lenders."

The group nodded in approval. Aaron pulled his
baseball cap down lower over his forehead.

"And right here, where we are standing on the
Mount of Olives, is where our New Testament says that
Jesus will descend from heaven and his feet will touch
the earth when he comes again in his glory."

"Amen, amen!" the group shouted.

"But we know that he won't come until the antichrist
returns and crowns himself in the Temple that the Jew
will rebuild."

Joe Mason raised his hand.

"Reverend Crosby, how can that be? How will the
Jew rebuild the Temple when the Arabs have what

looks like a pretty important mosque sitting right there?"

"Who knows? We heard about that old Wailing Wall collapsing. Maybe the next thing that collapses will be that mosque. Then they can have a war, Israel can take over the whole area, and the Jew can rebuild the Temple."

Many in the group nodded, as if this was an acceptable solution.

Aaron felt queasy. He knew that many evangelical Christians believed that a devastating Arab-Israeli war would set the stage for the rebuilding of the Temple and the return of Christ. It was one thing to hear such a prediction espoused on Cable TV. It was another to stand on the Mount of Olives with people who actually hoped it would happen.

Reverend Crosby continued, "I've heard that there is a group right here in Jerusalem training young men to serve as priests in the Temple when it is rebuilt. They are learning to perform the sacrifices, too."

Amy leaned closer to Aaron, her eyes wide with excitement.

"Is it true, Aaron? Are the Jews planning to rebuild the Temple?"

Aaron whispered to her, "Amy, *the* Jews aren't planning anything. *Some* Jews might be thinking about it. There hasn't been animal sacrifice since the destruction of the Temple almost two thousand years ago."

"But Reverend Crosby just said they are learning to do it again. That's very exciting."

Aaron nodded, but was silent.

Avi drove the bus over to the front of the hotel while the group stood at the overlook. He and Yair began unloading the luggage onto carts. Avi handed Yair a wad of bills.

"Here's your share of the tips. Some of them tipped me again when they got off the bus, but it's not much."

Yair stuffed the bills into his pocket.

The Zion Baptist Temple members began drifting across the road to the hotel. Aaron walked with Amy to the hotel entrance.

"Thanks for arranging the ride on the bus, Amy. It has been nice traveling with you. I have an appointment at one o'clock, so I need to get going."

"Do you have plans this evening, Aaron?" Amy asked.

"Well, no. I don't."

"Why don't you come back here? We could have dinner."

Aaron paused.

"Aren't you having dinner with the group?"

Amy shrugged.

"We can opt out of group meals at any time. We just have to stay together on the tours."

Aaron thought for a moment.

"My grandmother doesn't know I am here, so she isn't expecting me. I suppose I could come back for dinner."

"That would be great, Aaron," Amy said. "Call me in my room. I'll be waiting."

She turned and walked into the hotel.

Aaron saw the bus driver and another man leaning against the bus. As Aaron approached, Avi noticed Aaron's red cap. He perked up, hoping another tip was coming his way.

"Avi, maybe you or your friend can help me."

"What can I do for you, sir?"

"I need to go to the Israel Museum."

"I have to drive the bus soon," Avi said. "My friend Yair can help you, I'm sure."

"Sure," Yair said. "Are you ready to go now?"

"I'm going into the hotel to change my shirt. I'll be out in a few minutes," Aaron said.

"That's my white Mercedes, sir," Yair said, pointing to his car across the road. "Meet me there."

Aaron went into the lobby and found the restroom. He entered a toilet stall and put on a clean polo shirt he had in his knapsack. He came out of the toilet stall with his Zion Baptist Temple baseball cap in his hand. He put it on the counter next to the sink and splashed water on his face.

"Hey, man. Are you a Zebe?"

Aaron swung around to find a sixty-ish American male standing behind him.

"Your hat, man. It has ZBT on it. That's Zeta Beta Tau, my fraternity in college."

Aaron picked up his cap and smiled.

"So, another Zebe, huh. What's your name?" Aaron asked.

"Sam Stein. Syracuse, class of 1982. I'm here on a synagogue trip."

"Well, Sam, this is your lucky day. Try it on."

He handed the cap to Sam, who eagerly scrunched it over his head and looked at himself in the mirror.

"Perfect fit, Sam," Aaron said as he slapped Sam on the back.

Sam turned around and held out his hand.

"Thanks, man. This is great."

"Don't mention it."

Aaron left the restroom. He could see several from the Zion Baptist Temple group in the lobby. He wished he could stick around to see Sam come out and greet his new fraternity brothers.

Aaron came out of the hotel and walked toward Yair's Mercedes. He looked at his watch and saw that it was

11:45 a.m. He had plenty of time to make the delivery to the Israel Museum by one o'clock.

Agent Tzion drove up the hill and spotted Aaron crossing the parking lot. He drove toward Aaron and stopped his car. He got out and approached Aaron.

"Mr. Aaron Kragen?" he asked.

Aaron nodded.

Agent Tzion showed him his ID card.

"You have a delivery for Mr. Aitza at the museum?"

"Yes. But —"

"You need to come with me."

Aaron looked across the parking lot. Yair was watching.

"Sir, I just hired someone to take me to the museum. I need to speak to him and cancel. He's standing over there."

"You may," Agent Tzion said. "But be quick."

Aaron walked over to Yair.

"Yair, I'm sorry. My friend just arrived, and he is going to take me to Jerusalem."

Yair shrugged.

"Maybe another time," Yair said, reaching into his pocket. "Here's my card. I'm a professional tour guide."

Aaron slipped Yair's card into his pocket.

"Thanks, Yair."

Chapter 36

Monday, April 24, 2017

The sky was a cloudless blue, and the midday sun caressed Samir's face. He cupped his right hand next to his mouth and his left hand over his ear, so he could hear his own voice as he chanted the call to prayer. He thought of the Prophet's slave, Bilal, the first to issue the call to prayer. Bilal had a dream, in the earliest days of Islam, when the Jews of the city of Medina used a ram's horn and the followers of Isa used a paddle with a clapper to call their faithful to prayer. In his dream, Bilal saw a Muslim walking down the street, calling his fellow Muslims to prayer with a loud, clear voice. When he woke, he knew that was the way to announce the time of prayer.

Samir felt that he was part of an unbroken chain from Bilal to the present, and yet he knew that over time, changes occurred. When Muslims constructed minarets on mosques, the *muadhin* would climb the minaret to deliver the *adhan,* rather than stroll through the street. Today, Jews no longer use the ram's horn, except on their holiest days, and the Christians' paddle and clapper have long since turned into bells. He wondered if more changes would happen soon.

Yesterday morning, the *yahudi* had been waiting for Samir again at the entrance to the Noble Sanctuary.

The *yahudi* got right to the point.

"Are you nervous?"

"You were there when I spoke with the prime minister. Did I seem nervous then?"

"No. But you also told him you had more to tell him at the hearing than you would tell him that day."

"Do you think they will tell me the purpose of the hearing?"

Amos shrugged.

"My guess is that you will find out tomorrow."

Amos put his arm on Samir's shoulder.

"Samir, tomorrow afternoon, you will go to the Supreme Court. I will meet you here and take you where you need to be."

Samir nodded. There was nothing else to say. The *yahudi* turned and walked away.

As he exited the Noble Sanctuary shortly after noon today, Samir saw the *yahudi* waiting to take him to the Supreme Court.

Samir felt calm. He believed what his father had told him, and what his grandfather had told his father, all the way back to the time of his ancestor who had come out of Arabia to this holy city. He would tell what he had always known, and he would return and climb the minaret until the end of his days, *in sha allah*. God willing.

Meir lay on his couch in his chambers, his eyes closed. He had eaten a light lunch that Ruth had brought from the dining hall, and he was listening to a recording of Yehudi Menuhin playing Tartini's *Devil's Trill*. He had five minutes before he had to return for the afternoon session. His private line rang. He knew it would be Channah.

"How is your day going?" she asked.

"Interesting, interesting. That's about all I can say. I may be late."

Channah hung up and left her apartment. She walked across the street to hail a taxi. Zara stood on the corner and watched Channah walk past her so close she could have reached out and touched her. Channah made eye contact and smiled. Zara froze and caught her breath.

A taxi pulled over and Channah got in.

"*allah hu akbar*," Zara whispered.

Amran waited in the basement for the hearing to resume. His phone rang and he answered, "Amran here."

It was Agent Aleph.

"The wife walked right past her. The girl didn't make a move."

"How close?"

"As close as you could get."

"I am going to call the prime minister. She is getting too close," Amran said.

Amos and Samir exited the basement elevator. Amran led them to the door of the courtroom corridor. Meir was standing at the door to the courtroom. Meir introduced himself. "I am Justice Meir Bar-Aben. A pleasure to meet you, Mr. ibn Abdullah."

Amos translated into Arabic for Samir. Samir grasped Meir's hand and shook it firmly. Samir was impressed by the man in the long black robe—*al faizal*, the judge.

They entered the courtroom. Samir thought the courtroom was beautiful. The designs on the walls appeared Muslim rather than Jewish to Samir.

Rabbi Avidan came forward with an extended hand and a smile.

"It has been quite a while, Mr. ibn Abdullah. I am Rabbi Avidan."

Samir nodded and smiled back.

"Rabbi Avidan, of course.We seem to meet under unusual circumstances."

Amos translated again.

Prime Minister Zadok and Eli Heifitz introduced themselves. Samir shook their hands and said, "I am certainly in distinguished company today."

Meir gestured to all of them.

"We are ready to begin."

Samir stood next to the witness chair while Meir administered an Islamic oath. He then sat and waited. Amos sat in a chair next to Samir. Prime Minister Zadok resumed his place at the podium.

"Good afternoon, Mr. ibn Abdullah. We met before when I interviewed you in my office. Mr. Eitan will translate my questions and your responses."

Amos translated and Samir responded.

"Yes, Mr. Prime Minister."

Zadok began his questioning.

"Please state your name, sir."

Samir answered in a clear, melodious voice.

"I am Samir ibn Abdullah."

"Where do you live?"

"I have lived all my life on Sharia al-Wad in the city of al-Quds."

"That is in the Muslim Quarter of the Old City of Jerusalem?"

"Yes."

"What is your occupation?"

"I own a shop in the Muslim Quarter. And I am the *muadhin* of al-Aqsa Mosque every Monday."

"Can you explain to us what a *muadhin* does?"

"The *adhan* is the Muslim call to prayer. The *muadhin* is the person who calls the faithful to prayer."

"And when did you become the *muadhin*?"

"In 1965, when I was twenty-eight years old."

"Were there days when you were prevented from giving the call to prayer?"

"During the war in 1967."

"What happened during that time?"

"The Israelis controlled the Noble Sanctuary for several days. We were not allowed to pray there. I was afraid the Israelis would destroy the Dome of the Rock and al-Aqsa Mosque."

"What did you do?"

"I left my house in the evening of the day they captured the Noble Sanctuary. I went there. I met with the Israelis and told them why they should not blow up the Muslim holy places."

"With whom did you speak?"

"Moshe Dayan, the army rabbi, and Rabbi Avidan. Mr. Eitan was there also."

"Can you tell the court what you told them that night?"

Samir spoke slowly and evenly.

"I told them what has been handed down in my family from the day my people captured al-Quds from the Christians shortly after the death of the prophet Muhammad. Peace be upon him."

Meir leaned forward and interrupted the prime minister.

"Mr. ibn Abdullah, it would please the court if you would tell us what you spoke about that night."

"I will, Justice Bar-Aben. But, first, would it be possible for you tell me what this proceeding is about?"

"The prime minister has not advised you of the purpose of the proceeding?"

"No. He interviewed me, and he cautioned me not to tell anyone that I had been interviewed or that I would be testifying, but he did not tell me the purpose of the hearing."

Meir looked at Zadok.

"Mr. Prime Minister, would you please advise Mr. ibn Abdullah as to the purpose of the proceedings."

"Yes. This proceeding is to determine whether the State of Israel will take back the administration of the Temple Mount from the Waqf."

Samir nodded.

"It seems we are back to where we were the night of the war," Samir said.

"It appears that way, Mr. ibn Abdullah. An apt analogy," Meir said, smiling at Samir.

"Should I continue?" Samir asked.

"Please," Meir said. "If there is any additional information you wish to tell the court that you believe will be helpful, please take your time and explain."

Samir nodded.

"I will tell you everything I know, more than I told that night on the Noble Sanctuary."

Samir began speaking in a voice that had the cadence of poetry. Amos translated when Samir paused. Again, those in the courtroom found themselves swept into the past.

Chapter 37

Five hundred and sixty-four years after the Romans destroyed Jerusalem and the Temple, Sophronius, the Patriarch of Jerusalem, stood on the Mount of Olives and breathed the morning air. He was seventy-four years old in his first year as patriarch, and he felt firm and strong. He attributed his state of health to the clean air of the city and his ascetic life.

He spent his days in peace, embracing the rituals of the Byzantine church. He woke each day before sunrise and climbed to the summit of the Mount of Olives. As the sun rose and illuminated Jerusalem below, he gazed on the dome of the Church of the Resurrection, the Anastasis.

Sophronius resolved that he would not leave the walls of Jerusalem again, except to follow in the footsteps of the Savior. He walked where the Savior had walked, and he contemplated the sunrise every morning from where the Savior had sweated blood in his final hours. He lived in sparse quarters in the Anastasis, built over the hill of Golgotha, where the Savior had suffered and vanquished the fear of death for all who believed in the resurrection.

Once a year, Sophronius would walk to Bethlehem to celebrate the birth of the Savior. The entire world that he knew worshipped the Savior, except for the few remaining Judeans in the countryside who remained as witnesses to their horrible, murderous crime. It had seemed that Sophronius would live out his life in this city and finally meet his Savior in peace at the end of his days. He did not realize that soon a sense of disquiet would appear in his peaceful world.

Several days later, Sophronius had just finished evening prayers when the emperor's messenger, Septimius, arrived with news from the eastern borders, as he did every month. Sophronius invited him into the courtyard garden of the Anastasis for dates and wine. Septimius appeared agitated, and he quickly reached for his wine goblet.

"I do not mean to cause alarm in the city, but there is a new threat from the east."

Sophronius relaxed in his chair, wondering what the new threat could be. Had not the emperor put an end, years before, to Persian aggression? Septimius placed a map on the table, and Sophronius leaned forward and attempted to appear interested.

Septimius pointed.

"Here we are. To the east is the Arabian Peninsula. A man there, an Ishmaelite, who called himself a prophet of God, said that the angel Gabriel had appeared to him. The man had many followers. Two years ago he died."

Sophronius munched on a date and wondered what difference any of this made. In Jerusalem, many claimed visitation by angels. Besides, Arabia was a wasteland. The kingdoms of Persia, Babylonia, and Egypt had ignored it since the beginning of time. Today, its inhabitants were mostly the pagan tribes descended from Abraham's banished son, Ishmael. There were also Judeans who had escaped the wrath of Rome when Titus had finally rid Jerusalem of those who had killed the Savior.

Septimius pointed again to the map. Sophronius did not bother to try to focus his eyes on it.

"This is our border with the Arab lands. After the prophet died, his followers elected a new leader. His name was Abu Bakr. He gathered an enormous army, and, in the past year, he has conquered Persia."

Sophronius nodded. He had heard of the Persian conquest but had not felt threatened. Did not the True Cross still reside in Jerusalem?

Septimius paused and breathed heavily.

"Abu Bakr is dead. The Arab tribes have united, and their armies march under the command of a new leader, Umar ibn al-Khattab. They are raiding across our borders at every opportunity. May the Savior have mercy."

The armies of Umar ibn al-Khattab moved slowly east. During the second year of Umar's reign, in the year 636 of the Christian calendar, Sophronius stood on the walls of Jerusalem in the evening. It was one month before the celebration of the Savior's birth, and he was thinking about his annual walk to Bethlehem. In the distance, he could hear what sounded like muffled thunder, but the sky was clear.

The following morning, after prayers, Sophronius altered his routine and did not climb the Mount of Olives. Instead, he stood again on the walls and looked north. A great cloud of dust hung over the horizon, and the rumbling was loud and constant. By the time the sun had set that day, the stars shone clear and bright. The night breeze brought the smell of animals and unwashed bodies wafting through the valleys surrounding the city. Everyone knew that a great army had camped not far away, and only the children, the sick, and the old slept soundly that night.

The next morning, after sunrise, Sophronius stood on the city walls with Demetrias, the commander of the

Byzantine garrison. They watched a soldier on a camel approach the city. The soldier wore a flowing headdress and robe, and had a long curved sword on his belt. He raised his hand in salute to the men on the ramparts and began speaking in Greek.

"I am Abu Ubayda ibn Jarrah, a commander in the army of Caliph Umar ibn al-Khattab. In the name of God, the merciful and compassionate, we call upon the inhabitants of the city of Aelia to surrender and open your gates. You will be allowed to live in peace and worship freely."

Sophronius eyed the soldier warily. In the second century, the Roman emperor Hadrian had subdued a revolt by the Judean rebel Bar Kochba and renamed the city "Aelia" after himself, Publius Aelius Hadrianus. Hadrian had plowed the remains of the city like a field and had undertaken a massive building project. Even after the Byzantines built the Anastasis as the center of the new Jerusalem, many still referred to the city as Aelia.

"Saracens, bastards of Abraham," Demetrias said to Sophronius. He used the Greek term *sarakenoi,* "without Sarah," the derogatory term noting that the Arabian tribes were not descended from Abraham's wife, Sarah. Sophronius, himself of Arab descent, blanched at Demetrias's remark.

Demetrias sniffed the air, still redolent with the smell of an unseen army.

"Father Sophronius, we will not negotiate with these pagan hordes who do not acknowledge the Savior."

Sophronius nodded. Demetrias cupped his hands over his mouth and bellowed.

"We will not open the gates. In the name of Christ, we will defend this Holy City." He held his sword in front of him, grasping the blade in the middle with hilt up, in the sign of the cross.

Abu Ubayda whirled his camel around and departed. Sophronius ordered Demetrias to inventory the rations of the city and prepare for a long siege.

The Arab army moved into view the next day, camping on the Mount of Olives and the surrounding hills. No one could enter or leave the city. Sophronius could not climb the Mount of Olives in the morning. When the celebration of the Savior's birth grew near, he preached a sermon beseeching God to remove the Saracen scourge so he could make his annual walk to Bethlehem. Each morning, he awoke to the smell and the distant clamor from the tents that covered the hills around the city.

While Jerusalem had its internal water supply, its store of food diminished with each passing day. The garrison of the Byzantine army could do little but fire arrows from the ramparts at the Arab scouts who ventured into the valleys below.

Despite requests to Emperor Heraclius, Jerusalem remained under siege for five months. The armies of the empire were engaged elsewhere. In April of the year 637 of the Christian calendar, Sophronius sent a messenger from the Byzantine garrison outside the walls into the camps of the caliph's army.

The guards of the camp escorted the messenger to Abu Ubayda in his tent. The messenger stood before Abu Ubayda and unrolled a scroll. Reading in Greek, he kept his eyes low, refusing to look up as he read.

"Father Sophronius requests that Abu Ubayda meet with him inside the walls of the Holy City to discuss the terms of surrender to the army of the caliph."

Abu Ubayda uttered one word.

"Tomorrow."

Jerusalem was conquered again—but without a bloodbath.

The messenger returned, followed by ten donkey carts piled with food.

The next morning Sophronius mounted a horse, rode outside the gate, and looked toward the Saracen camp. Again, as he had five months before, he saw a single camel and rider coming toward him. Abu Ubayda had no sword hanging from his belt. The camel sailed lazily to the gate, and, seemingly without a command from its rider, lowered herself on her knees and allowed her rider to dismount. She stayed on her knees, gurgling and snarling her contentment just to sit without her rider on her back.

Sophronius dismounted from his horse and approached Abu Ubayda, his hand raised in greeting. The soldier came to meet him, speaking in Arabic, and then translated into Greek.

"*assalaamu aleykum.*" Peace be with you.

Sophronius responded in Greek.

"Welcome, General. Please accompany me into the city."

A soldier came out of the gate and took charge of Sophronius's horse. Abu Ubayda's camel remained kneeling and gurgling in the sun.

Abu Ubayda began to walk along with Sophronius through the gate. He noticed soldiers of the Byzantine garrison lining the street as he and the patriarch entered. Sophronius guided Abu Ubayda toward the Anastasis, where he had a small table with refreshments set up in his courtyard garden. He was anxious to discuss the terms of the surrender, but he wanted to find out more about his adversary first.

"We appreciate the food you sent last night, General. Tell me, how is it that you speak Greek?"

"We are a tribe of merchants. To do business, it is best to speak the language of the people with whom you deal."

Abu Ubayda smiled broadly.

Sophronius smiled back.

"I have a proposal for your consideration," Abu Ubayda said.

The garden of the Anastasis was already warm from the morning sun, and birds sang in the trees. Abu Ubayda sat at the table with Sophronius, who poured wine for both of them. Abu Ubayda declined the wine, but he reached for several dates from the supplies he had sent yesterday.

"Forgive me, but the teachings of the Prophet— peace be upon him—forbid our drinking wine."

For five months, a force they did not understand had besieged Sophronius and the inhabitants of Jerusalem. Sophronius now had an opportunity to satisfy his curiosity.

"Who was the Prophet? I hear that you believe he was commanded by angels."

Abu Ubayda answered, "The Prophet's name was Muhammad, and he was a merchant, until one day when the angel Gabriel appeared to him. The angel said one word to him and left."

Abu Ubayda reached for another date and gazed up at the sky. Sophronius sipped his wine and leaned back.

"What was the word that the angel said?"

"He said, 'iqra.'"

Sophronius did not understand. This was not a Greek word.

"Gabriel spoke to Muhammad in Arabic. 'iqra' means 'recite.' Muhammad began to recite revelations from God, the same God who is the God of the Jews and the Christians. Muhammad commanded his followers to memorize, recite, and write down these revelations. After Muhammad's death, his companions collected these revelations from those who had memorized them and from written records. A group of scribes wrote down the revelations in our holy book, the Quran, the 'Recitation.'"

"And how do you live this faith?"

Abu Ubayda stroked his beard and gazed into the trees, listening to the birds singing in the early morning sun.

"We live in a community, the *ummah*, in which we surrender our entire being to God and demand that everyone treat each other with justice, equity, and compassion. Those who practice this surrender, *islam*, are known as *muslims*."

Sophronius stroked a small gold cross that he wore on a chain around his waist.

"And is it your wish that the people of Jerusalem become *muslims*?"

Abu Ubayda shook his head.

"No, we want you to become taxpayers. You can worship as you please."

Sophronius was shocked and relieved. They ate slowly, and Sophronius watched Abu Ubayda drink sparingly from a water pouch he carried with him. Sophronius finished his wine and placed the empty goblet on the table.

"General, I sent my messenger to you last night to tell you I wished to discuss the terms of the city's surrender. Tell me about your leader, Caliph Umar."

"The Prophet had many wives. Two were the daughters of his close allies, Abu Bakr and Umar ibn al-Khattab. When the Prophet died, Abu Bakr became the first successor, or *caliph*, of the Prophet, and the head of the *ummah*. When Abu Bakr died, Umar became caliph. He calls himself the Commander of the Faithful."

Sophronius rose and walked toward a row of rosebushes, motioning for Abu Ubayda to join him. Bees flew among the roses. Sophronius inhaled the roses' scent and sighed.

He turned and faced Abu Ubayda.

"If I am going to surrender this city, I will only do so when your Commander of the Faithful presents himself to me. If he is worthy to conquer Jerusalem, he must humble himself to receive this Holy City."

Chapter 38

Samir paused in his testimony and breathed deeply. He looked first at Meir, and then he turned to face Prime Minister Zadok and Rabbi Avidan.

"I, Samir ibn Abdullah, am a direct descendant of Umar ibn al-Khattab, the second caliph, Commander of the Faithful. What I have told you has been handed down in my family from generation to generation. It is based upon the knowledge of the caliph and what he was told by his general, Abu Ubayda, and the patriarch Sophronius.

The courtroom was silent. Everyone looked at Samir with reverence and respect.

Meir had read the summary of Prime Minister Zadok's interview with Samir and knew of Samir's ancestry. Amos and Rabbi Avidan had heard it that night on the Temple Mount. Even so, Samir's declaration of his family history had a profound impact.

Prime Minister Zadok looked down at his notes.

"Mr. ibn Abdullah, what was Caliph Umar's connection to the place that Muslims refer to as al-Haram as-Sharif and that the Jews call the Temple Mount?"

Samir smiled.

"I will be pleased to tell you what I know."

Samir continued speaking in his melodious Arabic, with Amos translating

When Sophronius told Abu Ubayda that he would surrender his city to a humble man, Abu Ubayda smiled to himself. Caliph Umar's ragged woolen cloak would have been the envy of any street beggar in Aelia, and yet he wore it as a badge of the austerity and simplicity of the message of the Prophet who guided his every action.

As Commander of the Faithful, he directed the movement of armies. When his armies moved, he carried his own baggage and told his officers to carry theirs. "If you cannot be responsible for your own weight, you cannot be responsible for anything else," he ordered. "You need only carry your sword, your food, and your prayer rug. More is only a burden."

Earlier that morning, Umar had been prostrate on his prayer rug on a plain in Syria, facing east toward Mecca. He thanked God for the good news he had received from Abu Ubayda's messenger the night before. Aelia was on the verge of surrender. He did not know that his presence had been demanded as a condition of surrender by the patriarch of the followers of the Christian God Jesus whom Muslims knew as the Prophet Isa.

He rose from his prayer rug and looked out onto the plain, surveying the tents of his army that stretched for almost a mile. Before becoming the caliph, Umar ibn al-Khattab had been called *al-farook*, the arbitrator, because of his persuasiveness in settling disputes among the Arab tribes. He now saw a unified army, very different from the tribes that had warred against each other for centuries. He knew in his heart that this unification had been brough forth by God's revelation to the Prophet. He felt that his appointment as caliph and his impending conquest of the city that was holy to the Sons of Israel and the Christians confirmed that Muhammad's revelation was true.

Another messenger arrived several days later, reciting Abu Ubayda's account of his meeting with Sophronius. The message concluded:

"The patriarch of the city will only surrender the city into the hands of Caliph Umar ibn al-Khattab, Commander of the Faithful, when he himself appears before the gates of Aelia."

The caliph, with his flaming red hair and quick temper, had often been compared to the Hebrew King David. The messenger kept his gaze lowered to the ground, expecting an outburst from the caliph. When silence followed, the messenger slowly raised his eyes, only to see a wistful smile on the caliph's face. The caliph remained silent for almost a minute before he spoke.

"Return to Abu Ubayda and tell him I will arrive in three days."

Umar watched as the messenger mounted his horse and rode off. He returned to his tent where his general, Tarik ibn Walid, and his advisor, Ka'ab al-Chabar, were finishing the evening meal. Umar sat and reached for a flat loaf of bread. He dipped it into a bowl of sesame oil and raised it to his mouth. He chewed and swallowed. Ka'ab was reaching for a bunch of grapes as Umar made his announcement.

"Aelia has fallen."

Ka'ab's eyes widened. "Finally. How many men did Abu Ubayda lose?"

Umar shook his head. "None. The followers of Isa could not fight on an empty stomach. They surrendered. Abu Ubayda sent them food."

"Has Abu Ubayda taken control?"

Umar shook his head.

"Their leader, the patriarch Sophronius of the followers of Isa, will only give up control to me. I must ride to Aelia tonight. Ka'ab, you will go with me. I will need you."

"Commander of the Faithful, I will saddle our horses," Ka'ab said.

Umar put his hand on Ka'ab's shoulder.

"Ka'ab, you are a wonderful advisor, but a miserable horseman. There is no time to waste. Tonight, you will ride with me."

Ka'ab mounted Umar's horse in front of Umar. Umar reached his arms around Ka'ab and grasped the reins.

"Don't go to sleep, Ka'ab," Umar warned. "If you do, you will pull me off the horse."

They rode through the night under a full moon. Umar's heart felt as if it would burst. Did it not say in the Quran that Muhammad himself had made a mysterious night journey on his winged creature, al-Buraq, from Mecca to the farthest place of worship, and then he ascended to heaven? Umar urged his horse onward and imagined that his horse had wings.

Ka'ab clasped his hands around the horse's neck and held tightly. When he was sixteen, he had stood on the Mount of Olives with his father and others and seen the desolation of Jerusalem. The Christians had forbidden the Jews to enter the city. Since then, Ka'ab had accepted the message of the prophet Muhammad and become a Muslim. Now, he was twenty-four years old, and he would return with his caliph and enter the city as part of a conquering army.

As they rode through the night, Umar punched Ka'ab on his shoulder.

"You are falling asleep, Ka'ab. Let us talk about something that has been on my mind. Tell me how the Sons of Israel count the years and the time during the year."

As usual, the caliph asked a question, and Ka'ab did not know why he was asking. It was not for Ka'ab to know the caliph's reason for asking. The caliph might ultimately tell him the reason for the question, or not. Ka'ab looked at the moon and answered.

"Years are counted from the creation of the world. This year is 4397 years from the creation. There are twelve months determined by the moon. In some years, an extra month is added so that the original twelve months stay within the seasons. Thus, the *haag* commemorating the Exodus from Egypt is always in the spring. Our other *haagim* remain in their respective seasons."

"And the Christians? How do they count the years and the months."

"They count the years from the birth year of the prophet Isa. This is their year 637. Their twelve months are determined by the sun and therefore their months always stay in season."

Caliph Umar looked at the moon.

"We need a calendar, Ka'ab. My commanders are complaining that they are receiving written instructions from me, and they cannot tell which are the most recent. We will start counting our years from the year of the *hijra* of Muhammad and his followers from Mecca to Medina. I will issue a decree as soon as we reach Abu Ubayda's camp."

As the sun rose hours later, Umar brought his horse to rest at a small stream. They both dismounted, and Umar led the horse to the water. Umar reached into the saddlebag for bread. He broke it in two and threw half to Ka'ab. Umar spoke as they ate.

"This city, Aelia. Your King David was the first to make it his capital. And his son Solomon built a Temple to God there."

Ka'ab nodded.

"O caliph, King David was a man of war. Even though he begged forgiveness from God, God told him he was not allowed to build the Temple. His son, Solomon, was a man of peace."

"But the Temple is no more, Ka'ab."

"Rome destroyed it and scattered my people. Years later, the Roman Empire converted to the worship of Isa."

Umar looked into the distance.

"We will need to build there a proper place of worship."

On the morning of the third day, at sunrise, the caliph and his advisor rode into Abu Ubayda's camp on the Mount of Olives. Abu Ubayda led them to the summit to view the city below. Umar turned to Ka'ab.

"Below is the city holy to your people. Where was the Temple of Solomon?"

"Look below, O Commander of the Faithful. My father told me that it stood on the desolate platform you see on the edge of the city."

As Ka'ab stood next to the conquering caliph and the general, he remembered his father's tears as they had viewed the place of desolation years before.

At noon that same day, the Byzantine garrison lined the streets inside the city. The soldiers were in ceremonial array, with brightly colored uniforms and gleaming helmets. Sophronius was dressed in his own ceremonial robes. As patriarch, he would not leave the city but would await Umar's arrival. Abu Ubayda had informed Sophronius that Umar would arrive shortly after sunrise, descending from the Mount of Olives.

Sophronius shielded his eyes and stared upward. He expected to see an entourage, but soon he saw an animal with a rider begin to descend. As the animal came closer, Sophronius saw that it was a white camel. The rider was very tall and slim, wearing a ragged cloak. He wore no headdress and had flaming red hair. As the rider entered the gate, Sophronius walked forward to greet him. He looked at a face burned almost black by the sun, with huge white teeth exposed by lips curled into a smile. The rider spoke in Arabic, then in Greek.

"I am Caliph Umar ibn al-Khattab, Commander of the Faithful."

Sophronius bowed his head.

Umar continued in Greek.

"In the name of God, the Compassionate, the Merciful, this is the covenant that I, Umar ibn al-Khattab, the servant of God, the Commander of the Faithful, grant to the people of Aelia. Security of your lives, your possessions, your churches and crosses. None shall be molested unless they rise in body against the *ummah*. They shall pay a tax instead of military service. Those who leave the city shall be safeguarded until they reach their destination."

Umar delivered a message of peace, security, and freedom. Sophronius was relieved. He remembered with horror the Persian destruction of the city in his own lifetime. Umar was telling him that life would continue in Jerusalem as before.

Umar dismounted and slapped his camel on its rear. The camel turned and started walking steadily back to Umar's camp. As Sophronius guided Umar through the city, the crowd lining the streets could not help but wonder at the sight of the ragged man. Sophronius was eager to learn more about this force that had come from the desert and overwhelmed his city. Umar seemed just as interested in learning about the city and the people he had conquered.

Umar pointed to the crowds.

"These people are followers of the prophet Isa?"

"Isa?"

"The man you worship as God's son, Jesus."

Sophronius swept his hand in a semicircle in front of him.

"How do you know of our Savior? You say you consider him a prophet?"

Umar looked at the gold cross hanging from Sophronius's belt.

"We consider him a great prophet, but we cannot understand how God would allow such a great man to die like that, beaten and hanged on a tree for vultures and flies to eat."

Sophronius blanched.

Umar leaned forward so Sophronius could hear him over the noise of the crowd.

"The prophet Muhammad considered the revelation of God to the Sons of Israel and the Christians to be valid. We Muslims regard these two peoples as 'People of the Book,' since they have their own writings inspired by God whom we call 'Allah.' We believe that the prophets of these peoples were all great prophets. Muhammad was the last prophet who received a pure revelation from God. We worship the same God."

"But you do not consider Jesus to be God?" Sophronius asked.

"We do not," Umar answered. "There is no God but God."

Sophronius led Umar down the Cardo Maximus, the main street built by Hadrian when he built the city of Aelia. They arrived at the Anastasis. Sophronius and Umar entered the complex alone.

Umar toured in respectful silence. Sophronius showed him the garden tomb enshrined in a large chapel next to an interior garden, with the place of crucifixion inside a smaller chapel. The prophet Muhammad and Umar had had many discussions about this, and they had concluded that Isa had only appeared to die on the cross. Instead, he had ascended bodily to heaven, just as Muhammad had done in his night journey.

Sophronius swept his hand in front of him and spoke.

"Our Emperor Constantine converted to Christianity in the third century after our Savior's death. He sent his mother, Helena, to Jerusalem. The Holy Spirit guided her to discover the site of Jesus' tomb. She found fragments of the very cross upon which the Savior had been crucified. She also identified the place of Solomon's Temple."

Umar listened respectfully, and then he placed his arm on Sophronius's shoulder.

"Patriarch, the time for my midday prayer has come. I need to go outside and pray."

Sophronius and he were alone in the garden adjoining the tomb.

"Caliph Umar, this is sacred ground. You are welcome to pray here."

Umar shook his head, politely declining.

"If I were to pray here, my fellow Muslims would take this property and build a place of worship to mark where I first prayed in this city. I will pray outside of your shrine, in full view of the inhabitants, so no one will be able to say that I prayed my first prayers inside here.

They exited the building. Umar looked at the sun, faced eastward, kneeled, and touched his forehead to the ground.

The brightly dressed Byzantine garrison stood at attention as the man in the ragged cloak knelt in the street and uttered the cornerstone of his faith in a language guttural and incomprehensible to all who watched.

"There is no God but God, and Muhammad is his prophet."

Chapter 39

Umar rose from his prayer rug. Sophronius felt he was losing his authority to a force he could not comprehend. Here was a conqueror who guaranteed freedom of worship, who respected the sacred sites of Christianity, and yet he prayed by throwing himself face down in the middle of the street.

"It is time for the midday meal, Umar. Would you join me in the Garden of the Anastasis?"

Umar was not hungry, nor had he completed his agenda for the morning.

"Perhaps later. First, you must take me to the place where the Temple of Solomon stood."

Sophronius was startled by this unexpected request.

Because of the total destruction of Jerusalem by Hadrian in the second century C.E., even the ruins of the Temple had disappeared from the face of the earth. Sophronius would not know where the Temple had stood but for Emperor Constantine's mother, Lady Helena. She had visited the city in the fourth century. Lady Helena had identified the desolate platform as the place where the Temple stood and commanded the Christian inhabitants to use it as a dumping ground for the city's refuse.

Sophronius had been present five years ago when a delegation of Jews had arrived from the city of Tiberias in the Galilee. The Jews had petitioned Sophronius's predecessor, Patriarch Modestus, to allow them to return with their families and live in the city.

Patriarch Modestus had folded his arms in front of his chest and thought for a moment.

"Follow me," he said.

Modestus had led the delegation of Jews through the streets to a gate leading to the large platform, which Lady Helena had identified as the Temple site. A retaining wall, made of huge ashlars, surrounded the area, and a horrible stench rose from within. Modestus had pointed to a gate to the ramp leading up to the platform.

"This garbage dump is the place where your Temple once stood. Not one of the murderers of our Lord will live in this city while there is breath in my body. Return to the hills of the Galilee and be glad that the armies of the emperor leave you alone to wallow in your guilt."

Sophronius smiled to himself. *Umar has no knowledge of the Holy City or where the Temple of the murderers stood.*

Sophronius folded his arms in front of him and spoke in a soothing voice.

"Caliph Umar, the Temple of Solomon is no more. Part of the Anastasis is the Martyrium, a church built to honor the holy martyrs of our faith. The Martyrium is built on the foundation of Solomon's Temple."

Umar fixed Sophronius with his gaze.

"I wish to have my vizier, my trusted advisor, join us. If you would send one of your soldiers to my camp and request the presence of Ka'ab al-Chabar, he waits for my command."

Sophronius felt relieved.

"I will do so. Let us return to the garden of the church for a midday refreshment and await the arrival of your advisor."

They returned to the Anastasis, and Sophronius led Umar into the garden in the inner courtyard. Several priests served fruit and wine. Sophronius, remembering

Abu Ubayda's admonition that Muslims did not drink wine, offered pear juice to Umar.

An hour later, two soldiers appeared at the entrance to the garden with a tall man dressed in a long white headdress, a cloak covering him almost to the ground. He clearly was not a soldier.

Umar motioned Ka'ab forward. He walked toward them, bowing his head as he came. When he stopped, both Umar and Sophronius remained seated. Sophronius could now see that the man appeared to be in his early twenties.

The man spoke in Greek.

"Commander of the Faithful, I await your orders."

Umar motioned the man to sit next to him. Sophronius was beginning to feel uncomfortable. To sit in the presence of Umar was one thing, but to have a common person join them was at best demeaning, if not insulting.

Umar could sense Sophronius's discomfort, and he was quick to speak.

"It is my pleasure to present to you Ka'ab al-Chabar, my trusted advisor. He was one of the earliest to accept the message of Muhammad."

Sophronius looked at Ka'ab.

"And before you accepted the message of the Prophet, you were . . .?"

"My family is of the Sons of Israel. Before the destruction of the Temple, we left this Holy City and settled with our cousins, the Sons of Ishmael, in Arabia. After hearing the message of the prophet Muhammad, I became a Muslim."

Sophronius's hand began to shake, and he abruptly put down his wine glass. *Christ, save me. The caliph's advisor is a descendant of the murderers of our Lord.*

"Have you forsaken the God of your fathers to follow your prophet Muhammad?" Sophronius asked Ka'ab.

"I have forsaken nothing. I worship the God of Abraham, as did your own prophet, Isa."

Sophronius gripped the arms of his chair.

Umar poured fruit juice into another goblet and handed it to Ka'ab. Umar turned to Sophronius.

"Ka'ab will tell us where the Temple of Solomon stood."

Umar looked at Ka'ab, who had reached for his goblet. Ka'ab drank slowly. He put the goblet on the table and took some grapes. Sophronius sank deeper into humiliation. Finally Ka'ab spoke.

"My father scheduled our caravans to Jerusalem to arrive in the Jewish month of Av, the month of destruction. We stood on the Mount of Olives and mourned the loss of the Temple with our merchant friends from the city of Tiberias. We were not allowed into the city."

Sophronius knew this all too well. Ka'ab continued.

"We were told by a rabbi from Tiberias where the Temple stood."

Umar rose and pulled his cloak tightly over his shoulders. When he spoke, Sophronius could not detect any anger in his voice.

"Ka'ab, show me this place."

Sophronius felt his heart sink.

As they exited the Anastasis onto the Cardo Maximus, Ka'ab led them in the direction of the desolate platform they had seen from the Mount of Olives above. No one spoke. Sophronius was glum, and Umar looked at the inhabitants who had come out of their houses to see them. They seemed surprised to see the stately entourage. A breeze from the east stirred through the street and with it a smell of rotting garbage and sewage. Sophronius held the collar of his robe over his nose. As the odors became more intense, Umar turned questioningly to Sophronius, who avoided his gaze.

Finally, Ka'ab stopped in front of a ramp rising through a tall arch. They could see mounds of refuse piled inside the arch, and enormous piles spilled down the ramp. To the right of the arch rose a tall wall made of immense stones. Ka'ab walked slowly toward the wall and placed both palms on it. As a Jew, he had never thought he would be in this place. As a follower of the message of the Prophet, he was miraculously here as the advisor to the caliph.

Umar stood respectfully behind Ka'ab. He spoke in Arabic.

"Ka'ab, what is this stinking place?"

Ka'ab turned with a mist of tears in his eyes. Pointing to the garbage billowing through the arch, he sobbed haltingly in Greek, so that Sophronius would understand.

"A place once holy and now made abominable. This is the entrance to the desolate platform we saw from the Mount of Olives. This is where I was told the Temple of Solomon stood."

Umar turned to Sophronius. He could tell by the look on the patriarch's face that Ka'ab spoke the truth. Umar did not display any outward emotion. He merely bowed to Sophronius and courteously said, "Please lead the way. We will follow."

The ramp to the reeking pile loomed in front of them.

The only way to navigate the ramp to the platform above was on hands and knees. Otherwise, one ran the risk of falling face first into the muck. Umar motioned them forward, and Sophronius began crawling up the ramp. Sophronius began to gag from the stench, and he wrapped his robe over his nose and mouth. Ka'ab and

Umar seemed not to notice the horrendous odor as they crawled behind him. When they reached the top of the ramp, they were able to stand and survey the area.

They could see mounds of garbage flowing over the tops of large stones. Sophronius knew that there had once been a Temple to Jupiter and a statue of the pagan emperor Hadrian on the northern end of the platform. Now, rotting food, building debris, and sewage mingled in a horrendous unimaginable sea. Rats scurried everywhere, and some approached the three men, hoping for new choice morsels. Ka'ab stood stunned. The view from the Mount of Olives could not convey this stinking chaos and degradation.

Umar said nothing. Instead, he took off his cloak and spread it on the ground. He slowly began mounding trash and waste onto his cloak. When the cloak was full, he grabbed the four corners together and hoisted the load onto his shoulder. He walked to the eastern edge of the platform and unfurled the cloak, hurling the contents into the valley below. Only then did he speak, again without any trace of emotion.

"Ka'ab, tell me, what can still be here that is sacred?"

Ka'ab's mind began to steady. Umar had asked him for advice, as Umar had done hundreds of times before. Ka'ab pointed to the center of the platform.

"O Commander of the Faithful, regardless of the ill-guided actions of men, no man could ever remove what is called in Hebrew *haaben hashetiya,* the cornerstone of the world, which is the peak of Mount Moriah, upon which our father Abraham was commanded by God to place his son for sacrifice. It was on that rock that King Solomon built the innermost holy of holies of his Temple. This rock must be here, in this holy place."

Umar continued to heap refuse into his cloak. When he had filled it again and emptied it into the valley below, he reached down and pulled a long, stained rag from the rubble. He turned to Ka'ab.

"The rock is here, waiting to be liberated by the hands of the faithful. As you have seen me do, one thousand of our army will clear this place and once again make this place a holy sanctuary."

Sophronius stood with his hand covering his nose. Umar walked over to him, threw the stained rag on the ground between them, and spoke.

"No longer will your women desecrate this site with their monthly uncleanliness."

For the first time, Sophronius heard Umar speak in anger.

The next morning, a thousand men of Abu Ubayda's army walked into the city, past the Anastasis, to the base of the ramp leading to the desecrated area. Under Ka'ab's direction, they repeated Umar's actions, filling their cloaks and unloading them into the valley below.

They worked first around the perimeter, clearing the area on all sides of the platform, then inward toward the center, exposing large masonry stones. On the afternoon of the tenth day, as Ka'ab inspected the cleared area in the center of the platform, the workers uncovered the top of a large rough rock. Ka'ab sent a messenger to Umar, who was in his command tent outside the city. By the time Umar arrived, the work crews had uncovered the rock, so that it protruded about fifteen feet above the ground. Ka'ab was standing a respectful distance away, and all work had stopped.

The thousand men stood surrounding the rock. They parted as Umar approached. He motioned to Ka'ab, who came forward and led him around the rock. Ka'ab spoke in a hushed voice to Umar.

"We have found the stone upon which Abraham was commanded to sacrifice his son and Solomon built his Temple."

Umar turned and surveyed the platform. He closed his eyes, and his brow furrowed. When he opened his eyes, he seemed to be seeing something that Ka'ab could not.

"Ka'ab, did not the Prophet say that in his night journey, his winged creature al-Buraq brought him from Mecca to *al-masjid al-aqsa*, the farthest place of worship?"

Ka'ab nodded. He had heard Umar speak of this mysterious journey many times, as told to him by Muhammad.

"You have told me so, O Commander of the Faithful."

"And the Prophet tethered al-Buraq, and from there he ascended to heaven. He met with Ibrahim, Musa, Da'ud, Sulemain, and Isa, whom the Jews know as Abraham, Moses, David, Solomon, and the Christian Jesus."

Again, Ka'ab nodded.

"So the farthest place of worship must refer to the place of Solomon's Temple. And the wall below is where al-Buraq was tethered."

Ka'ab nodded in agreement. Where else would the place of worship be for all the prophets since Abraham?

Umar turned to his men.

"From today, let it be known that I, Umar ibn al-Khattab, the successor of the Prophet and Commander of the Faithful, have liberated and purified *al masjid al-aqsa*, the farthest place of worship."

In unison, Umar, Ka'ab, and the thousand men prostrated themselves on the ground, using their cloaks as prayer rugs.

"There is no God but God."

As Ka'ab pressed his forehead to the earth, he was surprised to hear himself praying in Hebrew, the words flowing from his lips for the first time since he had accepted the message of the Prophet.

"*shema yisroel, adonai elohainu, adonai echad.* Hear, Israel, the Lord is Our God, the Lord is One."

Umar took Ka'ab aside.

"We need to build a *masjid* here. Where do you think we should build it?"

Ka'ab surveyed the platform and spoke.

"If the *masjid* is built west of the rock, we can face the rock from the west and pray over the rock toward Mecca in the east."

Umar looked at Ka'ab with obvious displeasure.

"Why should we do that, Ka'ab?"

Ka'ab spoke slowly.

"Commander of the Faithful, remember that in the early days, the Prophet—peace be upon him—directed prayer toward Jerusalem before he changed the direction of prayer toward Mecca. If we pray here as I suggest, we face both the rock in Jerusalem and Mecca."

Umar waved his hand, dismissing Ka'ab's suggestion.

"Ka'ab, you are still thinking like a Son of Israel. There is no need to pray facing the rock. We will build our *masjid* on the southern side, and we will pray east toward Mecca as the Prophet commanded.

For the first time, Ka'ab's advice had not pleased Umar.

That evening, Sophronius rode out to Abu Ubayda's camp unannounced and asked to meet with the caliph. Two soldiers escorted him to a small tent in the rear of the camp. He found Umar roasting a small quail over a fire.

Umar motioned Sophronius to have a seat and reached for the spit. He flipped the charred bird onto a large stone and hacked it in two with a long knife. He took a stick and speared half, then handed the stick to Sophronius.

"Please eat, Patriarch."

Sophronius found the aroma of the burning flesh pleasing, and he took the stick from Umar. He picked a portion of the skin from the meat and nibbled. He pulled the meat apart and began to chew. Umar picked up the other half of the bird with his hands and began to chomp slowly and methodically. As he ate, he looked expectantly at Sophronius.

"I have not slept decently for days, Caliph. You mentioned that Christians would have freedom of worship, and you have kept your word. I invited you to pray in the Anastasis, and you refused. But now that you have cleared the platform, I fear that you will allow the Jews to return and build their Temple again."

Umar continued to munch on the roasted quail, remaining expressionless.

"Patriarch, you know a little about our religion, but nothing about our administration. We seek to preserve what the Romans call in their language the '*status quo.*' You know the Roman language?"

Sophronius nodded, translating the phrase into Greek.

"The conditions which now exist."

"Correct. The Christians practice their religion and live in the city. The Jews practice their religion but are banned by the Christians from living in the city."

Sophronius nodded. Umar tore a chunk of quail with his teeth and chewed. Then he spoke.

"These are the conditions that exist. In your lifetime, Patriarch Sophronius, all will remain as it is. There will be no Jews living in the city, no Temple rebuilt. The place of the Temple is sacred to Muslims. We will build a place to worship there, our *masjid*. You may rest assured that all will remain the same."

Sophronius left the camp feeling tired and depressed. Despite Umar's promises, he knew that nothing remained the same. He could do as he wished, but the Church no longer controlled the city or the rest of the surrounding cities. This desert wind had quenched the power of his emperor without strain.

The next morning, he climbed the Mount of Olives. He had not done so since Abu Ubayda had laid siege to the city. From the Mount of Olives, he looked down upon the cleared platform that the Christians had used as a dump. He saw the uncovered rock in the middle of the platform. A wooden frame was rising on the southern edge of the platform, the beginning of the place of worship that Umar was building for his people.

As Sophronius descended the Mount of Olives, he clutched his heart and felt deep sadness. He died eleven months later.

Samir folded his hands in front of him and paused. Meir leaned toward him and spoke.

"Let me ask you several questions, sir. Caliph Umar's advisor, Ka'ab al-Chabar, who you say was a Jewish convert to Islam, told the caliph where the Temple had stood. Do you know where Ka'ab was from?"

"It has been handed down through my family that Ka'ab was from a *yahudi* tribe that lived in Arabia," Samir said. "How Ka'ab became advisor to the caliph, I do not know."

"Also, Mr. ibn Abdullah, let me clarify. You testified that Caliph Umar referred to the entire platform where Ka'ab told him the Temple stood as *al-masjid al-aqsa*, 'the farthest place of worship.' Today, isn't that name only associated with al-Aqsa Mosque, instead of the entire platform?"

Samir nodded.

"That is correct. The literal translation of al-Aqsa Mosque is 'the farthest place of worship,' which originally referred to the platform itself, and later to the mosque built on the southern end of the platform. After a future caliph and others built additional Islamic structures on the platform, Muslims began to refer to the entire platform as al-Haram as-Sharif, the Noble Sanctuary, and to the mosque as al-Aqsa Mosque. Also, Muslims refer to the wall the Jews call the Kotel as 'al-Buraq's Wall,' as they believe that Muhammad tethered his winged creature al-Buraq to the wall during his night journey to the site of the Temple."

Meir turned to Prime Minister Zadok.

"Do you wish to continue the examination of Mr. ibn Abdullah?"

Zadok replied, "One further question. You testified that Caliph Umar sought the location of Solomon's Temple as he believed it was the destination of Muhammad's night journey."

"Correct," Samir said. "As a matter of fact, two evenings ago, Muslims celebrated *leilat almiraj*, the Night Journey."

"Thank you, Mr. ibn Abdullah," Zadok said. Zadok looked at Meir.

"I want to emphasize to the court that the testimony of Rabbi Avidan and Mr. ibn Abdullah supports the Jewish claim to the Temple Mount. It is clear that the Temple was built there, and that the Muslim Caliph Umar sought the location of the Temple and believed the Temple stood there."

"Thank you, Mr. Prime Minister," Meir said.

Zadok continued.

"Justice Bar-Aben, it is undisputed that the Muslims from their first days in Jerusalem believed the Temple stood on the Temple Mount and acknowledged the Jewish history of the site. I don't see that it is necessary to take additional testimony in this proceeding to establish the Jewish right to the Temple Mount."

Amos rose from his chair.

"Justice Bar-Aben, if I may address the court."

"You may," Meir responded.

"There is more to be told on this subject. Rabbi Avidan and Mr. ibn Abdullah have not told all that occurred on the Temple Mount that night in 1967. You have read the interview summaries. Both told Prime Minister Zadok they had additional information they would reveal during these proceedings."

"Mr. Prime Minister, I won't rule until I hear all the evidence," Meir said to Zadok.

"I understand," Zadok said. "I will present another witness who will testify tomorrow afternoon on this subject in detail."

"Thank you, Mr. Prime Minister," Meir said. "Mr. ibn Abdullah, I suspect that we will need additional testimony from you. I think it would be helpful if you could hear the testimony of the next witness tomorrow. Mr. Eitan can bring you again, I hope."

Samir looked at Amos.

"I can pick you up at noon tomorrow," Amos said.

Meir cracked his gavel.

"This hearing is adjourned until tomorrow at one o'clock."

After the hearing adjourned that afternoon, Amos dropped Rabbi Avidan in Meah Shaerim to visit friends and continued to the Old City with Samir.

"You have more to tell, Samir. I know what the next witness has to say. You will find it very interesting. I'm glad Justice Bar-Aben asked you to listen tomorrow."

"I like him," Samir said. "He listens intently, but he appears very troubled."

Amos nodded.

"He is trying to decide the future by understanding the past."

Samir sighed.

"We have a saying, 'Leave trouble alone, and trouble will leave you alone.'"

"Unfortunately," Amos said, "he doesn't have that choice."

Aaron Kragen had arrived at the Israel Museum with Agent Tzion earlier in the day, a little after noon. Despite Aaron's assurances, Hiram Aitza had the stone carefully inspected to make sure it had not suffered damage in transit. He called Amran, who was waiting in the corridor outside the courtroom, and let him know the stone had been delivered to the museum and was in a vault until the prime minister needed it.

Agent Tzion then took Aaron to a Mossad office in Jerusalem for debriefing. Aaron discussed his trip in detail, from the time he picked up the stone until his arrival at the Hotel of the Seven Arches. Agent Tzion told Aaron that the person whom Aaron had reported to border control was an undercover El Al security agent. Agent Tzion finished the debriefing at three in the afternoon, excused himself, and called El Al Security at Ben Gurion Airport. When he came back into the office where Aaron was waiting, Aaron had fallen asleep in his chair. Agent Tzion shook him awake.

"Mr. Kragen, since you identified an undercover El Al security agent, El Al needs to debrief you. I am going to take you back to the airport to meet with El Al security."

"I have dinner plans this evening, Agent Tzion. How long will the debriefing take?"

"Sorry," Agent Tzion said, "if I know El Al, they are quite thorough. You should cancel your dinner plans. I'll take you to a hotel after the debriefing, and tomorrow I need to take you briefly to another location so you can affirm that the package was in your custody at all times before you delivered it."

"I thought I had done that with Mr. Aitza today."

"You did, but tomorrow you have to meet with a Supreme Court justice and the prime minister and do the same thing."

Aaron was stunned.

"I really do need to cancel my dinner plans."

Amy returned to her room that evening about six o' clock after a walking tour of the Garden of Gethsemane and surrounding area. She took a quick shower. The hot water felt invigorating after such a long and exhausting day. She shut off the water and reluctantly got out of the shower. She quickly dried off, wrapped a towel around herself, and then sat down to dry her hair at a small vanity in the bedroom.

As she brushed her hair, she noticed the TV remote on the vanity. She picked it up and pointed it at the TV. *Click.* A nice looking man filled the screen. It looked like a news show. He was speaking very rapidly, with words that sounded every now and then like he was trying to clear his throat. Hebrew, she supposed.

She remembered that Reverend Crosby had told them that Jesus had spoken Hebrew and another similar language called Aramaic. She wondered if Jesus had really talked like that.

She dressed and waited. After thirty minutes, she became restless. She flipped channels and found a rerun of *Desperate Housewives* with Hebrew subtitles. After another thirty minutes passed, she picked up the phone and called the front desk.

The desk clerk answered in English.

"Yes, Ms. Collins. How can I help you?"

"Do I have any messages, by any chance?"

There was a pause.

"I'm sorry, Ms. Collins, there are no messages."

"Are you sure? I thought maybe there would be a message from Aaron Kragen. It's Aa-ron Kra-gen," she said speaking slowly.

"I'm quite sure, Ms. Collins, there are no messages here for you."

"Thank you," Amy said, as she hung up the phone.

Fifteen minutes later, the phone rang.

"Hello, Amy, it's Aaron."

"Hi, Aaron, are you here?"

"I'm not, Amy. I'm sorry, but I can't make dinner tonight. My business appointment is taking much longer than I expected."

Amy was silent.

"It was a pleasure meeting you, Amy. I want to thank you again for arranging the bus for me today. It was a big help."

"You're welcome, Aaron. Thanks for calling. What about tomorrow . . . maybe?"

"I'm sorry, Amy. I just can't plan ahead now."

Amy hung up.

All men were liars. All of them.

Joshua Galilee had spent the entire day meeting with, and being chastised by, his superiors in El Al security. When he finally left the airport in the early evening, he took a short taxi ride to the Sadot Hotel, one of the few hotels near the airport. It was a small hotel on the third floor of a shopping center, very popular with pilots and other airline crew members. Joshua was hungry. He had barely eaten all day, except for a quick sandwich while he was debriefed. He walked through the lobby and into the dining room. The hostess greeted him as he entered.

"Mr. Galilee, good morning. A pleasure to see you again."

Joshua smiled.

"I see my usual table by the window is available," he said.

"Sure, enjoy."

He went to the table and sat down. A server poured coffee.

Joshua walked over to the dinner buffet. They had his favorites, sweet potato tortellini and mushroom ravioli. He ate quickly and then went to the front desk to check in.

The desk agent smiled as he approached.

"Mr. Galilee, your room is ready for one night. Will you need anything during your stay?" she asked, as she handed him the key.

"No, thanks," Joshua said. "I'll be checking out early in the morning. I'll leave the key in the room as usual."

Joshua took the elevator to his room. Despite feigning sleep for most of the flight, he had never slept. The caffeine pills he had taken to keep awake were wearing off, and he was now very tired. He dropped his carry-on bag on a chair, closed the curtains, undressed, and got into bed. In minutes, he was asleep.

Chapter 40

Tuesday, April 25, 2017

Joshua Galilee woke in his hotel room and looked at his watch. It was six in the morning. He rose from his bed and stretched. He went to the bathroom sink and cut his beard as short as he could with a pair of scissors. Then he lathered what remained, shaved it smooth, and took a shower.

Joshua returned to the bedroom, opened his carry-on bag, and removed a pair of casual slacks and a polo shirt. He stuffed his Orthodox garb, including the fur-trimmed hat, into the bag. He called the front desk and told the desk clerk that he was checking out.

He grabbed his bag, left his key in the room, and took the elevator to the lobby. He walked to another bank of elevators and descended to the shopping center level. He entered the Assaf Center Mall and went to the Aroma Cafe, a coffee shop on the main level.

Joshua ordered coffee and a chopped salad and took it to a table. As he was eating, Hiram Aitza walked up and sat down at the table across from him.

"Good morning, Joshua," Hiram said. "You're looking well. Thanks for your help yesterday. I hope it wasn't too much of an imposition."

Joshua smiled.

"Any time, *abba*. Any time."

Meir and Channah slept late. After they ate breakfast, Channah began feeling ill. She got back into bed.

"It's just a bad headache, Meir."

"It's tension," Meir said. "Because of Ori's *yahrzeit* tonight."

Channah nodded. "You go to work. I'm fine."

"I don't have to be there until after lunch today. I'm staying home this morning."

The phone rang, and Channah reached for it.

"Hello?" She smiled.

"Yes. He is. A pleasure to speak to *you* again."

She handed Meir the phone.

"Your friend, Amos."

Meir took the phone and walked out of the bedroom. Amos was brief.

"Please meet me in your lobby at 10:00 a.m."

Meir hung up and came back into the bedroom. Channah asked him to lie down next to her again.

"Well, it seems that you are friends again."

Meir looked away, trying to end the conversation.

"Does it have to do with what happened on the Temple Mount that night? Are you and Amos involved in a historical mystery?" Channah asked.

Meir was beginning to feel uncomfortable, and Channah was not going to let it go. He did not respond, and Channah continued.

"Well, Meir, in most historical mystery novels, you have a handsome guy teamed up with a hot girl. They run around, chased by mysterious people. The reader begins to wonder when they will sleep with each other. At some point they do, then their lives are in danger, and then they solve the mystery."

"Well, that's not happening."

"And, also, that guy is really smart and decodes weird symbols and clues from ancient languages that nobody speaks anymore"

Meir thought a moment and laughed.

"Well, possibly."

"What about ancient documents or manuscripts or maps?"

"No, none of that yet."

"What about kabbalah, Jewish mysticism. Aren't you going to interview mystics?" Channah was laughing loudly now, and Meir looked serious.

"Maybe I should. Maybe some hundred-year-old rabbi?" Meir said.

"Right, and what about clues?" Channah asked. "Historical mysteries always have clues to be decoded by future generations."

Meir shook his head.

"I think you are really stretching it, Channah. Can you imagine me dealing with something as exciting as that?"

"You, Meir? Not in a million years. I'm sure whatever it is, it would bore me to tears."

An hour later, Meir met Amos in the lobby. Amos was apologetic.

"Sorry to bother you this morning, but you don't know much about the witness who is going to testify this afternoon, and I thought I should let you know she is very nervous. You might want to meet with her before she testifies."

"That's a good suggestion," Meir said.

"I can tell you that even though Arabic is her native language, she is fluent in Hebrew. She is feeling intimidated because she doesn't understand what this hearing is about."

"I can explain it to her before she testifies. Rabbi Avidan and Mr. ibn Abdullah know. It's only fair that she should also."

Later that morning, Agent Aleph called Amran.

"It's about the wife. She recently went to Hadassah Hospital with the daughter-in-law. I think the prime minister should know why."

"You can tell me," Amran said.

"Sorry, I think I should speak directly to the prime minister."

Amran shrugged.

"He's busy this afternoon. I'll tell him you will come to see him later this evening."

"Please tell him. It's important."

Chapter 41

Two nights before, Fatima had fallen asleep in her large armchair after dinner. The phone had jolted her awake. She did not recognize his voice when she answered.

"marhaba, Fatima!*"*

The familiarity in his voice made her pause.

"Yes?"

"It's Amos Eitan."

She roused herself into a sitting position. He continued speaking before she had a chance to say anything.

"The day after tomorrow, you must be at the Supreme Court building by twelve-thirty in the afternoon."

"And what —?"

"Your testimony will begin about one. It may go late into the evening."

"I'll have to cancel my class —"

"You might want to cancel for several days."

Fatima rarely missed class. After her first meeting with Amos, she had devised an excuse. Her aunt in Hebron had suddenly become ill. She had to go take care of her. Once her faculty colleagues thought she was in Hebron, they would not bother to call her at her apartment.

"How should I —?"

"Have an early lunch at Shlomo's Pizza and Pasta on Ben Yehuda Street. I will pick you up there at eleven thirty."

"Why don't you join —?"

"I'd be delighted. But I really can't."

"A pity. I was hoping —"

"Hoping what, Fatima?"

"That maybe we could sit and talk. I would actually have an opportunity to speak a complete sentence."

"Later, maybe"—he laughed—"*ila likaa.*"

He hung up.

Today, Fatima sat outside Shlomo's Pizza and Pasta on Ben Yehuda Street. A large green umbrella shaded her from the sun. She took off her sunglasses and flicked her hair from her neck to cool off.

Despite her nervousness, Fatima was hungry. She had ordered a large portion of her favorite penne pasta baked with tomato sauce and cheese. She ate it slowly, and it soothed her jumpy stomach. She knew that she might not have a chance to eat dinner, so she sopped up the tomato sauce with a large garlic roll.

As she waited for Amos, she reflected upon her childhood. Fatima had fond memories of growing up in the Muslim Quarter of Jerusalem. Her parents, now deceased, had owned a shop in East Jerusalem, selling nuts, tea, coffee, spices. Until 1967, East Jerusalem was part of the Hashemite Kingdom of Jordan, and Fatima's parents had sold silver crucifixes to the Christian pilgrims from abroad who entered Jordan to visit the Church of the Holy Sepulcher and the Via Dolorosa. With the Israeli victory in the Six-Day War, the shop was closed for only a week. When it reopened, her parents had a new display case of *magen david* necklaces and *mezuzot.*

Fatima's parents already knew English, as they had always had many English-speaking customers. They quickly learned Hebrew. You could not sell if you could not quote a price. By the time Fatima was born in 1976, her parents were fluent in Hebrew. She learned

Hebrew with her parents, perfecting it while talking to customers as she worked in the shop after school.

When Fatima was young, she lived with her parents and her grandmother, Umm Tawfiq, in a small apartment in East Jerusalem. Fatima's parents had a bedroom, and Fatima had shared a room with her grandmother. The largest room was the living room. Fatima's earliest memory of her grandmother was of her sitting in the living room in a large cushioned chair, sipping thick coffee and reading. Umm Tawfiq would mark her place, put the book down, and go into the kitchen to boil more water for coffee. It was her ritual: read, boil water, make coffee, drink coffee, and read some more.

One morning, when she was in high school, Fatima rose earlier than usual and found her grandmother in the kitchen having a light breakfast of pita with butter and coffee. Fatima sat down at the table with her grandmother. Umm Tawfiq smiled at her granddaughter.

"How are your studies coming, Fatima?"

Fatima was puzzled by the question, because her grandmother knew she was a good student.

"My grades are good, very good."

"Study history, Fatima. Study it well."

"I do. I like history. It is my favorite subject."

Umm Tawfiq smiled at Fatima and spread more butter on her pita. She stirred a teaspoon of sugar into her coffee.

"One day, I will tell you the history of our family."

Fatima studied, and every now and then she would ask Umm Tawfiq if she would tell her about her family's history. Umm Tawfiq always looked mysterious; she shook her head.

"Now is not the time."

In the summer after Fatima's first year at the university, Umm Tawfiq celebrated her ninetieth birthday. That evening, as she sat drinking coffee in the kitchen, she reached across the table and grasped Fatima's hand.

"I think that soon I will visit paradise. It's time that I tell you our history."

Fatima listened, fascinated.

When Amos had come to interview her at her office, she had refused to discuss her family history.

"Unless you can explain how my family history would be relevant, I won't discuss it with you or anyone else," she had said.

Amos had closed his notebook and ended the interview.

Amos found Rabbi Avidan and Samir waiting at the Jaffa Gate of the Old City and drove them to the Supreme Court. He then drove to Ben Yehuda Street to find Fatima. As Fatima finished her meal, she saw Amos park his car across the street. She left money on the table and walked slowly to the corner. She got into the car, and Amos drove quickly through the streets of Jerusalem. Even though it was spring, Jerusalem was in the midst of a heat wave. He had the windows closed and the air conditioning on. He glanced at Fatima and realized that she was sweating heavily and shivering at the same time.

"Would you like the window open?"

"Please. I am not used to air conditioning."

Amos opened the window.

"Better?"

"Yes. How long will I have to testify?"

"That depends on what you have to say."

"So why am I doing this? I'm just minding my own business, living my life, teaching history, and you show up. The next thing I know, I'm going to the Supreme Court."

Amos shifted into a lower gear as they climbed upward into the hilly part of the city, the location of the Supreme Court and the Knesset.

"Calm down, Fatima. Pretend you are teaching a class. You are in control."

"I'm in control? Of the prime minister and the Supreme Court of Israel? You can't be serious."

Amos shoved the car into first gear and climbed the hill toward the gate to the Supreme Court.

Amos showed his ID to the guard at the gate, and then he turned to Fatima.

"He needs to see your Hebrew University faculty card. They've got your name on the list."

She reached into her purse for a lanyard with her faculty card and handed it to the guard. He looked at her picture and then at Fatima. Fatima smiled at him, and the guard smiled back before checking his list.

The guard pointed to the entrance of the parking garage.

"You can park in the garage, but the only access to the court is through the main entrance today. The garage elevator is malfunctioning, stuck at the garage level. Please discharge your passenger before you enter the garage. You can walk back up the ramp after you park."

The electric gate opened, and the guard waved them through. Amos pulled up behind a tourist bus unloading passengers.

Amos stopped the car for Fatima.

"Wait for me in the lobby. I'll be back after I park the car."

Fatima got out of the car and watched Amos drive away. As she walked toward the entrance, she saw a line of tourists wearing red baseball caps and tee shirts. Before she approached them, she could tell they were Americans. Most were overweight and wearing tennis shoes. Almost all appeared to be in their sixties or older. They waited patiently as the guard at the door checked their purses and backpacks.

Fatima stood at the end of the line and let the sun warm her. The line moved forward, and she listened to those in front of her. Even though she considered herself fluent in English, she was having difficulty understanding them. The lilt of their voices and their drawn-out syllables told her they were probably from the southern part of the United States.

One particularly large woman was wiping her neck with a soggy handkerchief and breathing heavily. Fatima barely understood her when she said she was "rearr-rly, rear-rly, rear-rly ho-t."

Fatima saw that the woman's tee shirt read, "Zion Baptist Temple." Zion and Temple sounded Jewish, but she knew that Baptist meant Christian. A group of five suddenly held hands and formed a circle in front of her. They bowed their heads and began speaking in low voices. Fatima heard "Jesus" repeated several times within the space of a minute.

While Muslims and Jews prayed at appointed times at their places of worship, Fatima often saw Christians praying in Jerusalem anywhere at any time. They seemed to be so thankful for everything, so cheerful, so protected, so free from fear. How lucky to be so optimistic, she thought. Once the group finished praying, they took out cameras and started taking pictures of each other in front of the words "Supreme Court of Israel" carved in English, Arabic, and Hebrew on the front of the building.

One of the women approached Fatima with a camera in her hand. She was younger and slimmer than the rest, about forty, with long brunette hair and a huge travel bag over her arm.

"Excuse me, honey, would you mind snapping one?"

Fatima wasn't sure what "snapping one" meant, but understood that the woman wanted a picture taken. She held out her hand for the camera.

"Thank you," the woman said, leaning against the wall.

Fatima held the camera up and found her through the viewfinder. She took the picture, held up her hand to tell the woman to stay there, and quickly took another.

"Thank you again!" the woman said as she came toward Fatima to retrieve her camera.

"What's your name, honey?"

Fatima smiled.

"Fatima. And you?"

"Amy. My, my, Fatima. That's a pretty name. Are you here all alone?"

Before Fatima could answer, she felt a hand on her arm.

"No, she's with me."

Fatima turned to find Amos grasping her arm.

"You never made it to the lobby?" He spoke in Arabic.

"No, the line didn't really move. I didn't want to break in line."

"Come on. We don't want to be late."

Amos smiled at Amy. She couldn't understand what he had said, but it sounded mysterious to her.

Amos led Fatima by the arm to the front of the line and nodded to the guard who checked Fatima's ID and waved them inside.

The Zion Baptist Temple group stood in line for almost an hour. Amy leaned against the wall of the building in the shade and fanned herself to keep cool. A group of Israeli teenage girls standing in line were singing a Hebrew song. It was a version of ninety-nine bottles of beer on the wall, which Israelis had changed to a countdown of ninety-nine apples falling from a tree and exploding. The repetition made Amy's head spin. She drank her entire water bottle and was still feeling dehydrated. She leaned against the wall and closed her eyes.

"Amy, are you feeling okay?" Emma Mason said. Emma's husband Joe dipped his handkerchief in cold water and draped it over Amy's shoulders.

"Keep your eyes closed and breathe slowly, Amy," Joe said.

As they were standing in line, a car drove up to the entrance. Agent Tzion got out of the car and opened the rear door. Aaron Kragen emerged. The car drove away. Agent Tzion escorted Aaron past the line of tourists and into the lobby. Aaron noticed the red tee shirts and turned his head. Emma Mason saw Aaron as he passed. Amy continued to lean against the wall with her eyes closed.

Emma Mason cleared her throat and nudged Amy.

"Amy, who was that young man that came on the bus with you?"

"Someone I met on the plane."

"I know that. I saw you sitting next to him."

"Don't remind me, Emma. Why are you asking me about him now?"

"I think I just saw him walk past us and go into the lobby with two other men."

Amy rolled her eyes.

"You're crazy, Emma. I'm sure he's long gone by now."

Chapter 42

Fatima and Amos entered the lobby. Fatima reeled from the blast of air conditioning. She pulled a bright red shawl from her shoulder bag and wrapped it around her.

She turned to find Amos staring at her.

"Not appropriate?"

Amos shook his head.

"I wasn't thinking about that. You look very nice."

Amos's remark had a calming effect.

Amos took her arm and steered her down a corridor to an elevator. He reached into his pocket and removed a small card that he placed on a metal pad next to the elevator door. The door opened.

They entered the elevator, and Amos pushed the button for the top floor. Fatima was shivering again even though she was wearing her shawl.

"Aren't we going to the courtroom? I thought you told me we were going to be in a courtroom in the basement."

"We'll go there next. Justice Meir Bar-Aben wants to meet you before you testify."

The bell rang and the door opened.

Amran was standing outside Meir's chambers. He snapped to attention when he saw Amos and Fatima come out of the elevator. Amos nodded. Amran opened the door to the justice's chambers. Ruth sat at her desk, sorting the contents of a large file. She smiled at Amos and looked at Fatima.

Amos said, "Please tell Justice Bar-Aben that Professor al-Fawzi is here."

Ruth picked up her phone and called Meir on the intercom.

"They're here."

Within seconds, a door opened behind her desk and Meir appeared. He was wearing a black suit, white shirt, and dark tie. Fatima scanned him from head to foot. Meir smiled and extended his hand.

"Justice Meir Bar-Aben. A pleasure to meet you, Professor al-Fawzi."

Fatima took his hand.

"Likewise, Justice Bar-Aben."

"Let's sit in my office for a few moments."

Meir stepped aside from the doorway and Fatima and Amos walked past him into a small hallway. They continued to the end of the hall to Meir's office. Fatima was struck by the bright sunlight streaming through the tall windows. A sofa and three large chairs were arranged around a coffee table on one side of the room. Meir's desk was perpendicular to the windows, with bookcases behind it filled with framed photographs.

Fatima was starting to feel calm.

"No books, sir? I thought lawyers and judges surrounded themselves with books."

Meir smiled.

"My law clerk surrounds himself with books. And, of course, there is a large law library in the building, I'm not so sure anymore that the answers I am looking for are to be found in books."

Fatima glanced at Meir's desk. Five crystal paperweights were lined up precisely on the desk.

"No paper?"

Meir laughed.

"I can't stand clutter. The empty paper weights are my reminder to clean up at the end of the day."

Meir motioned them to sit. Fatima sat on the sofa, and Amos and Meir sat on chairs facing her.

"I wanted to meet you, Professor al-Fawzi, before you testify. Mr. Eitan has explained to you that this is not an ordinary proceeding, and we are going to be in a special courtroom for security purposes."

"I understand," Fatima said.

"Three people will be in the room besides Mr. Eitan, Chief Justice Eli Heifitz, and me. One is Prime Minister Zadok."

"Mr. Eitan told me it was the Prime Minister's Office that wanted my expertise as a witness. I assumed the prime minister would be there."

"Rabbi Ashur Avidan will also be there."

Fatima replied, "I have read about him. He is a descendant of Jochanan ben Zakkai.

"Correct. He has offered testimony in this proceeding, and he will offer additional testimony. I think it will be helpful to the court if he hears your testimony."

"The third person is Mr. ibn Abdullah. He is a *muadhin* of al-Aqsa Mosque. Are you aware of his family history?"

Fatima nodded.

"As a scholar of the early Islamic period of Jerusalem, I know that he is a descendant of Caliph Umar."

She paused and then asked, "Justice Bar-Aben, can you tell me why I am being called as a witness in this proceeding?"

"Certainly," Meir said. "The prime minister is calling you as a witness to describe the history of the Temple Mount during the Early Islamic period, after Caliph Umar captured Jerusalem. I believe he will ask you why Caliph Umar built al-Aqsa Mosque on the Temple Mount."

"I can answer the prime minister's questions," Fatima said. "But may I ask the reason for the hearing, sir? What decision will you make after the hearing concludes?"

Meir looked at Amos, and then he turned to Fatima.

"I had planned to tell you this before the hearing began. I must determine whether the State of Israel will revoke the Waqf's authority over the Temple Mount."

Fatima was stunned.

"And the prime minister believes my answers to his questions will support the revocation of the Waqf's authority?"

"I can't speak for the prime minister, Professor al-Fawzi," Meir said.

"He didn't interview me," Fatima said. "Mr. Eitan did."

"I know that," Meir said. "I read the summary of the interview. He apparently asked you some questions about your ancestry that you would not answer."

"Yes," Fatima said. "He couldn't tell me the reason for the hearing, so I didn't think the questions were relevant."

"You did tell Mr. Eitan that your interest in Islamic history initially came from your grandmother. Something she told you before she died," Meir said.

Fatima nodded, and her heart began to beat faster.

She could see Umm Tawfiq standing in the sunbeam that streamed through the window behind Meir.

"That's right."

"Have you ever told anyone what your grandmother told you?"

"No. When Mr. Eitan asked me, I refused to tell him. I did not see how it would possibly be relevant to anything I would be asked to speak about."

Meir looked at Amos then at Fatima.

"Now you know the purpose of the hearing, Professor al-Fawzi. Do you think it would help me make my decision if I knew what your grandmother told you?"

Fatima was not prepared for this question. She thought for several moments.

"I believe it would help. You would have to be the judge of that, obviously."

Meir smiled.

"Obviously. I believe we are ready to begin."

Umm Tawfiq smiled at Fatima from the sunbeam.

Meir stood and Amos and Fatima followed him.

Aaron Kragen sat in the justices' dining room, eating from the breakfast buffet and telling Agent Tzion about his security company. Agent Tzion listened politely and tried to act interested. He had just heard from Amos Eitan, who had told him to wait in the dining room until he called for them. Agent Tzion hoped it would be soon.

The elevator opened on the basement level. Amran took his usual seat by the elevator. Fatima waited in the hall with Amos, while Meir went into his office to put on his robe. Meir returned and escorted Fatima and Amos into the courtroom. Amos walked with Fatima to the front row. Fatima, feeling cold and disoriented by the lighting, pulled her shawl tightly around her shoulders.

Amran came into the courtroom several moments later, leading Rabbi Avidan, Samir, Prime Minister Zadok, and Eli Heifitz.

Meir introduced them to Fatima. Her calm vanished as she shook hands with them.

What was she about to do? Amos had told her to act like a history professor and teach. Fatima rubbed her eyes and opened them wide, focusing on Justice Bar-Aben. Prime Minister Zadok rose and stood behind the podium. He leaned forward and spoke.

"The next witness is Professor Fatima al-Fawzi. Professor al-Fawzi, would you please take the witness stand."

Fatima rose from her seat and entered the witness stand. Meir administered an Islamic oath. Fatima sat down and breathed deeply, looking at Amos.

"Professor al-Fawzi, before we begin, would you prefer to testify in Arabic?"

Fatima was surprised by the question. As a professor at Hebrew University, she was required to lecture in Hebrew. She had assumed she would testify in Hebrew.

"My Hebrew is fluent, but perhaps it would be better if I testify in Arabic for the benefit of Mr. ibn Abdullah, and Mr. Eitan could translate my testimony into Hebrew for everyone else."

"A good suggestion," Meir said. "Mr. Eitan will translate. Mr. Prime Minister, you have called Professor al-Fawzi as a witness. Please proceed."

Zadok began the examination.

"Professor al-Fawzi, I appreciate your participation in this hearing. Please state your occupation."

"I am a professor at the Hebrew University. I teach courses in Islamic history from the time of Muhammad until the present. But I do have a particular period of time that has been the focus of my academic research."

"And that period is . . .?"

"The first and second century of the Muslim calendar, the seventh and eighth century A.D. of the Christian calendar or of the Common Era, as many scholars prefer the terminology."

"Do you consider yourself an expert in this period of history?"

"I consider myself very knowledgeable, probably more knowledgeable than most."

"And the source of your knowledge?"

"I have conducted extensive academic research in original Arabic source materials."

"I see from your resume that you have written extensively about the Muslim conquest of Jerusalem in the seventh century of the Common Era."

"I have."

"Professor al-Fawzi," Zadok said, "I don't want to keep you here longer than necessary, so I will be brief. Yesterday, we heard testimony from Mr. ibn Abdullah concerning the Muslim conquest of Jerusalem. He testified at length about Caliph Umar's determination to find the location of Solomon's Temple. The caliph was told by his advisor Ka'ab al-Chabar—who was a Jewish convert to Islam—where the Temple had stood. Caliph Umar then cleansed the Temple Mount and built al-Aqsa Mosque on the southwest corner. Can you confirm the facts as stated by Mr. ibn Abdullah in his testimony?"

"I can, Mr. Prime Minister," Fatima answered. "Mr. ibn Abdullah's testimony is historically correct. Caliph Umar asked his advisor to identify the place where the Temple had stood, and he relied upon what his advisor told him. Did Mr. ibn Abdullah also explain the connection of Muhammad's night journey to the Temple Mount.?"

"He did," Zadok answered.

Fatima paused and waited for the next question. Zadok looked down and read his next question slowly.

"Professor al-Fawzi, you have been called as an expert witness in Islamic history. Based upon your expertise and knowledge, can you, therefore, confirm that the Muslim conquerors of Jerusalem were aware of the Jewish people's prior historical claim to the Temple Mount?"

"Yes," Fatima answered. "It is well documented that Caliph Umar specifically sought to discover the location of the Temple. He was advised that the Temple stood on the place that the Jews call the Temple Mount and the Muslims call the Noble Sanctuary."

Zadok looked at Meir.

"May it please the court—the testimony of Rabbi Avidan clearly established the Jewish people's historical claim to the Temple Mount. The additional testimony of Mr. ibn Abdullah and Professor al-Fawzi has established that from the first century of Islam, Muslims recognized that the Temple had stood on the Temple Mount before they claimed the area as their own. Whatever agreement Moshe Dayan may have made with the Waqf ignored the Jewish people's historical claim to the Temple Mount. The actions of the Waqf that have resulted in the collapse of the Kotel have violated the Law of the Holy Places. I believe that based upon the Jewish people's undeniable historical claim to the Temple Mount and the Waqf's violation of the law, this court has sufficient justification to revoke the Waqf's authority over the Temple Mount, and no further testimony is necessary. I request that we adjourn, and that you issue your decision based on the evidence you have heard."

Meir leaned forward and spoke.

"Mr. Prime Minister, this is the second time you have requested the court's decision during this proceeding. I denied the request after Mr. ibn Abdullah testified. Let me remind you that your office initiated these proceedings. You have brought four witnesses here, including Mr. Eitan. Rabbi Avidan and Mr. ibn Abdullah have indicated in their interviews with you that they have additional information they have not revealed to you, and that they still have not revealed in this hearing. Mr. Eitan has not finished his testimony with regard to his involvement with these witnesses, Moshe Dayan, and the Waqf."

Meir then turned to Fatima.

"Also, let me ask Professor al-Fawzi. Do you have any additional information you believe would help the court make its decision?"

Fatima inhaled slowly and looked at Zadok, then turned and faced Meir.

"I have answered the prime minister's questions based upon my research of public historical sources. I have additional information from a personal source that I believe would be relevant."

Zadok interrupted. "And who might that be?"

Meir banged his gavel lightly.

"Mr. Prime Minister, let me finish my inquiry, please," Meir said. "Professor al-Fawzi, are you willing to offer information from this personal source?"

"I am," Fatima answered.

"Can you identify your personal source?"

Fatima nodded.

"That source was my grandmother."

Fatima gave a long sigh. It was as if Umm Tawfiq had finally granted her permission to speak.

"Tell the court about your grandmother, please."

Fatima looked up at Meir. *Umm Tawfiq stood at his right shoulder and smiled.*

"My grandmother's name was Umm Tawfiq. She told me that I needed to learn the history of my people. She was fond of quoting Caliph Umar ibn al-Khattab, the caliph who conquered Jerusalem in the early years of Islam after the death of Muhammad."

"And what was the caliph's saying that your grandmother quoted?"

"Caliph Umar was a firm believer in knowing your lineage. When the Arabs came out of the desert to spread Islam, they lived in many places far from Arabia, never to return. Umar exhorted them to know the names of their ancestors."

"So, in other words —"

Fatima interjected, "Know your ancestors. By name. From the earliest times. . . ."

Fatima's voice faded. Meir waited for her to continue, but she looked at him, waiting for the next question.

"And do you know your ancestors, Professor al-Fawzi?" Meir asked.

"Yes. My grandmother told me, and I believe her. I know my ancestors from the earliest days of Islam. Our family has lived in Jerusalem for centuries."

Meir looked puzzled. He continued.

"Why do you think your ancestry would be relevant to these proceedings, Professor al-Fawzi?"

Fatima answered slowly and deliberately.

"Justice Bar-Aben, you told me the purpose of this hearing this morning. I have never revealed to anyone what I am about to tell this court. I am going to answer your question because I believe what I know will help the court make its decision."

"I appreciate that, Professor al-Fawzi," Meir said.

Fatima turned to Prime Minister Zadok and continued.

"My earliest ancestor in Jerusalem has already been mentioned in this hearing. My grandmother told me that he was the man known as Ka'ab al-Chabar, who came to Jerusalem as the advisor to Caliph Umar."

Fatima folded her hands on her lap. They were not shaking anymore. She breathed deeply and felt a calm come over her. Everyone in the courtroom was visibly surprised at her answer. Finally Meir spoke.

"Mr. Prime Minister, I am denying your request to conclude the hearing. I will need to hear the complete testimony of all the witnesses before I deliberate and make a decision."

Meir turned to Fatima.

"Professor al-Fawzi, I believe that whatever you may know about the life of your ancestor will be highly relevant. Mr. ibn Abdullah testified yesterday about Ka'ab's traveling to Jerusalem with Caliph Umar and advising him where the Temple stood. Can you tell us more about Ka'ab's life?"

"I can," Fatima said. "Ka'ab's ancestors left Jerusalem several decades before the destruction of the Temple by the Romans. They were prominent merchants who had established trade routes to Arabia and beyond. They occupied an oasis known as Chabar about a hundred miles from the city of Yathrib, later known as Medina. There they built a fortress around the oasis and used it as a base of trade.

"For centuries after the destruction of the Temple, these Arabian Jews traveled to the Galilee to trade with the Jewish population that survived. As a youth, Ka'ab traveled with his father, a prominent merchant. When he converted to Islam, Ka'ab took the name al-Chabar, which designated his origin as the oasis of Chabar.

"You mentioned that Mr. ibn Abdullah described the construction of the al-Aqsa Mosque. I can begin at that point in time and give you details of Ka'ab's life."

She paused and looked at Meir.

"That will be very helpful, Professor al-Fawzi. Please proceed," Meir said.

Fatima's testimony took everyone in the courtroom back to the time of Caliph Umar.

Chapter 43

Muslim Calendar, 16 A.H.
Christian Calendar, 638 A.D.

Umar appointed Ka'ab to supervise the clearing of the platform and the construction of the mosque. Ka'ab found himself drawn to the large rock in the center of the platform. Umar had ordered the erection of a low wall around the rock. Ka'ab had personally chosen the stones to be placed around the rock after the workers had found them in the muck.

Each morning, for eleven months, Ka'ab went to Umar's tent to report the progress of the previous day. One morning, several weeks after the death of Sophronius, Ka'ab found Umar sitting in front of his tent, speaking with someone in Greek. Ka'ab stood at attention and waited. Umar finally looked up and motioned to Ka'ab.

"Come, Ka'ab. Sit with us."

Ka'ab sat down across from the man and politely waited. The man appeared to be about forty years old. Ka'ab noticed a fringed garment protruding from the man's cloak. Ka'ab used to wear such a garment, whose fringes signified the commandments given by God to the Sons of Israel.

Umar spoke in Greek.

"This is Rabbi Simon ben David. He has arrived this morning from the city of Tiberias in the north."

Ka'ab cast his eyes down and spoke in a low voice.

"The rabbi and I have met before."

The rabbi spoke to Ka'ab in Hebrew, calling him by his Hebrew name.

"*shalom*, Yakov. I haven't seen you since you and your father visited me in Tiberias many years ago. You remember. I traveled here with you and your father on *tisha b'av*."

The rabbi's remarks startled Ka'ab. He had not been addressed by his Hebrew name in years. The rabbi's eyes were kind. There was no hint of animosity in his voice. Ka'ab looked down at the ground.

"Since I accepted the message of the Prophet, my father says *kaddish* for me every day, as if I were dead."

"I am sorry that you and your father are estranged," Rabbi Simon said. "The caliph tells me you are his advisor. Perhaps you can help me. You remember your visit to Tiberias and how many in our community longed to return here. We are asking the caliph to allow Jews to return to Jerusalem to live here again."

A small group of families had escaped the destruction of Jerusalem by the Romans and followed Rabbi Jochanan ben Zakkai to Yabneh, where he had established an academy for the study of Torah. During the generation following the destruction of Jerusalem, the Sanhedrin reconstituted itself with Torah scholars. It continued to meet in Yabneh under Roman rule.

In time, some of the descendants of this group had moved, along with the Sanhedrin, to Tiberias. During the celebration of the Passover meal every year, the concluding prayer was "Next year in Jerusalem." For most Jews scattered throughout the world, this was a spiritual yearning. For the community of Tiberias, it was a very real urge to return to their origins.

Jerusalem was a three-day journey from Tiberias. Rabbi Simon ben David led a small group, including his own family, every summer to the Mount of Olives. When Ka'ab was sixteen, he had traveled with his father's caravan to Tiberias. The families from Tiberias went with the caravan from there to the Mount of Olives. When they arrived at the summit, the group from Tiberias threw themselves on the ground and wept. They tore their garments and fasted from sunrise to sunset.

Rabbi Simon read the scroll of Lamentations, with his twelve-year old daughter, Deborah, standing next to him. As Rabbi Simon read the verses that mourned the first destruction of Jerusalem by the Babylonians, Deborah looked at her father with tears in her eyes. When he concluded the reading, Rabbi Simon spoke.

"Look upon the desolate platform you see below. It is where the Temple once stood."

Ka'ab and his father stood where Vespasian and Titus had stood. They looked down upon a huge desolate platform piled with rubble on the western side of the city. Until that day, Ka'ab had only heard of the destruction of the Holy City by the Romans from across the Middle Sea. Today, he could see it with his own eyes.

Ka'ab's father held his son to him.

"Never forget, my son, that you are Yakov ben Moshe of the tribe of Judah."

Then he told Ka'ab something that Ka'ab could not understand.

"The same people from across the sea who destroyed the Temple still rule the city, but they no longer worship many gods," he said, pointing to a large gray dome rising next to the desolate platform below.

"That dome covers a hill that used to stand outside the walls of the city. Our ancestors called it 'the hill of the skull,' because it looked like a skull rising from the earth. Six hundred years ago on that hill, the Romans executed a rabbi, Yeshua Bar-Yosef from Nazareth, because he challenged their authority. His followers believed he was the *meshiach,* the anointed one who would free us from all oppression. Since that time, many people began to worship this rabbi as a risen god, including the Romans. They call themselves Christians. They blame our people for killing the rabbi and forbid our people to enter Jerusalem or visit the place of the Temple. We are only allowed to come to this place once a year to look upon the destruction."

Ka'ab was saddened as he watched those from Tiberias mourn for their lost kingdom and their Temple that they had never seen. As the caravan crossed the desert on the journey home, he felt soothed by his life bounded only by the sand, the wind, and the sun. Little did he realize that he would soon hear a message that would transform him.

Ka'ab remembered his visit with his father to Tiberias and the journey to the Mount of Olives. He turned to Caliph Umar and spoke.

"I visited Tiberias with my father. The community is industrious and well respected. I support Rabbi Simon's request."

Umar was silent for a moment, and then he spoke in Greek to the rabbi. As usual, he was blunt and expressed himself with few words.

"Rabbi, Jewish trade can resume in Aelia. I will consider your request to have your families return."

Several days after Rabbi Simon's departure, Ka'ab rode with Umar into the city for Umar's weekly inspection of the mosque's construction. They dismounted their horses and climbed the ramp onto the platform. A mob of children swarmed toward them. Umar turned to Ka'ab, his temper rising.

"You allow this? Where are the parents?"

"The children are well behaved, O Commander of the Faithful. They are willing to go down into the city and bring us what we need. Besides, they are safer up here. In the narrow streets, they are always in danger of being trampled by the animal carts. And they are good sources of information. The followers of Isa still do not think kindly of us."

The children approached warily. They had never seen Umar. Ka'ab reached into his pocket and threw a handful of coins at them. They scrambled on the ground for the coins and began wrestling for them. Umar and Ka'ab walked toward the construction site of the mosque. Umar inspected the beams rising from the foundation. The outline of the mosque was now clearly visible.

Umar listened while Ka'ab described the mechanics of building the roof in sections on the ground and raising them in sequence. As Ka'ab spoke, Umar walked to the southern end of the platform. He looked down onto a sloping hill containing an abandoned neighborhood.

Ka'ab paused and followed Umar's gaze. Umar swept his hand in front of him.

"Do you know why this area is abandoned, Ka'ab?"

"I have never been down there. The children sometimes run down there and come running back, yelling."

Umar scanned the neighborhood again. He placed his hand over his eyes to block the sun.

"I believe this is what Rabbi Simon requested."

"What did he request? What do you mean?"

Umar did not answer.

"You said the children know about this, Ka'ab?"

"Yes. See the tall one? His name is Jason. He is the oldest, the leader."

"Call him over here."

Ka'ab whistled, and the children looked his way.

"Jason!"

Ka'ab waved his hand, and the tallest of the group came toward them. The others followed but stayed a respectful distance behind.

Jason was dressed in rags but stood tall and proud. He appeared to be about fourteen, with a faint hint of facial hair. The girls stole glances at him, and the boys tried to emulate his walk and self-confidence.

Jason bowed low, and Umar could detect no hint of disrespect. Jason respected authority, as he himself was an authority figure. He looked directly at Ka'ab, as if expecting an introduction. Ka'ab complied.

"Jason, this is Caliph Umar ibn al-Khattab."

Jason's eyes widened. He bowed again, even more courteous than before. As he rose, he looked straight into the caliph's eyes.

Umar pointed down the hill.

"Jason, you have been down there?"

Jason nodded and spoke in a clear strong voice.

"Yes, Caliph Umar."

"And what is down there?"

"Spirits of the murderers."

"The murderers?"

"Those who killed our Savior."

"And they are . . .?"

"The Sons of Israel. This was where they lived."

Ka'ab flinched. Umar continued to question the boy.

"Do you and your friends go down there often?"

Jason shook his head.

"I am the only one who does not fear the spirits of the murderers."

Umar reached into his pocket and held out a large silver coin to Jason, who graciously accepted the coin and bowed again. Umar waved his hand, indicating he was through. Jason walked back to his friends who stood wide-eyed with wonder at the bravery of their leader.

Ka'ab looked down the hill and then up to the summit of the Mount of Olives. He remembered standing up there with his father and Rabbi Simon's entourage, viewing the destruction on the platform where he now stood.

The caliph looked toward the neighborhood below and did not speak. He remained silent for several minutes. Finally, he turned and placed his hand on Ka'ab's shoulder.

"Before he died, Sophronius told me of this place. For a brief time, during the rule of the emperor Constantine, the Jews were allowed to return to Jerusalem. They settled in this neighborhood but were banished again after twelve years. They returned to live in this neighborhood briefly when King Kroshes of Persia conquered Jerusalem. But eight years later, the Byzantine emperor Heraclius took back the city, and the Jews were banished yet again."

Ka'ab looked again at the abandoned area. Umar continued.

"My promise to Sophronius has been fulfilled. I did not allow Jews to live in this city in his lifetime, but he is now dead. When the roof of the mosque is complete, we will send a messenger to Tiberias and tell the rabbi that his request has been granted. I will allow seventy families of the Jewish community of Tiberias to return and rebuild the neighborhood below."

Ka'ab urged the soldiers to work at a furious pace. A week later, Umar's soldiers completed the roof of the mosque.

Fatima paused in her testimony and looked at Meir.

"That is what my grandmother told me. While our family has been Muslim since the beginning of Islam, our ancestor was originally a Jew from Arabia and the advisor to Caliph Umar. He advised the caliph as to the location of the Temple Mount; he oversaw the construction of the mosque that Umar built; and he was present when the caliph allowed the Jews to return from Tiberias to Jerusalem."

Meir nodded, fascinated.

"Was it your ancestor's early connection with the city of Jerusalem that sparked your academic interest in the period of the Muslim conquest?"

Fatima nodded.

"Yes."

"Was that the extent of your family's knowledge?"

"No, Justice Bar-Aben. There is more to tell."

Amos finished translating and then addressed Meir.

"Justice Bar-Aben, may I request a short recess to speak with you and Prime Minister Zadok on another matter?"

Meir banged his gavel. "We are adjourned for forty-five minutes," he said.

Chapter 44

Meir, Amos, and the prime minister took the elevator to Meir's chambers. They went into Meir's office. Amos spoke.

"Justice Bar-Aben, we have had some evidence delivered that Rabbi Avidan has requested. The courier is here in the justices' dining room, and I need to speak with him."

"You can use my library," Meir said.

"I'd like to meet the courier also," Zadok said.

Amos nodded.

"Why don't you wait in the library, Mr. Prime Minister, and I will bring him in."

Agent Tzion escorted Aaron Kragen to Meir's chambers. Amos met them in the reception area, and he and Aaron went into the library where Zadok was waiting. Aaron shook hands with the prime minister and spoke in Hebrew.

"It is a pleasure to meet you, sir."

"The pleasure is mine, Mr. Kragen. Thank you for your service."

"You can't tell me what this is about, can you?" Aaron asked.

"No, we can't," Zadok said. "I appreciate your talents, Mr. Kragen."

They shook hands again.

Amos turned to Zadok.

"I need to talk to the courier, sir."

"Thanks again, Mr. Kragen," Zadok said. He left the library.

"Please sit," Amos said, as he sat down at the conference table. Aaron sat across from him.

"So, Aaron, first, let me ask you about the package that is now in the vault at the Israel Museum. Was it in your custody at all times until you delivered it to Mr. Aitza?"

"Absolutely. It was in my backpack the entire time, except for when the El Al agent examined it at JFK and the border control agent confirmed the custom information at Ben Gurion Airport."

"Fine. Now, I know you've been debriefed by Agent Tzion, but tell me what happened yesterday."

"Soon after I boarded the plane, I noticed someone acting strangely," Aaron said.

"How was he acting strangely?" Amos asked.

"He was an Orthodox man. He kept changing seats, and he prayed without a *tallit*. Actually, he didn't pray. He just stood near those who were praying. I also noticed that at the end of the flight, he slept through the morning prayers," Aaron said.

"What did you do, Aaron?" Amos asked.

"I wavered whether to say anything during flight. As a security professional, I know the criteria for suspicious activity, and his was arguably borderline. However, the more I thought about it, I realized that he might have been someone training for a future terrorist attack. I have read about incidents where persons move around the cabin in flight, testing the reaction of flight attendants and trying to make undercover air marshals react and identify themselves.

"Before we began our descent, I got up from my seat and noted the seat number where the person was sitting when we landed. When I went through the line in passport control to confirm my arrival with the package, I mentioned my concerns to the border control agent. I told him that I saw a person acting suspiciously, and he could have been someone practicing for a hijacking. He made a phone call to El Al security and thanked me for the information. He told me that El Al might contact me for further information. I reiterated I was under a deadline to make my delivery, and I left. I didn't know that he was an El Al security agent until Agent Tzion told me later."

"Why didn't you go directly to the museum with the package?" Amos asked.

"I had become friendly with a young woman in a church group from the United States. She sat next to me on the plane from Washington to New York, and I sat with her on the flight to Israel. After I had passed through passport control, she told me that she had asked the group leader if I could go on the bus with them to the Hotel of the Seven Arches."

"So what were you going to do when you arrived at the hotel?"

"I was going to go to the Israel Museum as quickly as I could. I hired a professional guide who was at the hotel to take me to the museum. As I left the hotel to go with the tour guide, I was surprised when Agent Tzion arrived. My instructions were to get to the museum from the airport on my own by one o'clock or call to report any delay. I had plenty of time to make the delivery."

"You believed you were on schedule?" Amos asked.

"I was on schedule. Agent Tzion and I arrived shortly after noon. Had he not intercepted me, the guide I had hired would have taken me to the museum by then, anyway."

Aaron paused and then asked, "I didn't realize anyone would track my movements once I arrived in Israel. How did Agent Tzion know I was on the bus?"

"Agent Tzion was able to track you on the airport security video from the time you landed until you got on the tour bus," Amos answered. "The bus dispatcher knows the destination of the buses when they leave the airport. Agent Tzion found that your bus was going to the Hotel of the Seven Arches and he followed."

"But why did he track me at all?" Aaron asked.

"We routinely track our couriers as they enter the country. He wouldn't have come after you if everything had gone accordingly to plan."

"Well, I'm sorry I identified the El Al security agent. He definitely needs more training. He is too obvious, and if he is trying to look religious, he ought to act religious."

Amos escorted Aaron out to Agent Tzion. Aaron and Agent Tzion took the elevator to the lobby. As they exited the elevator, they walked by the Zion Baptist Temple group that had completed their tour. Aaron found himself staring at Reverend Crosby who looked surprised and raised his hand in greeting. Aaron walked rapidly past Reverend Crosby and out the door.

Amy came out of the restroom and rejoined the group. Reverend Crosby came over to her, grinning.

"Hey, Amy, I just saw that guy you met on the plane."

Amy snorted and walked away.

As Agent Tzion and Aaron left the building, Agent Tzion called the other agent who had driven them there.

"It will be a few minutes before he returns to pick us up," Agent Tzion said.

Aaron reached into his shirt pocket and found Yair's card.

"That's fine. I need to make a phone call."

Aaron walked down the hill, called Yair, and spoke to him briefly.

When the other agent arrived with the car, Agent Tzion turned to Aaron.

"Your luggage is in the trunk. Where can we take you?"

"Just leave it here. I've arranged for someone to drive me north to visit my grandmother."

Hiram Aitza relaxed as he drove toward Ben Gurion Airport. He had sent Mr. Haskell at the Freer Gallery a delivery confirmation for the stone. Joshua sat next to Hiram, breathing the air from the open window.

This is much better than the air in Brooklyn, *abba*."

"I'm sure it is, son. I want to tell you again—I'm sorry that I asked you to follow the courier. The prime minister was not happy with me when he found out, but he wouldn't tell me the details. He said I should have left well enough alone. Did anything happen?"

Joshua shook his head. He was not going to tell his father his troubles.

"I'm just glad everything turned out fine for you, *abba*. Apparently, you had nothing to worry about."

Hiram turned and looked at Joshua.

"I like you better without the beard. I don't like the Orthodox look," Hiram said.

"I have three identities and three passports for my job. Now, I am Joshua Arad. A month from now, I will have a nice trimmed beard, and I will be Joshua Shamron. Two months later, when my beard is long, I will be Joshua Galilee again for two more months. Then I will shave it completely, and the cycle begins again."

Hiram laughed.

"You will always be Joshua Aitza to me."

Zara was waiting on the corner across the street from the Bar-Aben's building. She had called Hamid a few minutes earlier.

"I am going to do this, Hamid. I cannot wait any longer."

She hung up. Hamid was frantic. He rushed out of Zara's parents' house in Silwan and tried to flag down a taxi. Ten minutes later, Channah came out of her building. She crossed the street and headed for the market a few blocks away. Zara let Channah pass her and then began to follow. As Zara closed the distance between them, a white armored van came around the corner and stopped on the curb next to Zara. Two men dressed in helmets and heavy vests jumped out of the back of the van. One quickly grabbed Zara, holding her arms in front of her and handcuffing her. The other man gently picked her up and put her in the back of the van, slamming the door closed. Zara had not said anything, nor had she struggled to escape.

Channah and others on the street recognized the bomb squad truck and began running in the opposite direction. Other cars converged on the scene, and the bomb squad cordoned off the area.

The commander of the bomb squad truck called Amran and informed him.

Amran called Zadok, who was waiting in Meir's chambers.

"The subject tried to approach the wife, but we stopped her."

"Does the wife know what happened?"

"No. She was too far away to realize the subject might be coming for her. She ran away with others on the street."

"Amran, call in a few minutes and make sure she is treated well. I told the bomb squad to be careful," Zadok said. "The subject is pregnant with twins."

Chapter 45

Meir, Amos, and Zadok returned to the courtroom where the others were waiting for them. Meir took his seat and called the proceeding to order.

"Professor al-Fawzi, we are going to have Rabbi Avidan continue his testimony. We will resume your testimony afterwards."

Fatima nodded. She felt relieved for the moment.

Rabbi Avidan took the witness stand again. Prime Minister Zadok rose to the podium to question Rabbi Avidan. Meir summarized the rabbi's previous testimony.

"Rabbi, yesterday you told us about your ancestor, Jochanan ben Zakkai, and how he survived the destruction of Jerusalem. At the conclusion of your testimony, you mentioned that you had additional ancestors who lived during the time Jerusalem was conquered by the Muslims several hundred years later."

The rabbi assumed his didactic tone.

"Yes. I listened with great interest to Professor al-Fawzi's testimony, because it took us precisely to the point where I concluded my previous testimony. My ancestor, Jochanan ben Zakkai, established an academy for the study of Torah in the town of Yabneh. After the destruction of the Temple, the Sanhedrin had established itself there. Several hundred years later, the Sanhedrin had moved to Tiberias until its dissolution in the fourth century of the Common Era. Professor al-Fawzi may know that Rabbi Simon ben David, whom she mentioned in her testimony, was a descendant of Jochanan ben Zakkai and also one of my ancestors, as was his daughter Deborah."

Fatima nodded.

Meir leaned back in his chair.

Zadok continued the rabbi's examination.

"Rabbi, are you able to tell us what happened to Rabbi Simon after he met with Caliph Umar and requested that the Jews be allowed to return to Jerusalem from Tiberias?"

"I can."

The rabbi continued his testimony.

Rabbi Simon had hope in his heart. He had been a member of the delegation from Tiberias that had met with the Christian patriarch Modestus years before when Modestus had denied their request to return to Jerusalem.

Now, the descendants of Abraham's other son, Ishmael, had stormed out of the desert to retake Jerusalem. Rabbi Simon had gone to Jerusalem more curious than hopeful. Umar's respectful manner had been a welcome relief from the unbearable dominance of the Christians. The caliph had granted Rabbi Simon's request for trading to resume. Now, it seemed possible that the caliph might allow some members of the Jewish community of Tiberias to live in Jerusalem.

After meeting with the caliph, Rabbi Simon departed from Umar's camp. He steered Balaam, his donkey, to the summit of the Mount of Olives. Rabbi Simon shielded his eyes and looked down onto the cleared platform. Rising on the southern edge were the supports of the building, which would soon be a Muslim place of worship. In the center of the platform, he could see a ring of smaller stones encircling a larger stone. He felt tears welling in his eyes as he recited the traditional prayer of thanksgiving,

"Blessed are you, O Lord our God, King of the Universe, who has kept me alive to see this day."

He would return to Tiberias and await the caliph's decision.

Rabbi Simon walked, leading Balaam. As he traveled home, he thought about his life. Rabbi Simon had been trained as a carpenter, but he had spent much of his time studying the Torah. By the time Rabbi Simon had married Rebecca, he was a well-respected Torah scholar. Rabbi Simon's home was on the outskirts of the city. Surrounded by tall rock walls, the house had been built by his father-in-law, a merchant who had gathered considerable wealth by traveling the trade routes through Arabia, Babylonia, and Persia. Rebecca's father had retired from the trade routes and built the house, which served as a way station for caravans traveling to the east and west. He had died shortly after her wedding. Rebecca was an only child, and her mother had asked her and Simon to move into the house.

After moving in with Rebecca's mother, Rabbi Simon realized that his mother-in-law needed more than companionship. She needed employees. Rebecca and Rabbi Simon were immediately busy making sure that the merchants, their traveling entourages, and their animals were tended to and made comfortable. The high walls surrounding the house protected the merchants' animals and wares, and the merchants themselves relaxed in the comfortable home kept immaculate by Rebecca's mother. In exchange for this hospitality, the merchants paid in goods.

Rabbi Simon's responsibilities at the way station occupied most of his time. He busied himself stocking firewood, obtaining food for the animals, and keeping records of the payments of money and wares. His family could not possibly use all of the goods they received, such as wool, silk, spices, and dried foods. He suggested to his mother-in-law that they should sell the excess. Rabbi Simon found himself helping his mother-in-law manage a thriving business. He also resumed his Torah study and became known for his wisdom.

Now, he wondered how his family would react to the possibility that they would return to Jerusalem. Rebecca would be silent at the suggestion, and it would be days before he would be able to fathom her reaction. She would give hints, weaved through her conversation in subtle strands, as if she were making a new garment on her loom. His younger daughter, Deborah, would immediately be in favor of any change. Twenty years old and well beyond the age when she should be married, Deborah had resisted every available male in the Tiberias community. Rabbi Simon could not determine why she was so critical of every suitor who had presented himself. She seemed genuinely unhappy living in Tiberias, the only place she had ever known. On the other hand, his older daughter, Mariam, happily married, would probably wish to stay in Tiberias with her husband and two children.

Three days after leaving Jerusalem, Rabbi Simon crested a hill and looked down upon Tiberias. Balaam tugged at the reins, knowing he was close to home. Rabbi Simon mounted Balaam and relaxed the reins, allowing the donkey to head for home on his own.

As Balaam trotted down the hill, Rabbi Simon could see his dog, Caleb, running to meet him. Caleb ran up the hill and circled Balaam, barking excitedly, running ahead, and then circling back. This was Caleb's signal that they had visitors at the way station.

"It will be good to hear news from the trade routes," Rabbi Simon thought.

Caleb ran ahead. As Balaam trotted through the gate of the way station, Rabbi Simon saw twenty camels in the courtyard feeding on large piles of wheat and oats and dipping their noses into the water troughs.

Rebecca, hearing Caleb's barking, stood at the door in anticipation. Rabbi Simon entered the gate, and she came to him, gesturing toward the camels with her hands on her hips. Over the years, guests constantly filled their house, so they had developed their own form of silent communication. This was her way of letting him know that business was good, the travelers were courteous, and they had paid their fee in advance.

Rabbi Simon dismounted from Balaam and embraced his wife.

"We have an old friend as our guest, Simon. He will be here for a while. He is waiting for others to join his caravan."

Rabbi Simon knew every camel that plied the trade routes. He looked at the camels in the pen in front of the house, and one in particular caught his eye. It was an older male standing alone against the wall of the courtyard, with large eyes and a mouth that appeared to be smiling. Rabbi Simon turned to Rebecca.

"An old friend indeed! I have good news for him."

The merchants had gathered in the dining room of the way station for the midday meal. Rabbi Simon dipped his head to enter through the low threshold, and Rebecca followed him inside. He could hear the Hebrew dialect of the Arabian Peninsula. The Jews of Arabia now spoke Arabic, rather than Aramaic, as their native tongue. To converse with their fellow Jews who still spoke Aramaic, they spoke Hebrew. Even so, the desert winds and sun had smoothed the third letter of the Hebrew alphabet, the *gimel*—similar to the Greek *gamma*—into a softer pronunciation like that of the

Arabic letter *jeem*. This clearly recognizable sound identified those speaking this Hebrew dialect as members of the Jewish tribe that lived in the Arabian oasis of Chabar.

Rabbi Simon went to the main table in the back of the room reserved for the leaders of the caravans. All of the men were engaged in animated conversation, except for one who sat at the head of the table. This imposing man was sitting next to Deborah. He saw Rabbi Simon enter, and he rose quickly, coming to the rabbi with outstretched arms, speaking in Hebrew.

"Simon, *shalom*. We were wondering when you would return."

Rabbi Simon threw his arms around the small man and almost lifted him from the floor.

"Musa ibn Ibrahim!" Rabbi Simon called the visitor by his Arabic name.

Rabbi Simon held the man at arm's length and almost shouted, using his Hebrew name this time.

"Moshe ben Abraham! I am delighted that the desert winds have blown you in my direction."

The other men at the table rose to offer greetings to their host. Deborah rushed to her father and kissed his cheek.

"*abba*, we expected you two days ago. We were beginning to worry."

Rabbi Simon hugged Deborah and grinned.

"There is nothing to worry about. I met with the caliph himself."

Immediately, the room became silent. Rebecca looked at her husband in amazement.

"The caliph. You didn't tell me that."

"You didn't give me a chance. You were so excited about our visitors."

Moshe looked very thoughtful.

"Simon, you saw Caliph Umar?"

"In his camp outside the city walls, Moshe. He told me that Jewish traders could return to Jerusalem!"

The other men became excited, but Moshe remained silent.

"And when you saw him, he . . ."

Rabbi Simon hesitated, but answered the unspoken question using Ka'ab's Hebrew name.

"He had his advisor with him. Your son, Yakov . . ."

Moshe waved his hand, and Rabbi Simon stopped abruptly.

"The person you call Yakov falls on his face toward Mecca to pray. He has forsaken his people Israel."

Deborah's eyes grew wide. She had been twelve years old when the caravan from Arabia had visited Tiberias. She remembered Yakov expertly riding his horse around the courtyard of the way station and traveling to the Mount of Olives to see the destruction of Jerusalem.

"Is Yakov really the advisor of the caliph?" Deborah asked.

Rabbi Simon gave her a sharp look.

"Our guest does not wish to talk of this. We will not offend our guest, Deborah."

Deborah looked at her father. "I'm sorry, *abba*."

Moshe turned to Deborah.

"You remember my son," Moshe said. "May his memory be a blessing."

Deborah felt great sadness. Moshe spoke of Yakov as if he were dead.

Rebecca motioned her husband to sit down.

"You've had a long trip. Deborah, please bring your father something to eat."

Rabbi Simon and Moshe sat next to each other. The other merchants rose to give the two men privacy. Deborah brought fruit, bread, and cheese for her father. Her father caught her eye and nodded. This was her signal to leave her father alone with his guest. She placed another pitcher of water flavored with apricots on the table.

"I will go tend to the camels, *abba*. Call me if you need anything else."

She left the room, wishing she could stay and listen to her father and Moshe ben Abraham.

"Ka'ab, advisor to the caliph," she kept repeating, not able to imagine that the boy she knew so many years ago could attain such a position.

Rabbi Avidan paused in his testimony and looked at Fatima.

"So, you see, my family knew your family, Professor al-Fawzi. What you know about your ancestor, Ka'ab, I know from my own family's memory. The day that Rabbi Simon ben David returned to Tiberias, Ka'ab's father unburdened himself about his son who had converted to Islam."

"Do you wish to take a short break?" Meir asked the rabbi.

"No, I would prefer to continue."

Rabbi Simon and Moshe sat alone in the dining room of the way station. Moshe was curious about Simon's trip to Jerusalem.

"So, you met the caliph. How is he governing Jerusalem?"

"I did not know what to expect, Moshe. I had heard that the Sons of Ishmael had taken the Holy City from the Christians. Apparently, they are there to govern and tax but did not slaughter the Christians as the Persians had done before."

Moshe nodded.

"My neighbors are not murderers or plunderers. I know them well."

Rabbi Simon knew Moshe's family history and sometimes envied it. Those who remained in Israel had been subject to the whims of the Roman tax collectors, and later to their successors, the Byzantines. Some Jews had been allowed to live in Jerusalem during the time of Emperor Constantine and after the Persian conquest, but most had been banished from their Holy City. Moshe's family had remained in Arabia to worship and prosper in freedom.

Moshe filled his glass again with the apricot-flavored water and drank slowly, savoring the simple drink as if it were the essence of a desert oasis. Rabbi Simon leaned back and rested, glad to be home again.

"Caliph Umar was not haughty like the Christians. He didn't treat me as though I'd killed his God."

Moshe laughed.

"You didn't. In fact, they profess to worship the same God we do."

Rabbi Simon grabbed Moshe by the wrist and whispered, "How did this get started? The Sons of Ishmael have lived in Arabia for centuries, worshipping many gods. Why now do they come out of the desert? How do they come to worship one God? Who was this Muhammad?"

"I knew him, Simon. Muhammad was an honest businessman, just like you or me. He began to receive revelations from God from the angel Gabriel, and his following grew."

Rabbi Simon looked into his friend's eyes and saw pain.

"And how did your son . . . ?"

Moshe put his hand over his eyes, rubbing them hard, as if to block out a vision.

"My son, my son."

Moshe seemed to be on a precipice, not wanting to speak about his son but desperately needing to unburden himself. Finally, he began speaking in a low voice even though the dining hall was empty.

"You know my son as Yakov ben Moshe. But we who live among the Sons of Ishmael are known by our Arabic names, so my son was called Yakub ibn Musa. He was a happy child, as free as the desert wind. He loved to ride his horse. You remember, Simon."

Rabbi Simon nodded.

"I remember when you brought him with you here. He was sixteen years old. He rode around the way station on his horse with no saddle, with his hands in the air, and I thought we would die from fright. He went with us to the Mount of Olives."

Both men sat in silence, remembering the image of a happy youth. Moshe's face fell, as if suddenly hearing bad news.

"Soon after we returned to home, his mother died, and Yakub became restless. Nothing pleased him. He just wanted to ride his horse across the desert. He would stay out there in the night, listening for something, searching for something."

Moshe could not look at Rabbi Simon, and he wondered if he had the courage to continue speaking. He took a deep breath and exhaled slowly.

"But that was also when I first saw him lose our faith. He would come to me at night, questioning why we spend our lives mourning over ruins, in a place where we never lived. I told him because the Temple in Jerusalem was where God dwelled among us. Yakub told me God dwelled everywhere, not just in a mound of rubble."

The dining room was quiet. A slight breeze wafted through the open window. Rabbi Simon leaned forward attentively, encouraging Moshe to continue.

"Yakub spent time trading in Yathrib. There Muhammad was spreading his message of peace, of submission, Islam. He called his followers Muslims, those who submit to the will of God. He believed it was the original religion of the One God. It was a simple message. 'There is but one God. Muhammad is his prophet.'"

Moshe was speaking faster now, facing his sorrow and anxious to finish his story.

"Yakub worked in the markets, buying goods from other merchants for our caravans. One of the merchants was Umar, a close friend of Muhammad. Umar befriended my son, and from Umar he heard the message of *islam*. Yakub said it gave him peace."

"And did it?"

"I don't know. That is when I lost him. He left with Umar to help him spread Islam. They traveled to the other cities of Arabia. I heard from my relatives in those cities that Yakub was actively spreading the message of the Prophet."

Moshe put his head in his hands and stopped speaking.

Rabbi Simon put his hand on Moshe's shoulder.

"And you have not seen him since?"

Moshe shook his head and spoke again, barely above a whisper.

"When Muhammad died, one of his followers, Abu Bakr, became caliph, and after him, Yakub's friend and mentor, Umar. I soon heard that Yakub, who now calls himself Ka'ab, was the advisor to the caliph. He may have found the peace he needed, but he is no longer a Son of Israel. I called my family together and said the prayer for the dead."

Chapter 46

Rabbi Avidan paused in his testimony and addressed everyone in the courtroom. "The Tiberias community would soon receive good news. May I continue?"

"You may, Rabbi," Meir said. "Please continue."

The morning after the roof was raised on the mosque, Umar summoned a soldier to his tent. The caliph was sitting in front of his morning fire with his advisor and his generals. Ka'ab rose, handed the soldier a rolled papyrus, and gave specific directions to a small town north of Aelia. The soldier's horse was swift and covered the distance in two days. When the soldier arrived on the hill overlooking the way station, he dismounted his horse and looked at the scene below. From the top of the hill, the soldier could see into the courtyard of the way station. A woman was carrying buckets of water from a well to a water trough, with many camels nuzzling around her. Eager to complete his mission, the soldier mounted his horse and rode down the hill at a swift gallop.

Deborah heard the hoofbeats, and she looked up to see a horse and rider descending the hill. Normally, she would not open the gates alone, but she knew that her father did not want to be disturbed, and her mother was already busy in the kitchen preparing the evening meal. One person on his horse did not seem threatening.

She lifted the plank that locked the gate and placed it on the ground. When she pulled the gate inward, she found that the soldier had already dismounted and was standing at the gate.

The soldier and Deborah looked at each other. He was tall and brown from the sun, with a white headdress draping his shoulders and a long curved sword hanging from his leather belt. He looked like the men who came in the caravans, except that he had a military bearing. He stood straight and looked her in the eye.

The soldier spoke first.

"assalaamu aleyka. ana hussein ibn jani."

Peace be with you, I am Hussein, son of Jani.

Even though he spoke in Arabic, he knew that this woman would understand him if he spoke in simple words. Arabic and Aramaic were so similar that he had no trouble understanding conversational Aramaic, and most of the people here could understand his Arabic.

Deborah was familiar enough from her dealings with the caravans to understand his Arabic, and she answered in Aramaic.

"asalam aleka. ani deborah bat simon."

Peace be with you, I am Deborah, daughter of Simon.

Hussein continued.

"rab simon, huwa huna?"

"Is Rabbi Simon here?"

Deborah turned and motioned toward the doorway of the way station to find her father and Moshe approaching with concerned looks on their faces.

Deborah held out her hand in front of her, signaling to her father that everything was under control.

"He wants to speak to you, *abba*."

Moshe addressed the soldier in Arabic.

"This is Rabbi Simon. What is it that you wish to say?"

"I have been commanded by the caliph, Umar ibn al-Khattab, to deliver this to Rabbi Simon of Tiberias."

The soldier held out the messenger's pouch and offered it to the rabbi.

Rabbi Simon had understood the gist of what the soldier had said.

"For me from the caliph?"

Moshe nodded.

"Take it, Simon."

Rabbi Simon took the pouch. The soldier looked at Moshe and spoke.

"I am to ensure that Rabbi Simon reads the message."

Moshe pointed to the pouch.

"Open it and read the message, Simon. He needs to see you read it, so he can report to the caliph."

Rabbi Simon opened the pouch and removed the folded papyrus. He handed it to Deborah, who unrolled it.

"It's in Hebrew, *abba*."

Rabbi Simon did not seem surprised. Moshe reached for the papyrus and quickly looked at it. He handed it back to Deborah. Deborah began to read. The message was short but powerful.

To the people of the Book, the Sons of Israel living in the city of Tiberias.

You, as protected subjects of the Caliph, are invited to choose seventy families to return to the city of Aelia to live and practice your religion in peace.

You may establish businesses, houses of worship, and schools. You may inhabit the abandoned neighborhood south of our place of worship.

Umar ibn al-Khattab, Caliph, Commander of the Faithful

She finished reading and handed the papyrus to Rabbi Simon. He read it to himself, marveling at the caliph's swiftness in granting his request. He read the papyrus again, understanding that the "place of worship" was where Umar was building a Muslim place of worship on the cleared platform.

Rabbi Simon realized that his life had changed in an instant. He had become comfortable in Tiberias, away from the politics of Byzantine emperors, the Christian Church, and warring armies. The way station was profitable and busy, regardless of who ruled in Jerusalem. Yet he had never felt settled. He had taken the easy path, fulfilling the need of his wife and mother-in-law to continue their family business. Could he leave here and go to live in Jerusalem? He and Rebecca were thirty-nine years old. Deborah was twenty and should have married by now. Mariam was twenty-two, married with two daughters.

Rabbi Simon looked at Deborah, and instantly he knew what would be. She had inherited his restlessness. For some reason, she had lived her life ready to leave here at a moment's notice. He could see excitement welling in her eyes. He put an arm around her shoulder and spoke softly.

"Let's not mention this until we tell your mother. Then we will inform everyone."

He turned to Moshe.

"What you have heard is for the ears of the people of Tiberias. I trust that you will tell no one until I have told them of the caliph's invitation. Please tell the soldier we have received the caliph's message, and he may go."

The soldier, eager to leave, was already mounting his horse as Moshe spoke to him.

That night, Rabbi Simon called a meeting of the heads of the Jewish families of Tiberias. They crowded into the dining room of the way station and spilled out into the courtyard. With Rebecca and Deborah by his side, Rabbi Simon read the invitation of the caliph. Reaction was mixed. Some were overwhelmed and excited. Others were reticent. Some who owned land were eager to sell the land and move. Many who did not were eager to buy the land and stay. An equal number of wealthy and poor wished to leave and to stay. Some of the poor would rather be poor where they were, in a rural environment. Others saw opportunity to overcome their lot in life by moving to the city.

By the end of the evening, seventy families had volunteered to go to Jerusalem. Rabbi Simon's daughter Mariam and her family decided to stay and continue to maintain the way station with Rebecca's mother. Rabbi Simon, Rebecca, and Deborah would lead the group that would move to Jerusalem. They agreed that they would leave in one month, allowing enough time to prepare for their journey.

Rabbi Avidan paused. His face shone. It was as if he were reliving the excitement of the Tiberias community.

"The caliph was allowing my ancestors, the descendants of Jochanan ben Zakkai, the family of Simon ben David, to return to Jerusalem. They would not be oppressed or scorned, as they had been by the Christians, nor would their holy places by desecrated."

Meir looked at his watch.

"Thank you, Rabbi. We have time for some additional testimony. Prime Minister Zadok, do you wish the rabbi to continue?"

Zadok turned to Fatima.

"Professor al-Fawzi, you have heard the rabbi testify about his ancestors' acquaintance with Ka'ab. Do you have any additional information about Ka'ab's father, Moshe ben Abraham?"

"I do. I know what happened to him. He returned to Jerusalem before the families from Tiberias."

"Please change places with Rabbi Avidan so you can testify."

Rabbi Avidan rose and stepped down from the witness stand. As Fatima passed him on her way to the witness stand, she was in awe. She had just heard an oral history of her own ancestors. She sat in the witness chair and faced Meir.

Fatima resumed her testimony.

"I can tell you what happened to Ka'ab's father when he returned to Jerusalem from Tiberias."

Fatima continued her testimony.

Two days later, others from Arabia arrived at the way station to join Moshe ben Abraham's caravan. The following morning, the caravan departed through the gates of the way station, heading south to Jerusalem. Moshe ben Abraham carried with him a letter from Rabbi Simon to the caliph, detailing the families who would arrive in Jerusalem the next month.

As the camels loped forward, Moshe ben Abraham mused about the previous days. The Tiberias community had been jolted into a frenzy of change. What had seemed lost in the distant past was now attainable. A return to Jerusalem was no longer a prayerful lament, but a reality. Moshe ben Abraham reached into his saddle pouch and took out the caliph's letter, which Rabbi Simon had also given to him. He unrolled it, and his eyes welled with tears as he read the Hebrew words, noting the curve and slant of each letter. In his mind, he saw himself sitting with six-year-old Yakub, teaching him how to write the Hebrew alphabet. Each day, Moshe had taught Yakub a new letter. At the end of the day, Yakub would write all the letters he had learned so far, and Moshe would reward him with his favorite hard candy from India.

As he read the caliph's letter, Moshe ben Abraham could see the writer's hand forming each letter of every word, precisely and correctly. The handwriting was unmistakable. While the words were from the caliph, Moshe knew that the scribe who had written the letter calling the Jews back to Jerusalem was his own son.

The camels walked slowly and reluctantly on the rocky roads that fell from the Galilee into the Judean hills surrounding Jerusalem. Moshe ben Abraham was aware that his herd was unhappy once they left the smoother deserts of the Arabian Peninsula, and he noted their choppy cadence, like ships in rough water. They plied the roads of Judea with constant moaning and farting.

The caravan stopped along the way to sell the more inexpensive goods. This lightened the camels' loads and afforded Moshe an opportunity to gather information. He found a hopeful mood in the Galilee. The Arab army had left the local population alone to practice their religion and transact commerce.

The caliph demanded only that taxes be paid. The Jews had paid taxes for the past seven centuries to the Romans, the Persians, or the Byzantines. They were used to paying taxes, but the religious freedom was invigorating. The Romans had constantly offended the Jews by building temples to their pagan gods. Moshe ben Abraham had seen the remnants of Roman paganism in his travels. The statues of their naked gods were everywhere. He could not understand worship of deities who fornicated and created havoc with the affairs of men, depending on their whim. It seemed illogical that the Roman Empire, which had stabilized the world for centuries through imposition of its own law and administration, could worship entities who acted immorally. When the caravan stopped in a village in the middle of the first day, Moshe ben Abraham sat in the shade of a tree and watched his merchants display their wares.

"Silk, silk from India," one cried, as the villagers fingered cheap colored cotton cloth from India that was unrolled and spread on a small table. No one in the cities would have mistaken the cloth for silk, and Moshe was not even sure that these rural people were fooled. They just wanted to buy something that looked different from their own white cotton robes. Moshe ben Abraham had told his merchants not to call the cloth "silk," but they had their own boredom to contend with, and they believed that they increased sales by their subterfuge. Finally, he motioned his merchants to wind up their sales and pack up their unsold merchandise.

Three days later, the caravan began traveling shortly before dawn. Within an hour, they crested the Mount of Olives and looked down upon the city. Even in the early hour, Moshe ben Abraham could see a swarm of men working on the platform below. On the south of the platform, he saw a large wooden structure. He also saw the stone in the middle, just as Rabbi Simon had described.

Moshe ben Abraham felt a swirl of emotion. He had traveled to this very spot before with his son and wept for the lost history of his people. Now, he was standing here again, having lost his son, seeing the history of his people restored. The irony was painful to him. He put his face in his hands and wept. The camel drivers waited for him. Finally, he uncovered his eyes and raised his hand above his head. The caravan began its descent.

Fatima paused in her testimony. Meir looked at his watch.

"We will adjourn for the day and reconvene at one o'clock tomorrow afternoon."

Meir came down from the bench and spoke to all the witnesses.

"Mr. Eitan will arrange for you to be taken home and picked up tomorrow."

Zadok approached Meir.

"May I speak with you alone?"

Meir led Zadok to the corner of the courtroom.

"I want to know if you have considered the consequences if you do not return the Temple Mount to Israeli control."

Meir looked off into the distance. His judicial temperament dissolved.

"I told you I have to hear all the evidence before I can render a decision. That is my responsibility. To do otherwise would be to abuse the process, Mr. Prime Minister."

"I understand that, but we've spent all this time listening to family history. I don't see where it is leading us. The witnesses have confirmed the Jewish people's historical right to the Temple Mount and that the Muslims knew the Temple had stood on the Temple Mount when they conquered Jerusalem. That is why the Muslims built al-Aqsa Mosque there. That should be the end of the story."

Meir tried to stay calm.

"Rabbi Avidan and Mr. ibn Abdullah have not completed their testimony. It seems that Professor al-Fawzi quite unexpectedly has information that is filling in the gaps of the rabbi's and Mr. ibn Abdullah's testimony."

Zadok shrugged.

"Justice Bar-Aben, why can't you give Israel what it wants?"

Meir felt his anger rising.

"In this proceeding, I only know what the Office of the Prime Minister wants. As for what Israel wants, I'm not sure. There are certain factions that are concerned about the Temple Mount, and many people who are not. It is not my job to give the people what they want. I am not a cog in the political machine."

Zadok shrugged.

"You're not? Judges think they are above everything. Don't you realize you are as much a cog in the machine as any politician? You all have your price."

"Mr. Prime Minister, you assume everyone has wants that can be met. What I want, no one can give me."

Zadok nodded knowingly.

"So, you do have a price."

"I don't care to discuss it," Meir said. "It is personal and painful."

Zadok's voice was even and short.

"I would like to know your price, regardless."

Meir paused and then answered, "Do you know why I am adjourning this hearing until tomorrow afternoon? Because tonight begins *yahrzeit* for my son. I am going to say *kaddish* this evening and go to the cemetery early in the morning. Then I am taking the morning off."

Zadok touched Meir's shoulder.

"I didn't realize Ori's *yahrzeit* was tonight."

Meir continued.

"I told you that what I want, no one can give me, Mr. Prime Minister. I would like to feel my son's heart beating next to mine."

Zadok was silent.

Meir shook Zadok's hand and waited until he left the courtroom. Eli Heifitz came to Meir, offered his condolences, and followed Zadok.

Meir entered the hallway to find Amran waiting for him.

"Amran, my wife is picking me up this evening. You may go home."

"I can take you home, and she wouldn't have to come here, sir."

"We're not going home, and we don't need an escort to the synagogue. You are excused, Amran. Tomorrow, I will be out in the morning until we reconvene in the afternoon. I'll find my way back here on my own. Please, for this one day, I would prefer to be on my own."

Channah and Meir drove to the synagogue. Sarah was waiting for them. The evening service was brief. They said *kaddish* for Ori and hugged and cried.

They asked Sarah to join them for dinner.

"No, I can't. I'll see you soon."

Channah hugged her again.

"At least let us drive you home."

"No, I'll be fine."

Sarah hugged Channah closer and whispered, "When will you tell Meir?"

"Soon."

Sarah turned to Meir and hugged him.

They watched her hail a taxi.

"Let's go home, Meir," Channah said. "I don't feel like having dinner. You probably would be better off getting to bed early. I know you're exhausted. And you're getting up early tomorrow."

Chapter 47

Wednesday, April 26, 2017

The next morning, Meir arrived shortly after sunrise at entrance to the cemetery on Mount Herzl. As he entered the grounds, his eyes followed the orderly graves that flowed toward the horizon. The morning mist rose in eerie spirals, as if he were walking through the *olam habah,* the world of the afterlife. He came to a point where the path snaked to the left and the right, circling an infinity of graves. Mourners followed him, walking off the paths as they reached their destinations. Some stood alone; others were in groups, embracing silently.

Meir took the left fork, and the path leveled out. Five more minutes of walking brought him to a cluster of graves beneath a large tree. Meir's foot stepped on something hard. He reached down and found two chipped pieces of Jerusalem stone. He cupped them in his palm and squeezed them.

"I'm here," Meir said softly.

Meir placed the chips of stone on Ori's headstone— one from him and one from Channah.

A shaft of sunlight trickled through the tree branches, warming Meir's shoulders. He leaned against the tree and closed his eyes. He waited for thirty minutes, until he felt he could face the day.

Meir returned along the path and was jolted by the sight of Prime Minister Zadok waiting at the entrance of the cemetery. As Meir approached, the scent of Zadok's cologne and tobacco mingled with the morning air, burning Meir's eyes.

"I apologize for disturbing you here."

Meir was so angry that his vision blurred.

"You apologize? What is so important that you can't wait until this afternoon?"

Meir's voice was shaking. Zadok stared at Meir for several moments and then opened his arms in a gesture of submission.

"I need to tell you something. Something I believe your wife already knows."

Meir was stunned.

"What are you talking about? My wife?"

Zadok pointed to Meir's car.

"I think your wife needs to hear what I am going to tell you. Let me go home with you, and I can speak to you and your wife. Amran will follow in my car."

Meir was confused.

"I don't understand, Mr. Prime Minister."

Zadok sighed.

"We had a conversation yesterday, Justice Bar-Aben. I believe I can give you what you want."

Meir returned home at eight o'clock and found Channah still in bed. She rose from the bed and hugged him.

"I'm sorry I didn't go with you, Meir. I just couldn't."

"I know," he said. "But I have to tell you something. The prime minister is downstairs."

"The prime minister?"

"He's in the lobby. He wants to talk to us. I'll go down and get him when you're ready."

Channah had never spoken to the prime minister. She remembered that he attended Ori's funeral with many members of the Knesset. When he entered the apartment, his imposing height filled their small living room. Meir introduced him.

"Mr. Prime Minister, my wife, Channah."

Channah shook his hand.

"A pleasure, Mrs. Bar-Aben."

She waited for Zadok to speak.

Zadok pointed to the couch.

"We should sit down."

Channah sat next to Meir on the couch. Zadok sat on a chair facing them.

"You heard that a woman was detained outside this building several days ago."

Channah and Meir nodded.

"We didn't think it had anything to do with us," Meir said. "We didn't hear anything about it on the news. We assumed it was nothing."

"It did have something to do with you. The woman lives in Silwan. She was stalking both of you."

"Why? What was she trying to do?" Channah asked.

"She wasn't trying to harm you. She just wanted to be near you. Actually, she desperately wants to meet both of you."

"I don't understand," Meir said.

Zadok sat back in his chair, and his eyes softened. Suddenly, he was no longer the politician.

"I think your wife does."

Channah looked away. "Why would I know?" she asked.

Zadok took a deep breath.

"Because of your recent visit to Hadassah Hospital. And your daughter-in-law's meeting with —"

Channah gasped.

"How do you —?"

Meir looked at her.

"You've been going to the hospital? Why?"

Zadok interrupted. "I'm sorry. Let me explain. Or, perhaps, your wife might want to tell you."

They spoke for several minutes. When they were finished, Meir stared at Channah and Zadok in disbelief. Meir and Channah held each other. They were both in tears.

"You need some time to think about this. Let me know what you decide," Zadok said.

Channah looked at Meir.

"I don't need time to think about this. I want to meet her today."

Meir blanched. Channah persisted. "It's still early. Can that be arranged?"

Zadok spoke.

"I thought that might be your reaction. You can go later this morning. I'll send Amran to take you in my car. But, first, I suggest you call Mr. Eitan. You will need his help."

Two hours later, Amran stopped the car on a narrow street in the neighborhood of Silwan. Meir and Channah got out of the car surrounded by Amran, two other members of the prime minister's security team, and Amos. A group of boys kicked a soccer ball against a wall. An old man waved a cane at them, chattering rapidly. The soccer ball skidded in front of Amos, who kicked it back to the boys, sailing it just above their heads. They chased it down the street, laughing and shoving each other.

Amran scanned the buildings and found a black metal door that faced the street. A dark blue tile with three Arabic numbers announced that they had found their destination. Amos knocked on the door. A small window opened in the door. Amos spoke to someone through the window.

"They are here."

The door opened slowly into a dark hallway. Meir looked at Channah. She took his hand and squeezed it tightly. They entered and Amos followed. The security team stood outside and waited for them.

A couple stood in the hallway. They appeared to be in their fifties. Amos stepped forward. Before he could make introductions, the woman in the doorway extended the traditional Arabic greeting.

"*assalaamu aleykum.*"

Channah extended her hand.

"I am Channah. My husband, Meir."

Amos translated.

"I am Khadijah, and this is my husband, Mumtaaz."

Khadijah motioned to follow them down the hallway. The room in the back of the house was flooded with sunlight through a large window. A stereo played soft classical music. As the couple led them into the room, Meir and Channah could see that they appeared happy, luminous, as if all burdens had been lifted from them. A younger couple sat expectantly on a worn couch in front of an open window.

"My daughter and son-in-law, Zara and Hamid," Mumtaaz said.

Zara and Hamid rose from the couch. Hamid reached for Zara's arm to steady her. She was obviously pregnant. Tall, somewhat thin, and with dark flowing hair, Zara stood silent. Meir and Channah were struck by her beauty and her dignity. Zara looked at Hamid, and a hint of a smile appeared on her face. Then her eyes became moist with tears.

Zara reached to her throat and unwound a silk scarf. They could see the top of a scar in the center of her chest just below her throat. She took a step forward and stopped.

Meir and Channah came to her. Channah hugged her in a cautious embrace for several seconds, and then Meir did the same.

Zara pulled away and looked at them both. She murmured something in Arabic and embraced them again. Amos translated.

"You are the parents of my heart. You have given me life."

Zara, an only child, had always been treated as her name suggested, like a princess. Her parents had protected her and doted on her. Her grandparents, aunts, uncles, and cousins all lived in Silwan, making the neighborhood a calm and caring world. She grew up playing on the steep sidewalks that traversed the hill upon which Silwan rose from the Hinnom Valley, southeast of the Old City.

Many times Zara's parents would take her to the Noble Sanctuary to pray in al-Aqsa Mosque. After prayer, she would relax in the courtyard in front of the Dome of the Rock, and then her parents would take her inside and show her the large rock. Mumtaaz would recite from the Quran: "Glory to the One who carried His servant by night, from the Holy Mosque to the Farthest Mosque." As he explained, this verse described the Prophet's mystical night journey from Mecca to this very spot.

One afternoon, when Zara was fourteen, she and her parents had emerged from the Dome of the Rock into the bright sunlight. Zara felt dizzy and her vision dimmed. She stumbled against Khadijah and then reached for her arm as she struggled to breathe. She didn't remember anything more until she woke up in a strange room, with her parents peering into her face. Zara felt weak and cold and could barely ask the question, "Where am I?"

Khadijah reached down and stroked her forehead.

"A hospital, *azizi*. Don't be afraid."

"What happened?"

"You fainted."

"When can I go home?"

"Soon, *azizi*, soon."

Zara liked the doctors and nurses at Hadassah Hospital. She saw her parents talking to the doctors and crying afterwards. Later that night, her father sat next to her and held her hand.

"*Baba*, what is wrong with me?"

Mumtaaz leaned over her and stroked her forehead.

"Zara, *azizi*, remember that before the Prophet— peace be upon him—made his night journey, the angel Gabriel removed the Prophet's heart, filled it with knowledge of science and faith, and placed it back in his chest?"

Zara nodded. She had heard the story many times.

"Well, the doctors tell us that you need a new heart. It may take some time before they find you one, but when they do, you will be well."

Zara nodded again. She was scared. She wished she did not need a new heart. But she would wait.

She went home two weeks later, but rarely left the house. Her condition gradually worsened. Her best friend Hamid brought her school assignments. He would visit after school and help her with her homework, telling her the news about her other classmates. Khadijah, who taught in high school, would tutor her in the evening.

Zara and Hamid graduated from high school and remained close. Hamid began working with Mumtaaz, who was a graphic artist and website designer. Four years ago, when Hamid and Zara were twenty-two, they married. They lived with Zara's parents. Hamid often worked at home, so he could be near Zara. One afternoon, a year after they were married, Hamid answered the phone in the afternoon while Zara was sleeping. He shook her awake. An ambulance would be there in a few minutes to take her to the hospital. He called Khadijah and Mumtaaz on their cell phones. They rushed to Hadassah Hospital and met Hamid there.

Inside the hospital, Channah and Meir stood next to Ori's bed in the trauma center. In another room, as Sarah discussed Ori's living will, a doctor handed Sarah an authorization for organ donation. She scrawled her signature, thinking that Ori's organs were useless, crushed by the force of the blast.

The shock wave had pulverized most of Ori's organs, but the laptop he had held in front of his chest had protected his heart. Three nights later, Sarah called Channah and Meir to tell them that she had authorized the removal of the life support equipment. First, Ori's heart was removed. Zara lay in an adjoining operating room, prepared to receive it. Once Ori's heart was removed, the life support equipment was removed, and Ori's body died. Not knowing how Meir or Channah would react, Sarah did not tell them about the organ donation. The doctors could not tell Sarah who received Ori's heart, or whether the transplant was successful.

Zara's father brought her newspapers during her recuperation. Zara read the coverage of the bombing that had occurred the day she came to the hospital, including a story about the *shaheed*, Hassan ibn Sadik. When she read an article about the son of the Supreme Court justice who had died later in the hospital, Zara clutched her chest and felt her heart leap. She handed the newspaper to a nurse.

"The newspaper says that this person is the only one who died in the hospital after the bomb. Is that true?" Zara asked.

The nurse did not answer.

"You know something you can't tell me, don't you?"

The nurse pursed her lips and remained silent.

Zara reached for the paper. The picture of Channah and Meir at the graveside filled half the front page. She could feel their crushing grief, as strongly as she had felt her parents' joy when she had awakened in the recovery room.

Suddenly, she was dizzy and confused. The *shaheed* had taken many lives, yet had given Zara her new life. She closed her eyes and breathed deeply as her new heart beat steadily. Somehow, some way, she would resolve this confusion, but today she needed to rest.

As the days passed, Zara had uncontrollable urges to contact Channah and Meir. Having grown up in Silwan, she felt that she lived in a different world. Her disguised visits to the synagogue and the Kotel convinced her that human similarities overcame cultural differences.

When Hamid realized he was unable to quell Zara's desire to make contact, he read the newspaper articles that Zara had kept and decided to approach Ori's widow, Sarah. He waited for her outside her school one afternoon and quickly told her that he believed his wife had received Ori's heart. He told Sarah about his wife's desire to meet Ori's family but did not tell her that Zara was watching Channah and Meir. After meeting with Hamid, Sarah called Channah several nights after the Kotel collapsed, before Meir began working on the Section 614 proceeding.

After Meir received the Section 614 assignment, Amran guarded Meir, and Shin Bet agents Aleph and Bet followed Channah and Sarah for their protection.

After Amran had spotted Zara and Hamid, the Shin Bet monitored their movements. When agents Aleph and Bet followed Channah and Sarah to Hadassah Hospital, Agent Aleph became concerned and investigated why Meir's wife and daughter-in-law had visited the hospital. He discovered that Ori had been Zara's heart donor and informed Amran and Zadok.

The prime minister believed that Zara and Hamid meant no harm. Even so, Zadok did not want anything to distract Meir during the hearing. When Zara approached Channah, he had her detained and questioned briefly to ensure she was not a threat. He never expected that he would be the one to reveal Zara's secret to Meir, but Meir's comments at the cemetery presented him with an unexpected opportunity. In the end, Zadok, the ultimate politician, could not resist taking advantage of what he knew.

Channah embraced Zara again. As she held Zara against her, she felt Ori's heart pulsing against her breast. Meir embraced her next.

Zara looked over Meir's shoulder at Amos.

"Tell them it is a good heart. I am now strong."

Amos translated. Channah and Meir wept. Hamid came forward, put his arm around Meir's shoulder, and spoke. Amos translated.

"Zara's heart cried out to meet you. She was determined to follow her heart."

Channah broke her embrace and looked down at Zara's bulging belly.

Hamid said two words that needed no translation.

"*walid wa-walida.*" A boy and a girl.

Zara's mother came forward and embraced Channah and then Meir.

Her father spread his arms toward them with tears in his eyes and cried out, "*ahlan wasahlan.*"

Meir and Channah turned to Amos.

"He says that you have arrived in the home of your kinsmen."

An hour later, Amran drove Meir and Channah home. He and Zadok waited in the parking garage while Meir went up to the apartment with Channah.

"I am going to stay in today. No running around with Tamar. Do you have to go to work this afternoon, Meir?"

"Today, of all days, I have to go."

He kissed her good-bye.

Amran was waiting with Zadok in the parking garage. Meir got in the back seat with Zadok.

"How's your wife?" Zadok asked.

Meir reflected on the morning.

"Sad, happy, numb. We'll tell our daughter-in-law. She and Channah knew about the transplant, but not about the twins."

Zadok looked out the window.

"Did I meet your price Justice Bar-Aben? Did I give you what you wanted?"

Meir was silent for a moment.

"Thank you, Mr. Prime Minister. Under the circumstances, I believe it was only a matter of time before Zara would have contacted us somehow."

"No doubt," Zadok said.

Chapter 48

When Meir and Zadok returned to the Supreme Court, they found that Amos had picked up Rabbi Avidan, Fatima, and Samir. They were waiting in Meir's chambers. Meir called Eli Heifitz and asked him to meet them in the courtroom below. Amran escorted them to the elevator, and they descended to the basement corridor. Meir stopped in his basement office to put on his robe, and then he waited outside the courtroom until Eli Heifitz arrived. Everyone entered the courtroom together.

Meir sat in the justice's chair and waited for the rest to be seated.

"Professor al-Fawzi, we are ready for you to continue your testimony. Please return to the witness chair."

Fatima rose and came forward. She was feeling calm and in control.

Meir continued.

"At the conclusion of Professor al-Fawzi's testimony yesterday, we had reached the point where Ka'ab's father, Moshe ben Abraham, or Musa ibn Ibrahim, had traveled to Jerusalem immediately before seventy families returned from Tiberias. I assume Ka'ab and his father were reunited in Jerusalem."

They paused while Amos translated for Samir.

Meir looked at Zadok, who rose to the podium.

"Mr. Prime Minister, I am going to examine the witnesses from this point forward. If you have questions, of course, you may ask. However, in the interest of time, I am going to proceed with the examination."

"I understand," Zadok answered.

Zadok returned to his seat.

Fatima continued in Arabic with Amos translating.

As the caravan descended the Mount of Olives, Moshe ben Abraham urged his camel forward. Today, he would enter Jerusalem for the first time. The Christians were no longer in control. His neighbors from Arabia ruled. He could speak to them in Arabic, as if he were still in his own town. And what of Yakub? Would Moshe see him, recognize him, acknowledge him?

Soldiers of the caliph's army stood on both sides of the gate to the city to inspect travelers who entered. As Moshe's camel sailed ahead of the caravan, a young soldier left the shadow of the wall and walked toward him, smiling broadly.

"*assalaamu aleykum*, Musa ibn Ibrahim."

Moshe looked at the youth, dressed in the robes of the caliph's army.

"Farid? Farid ibn Salim?"

The soldier nodded and laughed. Moshe dismounted and embraced Farid.

Farid ibn Salim was one of Yakub's friends whom Moshe had employed. Farid had helped Moshe load his camels with goods before their journeys. He was always the first to come to the market when Moshe returned with foreign goods to help him unload.

"Farid, my caravan will camp outside the walls. I have a message for the caliph. Can you take me to him?"

"Of course. The caliph welcomes the traveler and offers protection to all."

Farid escorted Moshe through the city to a row of tents pitched against a high wall. The caliph's tent was the last in the row. Except for the two guards standing at attention in front, it looked like the other tents. Farid spoke to the soldiers as Moshe stood behind him. Farid turned and gestured to Moshe, while one of the guards entered the tent. The other guard approached Moshe.

"It is an honor to meet you, Abu Ka'ab. We are arranging your meeting with the Commander of the Faithful. Your son is an honored servant of the Prophet, an advisor to the caliph."

The other guard exited the tent.

"The caliph will see you now. Do you have knives with you?"

Moshe withdrew a case with a long knife from his robes and handed it to the guard.

"When you enter, you must address the caliph as 'Commander of the Faithful.'"

Moshe became nervous.

"Is there any other protocol?"

"You speak Arabic, so a translator is not necessary. Be brief. The caliph is very busy. You sit when he sits; you rise when he rises."

Farid nodded. "I will wait here."

Moshe entered the tent. Caliph Umar was standing in the gloom. His bright red hair hung loose down his shoulders. His beard was long and untrimmed, and his cloak was tattered. The tent was devoid of furnishings, except for a prayer rug and a blanket on the floor. Moshe had heard of Umar's austerity, but he was surprised to find him in a bare tent without attendants.

Before Moshe could speak, the caliph stepped forward and boomed, "Welcome, Abu Ka'ab. Peace be upon you and your household."

"And unto you, O Commander of the Faithful, peace be unto you and your household."

"The guard tells me you have a message from Rabbi Simon in Tiberias."

"I do. It is written in Hebrew, but I can translate."

At that moment, the tent entrance was drawn back and Ka'ab entered.

Much taller and thinner than the last time Moshe had seen him, Ka'ab, like Umar, was dressed in worn clothes. He stood still and looked at his father. All three were silent until Ka'ab spoke softly.

"*shalom, abba.*"

Moshe stared at Ka'ab but found it difficult to speak.

Neither moved toward the other. Moshe held the letter from Rabbi Simon.

"Perhaps my son could translate this letter for the caliph."

The caliph nodded, and Ka'ab took the letter. He unrolled it and scanned the Hebrew script. He read slowly, sentence by sentence, first in Hebrew, and then in Arabic.

"To the Commander of the Faithful, Caliph Umar, from Rabbi Simon ben David of Tiberias . . ."

Moshe closed his eyes and listened to his son reading the Holy Tongue.

When Ka'ab finished, Umar spoke.

"Ka'ab, I appoint you my ambassador to the families from Tiberias. You will arrange to collect the head tax from them. Now, go and walk with your father."

Umar waved his hand and dismissed them.

Ka'ab and Moshe walked in silence. The Christian inhabitants, accustomed to the Arab conquerors, ignored them. Arab soldiers nodded to Ka'ab, wondering who the stranger was at his side.

Moshe finally spoke. "Yakub, you are happy with this life?"

"It is my life. I wasn't happy before. Now, I am part of something. I have responsibility and respect."

"And God, Yakub? You still believe in God?"

"We believe there is no God but God, *abba*. If you believe in one God and I believe in one God, we believe in the same God."

Moshe felt reassured. He knew that the Muslims worshipped the God of Abraham, as did the Jews.

"And your people, Yakub? You have forsaken your people?"

"I have gone where our people are not. I will continue to ride with the caliph wherever he goes. When we conquer, we do not kill women, children, the old, the sick, or livestock. We do not destroy wells or break city walls. The conquered pay a tax and keep their religion."

"And a family? Do you think of having a family?"

"I think that if that is God's will, I shall have a family, *in sha allah*. But, *abba*, I also think it is God's will that you are here."

"Why, Yakub?"

"So you can see what you never expected to see."

The entrance to the platform had been cleansed from the Christian desecration. The ramp leading to the top had been trenched on either side and lined with stones to allow the winter rains to drain into existing cisterns that had been cleared of rubble. The guards nodded to Ka'ab as he and Moshe ascended. Ka'ab pointed to the large stone in the center of the expanse above.

"We saw this desolate platform, *abba*, when we stood on the Mount of Olives. Rabbi Simon told us this is where the Temple stood."

"And how did Umar's army know to find this stone?"

"I told the caliph the stone was there. The soldiers found it when they cleared the rubble."

Moshe walked around the stone, looking upward to the Mount of Olives, breathing in the clear air. Except for Ka'ab, he was the first of the Sons of Israel to walk here in centuries. Moshe finished his circling of the stone and returned to Ka'ab.

"Will Umar allow the Jews to pray here?"

Ka'ab shrugged. "I don't know. Look, on the far side of the platform, we are building a *masjid,* a place for Muslims to worship. It is *al-masjid al-aqsa,* the farthest place of worship. The Quran says that the Prophet traveled here on his winged creature al-Buraq and ascended from here to heaven."

Moshe looked in the other direction at the dome where the rebel Yeshua Bar-Yosef had been crucified. He was tired and confused. The city was now sacred to those who worshipped the crucified and others who believed that their prophets had flown here on a winged creature. What would Rabbi Simon think when he returned?

Chapter 49

Fatima paused in her testimony.

Meir spoke, "Thank you, Professor al-Fawzi. I am going to ask Rabbi Avidan to speak of the return of Rabbi Simon and the seventy families to Jerusalem."

Fatima rose from the witness chair and took her seat in the gallery. Rabbi Avidan came forward and sat down.

The rabbi began speaking.

Rabbi Simon and the seventy families left Tiberias a month after Ka'ab's father arrived in Jerusalem.

Deborah walked beside her parents, who were riding on Balaam. They had departed Tiberias, leaving behind their home, their friends, and their livelihood.

"How will we earn a living, *abba*?" Deborah had asked.

"The same way we always have. We will run a way station for travelers."

"And how will we start? Is there a way station for us in Jerusalem? We can just move in with supplies and go into business?"

Balaam turned his head toward her and nodded. Simon and Rebecca laughed.

"Balaam is wise. You shouldn't worry," Rebecca said.

Simon patted the leather bag strapped to Balaam's back. They had enough silver to start their Jerusalem location.

Three days later, at noon, the seventy families stood on the Mount of Olives. Those who had come before to commemorate the day of destruction marveled at the transformation of the city below. To the south of the cleansed platform, they could see the empty neighborhood that would be their home. Deborah looked at her father.

"What are you thinking, *abba*?"

"We have survived Egypt, Babylonia, Persia, Greece, Rome, and the followers of Yeshua Bar-Yosef. Now, the sons of Ishmael, who have allowed us to return in peace, rule Jerusalem. I just wonder how long we will be at peace here."

Deborah hugged her father.

"We will be at peace until another nation conquers our cousins."

Rabbi Simon looked down at the city.

"Let's hope that won't be for many generations."

The caliph's soldiers met the families from Tiberias at the gate and quickly escorted them to the lower district. Crowds of Christians lined the streets, peering at the Jews. Murmurs and whispers followed the procession.

"Murderers."

"Killers of our Lord."

Rebecca and Rabbi Simon pulled Balaam through the narrow street. Balaam walked steadily, as if he knew where he was going. Deborah walked on the other side of Balaam, peering defiantly into the crowd. Many of the Jews began to sing softly to calm themselves.

hnei ma tov u manayim shevet achim gahm yachad.

Here it is good and pleasant for brothers to live together.

As they sang, the Jews instinctively gathered closer together. The crowd thinned as the Tiberias families approached the abandoned houses in the lower district. Except for the children who had played here, no

Christian had ever ventured into the neighborhood. The Jews were surprised to see more of the caliph's soldiers patrolling the neighborhood. The houses were dilapidated, but all had roofs.

Moshe ben Abraham was there to greet them. He hugged Rabbi Simon.

"Every house has food, compliments of the caliph."

"Join us for dinner, Moshe, in our new home."

Moshe hesitated. "Tonight, I dine with the caliph and my son."

Rabbi Simon gathered the heads of the seventy families around him.

"This evening, we will choose houses. As we have agreed in Tiberias, my family will choose our houses first. Then you can take your families through the houses and choose several suitable for you. There will be a lottery for each house for those who want it."

The families left their possessions piled in the streets and began to drift in and out of the houses.

Rabbi Simon grasped Moshe's arm.

"I need you to take me into the city above. Can you do that?"

"Yes. But Yakub knows the city well. Could he help?"

"Definitely."

Moshe and Rabbi Simon retraced the route up the hill into the city. Moshe was silent as they walked. Rabbi Simon broke the silence.

"Moshe, you have met your son here. Have you had a change of heart?"

"He is happy and productive. I cannot close my heart to that. It is better for me to have a son than not to have a son."

"Then this is a good day for both of us."

Ka'ab stood at the entrance to the platform. He was overseeing the construction of the mosque. No one was allowed to ascend to the platform unless he granted permission. He saw his father and Rabbi Simon approaching and smiled. He had known that Rabbi Simon would not wait long to visit.

"*shalom*, Yakov," Rabbi Simon said, calling Ka'ab by his Hebrew name. "I need a favor."

Ka'ab nodded.

"I know what you want. I have already received permission from the caliph to take you up on the platform."

Rabbi Simon embraced Ka'ab.

"You are too kind. But I need to do something first."

Ka'ab and Moshe were surprised.

"I thought you would want to go up on the platform immediately," Moshe said.

"Today, I wish to walk along the wall that surrounds the platform and spend some personal time in prayer. May I do that?"

Ka'ab was puzzled, but he certainly could not refuse Rabbi Simon's request.

"Certainly, Rabbi Simon."

Rabbi Simon turned to Moshe.

"I believe I can find my way back to the lower district. Stay here, Moshe, and enjoy the rest of the day with your son."

Two hours passed. The Tiberias families had inspected the houses of the lower district and made their choices for the lottery. They waited for Rabbi Simon to return to choose houses for his family.

Rabbi Simon returned to the neighborhood with a determined look on his face. Some waved at him, and he nodded without breaking his concentration. Rebecca and Deborah saw him coming, walking quickly, his lips moving.

"*immah*, is he praying?" Deborah asked Rebecca. Rebecca watched her husband and remained silent.

Rabbi Simon continued down the central street and stopped in front of a small house. Deborah ran to him.
"This can't be our house, *abba*. It is too small."
"It's not our house. I am going to choose the large house in the center of the neighborhood that everyone expects me to choose."
Deborah looked relieved.
"But why did you stop here, a*bba*?"
"Because, my daughter, you are going to choose this house. And the house next to it, the smallest house in the district, will remain vacant."
Deborah was surprised and thrilled.
"A house of my own? Why?"
Rabbi Simon took her hand and led her to the door of the house.
"I made an agreement with the elders. My daughter would have a house of her own. When you marry, this house will be yours."

Rabbi Avidan paused in his testimony.
"Do you need to take a break?" asked Meir.
The rabbi shook his head. Everyone was surprised to see his eyes fill with tears.
The rabbi continued.
"It was an awesome moment for the seventy families. The Jews returned to Jerusalem and settled in the lower district."
He continued.

Deborah spent her days cleaning and repairing her new home. The neighbors kept an eye on her, wondering if she was betrothed, but there was no suitor. In the evening, she returned to her parents' home, where she spent the night.

The families spent the first days in the city creating a community. They discarded broken furniture, swept floors, and patched walls and roofs. They established a marketplace on the central street. They started trade with the Christian merchants in the upper city.

A month after they had arrived, Rabbi Simon convened a meeting of the heads of families at his house that he had established as the new way station.

"I have to respond to a growing concern. Some of you have asked to go up on the platform where the Muslims are building their place of worship."

A young Torah scholar named David stood.

"We have returned to Jerusalem. We should be able to pray where the Temple stood."

"David, are you the high priest?" Rabbi Simon asked.

Some laughed. Rabbi Simon waved his hand for silence.

David looked defiant.

"No, but I am a *kohain*, and I want to pray there."

"Do you know where the Holy of Holies stood?"

David did not answer.

"Of course you don't. The Romans utterly destroyed the Temple and leveled this city to its foundations. So if you go up to the mount, what might happen, David?"

"We might walk where the Holy of Holies stood."

Rabbi Simon looked at the gathering.

"Then why would you risk going up there? You know that to walk where the Holy of Holies stood is forbidden."

Everyone was silent. That was the end of the discussion. No one asked to go up to the platform again.

Rabbi Simon continued.

"The house next to my daughter's house is vacant. We need a synagogue for prayer and a study house for Torah learning. We can convert that house to meet our needs. Let us focus our efforts there."

After Deborah restored her house, Rebecca and Rabbi Simon gave her a *mezuzah* to place on the doorpost. As Deborah stood on the porch of her house, she held the carved stone container and placed a small scroll inside. Rabbi Simon helped her affix it to the doorpost, and they said the prayer for fulfilling the commandment for affixing the *mezuzah*. Rabbi Simon, Rebecca, and Deborah entered the house. Rebecca nodded her approval.

"A nice house for a family, my daughter."

Deborah sighed.

"A family? And who is here for me?"

Rebecca and Rabbi Simon were silent.

"I know everyone who came from Tiberias. I rejected them there. Why would I accept anyone of them here?"

Rabbi Simon hugged her gently.

"We have a new life here. Who knows what opportunities will come?"

Deborah looked around. Her parents had given her a table, two chairs, and some cooking utensils.

"I need something else for my house, *abba*."

"Anything. Just ask."

"This really is my house?"

"When you have a family, you can live here."

"Well, *abba*, I was thinking. If I had a bed, I could live here now."

Rebecca gasped.

"You can't live alone. You're not married. You wouldn't be safe."

"I might never be married. I can't live under your roof forever. And I am safe. No one comes into the lower district except the Muslim tax collectors. We are safer here than we were in Tiberias."

Rabbi Simon looked at Rebecca then spoke.

"We'll get you a bed. Stay for one night and tell us how you feel."

The community gossiped. Rabbi Simon's unmarried daughter was going to move into her own house. Even though they were grateful to him as a leader, they were puzzled. There were still vacant, unwanted houses in the lower district, yet they could not conceive of a reason that an unmarried, eligible woman would live alone.

Deborah had no qualms. She would continue to work at her parents' way station during the day. While the seventy families were the only Jews allowed to live in Jerusalem, others were allowed to come to the city to trade.

Deborah had moved her belongings into her house. She made the smaller room her bedroom. It had no window, and it was behind the larger room that fronted on the street. After a long day at the way station, Deborah decided to stay at the house for the first time. She entered the house and barred the door.

There was nothing to fear. The lower district was quiet. The stone walls of her house cooled her bedroom. She lay on her bed and closed her eyes. She awoke refreshed before dawn and returned to her parents' house to help prepare breakfast for travelers.

"You slept well?" Rabbi Simon asked.

"Very well."

"The house was quiet?"

"Yes."

Rabbi Simon smiled.

"And you feel safe?"

"I do."

"You should," Rabbi Simon said.

Two months passed. Deborah grew restless with the sameness of every day. She rose early and went to the way station. She helped make breakfast and then cleaned up. She shopped at the market and bought food and supplies. She watered camels and washed clothes. One afternoon she left early. When she arrived at her home, she realized she had no food. She left the house and wandered. She recognized every person she saw. Feeling trapped, she walked faster, until she was standing at the gate that led north from the lower district into the city. Taking a deep breath, Deborah exited through the gate and walked up the incline to the city above.

The upper city was crowded and noisy. No one paid attention to her. The Christians went about their routine, oblivious to the Muslim administration. Like the Jews, as long as they paid the head tax, they were not bothered. Because of the Roman destruction and the following Byzantine oppression, nothing in Jerusalem signified a previous Jewish presence. The Roman emperor Hadrian had built a long avenue known as the Cardo Maximus after he leveled the city. The Christians, and now the Muslims, used it as a market area.

Deborah came to the end of the Cardo and kept walking. Soon she saw a high wall of ashlars with a gate blocked by Muslim soldiers. Workers were carrying stones and boards through the gate.

She peered through the gate and saw a ramp ascending. A man stood directing workers up the ramp. He looked at her and spoke in Hebrew.

"Good evening, Deborah."

Deborah was startled. She did not recognize the person who spoke to her.

"I am Ka'ab. Do you remember me? I was called Yakov when I visited Tiberias when I was sixteen, and we traveled to the Mount of Olives with your family."

Deborah looked at him. Years had passed, and he was no longer a boy.

"Of course, I remember you, Yakov. Your father spoke of you recently when he visited us. He said you are advisor to the caliph."

"I am," Ka'ab said. There was an awkward pause. Finally, Deborah spoke.

"Would he forbid you from showing me what you are building?"

"The caliph does not restrict access here."

Ka'ab opened the gate and held out his hand to Deborah.

"Come with me."

When they reached the top of the ramp, Ka'ab made a sweeping gesture. Deborah was fascinated. The platform she had viewed only from the Mount of Olives seemed much larger as she stood here. Umar's soldiers had cleared the entire surface. Large flagstones covered some areas, while other areas consisted of exposed earth. There were also gaping holes in places, with large stones placed as barriers to prevent anyone walking on the platform from falling in. A low wooden building stood on the southern corner. Deborah saw a large stone rising from an outcropping in the center of the platform.

She turned to Ka'ab.

"You have changed, Yakov. You are now Ka'ab."

Ka'ab was surprised by her directness.

"I am the same as before, Deborah, except I am at peace."

"Before, you were not at peace?"

Ka'ab shook his head.

"Before, I felt lost. I don't know how to describe it."

"But you are still a Son of Israel?"

"I will always be a Son of Israel. I told my father that, and he still said *kaddish* for me. He said the early followers of Isa were Sons of Israel in the beginning, and now they are not. They accepted the nations as themselves, and now they persecute us."

Deborah looked away.

"That sounds logical. He sees the future, and he fears for you."

Ka'ab shook his head.

"My father should not be concerned. We are not like the followers of Isa who believe that a man could be God. We believe in one God, as the Sons of Israel believe."

Deborah pointed to the large rock in the center of the platform.

"What do you believe that rock is, Ka'ab?"

Ka'ab answered, "On the day we stood on the Mount of Olives, your father told us that this platform was the Temple Mount, where Abraham came to sacrifice Isaac. I believe that is the stone of sacrifice upon which the Temple was built."

"And what are the soldiers building on the edge of the platform, Ka'ab?"

"It is our place of worship, our *masjid*. From there, we will face east and pray toward the holy city of Mecca."

"Tell me about the *masjid*, Ka'ab. What does it mean?"

"Our Quran tells us that the prophet Muhammad traveled to a place known as the Farthest Mosque, *al-masjid al-aqsa,* on his winged creature al-Buraq. From there, he ascended to heaven to converse with Ibrahim, Musa, Isa, and the other prophets. Where else would he have come to meet the prophets except where the Temple stood? We, therefore, refer to this place as *al-masjid al-aqsa.* Caliph Umar believes that the rock confirms that this is the place of the Temple and therefore the destination of the Prophet's night journey."

"Why are they building the place of worship there and not near the rock?" Deborah asked.

Ka'ab looked at Deborah.

"The day the rock was finally cleared, and the soldiers placed the circle of stones around it, the caliph found me contemplating it at sunrise. I was awed. I stood before it, not believing that I was here, and Caliph Umar asked my advice as to where to build the mosque. I suggested it be built in a location on the platform so that as we faced east to pray toward Mecca, we would also be facing the rock."

"And what did he say?"

"I was still thinking as a Jew. We did not have to pray over the site of the Jewish Temple."

"And so he is building the mosque on the southern edge of the platform instead of where you suggested."

"Yes. Closer to Mecca."

"And as far away from the rock as it can be on this platform."

"So when you pray toward Mecca, you turn your back to where you believe the Temple stood."

Ka'ab's shoulders slumped and his eyes shone.

"You see my dilemma."

Deborah nodded.

"I do."

"I heard that your father told your community to avoid the platform for fear of walking on the Holy of Holies," Ka'ab said. "I did not realize that when I first ascended the platform. I now avoid walking near the rock."

"I will honor my father and not go near the rock. But you are drawn to the rock, aren't you, Ka'ab?" Deborah asked.

"I am. When I heard that the families from Tiberias were returning, I thought they would pray here, and this place would be holy to both Jews and Muslims. Now, the Jews have returned, and they do not come here. Even so, my father and I are now reunited."

Deborah smiled at him.

"Then be happy. Come to Shabbat dinner with my family, Ka'ab. Bring your father. It is time we are all together again.

The narrative stopped as Rabbi Avidan reached for a glass of water.

Meir looked at Zadok, who was fidgeting and scowling.

"Is there a problem, Mr. Prime Minister?"

Zadok flushed and was silent. Meir addressed Rabbi Avidan.

"Rabbi, I believe we are nearing the end of your testimony on this subject, are we not?"

Zadok interrupted.

"That is the problem. I don't know what the subject is. We have been traveling through the past for days."

Rabbi Avidan spoke. "It will all be clear shortly. Patience, patience."

"Please continue, Rabbi," Meir said. Rabbi Avidan leaned forward and began to speak.

Deborah returned to the lower district late in the afternoon. She found her father pacing nervously in her house.

"Where have you been? You've been gone most of the day."

"I went to the upper city. I was curious."

"And where did you go?"

Deborah was silent.

"I'm sorry, Deborah. Matthew, the wool merchant, saw you enter the gate to the platform."

"Matthew, the wool merchant, should have been buying wool instead of following me."

"He wasn't following you. He just happened to see you. Now everyone will want to go where you have gone. How did you get up there?"

Deborah paused.

"I saw Yakov at the entrance. He calls himself Ka'ab now. He took me up there."

Rabbi Simon was curious.

"What did you see?"

"They are building a place for worship. They call it a *masjid* in Arabic. It is on the southern edge. A large rock is in the center, surrounded by a ring of stones. The platform is clear, with large holes all around. They look like cisterns. The Muslims ignore the rock. The *masjid* is not near it."

"And Yakov?"

"He was rebuked by the caliph for revering the rock."

Rabbi Simon shook his head.

"I am sorry for Yakov," he said. "He is still living in two worlds, whether he realizes it or not."

Deborah smiled.

"*abba*, he and his father are coming tomorrow night to the way station for Shabbat dinner. I invited him."

Rabbi Avidan paused again.

"If you think you know where this story is heading, it isn't. This is not a romantic tale."

Fatima looked at the rabbi and nodded.

Rabbi Avidan continued.

Ka'ab and his father visited the lower district that Shabbat and had dinner at the way station. Deborah sat next to him as he regaled the guests with stories of his journeys with Caliph Umar's army and his relationship with the caliph. At the end of the evening, he told them that he was engaged to the daughter of a wealthy Arab merchant from Yemen who had supplied the army during the siege of the city. A year later, Deborah married David, the Torah scholar. They had two sons.

Chapter 50

Rabbi Avidan turned to Meir.

"At this point, the story is about Ka'ab."

Meir asked, "Professor al-Fawzi, do you know what happened to Ka'ab after he married?"

"Yes," she said. "Should I continue?"

"Please come up to the witness chair."

Fatima continued with her testimony.

In the fall of 644 C.E., seven years after the conquest of Jerusalem, Umar decided to perform the *hajj* to Mecca. Ka'ab was thirty-five years old and at the height of his power as the respected advisor to the caliph. Ka'ab had planned to go with Umar on the *hajj*, but his wife was at the end of her first pregnancy, and Ka'ab did not want to leave her. He sent a messenger to inform Umar. Umar summoned him the day before the morning of departure.

"Ka'ab, you have never made the *hajj*. It is your obligation as a Muslim. You must come with me."

"We are expecting our first child, and my wife does not want me to go. I must attend to her," Ka'ab said.

Umar's temper flared. "I have had eight wives and I must go. Come with me. I need you."

Ka'ab did not want to anger Umar. "Commander of the Faithful, please forgive me. I will go with you."

Mount Arafat, seventy meters tall and made of granite, stands several miles east of Mecca. On this mount, Muhammad gave his last sermon to his followers near the end of his life. According to Islamic tradition, Adam and Eve met and recognized each other at the base of the mount after two hundred years of separation following their expulsion from the Garden of Eden. The mount is also known as the Mount of Mercy, because here Allah granted Adam and Eve forgiveness, and they reunited.

As Umar, Ka'ab, and the rest of the entourage approached Mount Arafat, Umar steadied himself on his horse. The ground felt as if it were shaking. He looked around, but none of his companions seemed to have noticed. Icy fear gripped his heart, and he glanced around to find the cause of it. Ka'ab noticed the caliph's distressed face.

"What is it, O Commander of the Faithful?"

Umar grasped his chest. "I don't know. I thought I heard a voice crying from the top of the mount that I would never return home."

Ka'ab shook his head. "I did not hear anything. Let us continue the *hajj*, *in sha allah*."

The *hajj* concluded in Mecca uneventfully. On the return journey, Umar stopped in Medina. The next morning, he led morning prayers at *al-masjid an-nabawi*, where Muhammad and the former caliph Abu Bakr were buried. As Umar prayed, a slave owned by the governor of Bosra rushed toward Umar and stabbed him in the back and in the chest. The slave killed himself as the crowd prevented his escape. Umar died four days later and was buried next to Muhammad and Abu Bakr.

The news of Caliph Umar's death enveloped the Jewish and Christian communities in sadness. He had treated the two communities with respect, allowed them to practice their religions, and protected the trade routes.

Soon after Ka'ab's return, Deborah saw him in the market. As she approached, Ka'ab saw her and waved her away.

Fatima explained why Ka'ab was avoiding Deborah and the entire Jewish community.

"He was accused as a conspirator in the caliph's assassination."

"How do you know that?" Meir asked.

"Ka'ab is a historical figure. Basic research reveals his background and the accusation."

"Was he charged with the crime?"

"No. We know that he continued to live in the upper city and prospered. His first son was born shortly after he returned from the *hajj*, and he had another son several years later. Both sons became wealthy merchants, traveling with their grandfather Moshe ben Abraham, and continuing to ply the trade routes after their grandfather died. Whatever faction accused Ka'ab of complicity in the death of Umar was not politically powerful."

Fatima continued testifying.

The Jewish community thrived in the lower district, building schools, synagogues, and increasing their numbers. Gradually, the community began to conduct commerce in the upper city. They prayed against the wall surrounding the platform. However, they continued to abide by Rabbi Simon's admonition not to ascend onto the platform for fear of inadvertently walking where the Holy of Holies had stood.

Ka'ab had made himself invaluable in the administration of Jerusalem, now known to Muslims as *al-quds*, the Holy City. Ka'ab worked in the Holy City during the reign of three more caliphs. Beginning in the year 661, the Umayyad Caliphate moved the administration of the Muslim empire from Mecca to Damascus. The Holy City, therefore, became closer to the seat of power of the caliphate and remained an important religious center because of al-Aqsa Mosque. Ka'ab moved to Damascus to be the advisor to Caliph Muawiyah. He lived there for nineteen years, returning to the Holy City every year to perform administrative duties and visit his sons and grandsons. When Muawiyah died in 680, Ka'ab returned to the Holy City as an administrator during the reign of the next three caliphs.

Ka'ab was seventy-two when Abd al-Malik became caliph in the year 685. He was living with his sons and grandsons in their compound in the upper district, enjoying his family's prosperity. Abd al-Malik issued a decree from Damascus that Arabic was to be the official language of government, and all record keeping must be accomplished in Arabic. Ka'ab's younger administrators, mostly local Christians, looked to Ka'ab for direction. He became very busy, awakening within him the feelings of his early days with Umar when he helped establish the administration of the caliphate. During the first year of Abd al-Malik's reign, Ka'ab reorganized the record-keeping structure into a model for the other provinces.

In the second year of his caliphate, Abd al-Malik entered Jerusalem at night with little fanfare. Traveling in unfamiliar territory, the caliph feared assassination. The next morning, an official messenger arrived at Ka'ab's family compound and summoned him to al-Aqsa Mosque before midday prayers. Ka'ab arrived at noon to find a richly dressed entourage surrounding the caliph. Four large soldiers stood in a circle around the caliph to protect him from assassination. The caliph's advisor, Ahmed ibn Zayid, motioned Ka'ab to approach.

"You are Ka'ab?"

Ka'ab nodded. The minister grasped his arm and escorted him to the caliph, who looked stern and deep in thought.

The caliph looked at Ka'ab with a blank stare.

"You were advisor to Umar and Muawiyah."

"I was, O Commander of the Faithful."

"And you are a Son of Israel?"

"I am, but also a Muslim."

"No doubt," he said. "I am told that you believe that the Temple of Solomon stood where that large rock sits."

"Yes."

"And how do you know this to be true?"

"In my youth, I traveled with my father to visit the Sons of Israel in Tiberias. We would come with them on the anniversary of the destruction of the Temple to stand on the Mount of Olives and view this platform. The Christians would not allow us to enter the city."

"And who said the Temple stood here?"

"Rabbi Simon ben David, a descendant of a Jewish elder who lived at the time of the destruction of the Temple. He has lived in this city since Caliph Umar allowed the Sons of Israel to return."

"And how did you find the rock?"

"Umar's soldiers uncovered it. The followers of Isa had desecrated it with garbage."

"Well, then"—the caliph turned to his entourage—"we will build here, with the rock in the center."

A building site was marked around the rock according to the plans prepared by the caliph's engineers, Yazid ibn Salim and Raja ibn Hayweh. Construction began in the year 687, and Ka'ab often visited the site. He watched as a large hexagonal building took shape in the center of the platform, eventually obscuring the rock.

When the walls reached their maximum height, Ka'ab saw the ribs of a dome rise from the perimeter. Finally, in the year 691, the building was complete. The structure was similar to the Church of the Holy Sepulchre and other Byzantine churches. During the construction of the Dome of the Rock, the engineers also expanded al-Aqsa mosque.

Fatima smiled.

"Most non-Muslims assume the Dome of the Rock is a mosque. In fact, it is often referred to as the Mosque of Umar even though Umar did not build it and it is not a mosque. It is a unique Islamic structure. Abd al-Malik enclosed the rock with a building whose structure and dimensions were very similar to the Church of the Holy Sepulcher. Its dome rose above the Dome of the Church of the Holy Sepulcher. Its hexagonal form is foreign to Islamic architecture.

"The inside of the dome contains Arabic verses that extol Islam while deriding the Christians for believing that Jesus was God. One verse reads: 'Allah has no companion,' clearly a polemic against Christianity. Also, inside the dome is the verse from the Quran that affirms 'Jesus was a prophet of God, but not God.' Many believe that this was Abd al-Malik's attempt to minimize Christianity.

"When it was first built, the Dome of the Rock did not look as striking as it looks today. The Ottoman sultan Suleiman the Magnificent added the blue tiles covering the exterior in the sixteenth century. The dome itself was made of lead and was not a golden color, until it was replaced in the early 1960s with an anodized aluminum cover. By the 1990s, rust had dimmed the dome. In 1993, King Hussein of Jordan donated funds to purchase eighty kilograms of gold to restore the color of the dome."

Fatima paused, and Rabbi Avidan raised his hand.

"Justice Bar-Aben, I believe I should fill in Rabbi Simon's history here."

"Please, Rabbi, take the witness chair."

Fatima and the rabbi switched seats.

"Let me pick up the story at this point," Rabbi Avidan said.

In the forty years that passed until Abd al-Malik arrived in Jerusalem, Deborah and David, the Torah scholar, raised two sons who married, and each had a son. These great-grandsons of Rabbi Simon grew to run the way station. The Jewish community expanded and filled the lower district, building houses in vacant spaces and raising the existing houses skyward with additional floors.

One morning, in early spring of the year 691, Deborah was sitting alone outside her house, watching her grandsons unload a wagon of goods they had bought in the upper city. The sun was bright, and her eyes had grown dim. She was seventy-four years old. A man appeared before her, wearing a white robe.

"Good morning, Deborah."

She shielded her eyes with her hand and looked at him. She had not spoken to Ka'ab in many years. He looked old, thin, and troubled.

"Ka'ab! Ka'ab!"

She rose and hugged him to her.

"What brings you here?"

"I must speak to your father. Is he well?"

"He is alive and well. You know that. He pays his taxes."

"He is still the leader of the community in his old age?" Ka'ab asked.

"His body is weak, but his mind is as sharp as ever."

Deborah called to her grandsons.

"Boys, let's go see your great-grandfather."

They stopped unloading the wagon and came to her.

As they walked to the way station, Ka'ab said, "I am sure you have seen the construction on the Temple platform."

"Yes. A magnificent dome."

"It is finished."

"What does that have to do with my father?"

"You will see."

Rabbi Simon sat in the cool shade of the way station surrounded by merchants and travelers. He was ninety-two years old. He rose to embrace his great-grandsons, and then he stared at the man with Deborah.

"My eyes are not too dim to recognize you, Ka'ab, even after all these years. Peace be with you, and may your father's memory be a blessing to you."

"Peace be with you, Rabbi Simon, and with all your house."

"What brings you here, Ka'ab?"

Ka'ab reached into his robe and pulled out a scroll.

"This is a decree from the caliph. He sent me here because I told him I was Umar's liaison with the Jewish community. For his new building, he needs a thousand glass lamps and one hundred Sons of Israel to serve as guardians at the gates to the platform. The caliph believes that no one else would better serve to guard the site of the Temple than the Sons of Israel."

Rabbi Simon nodded and agreed.

"Ka'ab, the caliph is correct, and he is very wise. The Sons of Israel will guard the site of the Temple always."

Deborah was silent.

"I will have a meeting with the community about the caliph's decree," Rabbi Simon said. "I am sure we will have volunteers to serve as guardians."

Ka'ab stayed that morning. He went into the way station and visited with Rebecca. He ate lunch with the merchants. After he left, Rabbi Simon sat with Deborah.

"One day, my daughter, when you decide the time is right, you must tell Ka'ab the truth. For his sake, we owe him that."

Rabbi Avidan paused.

"What was the truth they needed to tell Ka'ab?" Meir asked.

Rabbi Avidan sighed.

"Gentlemen and Professor al-Fawzi, we are almost at the end of the story."

Part Six – Realization

Jerusalem
November 2035

My grandfather and I had been drinking coffee and nibbling baklava all morning. The call for midday prayer interrupted his story.

"Let me go to *salat* at al-Aqsa Mosque, *jiddo.*"

My grandfather stood.

"I will go with you today, Nuri."

We walked out to the narrow street and made our way past the shops and residences to the staircase of the Noble Sanctuary.

The security guard recognized my grandfather again and waved us through the checkpoint. It was hard for my grandfather to climb the stairs. We reached the platform and joined the others who were going to pray. We entered the mosque, and I found my place on the floor. I helped my grandfather down onto the thick carpet. Today, I prayed for my grandfather's health. I could not imagine my life without him. I also offered a special prayer that the soul of my uncle, after whom I am named, may rest in peace in paradise.

We came out of the mosque, and my grandfather put his arm around my shoulder.

"Let's walk while I finish the story. We will go to where the story ends."

We returned to the staircase and left the Noble Sanctuary. I knew where we were going now.

Chapter 51

Rabbi Avidan turned to Meir.

"I think it would be appropriate now to tell the court what happened on the Temple Mount in 1967. Mr. ibn Abdullah arrived first, so perhaps he should begin."

Meir nodded to Samir.

"Mr. ibn Abdullah, you've been waiting patiently. I am going to ask you, Rabbi Avidan, and Professor al-Fawzi to sit at the table in front of me. At this point, we may hear from all of you, and it will save you from walking back and forth to the witness chair. I'll direct the examination, and Prime Minister Zadok may also ask questions."

Meir waited as the witnesses took their seats at the table.

"Mr. ibn Abdullah, please tell us what happened the night the IDF took the Temple Mount in 1967.

Samir took a deep breath and began to speak.

"We were huddled in our houses, listening to gunfire, planes flying. After dark, young boys crept through the streets and saw the Israelis guarding the entrances to the Noble Sanctuary. Everyone expected that the Israelis would destroy the Dome of the Rock and al-Aqsa Mosque."

"I couldn't let that happen, at least not without confronting the Israelis. My wife begged me not to go, but I left the house. I encountered soldiers. I put my hands above my head. They did not speak Arabic, and I couldn't understand Hebrew, but I asked to speak to their leader. Even though I was not an *imam*, I kept saying '*imam*.' They knew what that was. They brought me up to the Noble Sanctuary."

Meir interrupted.

"Is that where you first met Mr. Eitan?"

"Yes. He served as translator during my meeting with Moshe Dayan and Rabbi Goren. I told them I was a *muadhin* of al-Aqsa Mosque, and I asked them, begged them, not to destroy our holy places."

"What did they say?"

"They said they had no intention of destroying anything. But I didn't believe them."

"Why not?"

"Before the Israelis captured the Old City, it was held by Jordan. When the Jordanians took control of what used to be the Jewish Quarter in 1948, they destroyed all the synagogues. Some were even being used as stables for animals."

"And you expected the Israelis to act in the same way?"

"I did. I knew that the Jews considered the Noble Sanctuary to be the site where their Temple once stood. So I thought that they would want to clear the area of Muslim holy places."

Meir was listening intently. He had been standing outside the command tent that night, wondering what was happening inside.

"What happened next?"

"To convince them not to harm the Muslim holy places, I wanted to tell Moshe Dayan and the army rabbi what had been passed down in my family from the early days."

"What did you tell them?"

"I told them I was a descendant of Caliph Umar, the caliph who had captured Jerusalem from the Christians, and that I had information they would want to know if Israel controlled the Old City."

"How did they respond?"

Samir paused. He looked at Rabbi Avidan.

"Well, before I could say anything more, Rabbi Avidan arrived."

Meir turned to Rabbi Avidan.

"Rabbi, what happened next?"

Rabbi Avidan cleared his throat. Prime Minister Zadok's eyes narrowed. Fatima suspected she already knew what the rabbi would say. Samir nodded in agreement as Amos translated the rabbi's words.

"As I mentioned before, Rabbi Goren knew that I wanted to be present if Israel ever reclaimed the Temple Mount. He arranged for me to come there that night. When I arrived, Mr. ibn Abdullah was there with Moshe Dayan and Rabbi Goren."

"Did you have any objection to speaking with Mr. ibn Abdullah there?"

"No. He told us he was a *muadhin* of al-Aqsa Mosque. I wanted Mr. ibn Abdullah to hear what I had to say."

"Please tell us what you told them."

"Well, I believe Professor al-Fawzi, who is a historian, will agree with me that there is not just one theory as to where the Temple stood."

Fatima nodded.

"Yes, Rabbi, I believe we all agree that no one is certain exactly where the Temple stood on the Temple Mount."

The rabbi continued.

"Most Jews assume that the Temple stood where the Dome of the Rock now stands. This is the 'central theory,' because it places the Dome of the Rock in the center of the Temple Mount. Also, some believe the rock under the Dome is the place of the Holy of Holies in the Temple. One archaeologist believes he has been able to identify the location on the rock where the Ark of the Covenant stood.

"Prominent archaeologists have proposed two other theories. The first theory places the Temple to the north of where the Dome of the Rock now stands. The second places the Temple south of the Dome of the Rock, in the area that is now the courtyard of the Dome of the Rock and al-Aqsa Mosque."

Zadok and Meir nodded in agreement.

"I know the archaeology. But, Rabbi, you didn't go to the Temple Mount that night to have a discussion about archaeological theories," Meir said.

"No. I went to tell them what I believe is fact."

"Which is?"

The rabbi paused.

"Justice Bar-Aben, at the beginning of this hearing, you asked me if I had any advice for you. Do you remember what I said?"

Meir smiled.

"You told me that the study of Talmud assumes nothing. Everything must be proven. I believe you were saying that we should not assume anything in this proceeding, and everything must be proven."

Rabbi Avidan nodded.

"Correct. That advice applies to those who attempt to determine the location of the Temple. They should not assume anything, but must prove even the most basic assumption. However, there is one thing that all the theories assume."

"And what is that, Rabbi?"

"All of these theories assume that the Temple stood on this platform that the Jews call the Temple Mount and the Muslims now call the Noble Sanctuary."

Everyone was silent. Fatima and Samir were nodding their heads in agreement. Prime Minister

Zadok frowned and looked at the rabbi. Meir was the first to speak.

"So, Rabbi, you are saying that we should not assume that the Temple stood on the place that is called the Temple Mount?"

Rabbi Avidan sat back in his chair and said softly but authoritatively, "I am saying more. I am saying that you should not assume it, because it is an incorrect assumption. It has been passed down through my family, from generation to generation, that the Temple did not stand on the platform we call the Temple Mount."

Chapter 52

After a long pause, Meir turned to Samir.

"Did you hear Rabbi Avidan tell all this to Moshe Dayan and Rabbi Goren that night?"

Amos translated and Samir nodded.

"Yes. I heard Rabbi Avidan say that he believed the Temple had not stood on the Noble Sanctuary," he said.

Samir looked down at the table and then looked at Rabbi Avidan.

"And that is what I also told them."

Zadok looked stunned.

"How did you know that?" Meir asked.

"Because," Samir said, "after the Dome of the Rock was built, Ka'ab told one of Caliph Umar's sons that the Jewish Temple had never stood on the Noble Sanctuary. Ka'ab did not say how he knew this nor did he say where the Temple stood, or even if he knew where it stood. This has been passed down in our family over the centuries."

Zadok turned to Meir.

"I don't understand this at all. This is ridiculous."

Zadok looked as if he were going to explode.

Meir knocked his gavel gently on the table.

Everyone was quiet. Meir leaned forward and spoke.

"Let me see if I understand this. Rabbi Avidan, you say that over the centuries, your family has handed down the knowledge that the Temple did not stand on the Temple Mount. Mr. ibn Abdullah, you say that Ka'ab told one of your ancestors that the Temple did not stand on the Noble Sanctuary. Even so, Ka'ab had told Umar that the Temple had stood on the Christian dumping ground that later became the Noble Sanctuary and that Ka'ab identified as the Temple Mount."

Meir turned to Rabbi Avidan.

"Do you know why Ka'ab believed that the Temple did not stand on the Temple Mount?"

Rabbi Avidan nodded.

"I do. And perhaps Professor al-Fawzi knows also."

Everyone turned to Fatima, who had been listening intently.

"I can speak for Ka'ab. I know who told him and when."

Zadok put his head in his hands.

"Please continue, Professor al-Fawzi," Meir said.

"Rabbi Avidan testified that after the Dome of the Rock was built, Ka'ab came to ask Rabbi Simon for one hundred Jews to serve as guardians of the Temple," Fatima said. "After that, the caliph enlisted Jewish males to guard the gates leading to the platform. On Mondays and Thursdays, one thousand glass lamps illuminated the Dome of the Rock. The sweet odor of incense and rose water mixed inside the dome drifted across the city. This practice continued during the caliphate of Abd al-Malik.

"Ka'ab lived as a Muslim for the rest of his life. He did not forsake the message of the Prophet. Even so, it weighed on him that he had revealed the site of the Temple to Umar, who had intentionally left the site bare. It also disturbed him that Abd al-Malik built the Dome of the Rock there, not as a place of worship for Muslims but as a message to Christians as to the dominance of Islam.

"And then one morning, a year after the completion of the Dome of the Rock, a messenger from the lower district came to Ka'ab and told him that Rabbi Simon had died in his sleep the night before. That night, after Rabbi Simon's funeral, Deborah told Ka'ab that the

Temple had not stood on the platform where the Dome of the Rock and al-Aqsa Mosque were built."

She paused. Zadok leaned forward.

"So, where did the Temple stand? I'm losing patience with this whole proceeding."

"I don't know," Fatima said. "Ka'ab never revealed where the Temple stood."

Rabbi Avidan interrupted.

"Please have patience, Mr. Prime Minister. I know where the Temple stood. And I will tell you."

The room fell silent.

The rabbi spoke slowly.

"Justice Bar-Aben, I know where the Temple stood, and that is why I came to the Temple Mount to meet with Moshe Dayan and Rabbi Goren. It was finally time for others to know."

"So what did you tell them?" Meir asked.

"I told them everything I've told you until now. Then I told them what Deborah told Ka'ab on the day of Rabbi Simon's funeral. Mr. Ibn Abdullah, remember when I asked to speak to them privately?"

"I remember," Samir said. "You confirmed that the Temple had not stood on the Noble Sanctuary, but I did not hear anything more."

"Let me tell the court what I told them," Rabbi Avidan said. He continued his testimony.

Two donkeys pulled a cart carrying Rabbi Simon's coffin up the same worn path that Rabbi Jochanan ben Zakkai had followed in his coffin the night he met Vespasian. Deborah, her husband, and sons walked behind the cart, followed by the entire Jewish community. Ka'ab walked respectfully behind. The procession arrived at the open grave. The funeral proceeded quickly. Everyone offered prayers, and then they lowered the coffin into the grave. The family shoveled dirt into the grave, and the members of the community each shoveled three times to fill the grave.

As the grave filled, Deborah turned and looked down on the city. In her grief, she remembered standing above with her father, looking at the destruction below. Today, the sun shone on the Dome of the Rock and al-Aqsa Mosque, which stood in the place of the destruction she had seen in her youth. She could see the lower district south of the Muslim shrines.

She noticed Ka'ab standing among the crowd—a distinguished public servant of the caliphate. She looked at Ka'ab and their eyes locked. He came to her.

"May his memory be a blessing always."

When she looked into his eyes, she knew what she must do—for herself and for him.

"Come to the *shiva* at my house tonight, Ka'ab. I have something to tell you."

As the sun set, Ka'ab walked into the lower district. The neighborhood was prosperous. The houses were larger, and the streets were narrower. Some houses were two stories, with balconies overlooking the streets. Deborah's house was enclosed by a wall that created a courtyard surrounding it. Ka'ab entered the house and found it crowded with those paying their respects. Deborah was sitting with her family at a table groaning with food. She rose and came to him.

Before he had a chance to speak, she said, "Let's go outside in the courtyard."

They walked into the cool night air. Ka'ab was puzzled.

"What is it, Deborah? You seem disturbed. Is this about your father?"

"Yes. My father kept a secret that he told me after we came to Jerusalem. I feel that I must tell you, because he wanted me to tell you."

Deborah took Ka'ab's hand.

"Remember the day we stood with you and your father on the Mount of Olives? My father told us that the Temple had stood on the desolate platform below, the one surrounded by high walls, the one where your mosque and Dome of the Rock now stand."

"Of course I remember. That is how I knew to tell Caliph Umar where the Temple stood."

"What my father said that day was not true. The morning after I slept in my own house in the lower district, shortly before I went up to the platform with you, my father finally told me the truth. He told me that I was the only one he would tell, his youngest child. I must tell it to my youngest child who must tell it to the youngest child of the next generation. *l'dor va dor.* From generation to generation."

"Why are you telling me this now?" Ka'ab asked.

"You took me up to the platform and told me you had revealed to Umar where the Temple stood. You told Umar, and he built a mosque there. Abd al-Malik built the Dome of the Rock there, also believing that is where the Temple stood. You felt conflicted for doing this. When you came to ask for guardians for the site of the Temple, my father realized we must tell you the truth. He left it to me to decide when to tell you."

Ka'ab looked at her, his face blank. Finally he spoke.

"And so, if the Temple did not stand on the platform, where did it stand?"

Deborah slowly swept her arm around the courtyard where they were standing.

"It stood here."

"Here?" Ka'ab asked. "Here in the lower district?"

"Here, where my house and courtyard are now. The Temple Mount extended from here. That is why my father asked the community to build a synagogue and study house next to my house. The community prays over the site of the Temple, although they do not realize it."

Ka'ab shook his head in disbelief.

"How did your father know that the Temple stood here?"

"Jochanan ben Zakkai, a member of the Sanhedrin when the Temple was destroyed, is our ancestor," Deborah said. "He knew the true location of the Temple, and it has been handed down in our family from generation to generation."

"So the platform is not the site of the Temple or of Muhammad's night journey?" Ka'ab asked, his eyes wide with amazement.

Deborah sighed. "I don't know if Muhammad was ever there, but I know the Temple was not."

"How did Jochanan ben Zakkai know where the Temple stood?" Ka'ab asked.

Deborah shook her head. "That is a secret that only my family will ever know."

Chapter 53

Meir leaned forward, fascinated. "Rabbi Avidan, can you answer Ka'ab's question? How did Jochanan ben Zakkai know where the Temple stood?"

"I will answer that. But first, let me tell you what stood on what we call the Temple Mount. Remember, a messenger came to Jochanan ben Zakkai in Yabneh after the Temple had been destroyed. The messenger said that the fire that had destroyed the Temple was so intense that all the precious metal on and inside the building had melted. After the destruction, the Romans pried every stone apart, looking for the congealed gold and silver. They destroyed the Temple to its very foundation, and they destroyed the walls of the city.

Many of the survivors were executed and the remainder who had not escaped were sent to Rome as slaves. There was no visual memory of the geography that had existed before the destruction."

Meir interrupted. "So if the Romans destroyed the Temple, the Temple's foundation, and the walls of the city, how do you explain that the Kotel and the other walls surrounding the Temple Mount are still standing? Would they not have been included in the destruction of the city?"

Rabbi Avidan put his finger to his forehead.

"Yes, these walls did exist before the destruction. However, they were part of an area next to the city that neither the Jews nor the Romans considered part of Jerusalem. This area was the Roman's Fortress Antonia, the headquarters for the Roman military and administration officials. The lower level was a prison. The Zealot rebels had occupied the fortress, and the

Romans destroyed its upper structure during the final assault. The Romans had no need to destroy this area further. In fact, they were careful to preserve the platform to allow the Roman Tenth Legion to camp there after the destruction. The wall that remains to this day, including that portion now known as the Kotel, is the wall of the lower structure of Fortress Antonia. That wall did not surround the place where the Temple stood.

"The messenger told Jochanan ben Zakkai that the desolate platform and the wall surrounding it were the remnants of Fortress Antonia. A year after the destruction, Jochanan ben Zakkai went from Yabneh back to Jerusalem and saw the destruction from the Mount of Olives."

Silence descended in the room. Meir felt the flash of understanding that struck him whenever he reached a decision. It came to him in an instant. It was a sense of order and rationality that later could be parsed into words and sentences.

Rabbi Avidan continued.

"Jochanan ben Zakkai knew that the Temple and the Temple Mount had been destroyed. This knowledge was passed down from generation to generation by Jochanan ben Zakkai's descendants to Rabbi Simon's generation. As the years passed, Jerusalem was destroyed again by the Roman emperor Hadrian and rebuilt. After the Romans, the Byzantine Christians changed the face of the city again. When Lady Helena, the mother of the Byzantine emperor Constantine, had identified the desolate platform as the site of the Temple, she possessed no actual knowledge of the past geography of Jerusalem. Jochanan ben Zakkai's descendants were the only ones who knew how to find where the Temple once stood. When Rabbi Simon came to the Mount of Olives and looked below, he knew that the desolate platform being used as a garbage dump by the Byzantines was not the site of the Temple. Rabbi Simon knew that the Christians incorrectly believed that the desolate platform was the site of the Temple, and he jealously guarded the true location, even from his own community."

Zadok sighed. "Rabbi, I am confused. Mr. ibn Abdullah told us that a delegation of Jews from Tiberias, including Rabbi Simon, came to Modestus— Sophronius's predecessor—even before the Muslim conquest and requested to return to Jerusalem. Modestus took them to the place that ultimately became known as the Noble Sanctuary and the Temple Mount."

Rabbi Avidan nodded.

"Mr. ibn Abdullah was correct. He related what Umar had been told by Sophronius. Sophronius had been present when the delegation met with Modestus. Modestus was the one who led the delegation to the desolate platform, because he assumed he knew where the Temple stood. Rabbi Simon himself never acknowledged to Modestus that the Temple stood on the desolate platform. Rabbi Simon remained silent."

"Let me ask another question, Rabbi," Meir said. "If the seventy families from Tiberias settled in the area where the Temple had stood, why didn't Rabbi Simon reveal to the community that they were living in the vicinity of the Temple and petition the caliph to allow them to rebuild the Temple?"

"Your question assumes that Rabbi Simon would want to rebuild the Temple," Rabbi Avidan answered. "Rabbi Simon wanted to keep the location of the Temple hidden from future generations."

"Why was that?"

"When the Jews were in exile in Babylonia after the destruction of the First Temple, the focus of Judaism shifted. While in captivity in Babylonia, the rabbis, or teachers, substituted prayer and Torah study for Temple worship. The priesthood without the Temple had no venue to perform its Temple rituals. When the Jews returned from exile and rebuilt the Temple, the religious elite, the priesthood, again controlled the Temple and the tax collection function in the form of sacrifice. But Torah study and prayer in study houses or synagogues evolved during the period of the Second Temple.

"Jochanan ben Zakkai declared, after the Second Temple was destroyed and sacrifice no longer possible, that acts of kindness and charity would substitute for animal sacrifice. Prayer and the houses of study, the synagogues, would replace Temple worship. The functionary priests in the Temple no longer had a major place in society, and it was the rabbis or teachers who would guide the people. The study and observance of Torah would strengthen them. This mindset existed in Yabneh after the destruction and thereafter in Tiberias until Rabbi Simon's generation.

"Except for Rabbi Simon, the Tiberias community that returned to Jerusalem had no knowledge of the geography that existed in 70 C.E. They believed what Rabbi Simon had told them—that the desolate platform they had viewed from the Mount of Olives was the Temple Mount. Therefore, they also believed that the wall around it was a remnant of the Temple. When Rabbi Simon led the Tiberias community back to Jerusalem, rebuilding the Temple was not a reality he wished to achieve. He, therefore, guarded the true location and did not reveal it to anyone except Deborah."

The rabbi paused for moment.

"That is why I have refused to be part of the new Sanhedrin that calls for the rebuilding of the Temple. We have survived against all odds for almost two thousand years because of our adherence to prayer and the study of Torah. The Temple and its practices belong to history. I do not yearn to rebuild the Temple."

Chapter 54

Meir asked another question.

"Rabbi, you testified that Deborah's house stood over the location of the Temple. How did Rabbi Simon and Deborah know that?"

Rabbi Avidan responded, "Rabbi Simon knew how to determine the exact location of the Temple. The night the messenger arrived in Yabneh to tell Jochanan ben Zakkai about the destruction of Jerusalem, the messenger gave Jochanan ben Zakkai a stone. He told Jochanan ben Zakkai that the stone had been chiseled from the foundation wall of Fortress Antonia the night before the Romans destroyed the Temple. The center of the Temple site was a certain number of paces south of that place from where the stone had been chiseled from the wall of Fortress Antonia. Jochanan ben Zakkai's descendants passed down the stone and the instructions to locate the Temple's site through the generations.

"Remember, I testified that the day the community arrived in the lower district, Rabbi Simon went to the upper city with Moshe ben Abraham and Ka'ab. He did not want to ascend the platform. Rather, he wanted to walk along the wall surrounding the platform. Rabbi Simon had the stone with him, and he found the indentation in the wall from where the stone had been removed. He returned to the lower district, counting the correct number of paces. This brought him to location where two houses stood—the one he selected for Deborah and the one that was later used as the community's synagogue."

Meir asked the ultimate question.

"So, today, based on everything you have said, where would you say the Temple once stood?"

The rabbi finally smiled.

"I will tell you what I told Moshe Dayan and Rabbi Goren in 1967. I told them that the Temple stood in what is now the neighborhood of Silwan, south of the Temple Mount. That is where the Tiberias families lived, in the lower district."

Prime Minister Zadok interrupted. "Rabbi, let me understand this. You are saying that the Temple actually stood in what is now the neighborhood of Silwan. The Kotel is not part of the original Temple Mount but is actually one of the walls that surrounded the Roman fortress, Antonia."

"Exactly. Today this is not as unbelievable as it may have seemed in 1967," Rabbi Avidan answered. "Extensive excavations have been ongoing since the 1990s in Silwan in the area that archaeologists call the City of David. This area contains archaeological evidence of habitation during King David's reign before the construction of the First Temple. One respected archaeologist believes that she has discovered the remains of King David's palace there. It seems plausible that the Temple actually stood in Silwan, rather than the place we now call the Temple Mount."

"When did you tell Moshe Dayan and Rabbi Goren that the Temple stood in Silwan?" Meir asked.

"Mr. ibn Abdullah stayed in the command tent with Mr. Eitan. Moshe Dayan, Rabbi Goren and I left the command tent and descended to the Kotel. I looked for an indentation at approximately shoulder height where a stone had been chiseled from the wall. After searching, we found it. I removed my stone from my bag and placed it on the indentation. Moshe Dayan shined his flashlight on the stone placed against the wall, and we could all see that the stone matched the indentation. I told Moshe Dayan and Rabbi Goren what the messenger had told Jochanan ben Zakkai and the significance of the stone. I told them that Rabbi Simon had counted his paces from this indentation, to determine the location of the Temple. Mr. ibn Abdullah and Mr. Eitan were in the command tent, and did not hear this. They heard nothing of the stone or the method for finding the Temple."

Meir asked, "You had the stone that was passed down in your family since the destruction of the Temple, given to Jochanan ben Zakkai by the messenger?"

"Yes."

Meir continued, "Did Moshe Dayan and Rabbi Goren believe what you were telling them? After almost two thousand years, you placed a stone in an indentation in the wall. How could they be sure that your stone came from the wall, or that it came from that place in the wall?"

The rabbi shrugged.

"I did not know if they believed me or not. They asked me how many paces Rabbi Simon had counted from the indentation to find what he had believed was the Temple site. I politely refused to tell them. I did not come there that night to reveal the true location of the Temple. You must remember that the consequences of capturing the Temple Mount, which had also been sacred to Muslims for many centuries, had the potential for more war and destruction. I suggested to Moshe Dayan and Rabbi Goren that they maintain the *status quo*, and return the Temple Mount to the Waqf. The only way I could convince them to do that was to tell them what I believed to be true, that the Temple never stood there.

When we returned to the command tent, Mr. Eitan and Mr. ibn Abdullah were waiting. The soldiers escorted Mr. ibn Abdullah and me off the Temple

Mount. I don't know what discussions Moshe Dayan and Rabbi Goren had after that.

"I never spoke with either of them again. When I saw in the next few days that the army had bulldozed the area around the Kotel to create a large plaza, I assumed they did not believe me. Then, several days later, I heard that Moshe Dayan had returned the Temple Mount to the Waqf. That is all I know. Maybe Moshe Dayan did believe me. Rabbi Goren continued to advocate that Israel take back the Temple Mount from the Waqf after the Six-Day War. He tried to pray on the Temple Mount on *tisha b'av* in August after the war ended. In 1986, he convened a forum of rabbis who concluded that a synagogue should be built on the Temple Mount for Jewish worship. This indicated to me that Rabbi Goren did not believe me."

Zadok looked annoyed.

Meir turned to Amos.

"Mr. Eitan, how much of this did you hear that night on the Temple Mount?"

Amos answered, "I heard Mr. ibn Abdullah and Rabbi Avidan state that the Temple had not stood on the Temple Mount. At that point, the rabbi left with Moshe Dayan and Rabbi Goren. I did not hear what he told them, and I did not know where they went. When they came back, Moshe Dayan and Rabbi Goren were silent. Rabbi Avidan said good-bye, and the soldiers escorted him and Mr. ibn Abdullah off the Temple Mount. I suppose that we have heard much more detail during this hearing."

Rabbi Avidan nodded.

"That is correct."

Meir continued. "Mr. Eitan, I am going to ask the prime minister to explain why he believes you have knowledge that you haven't told us."

Zadok cleared his throat and spoke deliberately.

"Mr. Eitan was present with Moshe Dayan during discussions with the Waqf. If there were an agreement between Moshe Dayan and the Waqf, he would have to know the substance of it. I am certain that the Waqf's excavations under the Temple Mount would be in violation of any agreement that existed."

Amos replied, "I know of no agreement. Once the rabbi and Mr. ibn Abdullah were escorted from the Temple Mount, I heard nothing else. When Moshe Dayan met with the Waqf, he returned the Temple Mount to their control without conditions."

"Mr. Prime Minister, have you attempted to discover any information from the members of the Waqf who were present that day?" Meir asked.

"No, we have not. Under the circumstances, we did not think it would be politically prudent to inquire. Such inquiry would only raise questions as to the reasons for the inquiry."

"Is there anything else you wish to ask about that subject, Mr. Prime Minister?" Meir asked.

"No, Justice Bar-Aben. Thank you."

Meir turned to Rabbi Avidan.

"Where is the stone, Rabbi?"

Rabbi Avidan sighed.

"The stone had been in my family for generations. Moshe Dayan asked for it that night. He said that it would help him decide what he was going to do. After he returned the Temple Mount to the Waqf, I expected that he would return it. I tried several times over the years to communicate with him, but I never heard from him."

"I'm surprised Moshe Dayan never responded to you," Meir said.

Zadok interrupted.

"I have to say that I'm not surprised. The director of the Israel Museum is my close friend When Rabbi

Avidan began looking for an artifact from Moshe Dayan's collection, I asked my friend how Moshe Dayan gathered his collection. He told me that Moshe Dayan was obsessed with antiquities and went to great lengths to create his personal collection. Archaeologists, journalists, and a former member of the Knesset have alleged that Moshe Dayan illegally obtained many antiquities in his collection. One of Dayan's biographers wrote that later in life, Dayan would sit for hours, transfixed by the sight of scratches on an ancient artifact. The Israel Museum paid a large sum to acquire a major portion of Moshe Dayan's collection from his estate after his death. The museum was criticized for paying for artifacts that many believed rightfully belonged to the State of Israel."

"I can't speak for Moshe Dayan's penchant for collecting artifacts," Rabbi Avidan said. "I was very disappointed that he did not respond to me. When Prime Minister Zadok interviewed me before this hearing began, I told him there was evidence that could support my testimony at the hearing. I did not tell him about my knowledge of the location of the Temple, nor did I tell him the significance of the evidence. I told him that I believed the evidence was in the Israel Museum."

"That's correct," Zadok said. "The rabbi told me that he believed an artifact in the Israel Museum would support his testimony. He even told me where it was in the museum. I did not mention the stone specifically in the rabbi's interview summary. Justice Bar-Aben, you may remember that the summary mentioned that Rabbi Avidan believed there was evidence to support his testimony."

"After Moshe Dayan's death," Rabbi Avidan said, "I read that his family sold a large portion of his collection to the Israel Museum. I visited the museum and saw a stone similar to mine, exhibited as an artifact from the Second Temple period. Of course, I could not examine it."

"Is it there now?" Meir asked. Rabbi Avidan turned to Prime Minister Zadok.

"It is," Rabbi Avidan replied. "Prime Minister Zadok arranged for me to examine it before the hearing, but it is not the one I gave to Moshe Dayan. However, I understand that since then we may have found the stone I gave to Moshe Dayan elsewhere."

"Yes," Zadok said. "A portion of Moshe Dayan's collection was auctioned in the United States. We were able to locate a stone from his collection that might be the rabbi's stone."

"Rabbi, would you be able to recognize the stone if you saw it again?" Meir asked.

"If I could hold the stone and examine it, I would be able to recognize it."

"If it pleases the court," Zadok said, "the stone has been delivered from the United States and is in a vault in the Israel Museum. I can have it delivered to your chambers immediately. Amran can go up to your chambers and bring it here."

"Please, Mr. Prime Minister, one more question and then I will ask you to have the stone delivered here," Meir said. "Rabbi Avidan, if you had the stone, could you find the indentation in the Kotel from where the stone was removed?"

"I do not think that would be possible, Justice Bar-Aben. It is likely that the indentation may not be intact after the collapse of the Kotel."

"Thank you, Rabbi. Mr. Prime Minister, will you please have the stone delivered to my chambers and have Amran retrieve it."

Prime Minister Zadok returned twenty minutes later with a briefcase he had received from Amran in the corridor. He placed it on one of the tables behind the podium and opened it. He lifted a pouch from the briefcase.

"This pouch has the stone from the United States. Rabbi."

Rabbi Avidan opened the pouch and took out the stone. He examined it closely, rubbing it with his fingers. Finally, the rabbi turned to Meir and sighed.

"This is not the stone I gave to Moshe Dayan."

"How would you know?" Meir asked.

"My stone had four Hebrew letters scratched on it. A *lamed*, a *heh*, another *heh*, and a *bet*. Rabbi Jochanan ben Zakkai scratched the letters on it himself. The letters were an abbreviation for *lehar habayit*, 'to the Temple Mount.' You can barely see the letters, but you can feel them with your fingers. The prime minister's comment from Moshe Dayan's biographer is intriguing. Perhaps the scratches on the ancient artifact that transfixed Moshe Dayan were the letters on my stone that he kept."

The rabbi picked up the stone again and rubbed it.

"This stone has no letters on it."

Zadok looked visibly relieved. Meir appeared startled. Rabbi Avidan looked at Meir.

"Is there something wrong, Justice Bar-Aben?" the rabbi asked.

Meir shook his head. "No, nothing is wrong," he said. "Before I close the hearing, does anyone have anything more to say?"

Zadok was silent. Meir turned to him.

"Mr. Prime Minister?"

"No, Justice Bar-Aben."

Samir turned to Amos and said something. Amos translated.

"He wants to say something."

"Please. I welcome anything he has to say."

Samir stood. Amos translated again.

"Justice Bar-Aben, you have listened carefully, and for that I am grateful. I want to tell you what my grandfather told me after he told me stories handed down from our ancestors. He used to tell us that the fire of memory burns brighter than the hardness of stone."

Fatima gasped. She turned to Samir and spoke in Arabic. Samir nodded knowingly, and Amos translated what Fatima had said.

"Professor al-Fawzi says that her grandmother used to tell her that memory speaks when stones are silent."

All in the courtroom were silent as they reflected on these words.

Finally, Meir spoke.

"I believe we have heard all of the testimony. I do have a question for all the witnesses before we adjourn. When I read the interview summaries, each of you described your family history in Jerusalem. I would like for each of you to describe your family's presence in Jerusalem since the Muslim conquest in the seventh century.

"Professor al-Fawzi, would you speak first."

"Certainly," Fatima said. "Generation after generation of Ka'ab's descendants continued to live in the city until the year 1099 when the armies of the First Crusade approached Jerusalem. My ancestors who were living in the city at that time fled to Yemen, where they had maintained trading relations. In the summer of 1099, the Crusaders conquered Jerusalem and massacred most of the Muslim and Jewish inhabitants. Jerusalem remained under control of the Crusaders for eighty years until Salah a-din defeated the Crusaders in 1187 and recaptured Jerusalem. Like Umar, Salah a-din granted clemency to the Christian inhabitants and allowed Jews to live in Jerusalem again. Members of my family who had been born in the intervening years returned from Yemen after the city was taken back from the Crusaders by Salah a-din, and I am descended from one of those family members."

"Thank you, Professor al-Fawzi," Meir said. "Mr. ibn Abdullah, would you tell me your family history, please."

"Yes. Similarly, generations of Caliph Umar's descendants continued to live in Jerusalem until the year 1099. The generation that lived in the city at that time escaped to Damascus before the Crusader armies reached Jerusalem. Members of my family born in the intervening years returned after Salah a-din recaptured the city. I am descended from one of those family members who returned."

Meir turned to Rabbi Avidan.

"Rabbi, what happened to your family?"

"Deborah's descendants also continued to live in Jerusalem until the time of the First Crusades. The generation living in Jerusalem in 1099 fled the country and eventually settled in Poland. As you might be aware, at that time, Poland was—for Jews—the most tolerant country in Europe, and remained so for centuries. Eventually, some of my ancestors settled in Lithuania. I was born in Vilna, Lithuania. I survived the Holocaust by fighting with Russian partisans. I immigrated to Israel in 1949 and settled in Jerusalem."

Meir said, "It is clear that this city has always been sacred to your families. Is there anything else anyone wishes to say before I close the hearing?"

Rabbi Avidan spoke.

"Our families' memories have survived the destructive forces of time. The witnesses have spoken the truth as they understand it. However, before you close the hearing, I have additional information that I would like to tell the court and the prime minister in confidence."

"Without the other witnesses present?" Meir asked.

"Yes. I apologize to Mr. ibn Abdullah and Professor al-Fawzi, but this information is strictly for the court."

"Then I can meet with you and with Prime Minister Zadok tomorrow," Meir said. He turned to Eli Heifitz.

"Mr. President, you should attend tomorrow."

Meir picked up his gavel and struck it three times.

"This hearing is adjourned. Mr. ibn Abdullah and Professor al-Fawzi, thank you for your time. I want to emphasize again that you are not to discuss with anyone what you have heard in this proceeding."

Samir said something in Arabic, and Fatima nodded and smiled. Amos translated.

"Mr. ibn Abdullah says he supposes he will learn the result of the hearing by watching the news."

Everyone stood up at once. Amos was the first to speak.

"I can drive Mr. ibn Abdullah and Rabbi Avidan to the Old City and Professor al-Fawzi home."

Fatima shook hands with Samir.

"How would you like to give a lecture at Hebrew University? I'm sure my students would appreciate hearing a direct descendant of Caliph Umar."

"I would like that," Samir said. "My grandfather used to say, 'a pound of talk, an ounce of understanding.' I could offer at least a pound of talk."

Fatima laughed and turned to Rabbi Avidan.

"It was a pleasure to meet you. Perhaps you could also give a lecture about the early Jewish community from Tiberias."

"My pleasure also. We can talk about it in the car."

Rabbi Avidan shook hands with Meir.

"I don't envy your responsibility, Justice Bar-Aben. Remember, what you need now is *hazak*. To be strong. We will talk tomorrow."

Meir squeezed Rabbi Avidan's hand.

"I will have Amran pick you up tomorrow and bring you here."

Meir turned and shook hands with Samir, Fatima, and Amos. When they left, Meir was alone with Zadok and Eli Heifitz.

"I am sorry we did not conclude the testimony today. We will meet with Rabbi Avidan tomorrow."

"I understand. Please go home, Justice Bar-Aben," Zadok said. "You have had quite a day."

Chapter 55

When Meir returned home that evening, Channah was sitting in the living room with Esther curled in her lap. She rose and came to him.

"You look exhausted, Meir. Are you finished with whatever you are doing?"

"Almost. I believe I know what my decision will be. It would help if I had the answer to one question."

Channah smiled. "I thought you could ask any question you wanted to ask. Why haven't you?"

"I didn't know the question until today."

"Then ask it soon, Meir, and be done."

After dinner, Meir went into Ori's room. He looked at the pictures on the dresser and let his mind wander through the years. Finally, he knelt next to the bed and pulled his violin case into the light. He put the case on the bed and opened it. He lifted the velvet cover from the violin. The violin's finish gleamed. Looking inside the violin's body through one of the f-holes, he could see that the sound post had not dropped even though the strings had lost their tension.

He put the violin on the bed and reached for the bow. He tightened the bow hair and held it in front of him. The bow was straight and true. He unwrapped the rosin cake that lay under the violin's neck. It was still clear after so many years. He rubbed the rosin on the bow, coating the hair lightly. He put the bow down on the bed and picked up the violin, gripping it between his chin and shoulder. It felt comfortable, smooth, and secure. He reached forward and tuned the A string to pitch and then tuned the other strings. His ear was still good, but he was not sure of his bow arm or fingering.

Meir placed the bow on the G string and pulled. The lowest note sounded rich and full. A warmth that he had not felt in many years welled up in his chest. He bowed an arpeggio across the strings, feeling the notes forming under his breastbone. He rocked his bow arm, keeping his wrist loose. He dropped his fingers on the strings firmly, remembering the placement with ease.

Meir closed his eyes, repeating the arpeggio, concentrating on the feeling in his wrist and shoulder. The notes sounded full in his ears, the violin vibrating softly under his throat. After a few minutes, he put the violin and bow on the bed. He turned and saw Channah standing in the doorway. There were tears in her eyes.

"Today, we felt our son's heart beating. Tonight, I hear music. What next?"

"I'm sorry, Channah. I didn't mean to play the violin when I came in here. I was looking at all the pictures of us and Ori."

Channah sat next to him and put her arm around his shoulder.

"You haven't played for so long. Why tonight?

"Maybe I am trying to recover something I thought I had lost. Today, I was looking at the picture of Amos Eitan and me at the Kotel. Where did the years go, Channah?"

"I don't know. There are things I remember, and things I choose to forget. Why were you looking at the picture today?"

"I was thinking about the war, the battle for the Temple Mount. I was looking at the stone frame. Remember the stone you gave me? I was trying to remember what you told me after you bought it in London."

"The first stone you used to frame the picture? The one . . . ." Her voice caught in her throat. She inhaled slowly.

"Yes."

"I told you I bought it in an antique store."

"How did you find it?"

"I was browsing in the shop, and the owner asked me where I was from. I told him, and he said he had a collection of artifacts from Israel and Egypt. I liked the stone. It wasn't expensive. I could see it framing your picture at the Kotel."

"Did he say how he acquired the artifacts?"

"He said they came from the private collection of Moshe Dayan. I didn't believe him, so I never told you that. I thought he was just trying to make a sale. I didn't care. It was Jerusalem stone. I knew you would like it."

She rose from the bed and walked to the door.

"Play some more. I'll listen from the living room."

Meir had not planned to play, but he had been distracted from his search by the sight of the violin and the urge he did not realize would overcome him.

He opened the small compartment in the case where he stored spare strings and rosin. He found the paper curled inside where he had left it the night before Ori's funeral.

That night, before going to the funeral home, he had wrapped the sheet of paper around the stone and carefully traced with a blunt pencil the letters *lamed, heh, heh,* and *bet* that had been carved into the surface of the stone. When he had traced the letters, they had no meaning for him. He was not sure why he had traced the letters. Perhaps he did it as a gesture to preserve what would soon be irretrievable.

He rolled up the paper and put it in his shirt pocket. He picked up the violin and bow and began to play the second violin part of the second movement of Bach's Concerto for Two Violins in D minor. Tears welled in his eyes as he played.

Channah listened from the other room and wept softly.

Chapter 56

The next morning, Amran escorted Rabbi Avidan and Prime Minister Zadok to Meir's chambers. Meir and Eli Heifitz were waiting.

"Gentlemen," Meir said, "Before we hear what Rabbi Avidan wishes to tell us, I need to take you to another location."

Meir asked Amran to drive them to the cemetery on Mount Herzl. When they arrived, Amran waited in the car, and the others walked to the entrance. Before they entered, Meir had a question for Rabbi Avidan.

"Forgive me, Rabbi. I forgot to ask you. Can you enter a cemetery?"

"Yes, I am not a *kohain*," Rabbi Avidan answered, indicating that he was not descended from Aaron, the brother of Moses, whose descendants are forbidden to enter cemeteries.

They entered the cemetery, and Meir led them on the path to Ori's grave. When they reached the grave, Rabbi Avidan read the inscription on the tombstone and said, "Your son. May his memory be a blessing."

Zadok, Rabbi Avidan, and Eli Heifitz waited respectfully for Meir to speak.

"I thought it would help if we came here for you to hear what I am going to tell you," Meir said. "I need to discuss something with you that I was not aware of until yesterday. First, let me show you something, Rabbi. Do you recognize this?"

Meir handed the rabbi a piece of paper. Rabbi Avidan looked at the paper, and his eyes widened.

"How did you do this?"

Prime Minister Zadok looked over Rabbi Avidan's shoulder.

"What is that?"

Rabbi Avidan handed the paper to Zadok.

"*Lamed, heh, heh, bet*," Zadok said. "Rabbi, you said these letters were on your stone."

"Yes, I did. The way these letters are drawn, they look the same as they did on my stone—the same size, the same spacing between the letters, the same shapes. Justice Bar-Aben, what is this?"

"It is a tracing from a stone that I had," Meir said.

"A stone you had? Where did you get it? You mean you don't have it now?" Rabbi Avidan asked.

Zadok handed the paper to Meir.

"What is this?" Zadok asked.

"During a business trip to London in 2008, my wife bought a Jerusalem stone in an antique shop. After the rabbi described his stone yesterday, I went home and asked my wife about our stone. She told me that the shopkeeper said it was from the collection of Moshe Dayan. She thought he was just making up a story to convince her to buy the stone. She never told me until I asked yesterday."

Zadok shook his head. "So, where is this stone?"

"It is here," Meir said.

"I don't understand. *Where* is it?" Zadok asked.

"In my son's coffin."

Zadok, Rabbi Avidan, and Eli Heifitz were silent. Meir answered their unspoken question.

"My father, who rejected tradition, instructed my mother and me not to bury him in a *tallit*. Instead, he asked to be buried with a stone, symbolizing the name he gave us, Bar-Aben, 'son of stone.'

"When Ori died, I did the same. I had the stone at home, framing a photograph of me and Mr. Eitan at the Kotel during the Six-Day War. Channah suggested we use the stone she had bought me. I took my stone to the funeral home and placed it in his coffin. When I removed the photograph from the stone, I felt the letters and traced them. I don't know why. I was numb with grief. I put the tracing away and forgot about it. Later, Channah and I found a similar stone to use as a frame for my picture."

"So you have unwittingly put crucial evidence out of reach," Zadok said. He turned to Rabbi Avidan. "Can you be certain that what is traced on this paper is from the stone that you gave to Moshe Dayan?"

"It seems that it would have to be my stone based on what the shopkeeper said and the letters scratched on it, but I can't be certain."

They looked at the grave.

Rabbi Avidan spoke again.

"I have always thought that perhaps Moshe Dayan believed what I told him, because the stone was something physical that had been passed down through my family."

"On the other hand, it was just a stone," Meir said. "It may have had some Hebrew letters scratched on it, but by itself it can't prove anything."

Zadok frowned. "Lawyers and judges always have to look at everything analytically. Just the sight of the stone may have convinced Moshe Dayan. It was something real, handed down through Rabbi Avidan's family. I would think that just seeing the stone would have had a powerful effect on Moshe Dayan, who was so enamored with antiquities."

Meir was silent for a few moments. Then he asked, "You think that makes the difference? Just seeing a stone?"

"It might make a difference to me," Zadok said.

Rabbi Avidan interrupted. "Ironically, all of this started with the sight of a stone."

Zadok was puzzled. "Rabbi, what do you mean?"

"The first day of my testimony," Rabbi Avidan said, "I spoke about God's command to Abraham to sacrifice his son, remember? Let me tell you the story again."

Chapter 57

Meir, Zadok, and Eli Heifitz listened as Rabbi Avidan told the story of Abraham's refusal to sacrifice his son.

Sarah's tears dropped onto the earth floor of her tent. She muffled her sobs in her hands. She paced the tent, not knowing what to do. She had always trusted her husband, Abraham. When they had left Ur Cashdim, with all its luxuries and comforts, for a life wandering as shepherds, she had listened intently as Abraham had explained that the One God had commanded them to go.

Years later, sitting in the cool desert night, Abraham had pointed to the heavens. He had spoken softly, holding her to him and telling her that the One God had appeared to him again. The One God had told Abraham that Abraham would father a nation, and his descendants would be as numerous as the lights in the night sky. Sarah could not bear children, and yet Abraham believed the promise of the One God. They had crossed the Twin Rivers and left the fertile plains of Ur. They had become the Ivrim, the Hebrews, those who crossed over the river. Even when Sarah's handmaiden, Hagar, gave Abraham a son, Ishmael, Abraham still yearned for his beloved Sarah to give birth.

Thirty-seven years after Ishmael's birth, when Abraham was ninety-nine, the One God had spoken to Abraham again, commanding him to place a mark of His covenant on all males on the eighth day of their life. She and Hagar did not question when they found Abraham and Ishmael lying shuddering in their tents, after Abraham had somehow managed to inflict the mark on Ishmael and then on himself. They nursed the men back to health, fearing that one or both would die from the pain.

Then the visitors from the One God had come to Abraham's tent, telling him that Sarah's womb would suddenly awaken, and she had laughed and laughed. She had laughed even harder later that night when she had seen the mark of the covenant on Abraham's body. Perhaps it was the laughter itself that had finally freed her body to produce a child. For the next thirty-seven years, she had watched Isaac grow to be a man.

And then, the One God had come to her husband again. Abraham heard two words in the night wind.

"ab, ben, ab, ben, ab, ben."

"Father, son, father, son, father, son."

The next night, Abraham heard the voice again.

"ab, ben, ab, ben, ab, ben."

The voice became more urgent, until the two words merged into one, with a different meaning.

"aben, aben, aben, aben."

"Stone, stone, stone, stone."

The night sky was sliced open by a streak of light, and Abraham saw a vision that drenched his being with confusion. He saw himself, a father, with his son and a stone. He had received a command from the One God that left him frightened and horrified.

When he told Sarah the next morning, the limits of her understanding were broken. How could the One God ask such a thing? How could the One God give and then take back? Had they left Ur to wander all these years so that they could offer their own child to the One God in return?

Sarah's tears fell without end, and she prayed to the One God to release her husband from his harsh demand. She heard Abraham saddle a donkey and call Isaac and Ishmael from their tents.

Abraham left from his camp in Hebron. With him were his two sons, Isaac and Ishmael, and his servant Eliezer. They loaded a donkey with wood. He told his sons and Eliezer that he had been commanded to go north and offer a sacrifice to the One God.

Abraham knew what he had been asked to do, but he did not know where he would do it. When he finally saw his destination, he left his fellow travelers in a cave. He traveled farther and found a large stone. On the stone was an altar in disrepair, which had been used by Noah to offer a sacrifice after the flood. Abraham rebuilt the altar and arranged the wood on it. He returned to the cave and asked Isaac to go with him.

Eager to please his father, Isaac returned with him to the stone and the altar, only to find that there was no animal there for sacrifice. Only then did Abraham tell Isaac that he would be the sacrifice commanded by the One God. He bound Isaac and laid him on the altar.

As Abraham raised the knife, a messenger of the One God called out to him and told him not to strike his son. Abraham found a ram with his horns caught in a thorn bush nearby, and he sacrificed it to the One God instead of his son.

"And the traditional explanation," Rabbi Avidan concluded, "focuses on the willingness of Abraham to obey the One God."

Zadok had listened intently, but asked impatiently, "And do you have your own explanation, Rabbi?"

"I do. This dilemma of Abraham to sacrifice his son disturbs me. I think the rabbis struggled to find an abstract and noble explanation. They assumed the voice that commanded Abraham to sacrifice his son was the voice of God. They also assumed that the second command not to sacrifice his son was from a messenger of God."

"And you believe otherwise?" Zadok asked.

"I believe the first command to sacrifice Isaac was not from God."

"Then who do you believe gave the command?" Meir asked.

Rabbi Avidan turned to Meir.

"Justice Bar-Aben, you have lost your son to violence. Do you believe God commanded it?"

"I cannot think abstractly about something so personal," Meir answered.

Rabbi Avidan nodded.

"I believe that the voice that Abraham heard was the voice of *hamalach hamavet,* the Angel of Death, not the voice of God. The Angel of Death is the personification of man's evil inclination, the root of hatred, prejudice, war, and the ultimate extreme—genocide. Who else would have commanded a father to murder his own son? I believe the very sight of the stone of sacrifice brought Abraham to his senses. No deity could rationally ask for such a sacrifice."

Meir nodded and asked, "What do you believe about the second command to Abraham from God's messenger as Abraham raised the knife. Was that not from God?"

"I believe it was Abraham's own conscience that called to him. Abraham saw the stone and refused to sacrifice his son. He gained strength from his own refusal."

"That is your interpretation?" Meir asked.

"Yes. I prefer a patriarch motivated by free will, not blind obedience."

Rabbi Avidan paused and looked at Meir, then turned to Zadok.

"I believe that Moshe Dayan understood that reality. However historically or religiously significant retaining the Temple Mount would have been, the fearful consequence of doing so was not acceptable to him. He chose the path that rejected war and saved lives. In the end, he acted not as a warrior, a politician, or a historian. He was a father. And he valued the lives of the sons and daughters more than stones of days past."

Zadok was silent for several moments. Then he spoke softly, looking at Meir.

"We will never really know why Moshe Dayan made his decision. However, he still had the benefit of seeing Rabbi Avidan's stone. If I could see the stone, at least I would have everything Dayan had when he made his decision."

Meir looked at Zadok, his anger rising.

"Are you suggesting that we disturb Ori's grave?

Rabbi Avidan put his hand on Meir's shoulder and intervened before Zadok could answer.

"There are strict prohibitions against disturbing the eternal rest of the departed. This subject is very disturbing, so let us not think about it further. Remember, I asked to meet with all of you this morning, because I had additional information that I believe would be helpful to the court. I would prefer to continue our discussion on the Mount of Olives."

Meir took a deep breath.

"Thank you, Rabbi Avidan," Meir said. "The subject is too painful for me."

Meir turned to at Zadok.

"Mr. Prime Minister, you have to decide whether you respect my son more than a stone."

Chapter 58

Amran drove through West Jerusalem, around the Old City, and up the Mount of Olives to the Hotel of the Seven Arches. Meir, Rabbi Avidan, Prime Minister Zadok, and Eli Heifitz walked over to the lookout point at the edge of the hotel's parking lot. From north to south they could see the Dome of the Rock, al-Aqsa Mosque, and the neighborhood of Silwan.

Rabbi Avidan leaned against the railing and spoke.

"Amos Oz, the famous Israeli writer, made a comment about the Temple Mount that I have always remembered. He said that he wished he could dismantle the entire Temple Mount, stone by stone, and send it to Scandinavia until the people of Israel could learn to live in peace. I think Rabbi Jochanan ben Zakkai would agree with that solution."

"Unfortunately," Meir said, "I don't have the authority to do that. It would be an easy solution. Don't you agree, Mr. President?"

Eli Heifitz, who had not commented during the entire hearing, smiled and said, "It would be wonderful if we had the power to do that."

"Why did we come here, Rabbi?" Zadok asked. "You said you had additional information for us."

"Before I tell you, I thought it would help if we came here to see the geography," Rabbi Avidan said. "From here you can see the neighborhood of Silwan adjacent to the Temple Mount."

Rabbi Avidan pointed to Silwan hugging the ridge to the south of the Temple Mount. He continued to point back and forth, between the Temple Mount and Silwan, and explained further.

"From here the angle of sight between the Temple Mount and Silwan is small, and it is easy to see how Rabbi Simon convinced his community and Ka'ab that the Temple had stood on the platform that came to be known as the Temple Mount."

Zadok frowned. "So Caliph Umar determined the place of Solomon's Temple and Muhammad's night journey based on erroneous information from his advisor, Ka'ab, who believed he was identifying the place where the Temple stood."

"History is a mixture of what is remembered, forgotten, hidden, and confused," Rabbi Avidan said.

Before Rabbi Avidan could continue, Zadok turned to Meir.

"We have heard the testimony of the witnesses. The hearing is finished. When do you think you can give me your decision?"

"We can speak about that now," Meir said. "I would like to tell you my decision here, with Rabbi Avidan present. But first, Rabbi Avidan, would you please tell us the additional information you wished to offer."

Rabbi Avidan thought for a moment and responded, "I did not expect to hear your decision today, Justice Bar-Aben, but my information would not be relevant to your decision. Perhaps it would be beneficial if I told you after I hear your decision."

"Then I will give a preliminary decision now, before I hear Rabbi Avidan's additional information," Meir said. He continued, speaking slowly and deliberately.

"First, the easiest issue to resolve, Mr. Prime Minister, is your allegation that there was a violation of unwritten agreements between Moshe Dayan and the Waqf. Amos Eitan was the only person who testified at the hearing who might know about any agreements. He testified that he had no knowledge of any agreements. If members of the Waqf who know about any agreements are still alive, we don't know. You haven't come close to meeting your burden of proof on this issue."

Zadok coughed and cleared his throat.

"I'll admit we have no evidence of any agreements between Moshe Dayan and the Waqf."

Meir continued.

"Mr. Prime Minister, you had two other bases for taking back the Temple Mount. The violation of the law of the holy places and the Jewish people's historical right to the Temple Mount. I can address both of these. The testimony of the witnesses has raised the question as to whether the physical site of the Temple Mount *is* a holy place to the Jewish people."

"It is considered holy by both Jews and Muslims," Zadok said. "There is no question about that."

"True," said Meir," but does that make it a 'holy place' under the law? If you believe the three witnesses, what we refer to as the Temple Mount was not a holy place at all, because the Temple did not stand there. Rather, it was the site of a Roman fortress, and later a garbage dump. The Muslim claim that the Temple Mount is the place where Muhammad traveled on his night journey to the farthest place of worship is based on the assumption that the Temple stood there. So if we accept the truth of the witnesses' testimony, what we call the Temple Mount was not the Temple Mount. Therefore, is the place we call the Temple Mount a 'holy place' under the law merely because it was *mistaken for a place that is holy?*"

Meir continued.

"On the other hand, there is a question of credibility. I believe that the witnesses were honestly telling us what had been handed down to them through many generations. But even if they believe what they said was true, and their testimony is believable, does that *make it true*?

"What I am asking is: does the 'fire of memory burn brighter than the hardness of stone,' as Mr. ibn Abdullah suggests? Is memory accurate or simply what people want to remember as true? If the Temple stood somewhere in Silwan, was the memory of its location preserved by Jochanan ben Zakkai and his descendants?"

Zadok was silent. Rabbi Avidan asked a question.

"Justice Bar-Aben, what are your thoughts on the question of the Jewish people's historic right to the Temple Mount?"

"That issue is preempted by the fact that we may not know with certainty the true location of the Temple," Meir said. "We have assumed the Temple Mount was the actual site of the Temple. I can't conclude that the State of Israel has the right to take back the Temple Mount based on a historic claim that the Temple once stood there if the Temple actually stood elsewhere."

"It seems that you have posed more questions than answers," Zadok said.

Rabbi Avidan spoke before Meir could respond.

"But questions lead to answers, Mr. Prime Minister," Rabbi Avidan said. "Asking the right questions is the first step."

"And the stone," Meir continued, "let's consider Rabbi Avidan's stone."

"We don't have the stone," Zadok said.

"We have Rabbi Avidan's testimony about the stone. That is credible evidence. Do you believe that Rabbi Avidan had a stone?" Meir asked.

"Yes," Zadok shrugged.

"The rabbi testified that it had four letters scratched on it, and that he gave it to Moshe Dayan. My wife bought a stone in London and she was told it was from Moshe

Dayan's collection. I traced the letters from it before I placed it in my son's coffin. Was it the rabbi's stone? We don't know, but what are the odds that there are two stones with the same lettering scratched on it?" Meir asked.

"Let's assume that it was the rabbi's stone," Zadok said. "How do we know it was what he said it was? Was it really from the Kotel? Did it mark the location of the Temple? Rabbi Avidan said himself that today he could not find the place on the Kotel from where the stone was chiseled. We don't have it. We can't prove anything with it."

"I agree with you," Meir said. "Since we don't have the stone and cannot locate the place on the Kotel from where it was chiseled, I have to say the stone is not relevant to my decision. But I find the witnesses' family memories to be persuasive evidence. While I can't be certain, I am convinced by the weight of the evidence that the Temple Mount is probably not the site of the Temple."

Zadok looked at Meir then at Rabbi Avidan. He turned his gaze to the Temple Mount, realizing the significance of what Meir had just said.

"So, if I understand what you just said, you will not grant my petition? You will not give me what I want?" Zadok asked.

Before Meir could answer, Rabbi Avidan spoke again.

"That was two questions, Mr. Prime Minister." He turned to Meir. "Remember that I have something I wanted to tell you, the prime minister, and President Heifitz in confidence. Before you answer the prime minister, please let me speak."

"You may, Rabbi," Meir said.

Rabbi Avidan turned to Zadok.

"Mr. Prime Minister, your petition seeks to reclaim the Temple Mount. But is that what you want?"

"I'm not sure what you mean, Rabbi."

"I mean, do you want to reclaim the Temple Mount or the place where the Temple stood?"

"I assumed they were the same."

"Correct," Meir said. "But if what the witnesses say is true, the Temple did not stand on what we call the Temple Mount. And if the Temple did not stand on the Temple Mount, the court cannot grant the petition or give the State of Israel the place where the Temple stood."

Zadok looked at Meir.

"Is that your decision?"

"It is, unless Rabbi Avidan's information gives me a reason to modify it," Meir turned to Rabbi Avidan.

"Please, Rabbi Avidan," Meir said, "tell us why we are here."

Rabbi Avidan sighed.

"I have waited patiently to tell you this. Hopefully you will be receptive to what I have to say. Justice Bar-Aben, the court may not be able to resolve the prime minister's petition by giving the State of Israel authority over the actual site of the Temple, but I believe I can."

"I don't understand, Rabbi," Meir said. "How can you resolve this?"

"Because I believe I know exactly where the Temple stood," Rabbi Avidan said.

Meir was puzzled.

"Rabbi, even if you know exactly where the Temple stood, how can you give the State of Israel authority over that place?" Meir asked.

"Justice Bar-Aben. Prime Minister Zadok, and President Heifitz," the rabbi said, looking at each as he spoke their names, "I not only know the place where the Temple stood; *I own it.*"

Chapter 59

"You *own* the place where the Temple stood? How?" Zadok asked.

Rabbi Avidan pointed across the valley.

"I bought property in Silwan."

Meir looked across the valley to where the rabbi was pointing. "When did you buy property in Silwan, Rabbi?" he asked.

Rabbi Avidan spoke.

"I was the first member of my family to return to Jerusalem since my ancestors fled the city before the Crusaders arrived in 1099. When I arrived in 1949, Silwan was part of Jordan, and I could not go there.

"The Six-Day War changed everything. The night I was on the Temple Mount with Moshe Dayan and Rabbi Goren, I had counted my footsteps from the staircase to the indentation from where my stone had been taken. Two weeks after the Six-Day War, I went to the Kotel. I'm sure you both remember the area had been transformed. The neighborhood had been leveled, creating the plaza and exposing the Kotel. I walked from the staircase and counted my footsteps again. Even though I did not have my stone, I was certain that I found the indentation. It was in the middle of a large ashlar, at about the height of my shoulder.

"I wanted to do what Rabbi Simon had done—to walk south, counting my paces from the indentation in the wall to find the location of the Temple. I was concerned about walking into Silwan so soon after the war. I waited almost two years. One morning, after I had prayed at the Kotel, I decided it was time. I started from the indentation in the Kotel that I had found that night during the war and walked south, counting my paces, into Silwan. When I stopped counting, I was standing in front of a large warehouse. A man was inside stacking boxes on shelves. He saw me looking into the warehouse and came out. I did not know what to expect, but he was friendly. I knew the word for owner and asked for *al melek*. He looked at me funny and answered in Arabic what sounded like 'in Amman.' I thanked him and left, assuming that the owner lived in Amman, Jordan.

"I hired a lawyer who spoke Arabic. Several days later, we returned, and the same man was inside the warehouse. My lawyer spoke to him briefly, and they started laughing. My lawyer told me I had asked for *al melek,* the king, not *al maalak,* the owner. The man was not the owner, but he gave my lawyer the name of the owner who lived in Silwan. After some lengthy negotiations, I bought the building."

"I am surprised," Zadok said. "I would think that the owner would be reluctant to sell the building to you."

"At first he was. My lawyer and I weren't sure if the reluctance was genuine or simply a negotiating tactic. But as my offer increased, the reluctance decreased."

"And you still own the warehouse?" Meir asked.

"It is the first property I ever bought. I still own the building. For years, I rented it to the man who was using it as a warehouse, but he died more than twenty years ago. The building has been vacant since then. I have had offers to purchase it from time to time through my lawyer, but I will not sell it."

"And you believe this building stands on the site where the Temple stood?" Zadok asked.

"I followed the directions that have been handed down through generations of my family."

"But you are not certain?"

"I know of only one way to be certain, Mr. Prime Minister."

Rabbi Avidan turned to Meir.

"Justice Bar-Aben, I assume what I have told you does not change your decision?"

"It does not," Meir responded.

Rabbi Avidan turned to Zadok.

"Mr, Prime, Minister, can you defer any consideration of disturbing Ori's grave to retrieve the stone?"

"Of course," Zadok answered. "I would prefer any resolution that would let Ori rest in peace."

"Excellent," Rabbi Avidan said. "Then let me propose a possible solution. But you must understand, Mr. Prime Minister, the state must agree to certain conditions before implementing the solution."

Rabbi Avidan began to speak.

Chapter 60

The next day, Prime Minister Zadok drove south from Jerusalem, past Masada and the Dead Sea, into the Negev. He longed for his small apartment on the kibbutz. As far as he was concerned, this stark landscape where the early settlers had coaxed prosperity from rock and dust was the true Israel. Jerusalem always seemed to him a remnant of the distant past, destroyed and rebuilt, the focus of religious yearning for a time that was lost. He could understand when Rabbi Avidan explained why Jochanan ben Zakkai was not in favor of rebuilding the Temple—prayer and study had replaced the Temple cult. Zadok had no affinity for the Temple Mount as a religious site. Yet the ultrareligious were a formidable force in Israel, and it would be a political coup if he could return the Temple Mount to the control of Israel.

As he approached the kibbutz, he mused about his acceptance of Rabbi Avidan's proposed solution. Zadok found the plan intriguing, especially if it succeeded, but he was not happy with the conditions the rabbi had imposed. He was deep in thought when he arrived. His wife opened the door of their apartment and hugged him tightly.

"You had a phone call from Hiram Aitza a few minutes ago. He is coming here to show you something."

"Now?"

"He said it couldn't wait."

When Meir told Channah that the case he had been working on was over, she sighed and hugged him. Channah did not ask any questions about the case. The revelation about Zara overshadowed everything else. Meir and Channah occasionally spent jumuah with Zara, Hamid, and their extended family. They awaited the arrival of the twins with joy.

The reconstruction of the Kotel proceeded. Meir's days settled into a routine. The basement courtroom faded in his memory. Two months passed. Early one morning, Ruth knocked softly on Meir's door.

"The prime minister is on the phone."

She closed the door as Meir reached for the phone.

"Mr. Prime Minister, *shalom*."

"*shalom*, Justice Bar-Aben. I want to invite you to the *siyum* of the Kotel next Thursday."

"The completion ceremony? May I bring Channah?"

"Of course. You can sit with me and the members of the Knesset."

"Thank you. *l'hitraot*."

Meir hung up. He knew Channah would not go.

Zadok, half the Knesset, and all of the Supreme Court justices sat on an elevated platform in the plaza in front of the Kotel. An IDF band played *"Hatikva,"* Israel's national anthem. The crowd watched as a crane lifted the last ashlar into place. The members of the new Sanhedrin stood together and prayed that the Temple would be speedily rebuilt. Groups of *haredim* surrounded portable arks and read from the Torah. Meir thought the Kotel looked strange. There were no vines, dove droppings, or notes crammed into the crevices. It was as if the Kotel had been washed clean of its history.

Zadok gave a speech. Meir felt that he might as well be listening to the dedication of a shopping mall.

After Zadok finished his speech, the IDF opened the barriers. A prayerful sigh rose as the crowd rushed toward the Kotel for the first time since the collapse. Many pressed their bodies against the Kotel, while others were more subdued, standing back and viewing the renewed expanse with awe.

Zadok approached Meir.

"Justice Bar-Aben, if you would come back to my office with me, Rabbi Avidan is waiting there for us. The rabbi did not want to attend the ceremony, because the new Sanhedrin members were here."

Zadok paused and then continued.

"I have something to show both of you. It is the reason why I believe Ori will rest in peace."

Amran drove Zadok and Meir to the Knesset. They found Rabbi Avidan waiting for them in the prime minister's conference room.

"Gentlemen, I want to show you some photographs that were taken of some ashlars after the Kotel collapsed," Zadok said.

He spread out large photographs on the conference room table.

"Hiram Aitza, director of the Israel Museum, was in charge of the reconstruction of the Kotel. He took these pictures," Zadok said.

Rabbi Avidan and Meir looked at the pictures. They could see words scratched into the stones. The words were in Latin, Greek, and Aramaic.

"Mr. Aitza translated these words. Here is a list of the translations."

Zadok placed a piece of paper on the table with a list of phrases written on it. *"I pray to Hades for death; Release me to the Elysium Fields; Death to Pagan*

Rome; Pray for the destruction of Antonia; Death to Caesar; Yahweh, have mercy, save me."

"What does this mean, Mr. Prime Minister?" Meir asked.

"Mr. Aitza told me these words appear to have been scratched on the stones by people who were imprisoned behind the Kotel. This lends support to Rabbi Avidan's testimony that the Fortress Antonia stood on the Temple Mount with a subterranean prison below. Mr. Aitza's computerized coding of the fallen ashlars placed these stones on the second and third tier of ashlars from the bottom of the Kotel plaza."

"Has anyone seen these inscriptions other than Mr. Aitza?" Rabbi Avidan asked.

"No. Mr. Aitza restricted access to the stones during the reconstruction, and he was the only one who photographed them. The stones are now in their previous position in the rebuilt Kotel, and the inscriptions are hidden from view."

"Mr. Aitza is supervising the implementation of Rabbi Avidan's proposed resolution of the Section 614 proceeding, isn't he?" Meir asked.

"Yes," Zadok said. "This has certainly encouraged him to move forward."

Chapter 61

The Temple Mount remained under control of the Waqf. The rebuilding and reinforcing of the Kotel cured the instability that had been caused by the Waqf's excavations and construction of the Marwani Mosque under al-Aqsa Mosque. Prime Minister Zadok ignored all political and religious sentiment to take back the Temple Mount and rebuild the Temple.

Zara gave birth to twins in Hadassah Hospital six months after the Kotel reconstruction was complete. Meir and Channah learned Arabic with the twins as the twins learned to talk.

A year after the reconstruction of the Kotel, Zadok, Rabbi Avidan, and Meir met with Hiram Aitza and a team of archaeologists who had conducted a secret dig in Silwan under Rabbi Avidan's abandoned warehouse. The archaeologists told them about a dramatic discovery.

A vertical shaft had been excavated deep into the strata below and had penetrated a layer of burnt wood and scorched stone. Within this layer of debris, they had found many small quantities of gold, silver, and other metals that had melted from intense heat.

The archaeologists continued their excavations in Silwan, tunneling deeper than any evidence of destruction by the Romans. Four years later, after slow and meticulous excavation, they found what they suspected to be the foundation of the Temple.

Additional archaeological analysis confirmed that they had found the Temple site under Rabbi Avidan's property.

Prime Minister Zadok and Hiram Aitza held a news conference to reveal the discovery of the Temple site in Silwan. The archaeology team answered the reporters' questions. The academic world soon accepted the conclusion that this was indeed the site of the Temple. The building above the site was demolished, and construction began according to the conditions agreed between Rabbi Avidan and the State of Israel before the excavations had begun.

Jewish worshippers abandoned the plaza in front of the Kotel. Shops and residences quickly filled the area.

Rabbi Avidan died in his sleep soon after the construction above the Temple site was complete. He was one hundred and six years old. Samir needed a knee replacement and could no longer climb the minaret. His eldest son, Salim, became a *muadhin* at al-Aqsa Mosque.

Chapter 62

Jerusalem
November 2035

My grandfather and I walked through Silwan toward my house. As he finished telling me this story, he said, "Remember, Nuri. Everyone's history is intertwined. To deny the history of others is to deny your own."

We stopped at a large playground surrounded by a park. Children and adults swarmed inside. We walked to the center of the park where a large pillar stood.

An engraved plaque on the pillar read in many languages:

You are standing at the place of the Temple, the House of God.

All your children shall be taught by God, and great shall be the peace of your children.
Isaiah 54

Behold, children are a heritage from God.
Psalm 127

Enter here and leave behind prejudice, hatred, feelings of superiority, violence, and war. Let your children play here. Yearn not for the past or stones buried below. Your children are the light of your future.
Rabbi Ashur Avidan, of Blessed Memory

This was the condition that Rabbi Avidan had imposed when he revealed the location of the Temple to Prime Minister Zadok. There would be no religious observance on the Temple site. The only activity allowed would be a public playground for all children.

My grandfather and I stood and watched the children play. He hugged me to him and said, "Nuri, your parents named you and your sister 'my light,' after my son who died before you were born. My grandchildren are truly the light of my future."

Outside the park, a long line of tourists waited to descend below and view the excavation of the Temple foundations. We sat on a bench and watched the children play.

Epilogue

I am Nuri ibn Hamid. My parents, Zara and Hamid, named me and my twin sister, Manari, after Ori Bar-Aben, whose heart gave life to my mother. Manari and I grew up with Meir and Channah Bar-Aben as our grandparents. In our tradition, parents take the name of their son. Our grandfather, Meir, is called Abu Ori, and our grandmother, Channah, is called Umm Ori. Because Ori was their son, Manari and I consider him our uncle.

Our grandfather, Abu Ori, retired from the Supreme Court at the age of eighty-eight when Manari and I were sixteen years old.

Every year, on the anniversary of Uncle Ori's death, according to the Jewish calendar, our family goes to a synagogue in the Jewish Quarter to say *kaddish*. Jacob Avidan leads his father's *minyan*, proclaiming to the Children of Israel, "God is One."

On the anniversary of the day my mother received the gift of Uncle Ori's heart, according to the Muslim calendar, our family goes to al-Aqsa Mosque for *salat*. Salim ibn Samir calls the *adhan*, proclaiming to the Children of Ishmael, "There is no God but God."

We pray that one day peace will come to all the Children of Abraham.

salaam, in sha allah. Peace, God willing.

Afterword

In the summer of 1970, after my second year of college at the Georgetown University School of Foreign Service, I lived in Israel at Kibbutz Gaaton in the Upper Galilee. I worked as a volunteer and studied Hebrew. I spent two weeks in Jerusalem. I wandered through the Muslim Quarter of the Old City, stood in the plaza at the Kotel, toured the Temple Mount, and visited the Church of the Holy Sepulcher. I tried to visualize Jerusalem as it evolved through its Jewish, Christian, and Muslim periods.

I returned to Israel the following summer as a volunteer at Kibbutz Nahal Oz, near Gaza. I spent another week in Jerusalem, duplicating my wanderings of the previous summer, lost in the flow of history. I listened to merchants and those lounging in the coffee shops of the Muslim Quarter of the Old City and realized, because I had a conversational knowledge of Hebrew, that I could partially understand Arabic. The poetic cadence of the language and the similarity of vocabulary to Hebrew struck a chord in me.

When I returned to Georgetown University for my senior year, I structured my curriculum to study the Arabic language and Islamic and Middle Eastern history and politics. I graduated at the end of the year and received a graduate fellowship to continue my study of Arabic during the summer before I began law school at the University of Toledo.

I did not return to Jerusalem until 1990. The renewal of the Jewish Quarter and the excavation and reconstruction of the Cardo allowed access to a thriving Jewish presence, but the Arab intifada restricted visits to the Muslim Quarter. My wife and I visited the Temple Mount with a private guide, and we only spent a few hurried minutes on the plaza in front of the Dome of the Rock. I could now read the Arabic script circling the Dome of the Rock and understand basic Arabic conversation. We also visited the Temple Institute, an organization founded in 1987 that had recreated the Temple vessels and thereafter published plans for rebuilding the Temple.

In 1999, my wife and I returned to Israel and toured the excavated tunnels that were recently opened under the Temple Mount. We could not gain access to the Temple Mount, but we were able to view it from various vantage points from the Jewish Quarter. Shortly after our return, I began to read reports of the Muslim excavations under the Temple Mount. I also became familiar with the ongoing political controversy concerning the excavations of the City of David in Silwan.

I based *Father, Son, Stone* on three historical topics—a place, a man, and an event. The place is the area known to Jews as the Temple Mount and to Muslims as the Noble Sanctuary. As a focal point of Jewish and Muslim sanctification and Christian desecration, this site has been a vortex of conflict and conflicting emotions.

The man is one whose history is bound to the Temple Mount and the Noble Sanctuary. He is Ka'ab al-Ahbar, an early Jewish convert to Islam who was the advisor to Caliph Umar.

The event that poses the dilemma to be resolved is Moshe Dayan's return of the Temple Mount to the control of the Waqf immediately after the Six-Day War. In light of the Jewish people's centuries of longing for access to the Temple Mount, the return of the Temple

Mount to the Waqf was, and still remains, inexplicable to many.

I use the fictional collapse of the Kotel and the family memories of the witnesses to examine the origins of the competing rights to the Temple Mount. The result is an alternative explanation to support Moshe Dayan's decision to return the authority over the Temple Mount to the Waqf.

I developed the resolution for the story after reading the book by Dr. Ernest Martin referenced in my bibliography. Using historical and archaeological analysis, Dr. Martin's conclusions are contrary to most theories. I neither accept nor reject his conclusions, but they did serve as a spark for my story.

I wrote this story as a legal dispute because I am a resolver of conflict. For seventeen years, I was an attorney in private practice. For more than twenty years, I have been a judge, a mediator, and an arbitrator. I have found that the resolution of conflict takes unexpected twists and turns. Evidence may be abundant, elusive, misleading, or nonexistent. Memories may be sharp or dim. Documents may be clear, vague, or ambiguous. Witness testimony may be eloquent or difficult to understand, credible or unbelievable. What is said in courtrooms may be a mere shadow of reality. What is commonly believed to be true may not be true. What is true may be undiscoverable.

In any conflict, the participants have their own view and understanding of events, framed by their background and vantage point when the events occurred. Conflict develops and compounds over time as events are remembered, forgotten, misinterpreted, and reinterpreted. The common method of analyzing a dispute is to return in time to the events that initiated the problem and attempt to see how the passage of time alters the view of these events in the present. Resolution of conflict results when the participants are finally willing to accept the reality of others.

During my first summer in Israel at Kibbutz Gaaton, I lived in an underground shelter within sight of the Lebanese border. Painted on the door of the shelter was a large peace symbol with a Hebrew inscription that read: *"Do not tell me the day will come. Bring the day."* For forty-four years, a framed photograph of the inscription has been with me wherever I have lived.

Father, Son, Stone expresses my hope and belief that people can live together in peace, despite their differences.

Allan H. Goodman

Fact and Fiction in *Father, Son, Stone*

While my story is fiction, the following events are historical.

First–Seventh Centuries C.E.

60–70 C.E.—Civil War in Judea among various Jewish factions threatens Roman rule and results in Roman suppression.

69 C.E.—Jochanan ben Zakkai escapes from Jerusalem and asks Vespasian to allow him to establish an academy for Torah study in Yabneh.

69–70 C.E.—Vespasian besieges Jerusalem and becomes emperor. His son Titus conquers Jerusalem.

130 C.E.—Roman emperor Hadrian suppresses the Bar Kochba revolt and plows Jerusalem like a field. He renames the city Aelia and bans Jews from living in Jerusalem. Jews are allowed on the Mount of Olives on Tisha B'av to observe the place of the destruction of the Temple below.

313 C.E.—The Edict of Milan grants tolerance to all religions in the Roman Empire. Christianity becomes the dominant religion in the Roman Empire.

325 C.E.—Emperor Constantine's mother, Lady Helena, identifies Christian sites in Jerusalem. She also

identifies the ruins on the Temple Mount as the previous site of the Temple. Christians begin using the Temple Mount as a garbage dump.

570 C.E.—Muhammad is born in Mecca in Arabia.

610 C.E.—Muhammad receives his first revelation from the angel Gabriel.

613 C.E.—Muhammad begins preaching his revelations, including surrender to God, Islam.

614 C.E.—Persia conquers Byzantine Jerusalem.

622 C.E.—Byzantine emperor Heraclius defeats the Persians, and Jerusalem is again under control of the Byzantines. The Jews are banned from Jerusalem.

622 C.E.—Muhammad migrates with his followers from Mecca to the city of Yathrib, later known as Medina. This migration is known as the *hijra.*

624 C.E.—Muhammad changes the direction of Muslim prayer to face Mecca rather than Jerusalem.

632 C.E.—Muhammad dies. Abu Bakr becomes first caliph.

634 C.E.—Abu Bakr dies. Umar becomes second caliph. Sophronius is Byzantine patriarch of Jerusalem.

637 C.E.—Caliph Umar captures Jerusalem after a six-month siege. His advisor, Ka'ab, a Jewish convert to Islam, shows Umar where he believes the Jewish Temple had stood in Jerusalem, the place today known to Jews as the Temple Mount and to Muslims as al-Haram as-

Sharif. Umar's army removes rubble from the area and builds al-Aqsa Mosque on the southwest corner.

Caliph Umar allows seventy families from Tiberias to live in Jerusalem in the lower district of the city.

During his reign, Caliph Umar mandates the Muslim (*hijri*) calendar, a lunar calendar that begins counting the years from the *hijra* of Muhammad and his followers from Mecca to Medina.

638 C.E.—Sophronius dies.

644 C.E.—Caliph Umar is assassinated while returning to Jerusalem after the *hajj*. Ka'ab is accused of conspiracy in Umar's murder. Uthman becomes third caliph.

661 C.E.—Muawiyah becomes the fourth caliph and moves the governing city from Medina to Damascus. Ka'ab becomes his advisor. The historical Ka'ab died in Damascus during the reign of Muawiyah. Muawiyah died in 680.

685–691 C.E.—Caliph Abd al-Malik builds the Dome of the Rock and begins the reconstruction and realignment of al-Aqsa Mosque. Reconstruction of al-Aqsa Mosque is completed by his son, Caliph al-Walid, in 705.

1099 C.E.—Armies of the First Crusade capture Jerusalem and slaughter the Muslim and Jewish population.

1187 C.E.—Salah a-din recaptures Jerusalem from the Crusaders and allows the Jews to live in the city again.

Twentieth Century

June 1967—Israel captures the Temple Mount during the Six-Day War. Minister of Defense Moshe Dayan, Rabbi Shlomo Goren, General Uzi Narkiss, and General Mordechai Gur are on the Temple Mount that day. Moshe Dayan orders the IDF to take down an Israeli flag that had been raised over the Dome of the Rock. Several days later, Moshe Dayan returns the Temple Mount to the Muslim Waqf. The neighborhood in front of the Kotel is bulldozed, creating a plaza.

June 1967—After the Six-Day War, the Law of the Holy Places is passed, protecting the holy places of all religions in Israel.

The Basic Law of Israel contains the following in the provision entitled "Jerusalem, Capital of Israel": The Holy Places shall be protected from desecration and any other violation and from anything likely to violate the freedom of access of the members of the different religions to the places sacred to them or their feelings toward those places.

August 1967—Rabbi Goren holds a prayer service on the Temple Mount.

1987—The Temple Institute is founded. Its website, *www.templeinstitute.org*, states the purpose of the Temple Institute as follows:

The Temple Institute is dedicated to every aspect of the Holy Temple of Jerusalem, and the central role it fulfilled, and will once again fulfill, in the spiritual wellbeing of both Israel and all the nations of the world. The Institute's work touches upon the history of the

Holy Temple's past, an understanding of the present day, and the Divine promise of Israel's future. The Institute's activities include education, research, and development. The Temple Institute's ultimate goal is to see Israel rebuild the Holy Temple on Mount Moriah in Jerusalem, in accord with the Biblical commandments.

At this site you may view photographs of the actual sacred Temple vessels that have been produced by the Temple Institute. Each vessel has been created by accomplished craftsmen. These vessels and priestly garments are being fashioned today according to the exact Biblical requirements, specifically for use in the future Holy Temple. They wait for the day when they will be called into the Divine service of the Holy Temple.

April 1986—The Israel Museum puts on display 1,000 artifacts previously owned by Moshe Dayan's family. The Museum had purchased the artifacts from Moshe Dayan's estate in 1981. Archaeological critics maintain that Moshe Dayan illegally acquired most of the artifacts, and the artifacts are, therefore, already the property of the State of Israel.

November 1992—The new building of the Supreme Court of Israel is dedicated. The description of the building in my story is based upon public information, as well as my own visit to the building in 1999. To my knowledge, there is not a courtroom in the basement of the building as described in my book.

May 1998—In an interview, reported in *Haaretz* and the Associated Press, Uzi Narkiss states that on the day the Temple Mount was captured, Rabbi Goren suggested that the IDF should blow up the Dome of the Rock. In a later interview in early 1999, Rabbi Goren's aide, Rabbi Menahem HaCohen contests that Rabbi Goren suggested blowing up the Dome of the Rock. Rather, Rabbi HaCohen alleges that he heard Rabbi Goren state that it would have been fortuitous if the Dome of the Rock had been destroyed in the fighting.

November 1999—The Waqf begins excavations under al-Aqsa Mosque to build the Marwani Mosque to hold 7,000 worshippers. These excavations are decried by many as an attempt to find and erase archeological evidence of the Temple. As the result of these excavations, there is geological evidence that the structural stability of the area has been compromised.

February 2000—An Israeli court rejects a petition to halt the Waqf's construction, saying the matter should be left to the Israeli government. Ehud Olmert, mayor of Jerusalem, orders a halt to the construction on grounds of archaeological damage, defying a decision of the Israeli government to allow excavations at the site. The Waqf does not halt construction.

September 2002—Part of the Western Wall (Kotel) develops a bulge that has not been historically evident until after the Waqf's excavations.

October 2004—The new Sanhedrin is reconstituted in Israel.

April 2005—The Temple Mount Antiquities Salvage Operation is established to recover archaeological artifacts from the 300 truckloads of topsoil removed from the Temple Mount by the Waqf during the construction of the underground al-Marwani Mosque from 1996–1999. Renamed the Temple Mount Sifting Project after its inception, the project is sponsored by

Bar Ilan University. The worksite of the project is inside the Tzurim Valley National Park on the southern slopes of Mount Scopus. The project has been in continuous operation since its inception in 2005.

May 2007—One hundred sixty-five artifacts from Moshe Dayan's collection in possession of a leader of a Jewish charity are auctioned in Maine, USA. The owner's estate affirms that the items were acquired from Moshe Dayan.

1997–2007—Archaeologist Eilat Mazar excavates what she believes to be King David's palace in the City of David archaeological site in Silwan.

October 2007—A petition is filed in the Israeli Supreme Court to enjoin the Waqf from further excavation on the Temple Mount.

May 2009—Members of the Temple Mount Faithful movement prepare a thirteen-ton cornerstone for the Third Temple and display it on Jerusalem Day, May 21, 2009.

November 2010—The Supreme Court of Israel denies the petition to enjoin the Waqf from excavation under the Temple Mount.

February 2012—After approval of the construction of a visitors' center over the archaeological excavation of the City of David in Silwan, an existing playground and community center serving Silwan residents is demolished.

Historical and Fictional Characters

Jochanan ben Zakkai (30 B.C.E. – 90 C.E.) was head of the Sanhedrin in 69 C.E. He was a man of peace who vigorously opposed the civil war between religious and political factions in Jerusalem. He realized that the internal strife of the nation and the resulting opposition to Rome would lead to more Roman oppression. He escaped the besieged city before the Roman destruction of Jerusalem and established a center of learning in Yabneh that did not depend on the Temple cult. According to the Talmud, he lived to the age of one hundred and twenty.

Rabbi Jochanan ben Zakkai's descendants, Rabbi Simon, Deborah, and Rabbi Ashur Avidan, are fictional. My research did not reveal anyone claiming to be descended from Rabbi Jochanan living in Tiberias during the Muslim conquest or any individuals who claim to be descended from him today.

Vespasian (9 – 79 C.E.) subjugated Judea during the Jewish rebellion of 66 C.E. While he besieged Jerusalem during the Jewish rebellion, Emperor Nero committed suicide and plunged Rome into a year of civil war. Three emperors perished in the following year, and the Roman legions then declared Vespasian to be their commander and emperor. He left his son Titus to command the forces surrounding Jerusalem.

Titus (39 – 81 C.E.), son of Vespasian, accomplished the capture of Jerusalem and the destruction of the

Temple in 70 C.E. While he did not want to destroy the Temple, the Temple caught fire during the fighting and was destroyed. He became emperor in 79 C.E. after Vespasian died.

Titus instructing his soldiers to chant "hep" during the siege of Jerusalem and using "hep"as a riddle for Vespasian to decipher are products of my imagination.

The origin of the battle cry hep—*"Heirosylma est perdita,"* or "Jerusalem is fallen"—is obscure. Some say that Hadrian uttered the phrase when he destroyed Jerusalem in the second century of the Common Era, and it was later shortened to *hep*. Others believe that *hep* was a Crusader battle cry. In 1819, anti-Semitic riots began in Wurzburg, Germany, and spread throughout the country. While mobs chanted *"hep,hep"* during these riots, some historic sources state that *hep* was a traditional herding cry of German sheep herders, and not a reference to the destruction of Jerusalem. Many believe that "hip, hip, hooray" evolved from *hep*.

Caliph Umar (approx. 586 – 589 C.E.) was a companion of the prophet Muhammad and instrumental in the early spread of Islam outside Arabia. His fairness and asceticism is well known. His conquest of Jerusalem, meeting with Sophronius, and permission for seventy families from Tiberias to settle in the lower district are documented in many sources.

Caliph Umar has many living descendants. The surnames Faruqui, Farooki, Faroqui, Farooqi, Faruki, Farouki, and Faruqi purportedly signify that one is descended from Caliph Umar, as he was called al-Farook, the arbitrator or redeemer. Caliph Umar is credited for creating the Muslim calendar and building the first mosque on the Temple Mount, where al-Aqsa Mosque stands today.

His fictional descendant in my story, Samir ibn Abdullah, is not based upon a real person. There is a family whose members for many generations have called worshippers to prayer at al-Aqsa Mosque, but to my knowledge they do not claim descent from Caliph Umar, nor do they proclaim the *adhan* from the minaret. They broadcast the call to prayer from an interior room of the mosque through loudspeakers on the exterior.

Sophronius (560 – 638 C.E.) was of Arab descent. After a monastic, ascetic life in Egypt, he was elected patriarch of Jerusalem in 634. His surrender of Jerusalem to Caliph Umar and subsequent meetings with Umar are documented in many sources.

Ka'ab al-Ahbar (559 – approx. 663 C.E.) was a learned Jewish scholar from Yemen. He was known in Arabic as *alahbar*, from the Hebrew word *haver,* a title for scholars below the rank of rabbi. He accepted the message of Islam and became an advisor to Caliph Umar. He came with Caliph Umar to Jerusalem and stood on the Temple Mount. Umar deemed the Temple Mount a holy place to Muslims based on the advice of Ka'ab al-Ahbar that Solomon's Temple had once stood there. Ka'ab al-Ahbar suggested to the caliph that Muslims direct their prayers toward the rock that stands at the center of the Temple Mount as they faced east towards Mecca, but the caliph dismissed his suggestion. Ka'ab al-Ahbar was accused of conspiracy in the death of Umar. There is no evidence that Ka'ab al-Ahbar had any contact with the seventy families that came from Tiberias to settle in the lower district.

Ka'ab al-Ahbar reportedly lived more than one hundred years. He moved to Damascus, became an advisor to Caliph Muawiyah, and died during

Muawiyah's reign. Therefore, he died before Caliph Abd al-Malik built the Dome of the Rock.

While some details of my fictional character's life are consistent with the life of the historical Ka'ab al-Ahbar, many details differ. I have named my character Ka'ab al-Chabar, as he was from the city of Chabar. I portray him as a young convert to Islam from an Arabian Jewish merchant family, rather than an aged, learned scholar from Yemen. He visits Jerusalem as a youth before his conversion to Islam. My character is much younger than the historical Ka'ab was when Umar conquered Jerusalem, and he is alive when the Dome of the Rock is built.

Ka'ab's fictional descendant, Professor Fatima al-Fawzi, is not based on any historical person. My research has not revealed any individuals today who claim to be descended from the historical Ka'ab.

Caliph Abd al-Malik (646 – 705 C.E.) is credited for building the Dome of the Rock, which stands to this day. No one knows for certain why this structure was built and what it was. The practices that prevailed at the Dome of the Rock in its early period were not distinctly Islamic. The Dome of the Rock is often mistakenly called the "Mosque of Umar." We know that Umar built the first mosque on the Temple Mount where al-Aqsa Mosque stands today, not where the Dome of the Rock was ultimately built.

Moshe Dayan (1915 – 1981), military leader and politician, was Israel's Minister of Defense during the Six-Day War. Many criticized him for returning the Temple Mount to the Waqf. In my bibliography, I have referenced the pages in his autobiography, *Moshe Dayan, Story of My Life*, in which he describes his reasons for returning the Temple Mount.

Members of the Knesset, archaeologists, academicians, and journalists have extensively criticized Moshe Dayan for allegedly illegally collecting antiquities in Israel and the territories acquired by Israel. The Israel Museum's acquisition of most of his collection after his death was also criticized. A portion of his collection was auctioned in the United States.

Rabbi Shlomo Goren (1917 – 1994), chief rabbi of the IDF, was one of the first to walk on the Temple Mount after its capture during the Six-Day War. He remained a strong advocate of the Jewish people's right to pray on the Temple Mount after the Six-Day War.

About Hebrew and Arabic

The Hebrew and Arabic alphabets do not contain uppercase and lowercase letters. The Hebrew alphabet has certain letters that are formed differently if they are the last letter in a word, but otherwise there is only one form of each letter regardless of whether the word is the first word in a sentence, a proper name, or any other reason that would require an initial uppercase letter in English.

Letters in the Arabic alphabet take various forms, depending on whether they appear at the beginning or end of a word, in the middle of a word, or adjoining other letters. There is no specific form of the letter that would be used for the initial letter of a word used as the first word in a sentence, a proper name, or any other reason that would require an initial uppercase letter in English.

I have transliterated Hebrew and Arabic dialogue into lowercase italics without initial capital letters. English translation of the transliterated Hebrew and Arabic appears immediately thereafter.

I have spelled Hebrew and Arabic terms and names that are familiar to English speakers with initial uppercase letters according to accepted spellings; these are also not italicized. Examples are Muhammad, Quran, al-Aqsa Mosque, and Kotel. I have transliterated the Hebrew word for stone, pronounced "ehven," as aben, to preserve the Hebrew spelling.

Bibliography

Jerusalem, the Temple Mount, life in the first century C.E., and Byzantine Jerusalem

Breger, Marshall and Ora Ahimeir, eds. *Jerusalem: A City and Its Future*. Syracuse: Syracuse University Press, 2002.

Caroll, James. *Constantine's Sword: The Church and the Jews*. New York: Houghton Mifflin, 2001.

Chilton, Bruce. *Rabbi Jesus: An Intimate Biography*. New York: Doubleday, 2000.

Cline, Eric H. *Jerusalem Besieged: From Ancient Canaan to Modern Israel*. Ann Arbor: University of Michigan Press, 1994.

Elon, Amos. *Jerusalem: City of Mirrors*. Boston: Little Brown and Company, 1989.

Goldwurm, Hersh. *History of the Jewish People, The Second Temple Era*. New York: Mesorah Publications, Ltd., 1982 (Jochanan ben Zakkai, pp. 183–185).

Graetz, Heinrich. *A History of the Jews*. Philadelphia: The Jewish Publication Society of America, 1946 (a history of the Jews who left Jerusalem prior to the Roman destruction and settled in the Arabian Peninsula and Yemen, the Destruction of the Temple, and Jochanan ben Zakkai's establishment of the Academy in Yabneh).

Grant, Michael. *The Twelve Caesars.* New York: Barnes and Noble, Inc., 1996 (Vespasian, pp. 211–225; Titus pp. 226–239).

Holder, Meir. *History of the Jewish People: From Yavneh to Pumbedisa.* Hersh Goldwurm, contributing editor. New York: Mesorah Publications, Ltd., 1986 (Jochanan ben Zakkai, pp. 11–15).

Kolleck, Teddy and Moshe Perlman. *Jerusalem, Sacred City of Mankind: A History of Forty Centuries.* Jerusalem: Steimatzky's Agency Limited, 1968.

Korb, Scott. *Life in the Year One.* New York: Riverhead Books, 2010.

Peters, F.E. *Jerusalem.* Princeton: Princeton University Press, 1985 (the direction of Muslim prayer (qibla) p. 189; Lady Helena's designation of the Temple Mount and use of the Temple Mount as a garbage dump, p. 195).

Ritmeyer, Leen and Kathleen Ritmeyer. *Secrets of Jerusalem's Temple Mount.* Washington, D.C.: Biblical Archaeological Society, 2006 (identification of the location in the Dome of the Rock where the Ark of the Covenant was allegedly placed, p. 112).

Vilnay, Zev. *Legends of Jerusalem.* Philadelphia: Jewish Publication Society of America, 1973.

Whiston, Wilson, trans. *The Works of Josephus.* Peabody: Hendrickson Publishers, Inc., 1987.

Islam

Armstrong, Karen. *Islam: A Short History*. New York: The Modern Library, 2000.

Brockelman, Carl. *History of the Islamic Peoples*. New York: Capricorn Books, 1947.

Katsch, Abram I. *Judaism in Islam*. New York: Sepher Hermon Press, 1980.

Nevo, Yehudah and Judith Koren. *Crossroads to Islam*. Amherst: Prometheus Books, 2003.

Ka'ab al-Ahbar, Caliph Umar, and the Conquest of Jerusalem.

Armstrong, Karen. *Jerusalem: One City, Three Faiths*. New York: Ballantine Books, 1996 (Ka'ab, pp. 230–31).

Elad, Amikam. *Medieval Jerusalem and Islamic Worship*. Boston: Brill Publishing, 1995 (Ka'ab recommends the qibla behind the Rock, p. 30; practices at the Dome of the Rock, including the Guardians of the Gates and employment of Jewish and Christian inhabitants, pp. 51 *et seq.*).

Lewis, Bernard. *The Jews of Islam*. Princeton: Princeton University Press, 1984 (Ka'ab, pp. 71, 96–97, 207n.39).

Makiya, Kanan. *The Rock*. New York: Vintage, 2001 (a fictional account of Caliph Umar's conquest of Jerusalem and the life of Ka'ab supported by extensive historical notes; the Guardians of the Dome of the Rock appointed from the Tiberias community; Jews light the lamps in the Dome of the Rock, pp. 252–253; 338).

Majdalwi, Farouk S. *Islamic Administration under Omar ibn al-Khattab*. Amman: Majdalawi Masterpieces Publications, 2002 (a detailed biography of Caliph Umar).

Martin, Ernest. *The Temples that Jerusalem Forgot*. Portland: ASK Publications, 2000 (extensive references to Caliph Umar and Ka'ab throughout the book).

Montefiore, Simon Sebag. *Jerusalem*. New York: First Vintage Books, 2011 (Umar, Ka'ab and Sophronius; Ka'ab suggesting praying north of the stone on the Temple Mount, pp.182–186; Amos Oz's comment about sending the Temple Mount to Scandinavia, p. 538; a description of the family that currently calls worshippers to prayer to al-Aqsa Mosque, pp. 543–44).

Rogerson, Barnaby. *The Heirs of Muhammad*. New York: Overlook Press, 2006 (Ka'ab, p. 273).

Jerusalem – The Crusader Kingdom

Kolleck, Teddy and Moshe Perlman. *Jerusalem, Sacred City of Mankind: A History of Forty Centuries*. Jerusalem: Steimatzky's Agency Limited, 1968 (First Crusades, Salah a-din, return of Jews and Muslims to Jerusalem, ch. 16, pp.175–196).

Israel and the Six-Day War

Dayan, Moshe. *Moshe Dayan: Story of My Life*. New York: Morrow and Company, 1976 (his pledge not to be separated from "the holiest of our sites," p. 16; detailed description of giving back the Temple Mount to the Waqf, pp. 385–396).

Eban, Abba. *Personal Witness: Israel through My Eyes*. New York: Putnam, 1992.

Gur, Mordechai. *The Battle for Jerusalem*. New York: Ibooks, Inc., 2002 (original Hebrew title: *Har Habayit Beyadeinu*).

Halevi, Yossi Klein. *Like Dreamers: The Story of the Israeli Paratroopers Who Reunited Jerusalem and Divided a Nation*. New York: Harper Collins, 2013 (hoisting the flag on the Dome of the Rock, p. 91).

Netanyahu, Benjamin. *A Place among the Nations: Israel and the World*. New York: Bantam Books, 1993.

Oren, Michael B. *Six Days of War: June 1967 and the Making of the Modern Middle East*. New York: Ballantine Books, 2002 (Rabbi Shlomo Goren's suggestion to Uzi Narkiss to blow up the Dome of the Rock, p. 246).

Segev, Mark. *1967*. New York: Metropolitan Books, 2007 (Rabbi Shlomo Goren's suggestion to Uzi Narkiss to blow up the Dome of the Rock, pp. 378–379; naming the Six-Day War, p. 449).

"Blow Up the Dome of the Rock," *Middle East Reality Magazine*, January 1, 1998—www.mideast. org/archives/1999_01/_05.htm—This article quotes *Haaretz* (December 31, 1997) and the Associated Press reporting Uzi Narkiss's interview in May 1997 in which he alleged that Rabbi Goren, on the night the Temple Mount was captured, suggested that the IDF blow up the Dome of the Rock. The article further quotes a subsequent interview on IDF army radio with Rabbi Goren's aide, Rabbi Menahem HaCohen, who denied that Rabbi Goren suggested using explosives. Rabbi HaCohen alleged that Rabbi Goren stated that it would have been fortuitous if the Dome of the Rock had been destroyed in the fighting. However, during the same radio interview, a tape was played that allegedly contained Goren speaking to a military convention in 1967 after the war ended. On that tape, the speaker says he told Moshe Dayan (not Uzi Narkiss) that, "Certainly, we should have blown it [the Dome of the Rock] up."

To Rebuild the Temple

Shragai, Nadav. "Present Day Sanhedrin Court Seeks to Revive Temple Rituals," *Haaretz*, February 28, 2007.

The Re-established Jewish Sanhedrin, www.sanhedrin.org

The Temple Institute, www.templeinstitute.org

"Detailed Blueprints for the Holy Temple," www.templeinstitute.org/blueprints-for-the-holy-temple.htm

Moshe Dayan's Acquisition of Antiquities

Barkat, Amiram. "Moshe Dayan's Antiquities to be Sold at Bargain Prices in U.S. Auction," *Haaretz*, May 27, 2007 (www.haaretz.com).

Cockburn, Patrick. "The Pictures that Prove the Guilt of Moshe Dayan—Hero and Thief," *The Independent*, February 14, 1997 (www.independent.co.uk).

Dayan, Moshe. *Moshe Dayan: Story of My Life*. New York: Morrow and Company, 1976 (pp. 416–421).

Friedman, Thomas L. "Dayan Legacy Prompts Dispute on Antiquities," *New York Times*, May 14, 1986.

Kletter, Raz. "A Very General Archaeologist— Moshe Dayan and Israeli Archaeology," *Journal of Hebrew Scriptures*, Volume 4, Article 5 (2003).

Van Creveld, Martin. *Moshe Dayan*. London: Weidenfeld and Nicholson, 2004 (Moshe Dayan transfixed by scratches on an ancient artifact, pp. 202–203).

Excavation of the City of David in Silwan

Faust, Avraham. "Did Eilat Mazar Find King David's Palace?" *Biblical Archaeological Review*, Vol. 38. No. 5, Sept.–Oct. 2012.

Na'aman, Nadav. "The Interchange Between Bible and Archaeology: The Case of David's Palace and the Millo," *Biblical Archaeological Review*, Vol. 40. No. 1, Jan.–Feb. 2014.

Reich, Ronny. *Excavating the City of David: Where Jerusalem's History Began*. Jerusalem: Israel Exploration Society and the Biblical Archaeological Society, 2011.

Shanks, Hershel. *The City of David: A Guide to Biblical Jerusalem*. Washington: Biblical Archaeological Society, 1973.

Zorn, Jeffrey B. "Is T1 David's Tomb," *Biblical Archaeological Review*, Vol. 38. No. 6, Nov.–Dec. 2012.

Acknowledgements

I could not have written *Father, Son, Stone* without relying upon my life experiences as a son, husband, father, father-in-law, grandfather, brother and friend. My family and friends have been my support team in this endeavor.

I must express my immeasurable love and gratitude to my wife, Susy, who has believed in me and encouraged me from the day I began to write this story. As writing fiction is not my vocation, but an avocation, the creation of this novel has taken countless hours in which we could have enjoyed life in other ways. Even so, Susy has recognized my desire to write as a passion that I—and therefore she—could not ignore.

At the end of my writing process, Susy traveled to Israel and toured the City of David excavations. Her observations confirmed my mental impressions of the geography of Silwan that I had previously formed through my research.

I am hugely indebted to my editor and dear friend, Adele Igersheim. Her patience, guidance, and persistence brought my novel to completion. I cannot thank her enough for her effort and support.

About the Author

Allan H. Goodman is a judge, a mediator, and an arbitrator. He lives in Rockville, Maryland, with his wife, Susy.

He is the author of two nonfiction books, *Basic Skills for the New Mediator,* second edition, and *Basic Skills for the New Arbitrator*, second cdition.

Father, Son, Stone is his first novel.